# Sand Hill Road

*A Novel*

*by*

*Patrick Krejcik*

Palo Alto Venture Publishing

*Published by Palo Alto Venture Publishing*

*Palo Alto, California 94306, USA.*

*http://paloaltoventurepublishing.com/*

*ISBN-10: 0692513698*

*ISBN-13: 978-0-692-51369-9*

**Disclaimer**

The following is a work of fiction. All characters appearing in this work are fictitious. Any resemblance to real persons, living or dead, is purely coincidental.

First edition 2015

Cover design by Catharine Retter

# Contents

# Prologue - Ad Venture Capital

*If you go down to the woods today you're sure of a big surprise. If you go down to the woods today you'd better go in disguise. For every heir that ever there was will gather there for certain because today's the day that TEDx has their picnic.[1]*

And that was the problem, for normally the Stanford TEDx talks were held in the auditorium but today's keynote speaker was such a big draw that the venue had been changed in favor of the much larger amphitheater down in the woods, across the other side of the campus.

A figure raced across the wooded area towards the Frost Amphitheater. He had considered driving across the campus from the auditorium but dismissed the idea when he realized he would never get there in time, with no parking within a mile of the new venue and security that would never let him through with a car. His partner was in mortal danger and he had to reach him before he was scheduled to give his presentation following the keynote speaker.

The theme of this year's Stanford TEDx talks was the rise of venture capital in Silicon Valley and the course it would chart in shaping the future. A smart move on Stanford's part since several prominent Stanford alumni could be counted amongst those who had made great fortunes in venture capital and with the right amount of pampering and indulgence they could be counted on to donate some of that wealth back to their alma mater. Not just the alumni, but their families would also have to be wooed today to relinquish part of their inheritance for the sake of having a building or institute named after them.

*Ev'ry heir who's been good is sure of a treat today. There's lots of marvelous things to eat and wonderful games to play.*

The red-faced figure, now heaving for breath, had a few minutes earlier been sitting in the cool air-conditioning of his office thumbing through the presentation notes of his partner. He hadn't laid much worth on his partner's TEDx presentation because it was sure to be overshadowed by the keynote speaker, the infamously outspoken head of West Venture Capital. The man was being treated like the rock star of venture capital. His presentation would be more akin to a performance than a lecture and sure to be enhanced with giant screens, lighting and all manner of special effects. Not a grain of real content would be revealed though, he'd grumbled to himself. It would all be a mastery of deception with no hint of where the real money was going.

*Beneath the trees where nobody sees they'll hide and seek as long as they please cause that's the way that TEDx has their picnic.*

On reading his partners presentation material he had suddenly dropped the papers and gasped in panic. If his partner went ahead with this address it would mean the end, the final nail in the coffin. Their fledgling startup had suffered greatly of late, and this preposterous presentation would blow it up completely. Born from the fertile nutrients of a Stanford think tank, it had attracted serious money at the beginning from big-name investors, but then the market made a spectacular crash. Worse, the IPO they had been managing was an unmitigated disaster and on opening day it closed below half of the opening price. People had lost a lot of money. In the postmortem that followed it was grudgingly conceded that no-one could have predicted the market crash. A black swan event[2], they had called it, just a feature of the chaotic behavior of stock markets, but the animosity had remained and the money dried up.

While reading the presentation he had also realized that the venue of the talks had been changed from the nearby auditorium to the other side of the campus. In a crazed panic the overweight figure had lurched into the hallway and skidded and dashed along the sandstone corridors and gravel pathways of the sedate campus. People stepped aside in alarm at the sight of his wheezing red face. He would have grabbed a bicycle and thrown the rider to the ground if any had come close enough, but all were wary of the crazed look upon his eyes. He was desperate to stop his partner from making the biggest mistake of his life, as much for his own sake as his. It would banish all hope of them ever recouping any of the fortune that was rightfully theirs.

The presentation material had started well enough; sticking to the allotted theme that failure was good in the venture capital world. Who better to give such a talk than someone who had failed so spectacularly and so publicly in recent times? It prepared one for greater things, steeling us for the tasks that lay ahead, he had said, and that we all have to learn from our mistakes. Nothing ventured, nothing gained, plus all the other corporate clichés they had heard espoused at dozens of company presentations. But his partner was a specialist in the turbulent behavior of markets and how catastrophes could be triggered by a series of seemingly innocuous events. What followed was a detailed analysis of the last stock market crash that would certainly go over the heads of most of the TEDx audience. He seriously doubted the sanity of his partner when the talk segued into musical composition, arguing that comparing musical discord with sublime harmonies was the perfect illustration of deterministic chaos that ruled the world and the market place. This was certainly going to lose them audience popularity, but what really frightened him was the leap his partner made on the next page.

The blood had drained from his face and pooled in a sickening blob at the pit of his stomach when he had read his partner's proclamation that the stock market had not evolved, as we all believed, but had gotten to this point before the crash by intelligent design. He actually used the words 'evolution versus intelligent design' on his slide to emphasize his point. The crash had been engineered by some of the largest companies on Sand Hill Road, he had declared. Sand Hill Road, the venture capital center of the world where the greatest accumulation of wealth and power was concentrated along a narrow strip of roadway running along the northern border of the Stanford campus. The buildings appeared modest but commercial real estate here was the most expensive in the nation, outpacing even Wall Street and Fifth Avenue. If you were in venture capital you had to have an address on Sand Hill Road. And the tenants of this exclusive office park would be here today in droves to hear their guru deliver the keynote address; a hostile audience, to say the least, to stand in front of and accuse of masterminding a financial crisis that had brought a nation to its knees.

His partner's paranoia would not find any sympathy with this audience. His body then began to shake with the realization that if he had managed to find an advance copy of the presentation then so might others; others who might have unsavory ties to the darker side of investment finance; those who might quite clearly point the finger of blame at his partner for all the losses that had been incurred by their cartels in the past months. His legs were buckling now as he reached the trees at the rear of the amphitheater and he stumbled fitfully, trying to make his way down the slope through the foliage to the main entrance. He had long since lost his glasses in the mad dash across campus but his blurred vision could still make out the giant screens and dazzling graphics of the keynote speaker's address. The audience was cheering enthusiastically.

*If you go down to the woods today you'd better not go alone. It's lovely down in the woods today but safer to stay at home.*

The security personnel, as one might expect, would not let him in. He had neither the requisite TEDx venue pass nor any kind of Stanford ID with him to back up his claims that he was a partner of the next speaker. They didn't know whether to call the police because he was acting like a lunatic terrorist, or whether to call for medical aid because he appeared to be on the verge of physical collapse. Instead they escorted him into an isolated room where all he could do was watch hopelessly as events unfolded on a monitor before him.

The keynote presentation concluded with the Stanford marching band striding across the grass in front of the stage carrying a towering Stanford tree mascot in their midst which they earnestly placed to one side in front of the stage in homage to the keynote speaker. A flurry of balloons was released and the speaker was whisked away to his limousine surrounded by his entourage of men in dark suits.

*Picnic time for TEDx heirs. The little TEDx heirs are having a lovely time today. Watch them, catch them unawares and see them picnic on their holiday.*

The audience already seemed bored as the next speaker was introduced. Whoever followed the keynote speaker had a hard act to follow, but the second speaker's slow, stumbling demeanor did nothing to allay the audience's fears and prejudice. Really, who wanted to hear about the lessons of failure after hearing and being promised that the new generation of venture capitalists could deliver them all the wealth they had ever dreamed of.

The lack of audience response made the speaker even more nervous and he made a lame joke about the interactive props he had lugged out with him onto the stage. A stick and a coil of rope, he'd said, were all he needed to demonstrate the snaking motion of market behavior, explaining that the organizers had encouraged him to use props wherever possible. No-one got it, of course, and a palpable silence fell over the audience. The proverbial crickets could be heard chirping in the surrounding trees while the speaker just stood there.

People were reaching for their cell phones in search of distraction by the time he got to the point in his presentation about the stock market analysis. Rather than a lesson in the importance of allowing failures in the financial world, the talk was now beginning to feel like an exercise in finger pointing and the shifting of blame. He was pacing around the stage turning his head away from the microphone numerous times rendering his voice inaudible, which was then followed by the excruciating noise of him twisting the mouthpiece of the headset to compensate. Those who were still half listening were totally baffled when he suddenly switched gears and told them that the stock market's turbulent behavior of late was completely analogous to modern music. Sweat began to trickle down the folds in his neck as he realized he had totally lost his lost his audience.

The whole presentation was the embodiment of failure. A long way from the upbeat talk the organizers had envisioned.

"Of course, I have some music to play for you. I wouldn't expect anyone to understand without hearing some examples." The microphone rumbled raucously from his labored breathing as he held it between his fingertips too close to his mouth.

A dark suited, thick set man sat uncomfortably fingering his collar in the first row below the speaker's gaze. He had been preoccupied with his cell phone for the duration of the talk. The name on his purple VIP lapel badge read *R. R. Raskolnikov - Nakazaniye Institut*. He tapped a few more times on his phone and winced as he finally put the phone away.

The music began, but it was not the piece the speaker had selected. It began brashly and discordantly as intended, in order to illustrate turbulence and chaos, but instead of transitioning gradually into a melodious ordered harmony it became louder and more discordant. The beat became more incessant and closed itself oppressively around the presenter.

*See them gaily gad about. They love to play and shout; they never have any care.*

R. R. Raskolnikov from the Nakazaniye Institute simply sneered. Others in the audience covered their ears against the cacophony while the presenter stabbed at the buttons on his podium trying to regain control. The coil of red rope that he had intended to whirl triumphantly through the air above his head at the jubilant conclusion to the music now hung limply at his side. As he stepped forward on the stage the podium lights began to flicker and he slowly repeated a mantra to himself, staring the whole time at the edge of the stage in front of him.

"When failure is imminent one must be creative and improvise with whatever is on hand."

The flickering lights were now timed precisely to the alpha rhythms in his brain. In some people this can induce a seizure. A grand mal. But the speaker just stood there feeling an unbearable weight of oppression and despair close in on him. His mantra changed.

"In chaos one must seek a deterministic change, but when all other means have been denied one can only demonstrate self-determination in a final act of self will."

6

At the conclusion to his words he raised his arm in one smooth motion and threw the coil of rope across the branch of the Stanford tree that bowed across the front of the stage. The other ends of the rope he coiled around his neck and in a running leap, jumped off the edge of the stage.

The Stanford tree swayed precariously under his weight, but the loud crack that could be clearly heard over the microphone came not from the overhead tree branch, but from the vertebrae in his neck succumbing to the load.

The music stopped and the audience was silent.

"You're killing us," cried a heckler, for no-one believed what had just happened could possibly be real.

In the isolated room at the side of the stage the speaker's partner who had been pounding with both fists on the door now lay collapsed and motionless on the floor.

The 911 emergency services would have been notified much earlier if they had paid heed to the social media storm that followed. Every cell phone in the audience recorded the image of the swaying body on the Stanford tree until the stage hands finally decided they should lower it onto the grass.

What *crime*, or what *punishment* had been enacted today? The man with the purple VIP pass was among the first to depart, and he now had a satisfied look on his face as he patted the cell phone in his breast pocket. Others in the audience were at a loss what to do next, now that the remainder of the talks had been cancelled. Some decided that to continue with a picnic wasn't such a bad idea.

*At six o'clock their mummies and daddies,*
*Will take them home to bed,*
*Because they're tired little TEDx heirs.*

# Chapter 1 – Massimo

The sky rippled across his vision, the water creating patterns in an otherwise featureless blue as he pushed back from the wall, turning into the final 50 meters of backstroke. His arms stretched out behind his head and his body undulated beneath the water with two dolphin kicks before breaking the surface.

Regular lunchtime swims beneath the blue Stanford skies were a luxury Massimo had become used to since moving to Silicon Valley. He had even come to find the monotony of the cloudless blue tiresome to stare at while doing repeated laps of backstroke, and had to remind himself of its gray counterpart which he had endured in Europe.

The occasional rogue cloud that broke past the maritime guardians of the Santa Cruz range stimulated his imagination far more than it might a rational, non-swimmer. A lone cloud had triggered a thought that had become a turning point in his research. Swimming and turning at the wall with each lap also seemed to tumble his thoughts, and he often emerged from the pool with new connections between the threads of his various research pursuits. It spurred him on to finish his swim at greater speed and return to the lab to start pursuing the ideas in earnest. More often than not though, rational thought processes would resume control of his mind on the journey back to his desk and, like waking dreams under the scrutiny of day, reveal themselves to be no more than incoherent murmurings of his mind.

Sometimes, just sometimes, as on that one lunchtime almost a year ago, the jumbling of thoughts would lead to a brilliant flash of insight. The tumbling of the cloud's vapors as it scudded across the sky had been recorded in a series of snapshots by his brain, each time he rolled his head in time to the rhythmic strokes of his arms. Regular patterns began to emerge from the chaos as his goggled vision broke up the cloud's motion into a sequence of movie frames in time to the slow motion of his swimming. The wisps of cloud he could imagine describing to some small child as shaped like ducks or horsies, were re-forming themselves in a random yet strangely deterministic way. Each glimpse, following two languid strokes in the water, revealed a new guest at the zoo of his imaginary child companion. After a while he could begin to predict what shape would appear 10 strokes further on, some order in the chaos, making not the patterns themselves repeat, but the types, or as he would later say, the classifications of the patterns, repeat.

It was that single lunchtime epiphany that caused him to look deeper into the subject of deterministic chaos[3]. The intriguing world of fractal geometry[4] had suddenly opened up to him, or as his esteemed Stanford colleague had put it, "It turns out that an eerie type of chaos can lurk just behind a facade of order - and yet, deep inside the chaos lurks an even eerier type of order."[5]

Alas, out of the pool, his creative mind was also susceptible to extended periods of daydreaming. Usually it was in response to being asked to do some domestic chore. It was not unheard of for him to pull into his driveway after work, not only unaware of the route he had just taken, but also without the bread and milk his estranged wife might have expressly reminded him to pick up.

"He can't even be relied upon to pick up fresh bread for dinner," she had complained to her friends at a party. "Not that I like the bread here. All they ever seem to have is that sourdough stuff, and never a good Italian loaf."

Massimo quite liked the hard crust of the sourdough baguette from his newly adopted home of San Francisco, but usually chose not to argue, and would remain sullenly silent.

"How could an esteemed university like Stanford hire such a scatter brain?" she would lament to her friends. "He needs to make an effort to get beyond science and converse with his colleagues about social pleasantries if he wants to advance his career."

He couldn't imagine his wife, Donatella, discussing baseball over burgers and beer with his American colleagues nor could he imagine their responses to her questions about what their wives might wear to a gala ball.

Oddly enough, he was standing at the counter of the coffee shop thinking of what his wife would say to him, as if she had somehow been a party to this present train of thoughts when a voice startled him.

"Hey, Massimo, how are you doing, alright?"

The voice ended with the staccato twang of a native Spanish speaker showing off his acquired English skills to another non-native English speaker. He looked up and focused on the barista at the end of the counter. The grinding and hiss of the coffee machine filtered into his consciousness.

"Oh – Carlos - hello, *va bene*, thank you, it goes well enough."

Carlos had already turned to his next customer. He made a point of engaging each customer in conversation, particularly if it was a young, attractive female

"Double latte made with passion," he said to the brunette sporting yoga pants and a loose exercise top. He finished the heart motif in the froth with a swirl and a flourish that extended all the way to his hips.

"Hey, you are looking sharp today!" Massimo called as he noticed that Carlos had tied his apron in such a way that his unbuttoned shirt could be more proudly displayed.

Carlos winked and turned his attention instead to two young mothers receiving their order of caramel lattes and a daily dose of safe flirtation. Their young offspring could merely grope futilely for attention.

The tall man in front of Massimo in the line caught his attention. He carried himself with an overly casual air. His hair was a little too long but expensively styled. The shirt with soft collar was clearly tailored to the slim form of its wearer. Not that the man was particularly thin; it was just that he had forgone the more typical comfort-first, tent-like clothing styles worn by the majority of males in this neighborhood. A pale yellow cashmere sweater was draped over his shoulders. His coffee order, on the other hand, was much less casual.

"One low-fat, *grande* latte with a shot of chocolate-hazelnut syrup, extra foam and grated nutmeg on top."

The crowd in the small coffee shop forced Massimo to stand close to the man's back. His vision was filled by the cotton fabric of the shirt. Up close the fine weave of the fabric looked like those thousand-count cotton sheets he had experienced maybe once or twice at a costly hotel. The jeans, too, were no ordinary off the rack brand, but tailored and pre-aged so as to be at once classy and hip, or maybe young and old at the same time, he did not know which.

The young cashier repeated the man's order back to him, her pierced eyebrow raised in a way Massimo thought was a little too cheeky for her own good.

"No, not chocolate, I want grated nutmeg" the striped shirt repeated back to her.

Massimo had to suppress a guffaw at what, in his opinion, Americans had done to his national drink with these frothy extravaganzas. He did not think the laughter had even left his lips, but the striped shirt turned away from the counter as his order was filled, raising a single eyebrow as he peered down at Massimo's diminutive frame.

Massimo tried to ignore the look.

"One *ristretto*, please!" he said to the cashier, mustering all the rightful authority he could command as an Italian ordering his native drink in the land of over-frothed and caramelized concoctions.

"One ristretto...?" she echoed with lips pursed, her face looking back at Massimo blankly.

"Yes, an espresso in a small cup with only just enough liquid to cover a sugar cube," Massimo blurted out, his eyes mesmerized by the slim tattoo that slid down one side of her neck towards her boney shoulder. "Oh never mind, just enter 'espresso' for the order and put my name on it, and Carlos knows how I like it: Massimo – M, A ..."

"Yes – S, S, I, M, O" she replied before he could finish.

"Well, enjoy your ris-tret-to," she added, drawing out the syllables as Massimo turned and moved off, not quite knowing what to make of her.

Carlos was all showman when it came to the striped shirt's elaborate concoction. He knew his customers, thought Massimo. It was like watching a maestro conduct the New York Philharmonic.

Carlos stood in front of his instrument, making grandiose sweeps with his arms, adding finishing touches, a fortissimo shake of powders here, an arpeggio of sprinkles. It was all to good effect, it seemed, because it produced the desired sizable deposit in Carlos's tip jar as the stranger removed his prize.

Massimo mentally applauded. His ristretto, in contrast, was slid with practiced ease, but little or no flourish over the counter to where he stood. In return Massimo dropped just one coin in the tip jar to Carlos's smiling wave as he turned to his next customer.

Massimo added one sugar cube, stirred twice, clinking noisily with a spoon before lifting the tiny cup to his lips to slurp down the contents and finish with a breathy "ahh."

Opposite him, across the bench top, the striped shirt was still fiddling with stirrers and lids.

"Seems hardly worth the effort, you don't get much for your money," he said in Massimo's direction.

Massimo felt the back of his neck heat up. "All the flavor is concentrated into a smaller volume and is much more pleasurable," he said, always prepared to take on the authoritative role of teacher on the subject of coffee preparation.

"Well, I don't know about that, I get to enjoy mine for the next half an hour, which is an enjoyment cost rate index of under $10.00 an hour, whereas your three second sip doesn't offer much bang for the buck."

"Hah, I wouldn't mind betting that also sums up your attitude to American cars." Massimo couldn't stop himself. He had already jumped with both feet to the conclusion that this man must drive an Escalade or some such monstrosity with matching super-sized cup holders to carry his oversized coffee order.

"And that remark could only come from someone who drives a two-seater Italian sports car."

The man was laughing, leaving Massimo in no doubt that he was being good-naturedly mocked. His thoughts flew back to his bachelor years when he had, in fact, driven an Alpha Romeo, or rather had spent his weekends under it, lying on the floor administering to its little quirks. When Donatella came into his life he had to decide which of the two should take precedence in his heart.

"I prefer German Engineering, actually," he said instead, not untruthfully. He remembered the secondhand BMW 2000 model that had replaced the beloved Alpha, and subsequently allowed them to take some memorable weekend trips in the Tuscan hills when they were courting.

"I'll take the superior handling of a compact German rear wheel drive sedan any day over the ride of your giant SUVs," he continued, convinced more than ever that the stranger was sure to drive an Escalade, or even worse, a Hummer.

"Well, why do you come to a coffee bar that sells the equivalent of SUV espresso drinks?" the stranger parried, deflecting the conversation away from cars and back to their drinks.

"Actually, they have the best espresso making equipment money can buy," he said, directing his gaze to the gleaming stainless steel of both Swiss and Italian roasters, grinders and high-pressure espresso makers, "and they can make quite a decent ristretto if you ask them."

But then as an afterthought he added, "The trouble is that Carlos, here, doesn't have the right attitude to be a really first rate barista in spite of the best equipment."

"Attitude?"

"Yes, in Italia the best baristas *know* they can prepare an espresso that will make you swoon." Massimo saw he had the striped shirt's full attention. "If they feel like it, they can meld the optimum grind of beans with just enough tamping of the powder to match the pressure of their machine and bring forth an espresso with perfect crema and an aroma to die for. But he will only make you such an espresso if, in his opinion, he thinks you can truly appreciate his art; so sadly, the experience of a perfect espresso is often denied to many Americans."

A contemptuous snort was all that Massimo received in reply before the man became preoccupied with his phone, scrolling through his messages.

Massimo knew his wife would have frowned at him if she had witnessed the exchange. She, too, often reminded him at dinner parties not to dwell on some detailed minutia of physics. "What might fascinate you and even occupy a year or more of your research might only interest a polite guest for about 5 seconds over drinks or dinner. You have to learn to make conversation about safe topics like sports, kids or movies."

"If its attitude you value," came the voice once more above Massimo's head as the man pulled himself up to his full stature and made to depart "then I recommend you try the French coffee bar on the other block. They'll give you a dose of attitude with your espresso. Especially if you try that Italian barista story BS with them," he laughed, but then his phone buzzed once more and he pronounced, "Yes, I'm on my way," before stepping out the door and giving Massimo a brief, perfunctory wave as he departed.

Massimo stood there a moment feeling a little foolish and wondering what he was doing since he had finished his espresso ages ago. Following suit, he headed for the door to a chorus of, "bye Massimo," and, "come again," from Carlos and the girl at the cash register. She definitely looks like a wind chime with all those dangling feathers and metal pendants, Massimo decided as he went in search of his car.

"Did I eat a salad at the deli before coming to the coffee shop?" he wondered, and answered the question almost immediately as his tongue found a lodged sesame seed between his molars that could only have come from the nearby deli's house salad dressing. At least that narrowed down where his car was likely to be, and he turned his gaze to the row of cars to his left, spying once more his coffee shop companion making a rapid exit from the car park. To his surprise, it wasn't an Escalade at all that he was driving, but a smart, black Tesla with vanity plates TESLA1. He felt a pang of jealousy as the car silently whooshed past him. The days of driving a two-seater car were long gone, and he certainly couldn't justify a Tesla on a university physicist's salary, but the primal automotive hormones that pulsed through his blood knew nothing of this.

# Chapter 2 – Sand Hill Road

If Sand Hill Road were a character in a story it might be described as suffering from a multiple personality disorder. The story it would feature in would be that of the growth of technology in the Silicon Valley area to the south. Silicon Valley tentacles now spread to the southern reaches of Santa Clara County, but the cortex, the nerve center had stayed here on Sand Hill Road, close to its maternal Stanford campus. Like any rich, complex character the Road hid most of her traits from the casual viewer. The trees that lined the modest four-lane avenue managed to conceal the low-rise office buildings on the northern side. The smooth skin of the pavement that linked the Stanford campus with the foothills in the west was frequently adorned with the spandex costumes of cyclists on their lunchtime jaunts.

Today, however, she lay indignantly indisposed while enduring some cosmetic surgery. Massimo sat patiently at the traffic light at the lower end of Sand Hill Road waiting his turn to pass through the single lane detour around the construction work. His lunchtime swim usually relaxed him and tempered his native disposition to lean on the car horn whenever the car in front did not immediately move forward to fill a gap. The traffic crawled past the utility upgrade project that spilled across the roadway in front of the new office complex, where he noticed large spools of fiber optic communications cable. No varicose veins of fiber were allowed to despoil the legs of Sand Hill Road, standing here at Stanford's portal. The fibers would be pulled through subterranean duct work hidden from view. As was his habit, Massimo did a quick mental calculation as to the capacity of these network communication fibers, based roughly on the diameters and numbers of fiber trunks that he saw being pulled into the conduits. He mentally shelved the absurdly large answer he came up with, wondering how he may have erred in his calculation. Not even the SLAC National Accelerator Laboratory where he was currently employed could use more than a fraction of such a bandwidth, and SLAC, being after all the founder of the World Wide Web on the North American continent, could be a very hungry user[6]. It was hard to imagine that the string of office parks spread along the flanks of the hill rising towards the freeway could use anything close to that network capacity.

Once clear of the detour, the traffic sped up again and Massimo was overtaken by several large and expensive sedans whose occupants were clearly in a greater rush than he was to return to work after lunch. A brief attention lapse as he fiddled with the radio volume to catch the last comments on the public radio station about a program the following day nearly caused him grief, as both a black Mercedes and a BMW sped past him and cut him off to make sharp right hand turns into the steep driveway of the office park. He pondered his wealthy neighbors' preference for black cars with tinted windows as he half listened to the radio commentator preview the upcoming show on Evangelism's fight against false gods in America.

Taking a little more care this time, Massimo maneuvered his car into the left turn lane as he approached the entrance to SLAC. Ahead of him, in contrast to the other traffic, were two sensibly sized Japanese sedans and a bicyclist waiting to make the turn into SLAC. The bicyclist was not one of the spandex crowd, but wore street clothes and clips at his trouser cuffs. As Massimo drew closer he noticed they were in fact clothes pins protecting the baggy pants from the chain; undoubtedly a visiting scientist from Europe. Blue jeans and casual shirts defined his American colleagues, but the northern Europeans seemed glued to their corduroy trousers and woolen sweaters no matter how much it warmed up during the day. He hoped someone had warned the young cyclist about the dangers of crossing at this spot as he watched him wobble across the intersection.

If Sand Hill Road was suffering from a multiple personality syndrome then one of these personalities had a decidedly vicious streak, for this same road had taken the life of another young cyclist making the same crossing not so many years ago. Late afternoons would see the sun low on the hills in the west and drivers would be hard pressed to make out a lone cyclist through their squinted vision. Not so right now for the sun was still high and the maritime cloud was cresting the western hills and would roll over the sun later in the day. The sun would not be blinding anyone today, the road would be well behaved for now and the only price to pay would be a cool evening. It came as a surprise to first time visitors to the Bay Area that even in summer one often required a sweater to dine *al fresco*, Italian style in the evening. "Our maritime air conditioning," Massimo had been told when he first arrived, thinking that all he would ever need were shorts and a tee shirt in sunny California.

A mark of the multiple personality syndrome is that each of the dissociative identities seems to know very little about each of the other personalities. Massimo was pulling into the lab where his coworkers were quite oblivious to their high-rolling neighbors across the street. The lab took up the most sizable single piece of land along Sand Hill Road, but it likewise provided a cloistered life style for its inhabitants. The linear accelerator from which the lab's name was derived stretched a full 2 miles to the west, passing beneath the freeway and extending well beyond to the forested foothills. Research labs and support buildings sprawled almost another mile in the other direction making this a very visible aerial landmark. Not many local residents knew the details about the inner workings of such a place. There were a few who had taken the Saturday public tours and were driven around the site in a bus while a grad student would try and explain how the wondrous world of quarks and leptons could be revealed by colliding beams. The grad students acted as tour docents to boost their meager research stipends, and the participants were mainly visiting relatives. Certainly none of the luxury cars from the affluent neighbors would ever be found on the SLAC visitor parking lot.

For their part, the lab acolytes confined themselves mainly to their own premises. A cafeteria served their lunchtime needs and a few would sometimes kick a ball around or throw it over a net on the lawns. Some would venture outside to a local sandwich shop, or run a brief errand to the bank or store before hurrying back, but no-one ever talked about "the other side."

The other side of Sand Hill road for all its modest appearance is *the* venture capital center of the western hemisphere. Not just for Silicon Valley and the technology hub it represents, but it has grown into the venture capital center for the world economy. No one with serious big money to invest could afford not to have an address here. Hollywood would have us believe that Wall Street was the business center of the western world. The impressive Manhattan high-rise lays credence to the impression, but Wall Street is just the public marketplace for the greater establishment. It needs the ostentation and rowdiness of New York to function. Any decision on where to put $10 billion to launch a whole new industry is not made in the rarified atmosphere of a 50th floor Wall Street boardroom, but rather around a table in a modest room of wood and glass sheltered behind the Coastal Live Oaks scattered along Sand Hill Road.

As Massimo walked across the parking lot he fell in beside another colleague also returning from a lunchtime outing. A lanky fellow with a drawl to match, who had joined SLAC after the Super Collider project had been cancelled in his home state of Texas. Massimo proceeded to tell him how he had just been cut off by two large cars near the entrance and how he was worried for the cyclist. His colleague nodded gravely in concern and talked a little about how SLAC could better instill bicycle safety in the minds of their coworkers.

"Those guys at West Capital Ventures or whatever they're called must have been in an awful hurry to close a deal after lunch," Massimo added, trying to make conversation as they headed across the quadrangle.

"I'm sure I wouldn't know," was the limited reply he received.

"Do you suppose NASDAQ considers its office across the way to be right in the middle of things nowadays?" tried Massimo again searching for a little conversation.

"NASDAQ?" was the only reply, if you could call it as much, Massimo received.

It wasn't that his research colleagues were totally ignorant of the world outside their gate, it was more a case of being so remote from the world of big business that it rarely fitted their daily perception of reality. Massimo turned the conversation back to the safer topic of their research ramblings and said,

"You know, I was thinking some more about our conversation on dynamic modeling of chaotic systems," returning to his earlier aquatic musings.

This time the response was much more animated and they were soon speculating that with enough computing power they could put to the test all the fanciful ideas Massimo had on predictive behavior.

"I did try linking all the on-site servers afterhours to make one massive parallel processor to try out my model" Massimo continued in a low a voice, "but it's still way too slow."

"Hah, now I thought as much. I noticed the system slow way down at about 2 a.m. on the weekend when we switched back from daylight savings time. There's an additional hour of time that does not appear in the computer server logs, so you thought no one would catch you, you dawg. Don't do it too often and I won't tell." He gave a playful nudge that almost sent Massimo's diminutive frame stumbling across the weedy verge of the path.

"There's no point in repeating it unless I tie in many more computers, like those from the Berkeley and Livermore Labs across the Bay, and then some."

The Texan's narrow squint widened in sudden expectation that he was about to become party to some great plan, so Massimo hastened to add, "But that's not going to happen anytime soon because even if you scale up a neural network to that size it gets bogged down by the available network speed linking all of the computer nodes."

"Well now, if only the lab could afford its own direct satellite uplink like WVC across the road, the problem would be solved!" drawled his friend.

"Wait, what?" said Massimo, stopping dead in his tracks.

"West Venture Capital, you just mentioned them before, and that triggered a memory of something I saw just last week." He stopped and turned to wait for Massimo to catch up before adding, "You know I like to go walking at lunch times to clear my head, just like you and your swimming; well I took a shortcut the other day through the lane behind WVC and saw a new pair of giant satellite dishes installed on their roof."

Indeed, Massimo often noticed his tall friend striding at a fearful pace along the verge of Sand Hill Road when he was either departing or returning from his own lunchtime excursions. The guy walked so fast that people could rarely keep up the same pace for long and he ended up walking alone.

"At first I thought they must be contracted to NASA, but those ones are pointed to low latitudes where the big-boy data communication satellites are sitting. So my guess is that those rich guys can afford the fastest data communication on the planet, so they just do it for no other reason than that they can."

Massimo didn't reply for some time. His thoughts had stopped flowing as though someone had hit the pause button; somehow things were out of kilter and made less sense than before. As he reached his office door he turned once more and asked

"Do you know if SLAC is getting a giant, new fiber optic trunk connection installed for our high-speed Internet?"

"Naw, in your dreams. I'd be the first person to know about something like that. I mean, really, who could afford to fund something like that around here?"

"Exactly," murmured Massimo, largely to himself as he drifted into his office.

Massimo did not immediately plunge into his research as he normally did after his free-roaming midday breaks. Instead, he brought up a Google map of the neighborhood on his computer and overlaid a network node map on top of it that should have showed all the fiber optics trunk cables. He learned absolutely nothing from the exercise. In fact, it was strange that so little information appeared on his map, for when he zoomed out, much more detail was available for neighborhoods further away. Could somebody exercise censorship on a utilities map?

Resignedly, he closed his browser and brought back up the documents from earlier in the day detailing the funding application his collaboration team was putting forward for new projects. The irony did not escape him that here some of the brightest minds in the world spent a huge fraction of their time begging for money for so many new projects while across the road their neighbors were always desperately looking for ways to spend their billions.

If this was not a case of extreme dissociative identity disorder, then what was?

# Chapter 3 – Laura

The sun had not yet broken through the bedroom blinds and Massimo slept late the next morning. His biological clock had told him it was Saturday and there was no rush to go to the office. Massimo did sometimes go into the lab on weekends for it would be quieter and he could work uninterrupted by phone calls or meeting requests from his online calendar. This morning he did not feel the urgency to rush back to his papers; there had been no great confluence of thoughts to culminate his week. The only legacies of the week were some doubts and uncertainties lingering at the back of his brain, refusing to come forward and clarify themselves.

Pushing the blinds aside he saw only a uniformly gray sky, silicon gray, he always thought to himself when it looked like this. Yesterday's fog bank poised on the crest of the hills had indeed rolled down into the valley during the night and now lay pooled on the valley floor. But the gray would soon take on the glint of its silicon namesake; for the sun was already at work polishing away the top layers of fog so that by lunchtime the valley would once again gleam like the silicon chips it was known for.

Massimo had not gotten completely accustomed to living alone, and he gazed at the nearly empty cupboards as he shuffled into the kitchen. Massimo's estranged wife, Donatella, had been very orderly and organized.

Not only had the cupboards been full during their years of marriage, but there would always be placemats under containers and decorative holders for everything. Massimo had always considered such decorative embellishments superfluous in a kitchen but he had remained silent for they had fallen into more conventional marriage roles where he had avoided the kitchen altogether. The move to the U.S. had proved a trial and she had not endured more than two months. Upon first arriving to take up his appointment at Stanford, she was unable to reconcile her traditional upper class Italian upbringing with the Californian lifestyle. The food in the markets was all wrong, despite the abundance that Massimo marveled at; and Donatella thought the people lacked a dress sense; while Massimo thought it was like being on vacation to be able to walk to the store in sandals and shorts.

These recollections did little to enliven Massimo's mood as he stood in the kitchen staring at the moka pot bearing evidence of yesterday's coffee still encrusted on its side. It would not magically clean itself in the sink and Massimo's frustration only increased as he saw that the discarded Lavazza packet was also empty. Not even bothering to look for bread in the cupboards, he instinctively reached for his phone to call Laura.

During the ardent love affair with Laura, that had lasted only a few precious months, the house had been warm and messy and the two of them had often spent hours together in the kitchen cooking and tasting, talking and laughing about their work and their lives over a bottle of wine. Laura was a postgraduate student, quite a bit younger than Massimo and they had met through the Italian club on campus that Massimo had been frequenting since his wife's departure. Their age difference had raised eyebrows among his colleagues whenever she was introduced, but, not being his student, no one could officially complain. Her work was in a whole different area, focusing on cellular biology, and she worked down on the university campus, not far from the pool where Massimo had his lunchtime swims.

Things had gone awry when Massimo had exclaimed, in a fit of passion how he wished he could make an honest woman of her.

She had given him a cold stare. "You think I was a dishonest woman before I met you? Am I somehow unworthy at the moment because of our relationship?"

Massimo attempted to explain that this was not what he meant; the term honest was just a turn of phrase. He tried to explain that Donatella had left to return to Italy with little hope of ever agreeing to a divorce because of her conservative religious background.

"You're missing the whole point!" she cried. "For a woman to be taken seriously in science, she has to work incredibly hard to be recognized as standing on her own two feet. I don't want to be perceived as some appendage, dependent upon an older man for support or advancement."

The quarrel had lasted for several days. It never actually turned bitter, and was in fact interspersed with some fervent love-making to the point that Massimo felt that he had won his case. Finally Laura had declared, "It's just no use living together. You'll always fall back into your conventional role of the male caregiver and assume that I'll take the role of homemaker." She'd gotten up and her voice trailed off as she left the room. "The trouble is you're too damn good at it."

By the next morning Laura had already packed her bags and announced she was returning to a shared student housing apartment.

"Wait till I've finished my dissertation," she'd said, "And see if you're willing to follow me to my first career appointment."

They remained friends and still saw each other from time to time. "Friends with limited benefits" Laura would teasingly say when she kicked him out of her apartment on evenings when she wanted to work.

Memories of all the good times with Laura flashed through his mind as he dialed her number, all the time staring despondently at the bare kitchen surrounding him. A sleepy voice finally answered after three rings.

"Massi, I only answered because I saw it was you calling and I had to get up anyway to go pee, but I'm going back to bed straight away. I pulled an all-nighter and now I have to sleep."

The image of Laura standing there in her night time attire of panties and a tank-top leapt into his mind. He managed to resist asking what she was wearing, knowing that she would find that a little creepy, even coming from him. He heard the toilet flush in the background and could imagine her padding back from bathroom to bedroom in her bare feet. His body yearned to be able to crawl into bed beside her and feel the warmth of her slumber. She responded to his silence by adding

"I'll bet you've run out of coffee again and are feeling sorry for yourself because it's the weekend."

"No," he stammered. "I just wanted to invite you to join me for breakfast at a French café someone told me might be good."

"Not this time," she yawned. "Call me back this evening and maybe we can cook dinner together at my place. You have to do the shopping, though," and the phone went silent.

Feeling a little dejected, Massimo reached for his cycling shoes thinking that the exercise of biking to the café might bolster his spirits. He did not normally wear full biking regalia, but in deference to his fellow cyclists who would be sharing the road on a Saturday morning, he reached into his closet and retrieved his cycling shirt. At the back of his mind was also the mischievous thought that its Italian colors of green, white and red would signal the right message if he was going to eat breakfast at a French café. A flashy pair of streamlined sunglasses completed his ensemble.

The bicycle had to be lifted down from wall hooks in the garage, and it took several minutes to inflate the tires to the correct pressure and check them with a gauge. The bike had once been his pride and joy. A custom frame built to fit the lean body of his youth when he had just graduated from university. It had been a reward to himself for completing his dissertation and was lovingly hand-fitted with authentic Campagnolo parts. He remembered painstakingly selecting each and every gear-wheel and brake lever to assemble the ultimate bike that was going to take him on an epic tour of the Italian Alps.

That trip never eventuated because first he was given the chance of a lifetime to go to CERN in Switzerland[7], and then later he and Donatella made the big move to the States. He had dutifully lugged the bike along on each move, carefully hanging it from wall mounts in each new domicile, always promising himself that the grand tour would one day happen. The alloy frame was no longer the most lightweight in today's world of carbon fiber bicycle technology, but it still gave him a thrill to crouch over the curved handlebars of his bike. Nobody, he thought, can come close to reproducing the svelte lines of a Campagnolo bike, and he pedaled off.

# Chapter 4 – The French Connection

Massimo's cycle shoes clattered as he crossed the black and white tiled floor of the French café. "Oh, that does smell good," he thought, as wafts of freshly roasted coffee beans intermingled with the yeasty aromas of croissants emerging from the oven. The café walls were adorned with the typical posters for such an establishment, depicting the Eiffel tower and black cats in various scenes involving coffee cups. There were also a couple of original jazz-themed posters that he found appealing. The place was quite busy so he claimed a seat by placing his bicycle helmet, sunglasses and bicycle pump on the table. He turned his full attention to the large glass display case featuring quiches and ham baguettes on one side and ornate looking gateaux and fruit tarts on the other.

"Monsieur, what would you like?" asked the cashier from behind an ornate zinc countertop.

"I would very much like a large cappuccino, a croissant and a bread roll with some jam," Massimo answered.

"One café au lait, one croissant, one buttered baguette avec confiture," repeated the cashier.

"Extra foam on the café au lait," Massimo added hopefully as he paid.

He took his order back to the table and marveled that it looked really promising and smelled even better. The croissant looked so perfectly flaky that he bit a piece off before even sitting down. The baguette was arranged on a plate with a tiny pot of jam sitting on a doily with a small silver spoon. It crossed Massimo's mind that even Donatella might have liked it here, but she probably would also have complained that he had already eaten off part of his croissant.

The tables were laid with a sugar bowl and a small arrangement of flowers floating in water. He sprinkled a spoonful of sugar lightly over the top of his cappuccino and observed how the thick foam was able to support the fine sugar granules. The taste combination of the sweetened foam and the bitter coffee beneath was always a treat but today he pondered over why the foam could support the grains when a liquid could not. A foam, after all, was just some empty space whipped into the liquid, so how could adding nothing do something? There was no magic involved, he knew it was all to do with surface tension and increasing the surface area, but the apparent paradox kept him amused as he munched on the baguette. The structure of the foam was the more interesting thing, he thought to himself. It was a fine example of his current research on how a microscopically random structure could have such regular and predictable macroscopic properties. He could just imagine making a presentation to his funding agency and saying that these new 'amorphic random vacancy structures' he was investigating could have vast practical applications like floating sugar on his coffee.

"Ah, I see you followed my café recommendation," came a voice from behind. Looking up, he recognized the tall, well-dressed figure from the previous coffee shop encounter.

"Oh, yes, thank you, it's very good. I'm particularly enjoying the croissant. It brings back fond memories of Geneva."

The man turned and signaled someone behind the counter without bothering to place an order at the cashier. Turning back, he pushed the bicycle pump aside and sat down uninvited.

"Think you are going to get a flat tire inside the café?" he asked. The corners of his mouth were upturned to give just the slightest hint of a laugh.

"You can't be too careful. I've had several pumps stolen when I left them attached to my bicycle," retorted Massimo, with his mouth half full of croissant.

"Is that your Campagnolo outside, then?"

"Yes, yes it is," smiled Massimo, his chest swelling with pride. He was also a little surprised that someone would recognize a custom bike like his.

"A fine piece of equipment or what's left of it after those kids were messing with it."

"What!" exclaimed Massimo jerking his head around and straining to look out the window until he noticed the man was quietly chuckling.

"Don't worry, just kidding. Nobody's going to bother with a bike around here unless it's all carbon fiber and titanium."

"Well it means a lot to me still," replied Massimo settling back down to the remains of his coffee and baguette.

"Oh, I know what it's worth," he replied. "I tried to build a custom Campagnolo once, but I could never find a frame big enough to suit me, if you know what I mean."

Massimo nodded, his esteem for this knowledgeable table companion rising up a notch or two.

"So I had to go the Shimano route, with a frame built here in the US. Technically speaking it was the better choice in the long run." Noting the cloud of disappointment that had passed over Massimo's eyes, he hastened to add, "But you have ended up with the real classic out there."

Appeased by his companion's concession to the classic style of his beloved bicycle, Massimo happily launched into a conversation about the real benefits of carbon fiber technology. The conversation became quite detailed and they were soon discussing the advantages of carbon nanotubes and the empty space they introduced into structures which paradoxically made them stronger.

Massimo could not resist telling his newfound companion that he had just been pondering that very same paradox for foams, which were, after all, just a random structure and shared nothing of the beautiful linear structures of nanotubes. With a flourish he sprinkled some sugar over the dregs of foam in the bottom of his cup, and held it up to demonstrate the effect. He encountered a disapproving stare in return, such as a parent might give a child caught playing with its food. Massimo scooped out the foam with his spoon, and ate any remaining evidence thus saving further embarrassment from his over-enthusiastic physics demonstration.

"I thought no self-respecting Italian would ever add milk to his coffee drink," said his companion cracking a wry smile.

"It's perfectly okay to do so before 11 a.m.," said Massimo, relieved to draw the conversation away from physics demonstrations. "It's just that after 11 a.m. the taste of pure coffee seems more appropriate."

"Well, in that case you are in for a treat," and his companion signaled to the barista once more. "They make a special single shot for me here with fresh Lavazza beans. You should try one and also help me finish this *pain au chocolat*," he suggested, pointing at his plate. Massimo took more notice of the activities behind the bar, and saw now that the coffee machines were the old fashioned kind with long pump levers that the barista was required to pull down to apply just the right amount of pressure to the coffee.

At that moment his companion stood and turned towards the door addressing a newcomer.

"Georges, come and meet my new friend. He's a coffee connoisseur and fancies himself as a bit of a mathematician as well."

He stood to extend his hand to the newcomer. "Hello, my name is Massimo," he announced, exchanging handshakes.

"And by the way, my name is Michel, or Mike if you prefer," added his new companion, sitting back down.

"But he also answers to Mickey or even Mikhailovich and a few other variants." Georges winked and joined the two others at the table. Georges had evidently been smoking outside before coming in to join them, for he carried the strong odor of Galloises into the café with him.

"Looks like you guys have been discussing some serious mathematics," observed Georges pointing with yellowed fingers to the paper table napkins where Massimo had been scrawling equations describing the patterns to be found in foam structures.

"Yes, our Italian friend here is someone to watch when it comes to emerging technologies," replied Mike, tapping an extended forefinger to the side of his nose.

At that point three espressos were delivered to their table along with another plate of croissants while the messy remains of Massimo's plate were quietly whisked away. Massimo eyed the perfect crema topping the espressos and immediately took up his cup to hold it under his nostrils. With closed eyes he took first a small sip and then finished with a single gulp.

"Truly, I don't think I have enjoyed an espresso this good since sitting at the Piazza di Sant' Eustachio in Rome," sighed Massimo and bit off another piece of croissant to round off the experience.

"Glad you liked it. I did tell you this was the place to find 'attitude' if that's what you value in your cup," affirmed Mike.

"Well I hope you tell me how I can be sure to receive the same service next time I visit. You said they prepared it especially for you. I'm curious how you are so well connected here."

"First of all, I would recommend that you not come in here flagrantly wrapped in the Italian flag," laughed Mike, gesturing at Massimo's shirt, "Especially when it's getting close to World Cup Soccer season."

"What, this old thing?" Massimo remarked with mock innocence, fingering the collar. "It's just my old cycling shirt. How could that offend anyone?"

"And it really suits you," chimed in the young waitress hovering behind Massimo waiting to clear the cups away and bring them anything else they might request. "Such pretty colors. Do they stand for anything?" the coquette asked, fluttering her eyelashes at him.

"Green, white and red stand for hope, faith and charity!" said Massimo in a flourish of that special patriotism reserved just for expats.

Mike and Georges rolled their eyes. It dawned on Massimo that he might have offended their national pride since Georges was clearly a Frenchman and Mike might also be a Francophile for all he knew. Maybe they even owned the place and these Gauls, he knew, could only tolerate the company of a Roman for a limited time.

"I suppose I should think about heading off. I won't be able to cycle up Sand Hill Road if I eat any more of these delicious croissants. You really know how to make the best 'bread and coffee' I have had the pleasure to enjoy in a long time," said Massimo with exaggerated politeness.

"Sand Hill Road?" asked Mike with one raised eyebrow.

"Yes, I thought I would go by my office and put in a few hours while it's quiet."

"Yes, we are heading back up there soon as well. Can't say it will be quiet, though; our office is hectic all the time now it seems," added Georges.

"You also work on Sand Hill Road? For a while there I thought you might be the owners of this place "

"Owners? No, not really. The two French brothers over there are the proprietors. We just bank-rolled them. That is to say Georges financed them, and I was the one who put Georges up to it," answered Mike flatly.

Massimo nodded his head in approval. "Well, congratulations, you've made a fine investment."

"Not really. I'm recommending that we not go beyond the start up financing phase. It has no *Series A* growth potential, so adding working capital for a second round would be a bad move," continued Mike.

Massimo's brow wrinkled as he looked around. Not only could he not make sense of their financial jargon, but every table in the establishment was now occupied with hungry patrons. "It looks like it is doing such good business, though."

"But what kind of business model is it? You capitalize on using a bunch of antique, leaky espresso machines for the sake of image, and then rely on some server's 'attitude' for the quality factor. How could you ever start a franchise from this model?" Georges sniffed.

"I'm sorry to hear that," said Massimo, meaning that it would be a shame for the neighborhood to lose such a fine establishment.

Mike leaned back in his chair and cocked his head to one side so that he was now looking down his nose at Massimo. "Oh, don't worry about us. We'll still make a tidy profit on Georges' initial investment. We'll make it look attractive on the books for someone, maybe even one of Georges' siblings, to do a leveraged buyout, and we'll be in the clear." The number of happy patrons spilling out onto the sidewalk clutching croissants and cappuccinos was of no consequence. "The thing is," he continued, "we don't want to turn Georges' $1 million seed money into just $1.5 million, we want to turn it into $10 million at the very least."

"So you work on Sand Hill Road too, huh?" said Georges, grinding his teeth in an irritating fashion and beginning to look a little bored. "Then how come you are writing out *Navier–Stokes equations*[8]," he said pointing once more to the paper napkins covered in Massimo's scrawl.

"Oh that," Massimo replied, feeling a little more comfortable that the conversation had returned to his subject area. "I was explaining that the structure of foam had a lot to do with turbulent flow and *Kolmogorov length scales*[9]."

This time it was Mike whose eyes rolled, half closed toward the ceiling. "Georges here studied mathematics at the Sorbonne."

"You know there is still the *Millennium Prize*[10] to be won for solving the *Navier–Stokes problem*." A touch of petulance crept into George's voice, in response to Mike's obvious boredom with the subject. "I would much rather make a million dollars from the Millennium Math's Prize than from my grandfather's legacy."

"Only in Palo Alto," marveled Massimo, "could you expect to have a conversation about higher mathematics in a coffee shop. Was your grandfather also a mathematician?"

"No, my grandfather is Georges Daria owner of Daria Financial Enterprises, and he has set up a trust fund for his five grandchildren so that we may get some experience, so to speak, in venture capital." The teeth grinding and sniffing became louder as he spoke of his grandfather.

"Not to be confused with *George Doriot*[11]," interjected Mike, "our famous compatriot and founder of venture capital here in the Valley, who invested $70 thousand in *Digital Equipment Corporation* in 1957 and turned it into a cool $350 million when he sold it 11 years later."

"And what is your grandfather expecting you to do with his trust fund?" Massimo looked around the coffee shop, so enamored with the conversation that he expected everyone present would want to lean over and join in.

Georges shrugged his shoulders. "We should each invest $100 million in startup ventures, and whoever gets the greatest return in five years will become the CEO of his new venture capital firm here on Sand Hill Road."

"Is this coffee shop a part of that financial venture?" asked Massimo, still amazed that he was having this conversation with these new acquaintances.

"Think of it more as a practice exercise for Georges to learn the tools of the trade," answered Mike.

"But what about you?" continued Georges, unfazed by Mike's sarcasm. "What is it that you do on Sand Hill Road that allows you to pursue this kind of mathematics?"

Massimo felt this deserved a serious answer but as he leaned forward he immediately recoiled from Georges' stale tobacco breath. "I'm an accelerator specialist, and I try to mathematically model complex phenomena which look random on the microscopic scale, but collectively bring about large and sometimes predictable changes on a macroscopic scale."

Georges was unaware of the effect his poisonous breath had on people, and grinned at Mike, revealing his yellow, unsightly teeth. "He should meet our Kate. Her department handles all the accelerator work for our company, but I can't say that we use these same mathematical models. Which company did you say you worked for?"

"I work for SLAC, on Sand Hill Road."

Georges was evidently very new to the area, for he asked with one of his increasingly annoying sniffs, "SLAC, I don't think I know it, do you Mike? Is it an Italian company?"

But Mike was now laughing. "He means the giant particle accelerator, Stanford Linear Accelerator, S.L.A.C."

"I don't understand the joke," said Massimo apologetically. "Are you investing in companies building compact particle accelerators for medical applications and so on?"

Georges responded as though he were speaking to a child. "No, no I was talking about investment accelerators. We accelerate a lot of startup companies through their growth phase by finding market synergies for them. I was wondering what your mathematical modeling had to do with *our* accelerators."

Mike put his hand out on the table to halt the over-zealous response from Georges. "But you should still meet Kate. We do a lot of research into, how did you put it, predicting the behavior of chaotic systems made up of billions of random interactions and trying to control the large collective swings."

"Really," said Massimo, "what kinds of systems to do you analyze?"

"The Stock Market."

A pause ensued as Massimo looked from one face to the other, but no further explanation seemed forthcoming. "You're serious? I would have thought a system driven by so many psychological factors wasn't really tractable in a mathematical sense."

"True. We are very specific in our area, though. Simply put, we want to predict and control when a startup firm can go public and how much can we expect to make from an IPO," answered Mike. "But I should leave the subtleties to Kate to explain. You would like her, and if I'm not mistaken she has a thing for short Italian guys," he smirked.

Massimo tried to ignore the innuendo and said politely that he would be delighted to learn more about their systems whenever the opportunity presented itself.

"Listen, we have these regular get-togethers at the *Rosewood* where we brainstorm over a few drinks in the evening after work. Why don't you give me your email or mobile number and I will text you next time we head over there. Love for you to join us and have you teach Kate a thing or two."

"Ah, sure, sounds nice, thank you," said Massimo fishing a business card out of his wallet with his contact information. He had never actually been to the upscale Rosewood, even though it was right next door to SLAC. It had a daunting façade designed to appeal to the well-to-do inhabitants of the office park rather than the SLAC academics.

"Where is it that you fellows work exactly?" inquired Massimo, still wondering if it wasn't a bit unusual for someone from SLAC to be invited into the world of the big business.

"We're at WVC. Just across the road from you guys," Georges responded happily.

Massimo just stared at them, at a loss for words.

"Great. We'll be in contact, then," Mike finally said, taking the card. "Gotta go. Georges - we have another meeting. Nice talking to you Massimo; enjoy your cycle up the hill. The bill for breakfast has been taken care of." And with that they swept out of the café leaving Massimo no time to respond or even say thanks.

The climb up the Sand Hill Road incline was not particularly steep, but it was already late in the morning and the sun was high, so that by the time he reached the SLAC gate he was in a sweat. It had been an interesting morning for Massimo, meeting such a different class of people at the coffee shop. Rather than going straight to his papers as he entered the cool air conditioning of his office, he began a methodical web search for all that he could find listed for West Venture Capital. The sweat began to dry on his neck and sent a shiver down his spine.

It was getting quite late when Massimo remembered his promise to Laura to do the shopping for that night's dinner, so he headed for the farmers market in search of something suitable. Not knowing exactly what would be on the menu, he strolled past the stalls and examined the fresh produce, selecting whatever he thought looked good. Foremost in any menu planning was the choice of which wine would go with the food. There was still time to go to his favorite wine shop and pick something appropriate. Laura and he could both enjoy a traditional Italian wine, but they liked to explore some of the local Californian varieties as well. Perhaps a crisp Italian white to start with, like a Friuli from the Venetian plains, and then a California pinot to follow. He always ended up buying way too many bottles, but on the other hand he liked to leave things at Laura's apartment to indicate that he would be returning frequently.

# Chapter 5 – A Musical Interlude

Massimo arrived at Laura's apartment as the sun was setting. The tops of the trees shone in the last remaining rays as the sun set behind the student apartments and the hills to the west. Laura's roommate, Eva, was just descending the stairs as Massimo arrived. Stretched pants over slightly plump thighs and a bare midriff greeted Massimo's eyes as she came down to his level.

"Laura is still in the shower," informed Eva, leaning provocatively on the railing. "You can get all wet with her, or, if you prefer, you can come party with me."

"I brought some dinner things to prepare," he responded, holding up the bags from the market to cover the embarrassment he felt every time he saw her.

Eva could instinctively sense weakness, just like a dog can smell fear on a man. "Are those carrots in the bag, or are you just pleased to see me," she leered, brushing past and pushing him up against the wall.

Fortunately, Eva spent most of her time out of the apartment when Massimo was there because he never knew what to make of her advances. The door to the apartment was open and he could hear the shower running in the bathroom. Trying the handle, he found it locked so he tapped lightly. "It's only me."

"Make yourself at home, Massi. I'm going to stand under the hot water for a bit to see if it helps the knot in my shoulders."

"I could help with that," but she seemed not to hear so he proceeded with taking the groceries to the kitchen. Passing her bedroom door he saw the still unmade bed with jogging shorts and underwear strewn on top. Laura favored the more sensible grey cotton of sports bras and panties, citing comfort over appearance, but Massimo found her equally sexy no matter what she wore. In fact, he enjoyed pulling those tight elasticized tops over her head in bed at night and getting a face full of her soft flesh. "Time enough for that later," he sighed thinking it was probably not wise to be found staring at her underwear, and he hauled the bags from the market into the kitchen.

Reaching up to the top shelf, he retrieved his two favorite wine glasses and gave them a rinse in the sink. They seemed to be safely out of Eva's reach up there and just needed a polish to get the dust off each time he came around. He struggled with Laura's cheap corkscrew and thought that could be something else he would purchase and leave here as a reminder. Laura walked in just as the cork popped and eyed the bounty of his market purchases.

"What do we have here?" she marveled.

"It's a young Friuli from Veneto," twirling the glass between his fingers and holding it up to the light.

"No, the food, silly. How many people are you planning on feeding?"

"Tonight we have fresh pasta with *cimelio pomodori*," pouring Laura a generous glass of the white wine. "Nobody ever seems to have cimelio pomodori when I ask," handing her the glass and holding onto her fingertips. "But today I spied them myself," proudly splitting open the bag and letting their ungainly shapes wobble across the counter. "The lady kept exclaiming something about 'hair looms', but I set her straight and explained that they are *vecchie varietà pomodori* and taste wonderful prepared just with good olive oil." He reached into the bag and pulled out a liter bottle of the same.

"You shouldn't tease the market ladies," giggled Laura, reaching up and putting her arms around his neck to kiss him long and gently with her soft and open mouth. They held the embrace long enough for Massimo to run his hands down over her smooth bottom, now covered in a stretchy pair of workout pants. "Mmm, no underwear," he murmured.

"First we eat," and she gave him a gentle shove.

"Well, the market ladies appreciated me," grinned Massimo, "and they let me taste some of their different olive oils. I must say these Californian olive oils are really good."

"I hope you didn't crack your old joke about the extra virgins," she retorted.

"No, I was such a gentleman and we got talking about our favorite foods and they went and found this for me at yet another stall." With a flourish he withdrew a small plastic container from the bag. "Bufala mozzarella!"

"Oh, my favorite!" she said, but then ran outside to the balcony, to return a few moments later clutching several broken stalks of a yellowing basil plant. "I knew I planted this for a reason. Mozzarella with fresh heirloom tomatoes, olive oil and basil. Yum."

"Good thing I bought this, then." He produced a large sized pot of fresh basil that he had also bought at the market. "I think I should come over each day to water this."

"I know you'd like to do that." She gave him a playful squeeze. "I'll prepare the mozzarella, then, and you can do the pasta because we don't have that much time before the concert starts," she pronounced, taking first a gulp of wine.

"Wait, what concert? I thought we were having a quiet night together, on our own," pouted Massimo.

Laura glared down at the cutting board. "I told you a week ago that my friend has a wonderful opportunity this evening to play with her chamber group at the Stanford Memorial Church. She needs our support in the audience. Besides you love that kind of thing."

Massimo was more than taken aback by Laura's sharp tone. "Look, I'm sorry. I know, you're right, but I've had a lot on my mind this week and I was looking forward to sharing it with you and telling you about this interesting pair I was conversing with at the French Café this morning," he replied.

"I suppose I should've reminded you on the phone this morning, but I was still asleep." Before he could get too complacent she added, "I want to be supportive to my student friends." Something was clearly still bothering Laura because after a few moments of silence she stuck the point of the knife into the cutting board. "You never ask me about my work, or what I've been doing with my friends, it's always about you."

The evening was definitely not going as he had planned it. The knife sticking up out of the cutting board was a little disconcerting, too. "I'm sorry, it's just that all this week I feel I've been on the verge of discovering something and today I learned some amazing things." He looked pleadingly into her eyes. "And you know I always want to share my discoveries with you."

Laura wasn't having any of his puppy-dog act, and said quite coolly, "After the recital there's a party, and, if you decide to join me this evening, you can meet some of my friends. There'll be plenty of time to talk then." Her voice softened just a little. "Some of my fellow students are in the mathematics faculty, and I am sure you can mesmerize them with your latest ideas, and ensnare them with your discoveries, just like you do me."

Massimo had prepared a thin wedge of mozzarella with a slice of the tomato and a sprig of basil which he now drizzled with the olive oil and just a drop of balsamico. Waiting for just the right moment, he popped it into her mouth as she looked up at him and followed in close to kiss her before she even had a chance to swallow. She relaxed into his embrace and returned the kiss. Closing his eyes the world spun for him as he took in the scents of her warm skin deliciously mixed with the herbaceous smells of tomatoes, basil and olives. His mind cast back to sunny days in the fields of Tuscany when he had rolled in the grass beneath olive groves amidst the wild herbs.

"Well, okay, I admit it, you can win me over with your mozzarella kisses," laughed Laura, straightening her clothes. She turned to busy herself with the rest of the meal preparation and did not notice a distant look of sadness that crossed Massimo's eyes. The girl he had romped with in the hills of Tuscany had been Donatella, not Laura.

Over the course of the meal Massimo related to her the events of the morning, starting with a description of the French Café with its most excellent coffee and croissants, to which Laura nodded in appreciation. He continued with the story of the chance second encounter with Mike and his friend Georges who seemed to be in the venture capital business and worked just across the road from SLAC.

"When I told them about my mathematical algorithms at the lab they seemed to be able to grasp it quite rapidly, but entirely from the point of view of money flow and market dynamics."

The thing that worried him, he explained to Laura, was that they seemed to treat a small business like the café just as an exercise in financing a startup. Only the profit line seemed to matter and they had no concern for the lives of the people involved.

Laura rose from the table and stooped to wipe a dribble of pasta sauce that lingered at the corner of his mouth. "That attitude never makes sense to me. Why not let it continue to exist as a small business, does every enterprise have to be franchised and become a chain?" But then she answered her own question. "I guess they can make a greater short term profit by writing the whole thing off as a loss and unloading it somehow."

"I'm glad you're not like that." She methodically scraped her dish and stacked it in the sink. "I'll take your absent mindedness any day over their ruthlessness. Could you take the rest of the things to the sink while I quickly change my clothes?"

He was polishing the wine glasses and restoring them to the top shelf when she reappeared in a full length dress of unusual oriental colors.

"Very becoming," he said appreciatively, admiring how it left her shoulders bare.

"It was a gift from an Indian friend who taught me how to wind it around in many different styles. This is the nontraditional style" she said lifting one leg high so that it parted her skirt at the front and revealed a milky thigh all the way to her crotch.

"Are you not wearing underwear?" he exclaimed in mock breathlessness.

"You'll never find out if we don't get a move on for the recital first," she winked, with one hand on her hip.

"I'm not really dressed for a recital in the Memorial, or the *MemChu*, as you insist on calling it," he grumbled.

"Just put your jacket on. You always look presentable, *si bell'uomo*," and she smiled at him in such a way as to melt any further resistance he might have.

As Massimo settled back in his seat beneath the great dome of the Memorial Church, he had to admit to himself this was not a bad way to spend an evening. The mosaics covering the walls glistened in the soft light. The discreetly lit stained glass windows were nicely proportioned between the soaring arches. It was not to be compared with the great cathedrals he had grown up with in Italy, but he could appreciate that care and attention had gone into its design and architecture so that the overall effect was pleasing and harmonious. Laura was taking pains to point out to him that the themes portrayed in the art were much more humanitarian than their counterparts in Italy. The statuary in an Italian cathedral focused much more on death and damnation compared to the aura of salvation illuminated here. Laura made sure he was aware that many more women were portrayed in the scenes here, thanks to Jane Lathrop Stanford's enlightened views in her time[12].

The program looked interesting. It was to begin with a Haydn string quartet and Laura pointed to the name of her friend amongst the players. He liked the musical form of the string quartet, especially the early classical compositions which appealed to his mathematical love for symmetry and patterns. The musicians came out to take up their positions, and as they checked the tune of their instruments one final time, he was relieved to hear that Laura and he were occupying the better seats under the cupola. The acoustics of this marvelous building were fickle, but fortunately just beneath the spherical dome the sound was very pure. In his early days at Stanford he had once stumbled upon a rehearsal during a tour of the campus and was horrified at the cacophony of sound that made its way down the transept towards the vestibule where he had stood. But now the opening notes of the first sonata movement swirled gloriously around the pendentive and fell softly on his ears under the watchful eye of the oculus of the dome above.

As the second movement took flight his thoughts began to wander while the notes of the allegro drifted slowly around him. Earlier thoughts and conversations reemerged on the similarities between his mathematical model of chaotic motion and the dynamics of money flow in volatile markets. Fortunately he had never turned his computational skills toward an analysis of the formal structures of the music he was now hearing, for that would have ruined the emotional pleasure; but he could not stop his mind's eye from visualizing little graphical charts of the tonal cascades that toppled around him. At the end of the movement he shared in the audience's collective hushed fidgeting to compensate for the period of enforced stillness. Necks and shoulders creaked as they were straightened, and bottoms were slid imperceptibly on the hard polished wood.

The livelier notes of the minuet that followed caused him to look up and take note of the players. Laura's friend on the second violin was certainly striking in appearance. Her earnest countenance as she deftly returned each cadence handed over to her by the first violin did not detract from the fine features of her profile. High cheek bones and a long straight nose were softened by wisps of blonde hair that had escaped the tight bundle at the back of her head. The overhead lighting played off the wisps of hair and gave her tall head an angelic halo that set her quite apart from the other players. She sat with a tall arched back and with each musical phrase would lean toward the other players in turn as though to receive their notes. Massimo felt quite unnerved after a while that she was returning each of her notes with such blatant acuity as though the piece had been written for the second violin and not the quartet. She should have been the first violin. It was startling to behold this Nordic angel not only dominate but captivate first her fellow players, and then the audience with her performance. Sitting there, head and shoulders above the others, hair and face aglow against the black of her dress, she was the Archangel, Massimo thought.

The final Rondo brought normality back to the performance as each of the players spun their refrains in intersecting circles. Massimo relaxed a little and slid slightly back in his chair to enjoy the remainder of the piece, delighted to suddenly feel Laura's hand slip softly into his.

As promised, after the show Massimo was led off to a party for the performers at the home of a fellow student. The house was quite humble, at least by Stanford standards, and was packed with students around Laura's age. They pushed their way through the throng toward the kitchen in search of a drink. Before they even reached the door, the tall, unmistakable blonde figure of the second violinist pushed her way toward them.

"Laura! How wonderfully sweet of you to come. I couldn't have faced my performance tonight without knowing you would be there in the audience." She hugged Laura with such intensity that Massimo immediately dropped any notions he held about the austerity of women from the northern latitudes. "When I spied you in the audience I felt compelled to play some passages just for you. I hope I didn't get too carried away in the third movement," she continued.

"No, it was breathtaking. You had us transfixed with your playing," responded Laura with genuine warmth.

When she was introduced to Massimo the air of warmth and affection abruptly changed. She fixed him with her icy blue eyes and gave him a slow, rigid handshake from an arm outstretched to hold him at a maximum distance. This archangel is a Norse goddess, he thought. Not to be tampered with.

"Massimo, I have heard much about you," she said, continuing to look down her long nose at him. Her seemingly friendly words of greeting were said with such cold precision that he reflexively put a hand to his chest, as she continued: "You must tell me more about your work and your relationship with Laura." He felt like a patient on a table being sliced open for examination.

"Hildr is also a mathematician," came Laura to the rescue. "I'm sure you two could discuss the subject for hours, but let's get some refreshments first. You must be dying for a drink after that performance."

"Oh Laura, always thinking of my welfare," and she turned her back on Massimo to escort Laura arm in arm to the kitchen. Massimo followed at a short distance, giving a little shudder at what had just happened.

In the kitchen more students were embracing Laura as Massimo entered, and this time he was greeted with warmer nods and smiles from the throng of students. He took up a position between two friendly looking fellows who immediately offered him a plastic cup of beer without his even asking. They both turned out to be in Laura's statistics class, a subject she did not relish but needed for her biology studies.

"I don't normally drink beer," yelled Massimo above the party noise, "but this is really good."

"It's Lars' school project," came the reply.

"What, you make beer in school now? That was never offered when I was a student," he laughed.

"No, no. I made the business plan for Whiskey Hill Brewing, and Stanford Startups procured the venture capital. A side benefit is that I get to 'promote' the beer at all the parties I go to. It's great, I get invited everywhere now," beamed Lars.

"And I am the quality control consultant," added Sven, Lars' friend. "I also came up with the name one day after we came back from a bike ride along Whiskey Hill Rd. You know that road at the far end of Sand Hill?"

Massimo nodded, explaining that he worked on Sand Hill Road, and the two young men were duly impressed. Lars and Sven were handing out cups of beer to each new face that appeared in the crowded kitchen and made sure that Massimo's cup never got below half full while they talked. They were very eager to talk about their business startup, and answered all of Massimo's questions about the stages of funding and how the money flowed through the different entities that were created around a new business. For his part Massimo told them his story of the French Café startup and his chance encounter with the two people from West Venture Capital.

"You are so lucky," shouted Lars above the party clamor. "The VC business is all about networking. My dream would be to go and work with an outfit like WVC when I finish with Business School. But you don't just get to meet people like them by chance. They seek you out when it's in their interest. What have you been doing that would attract attention from people like them?" laughed Lars, giving Massimo a friendly jab.

"Me too," chimed in Sven. "They have one of the best computer centers for financial analysis in the industry. Imagine having those resources available when you graduated." Sven was a computer science major and evidently his friendship with Lars had grown out of their mutual fondness for the cold amber liquid they were now pouring into everyone's cups.

"I have nothing to do with the world of Venture Capital," answered Massimo. "My field is dynamic modeling of chaotic systems, at SLAC. For particle accelerators," he added, noting with pleasure that the topic appealed to the two young men as he launched into a full description of simulations that could be done with fractals to predict the outcome of turbulent flows. He saw out of the corner of his eye Laura pulling silly faces at him to indicate that he had gone into his lecturing mode. But what the heck, there was no way he was going to be able to pry her out of the clutches of the Nordic goddess, so why not indulge a little on his favorite topic if the beer was flowing and his audience was keen.

"Say, what do you know about Hilda, or whatever her name is, the beautiful violinist," hiccupped Massimo between gulps of beer.

"Ah, *Hildr*, the Ice Queen: Beauty, brains and musical talent. She is pursuing a PhD in math," answered Lars.

"Well, the Ice Queen is acting like she wants to abduct my girlfriend to her ice palace," muttered Massimo.

"Laura is safe if she is not a violinist," winked Lars. "Hildr had her own string quartet in Sweden, at a very young age, and they went on tour in Europe. Quite the prodigy according to newspaper articles. The quartet broke up, under a dark cloud, but nobody knows the story exactly. She terminated a rising career in music and came to Stanford to take up a career in mathematics instead. You could talk safely to her about math. That's your field as well, and she doesn't feel threatened there."

Massimo took the cue to continue talking about his computer simulations and how it could be generalized to analyze any chaotic systems. "Even the flow of money in markets," he laughed half jokingly, but Lars and Sven took him seriously at his word, egging him on with pointed questions. "It's just a matter of finding the correct canonical variables to describe the flow of money." Had there been a podium and chalk board available then Massimo would have completely transitioned into his lecturing mode, but he made do with his second favorite recourse to paper napkins and marker pens. "In physics when we describe the flow of a stream of water, or a beam of high energy particles, for that matter, we use the position and momentum of the particles, so in a financial transaction we need to track the volume and speed, or frequency of transactions to analyze the market behavior."

"That's right," cut in Lars. "One transaction of $10 in a day generates the same wealth in the economy as 10 separate $1 transactions in one day. The speed of the money flow is just as important as the size of the transaction."

"So what you are saying is that your program could predict when the money flow would become chaotic, or turbulent as a result of the speed of the transactions becoming too high?" added Sven excitedly at the thought of seeing such a simulation run on the computer.

"Where it gets really interesting," continued Massimo, "is in being able to predict the size and number of the whirlpools and eddies that occur in turbulent flow. Just like the eddies you can see in a fast moving river as it passes a rock or a pylon."

"Whoa, you lost me there, guys," interrupted Lars. "What's an eddy look like in the money market?"

Massimo slowed down to explain more carefully. He realized he was enunciating for the first time the thoughts that had been swirling around his head during the concert that very evening. He took a deep breath and described with little diagrams how an eddy occurred when the water spun off from the main flow and would take a whole new trajectory.

"In a financial market an eddy is a spinoff where a portion of the money gets concentrated around a new venture. Some spinoffs grow and end up becoming large new corporations, others shrink and disappear."

Lars and Sven were eagerly nodding their heads, refilling Massimo's beer cup with greater and greater frequency to make sure he wouldn't tire of their questions.

"Ooh, this stuff goes to your legs, doesn't it," he huffed, while heaving himself up on the counter for a seat, and also to gain a little height on his tall, blonde companions. "A good analogy is in the simulations done by atmospheric scientists. The winds that circle our planet are always creating little eddies of low pressure. When one of those eddies passes over a body of warm water like the Caribbean, it can pick up more and more energy and grow until it becomes a hurricane. An eddy so big you can see it from outer space."

"A perfect storm!" enthused Lars. "I can just imagine that spinoffs would sometimes become new corporations, even whole new industries, like you said, but other times the money flow would be just too fast, and it would wreak havoc in the financial market."

"But you can't predict all that?" argued Sven. "Nobody can do that."

"Some features you can," countered Massimo. "The meteorologists do a great job predicting the number and size of hurricanes that are likely each year, and the general areas that are susceptible. They're just not very good at predicting tomorrow's weather," he sniggered.

Scientists were always keen to make fun of their colleagues in other fields, and Massimo was on a roll: "I bet I could even come up with a formulation of the Uncertainty Principle for financial markets. It would be something like, 'you can know either exactly how much money you have, or how fast it is being spent, but you can't know both precisely', I think," he said very loudly for the whole kitchen to hear, in the belief that this was such a profound thought that everyone would want to hear. "At least, I never know where my money is going," and he laughed heartily at his own joke. But, as was often the case, no one else seemed to get it, or worse, no one appeared to be listening either.

Trying to regain a little composure, he turned to Lars and asked, "In your opinion, what would be the implications of being able to make broad predictions on the stock market?"

Lars drew himself up and answered with such sobriety that Massimo wondered how he did it. "There is a fundamental principle that we are taught in Econ 101 which states that a free market, like the stock market, is always perfectly informed. That is to say, that if one person knows something that gives him an advantage in a trade then the price reacts accordingly, and everyone finds out about it and the level of the playing field is restored automatically."

"That sounds reasonable," agreed Massimo, "but what's that to do with predictions?"

"Well, suppose you make a prediction that gives you an advantage over other traders. If you act on it the price will change and other traders will act accordingly. The outcome will therefore change and your prediction will no longer be valid."

"It is true then," Massimo exclaimed. "That is exactly the underlying logic of the Uncertainty Principle[13]. It's Schrödinger's Cat all over again!"

Lars and Sven did not quite follow Massimo's sudden mirth, and exchanged a look suggesting that Massimo was indeed a little crazy in the cat department.

"There is one thing, though," broke in Sven, "and that is the fact that the Venture Capital market is not a free market where everyone is perfectly informed. If you had enough data you could test your theory of modeling the financial flow in the VC market and look for deterministic chaos associated with startup companies."

The three of them looked at each other in silence, each of them stroking their chins as the import of what had just been stated sank in.

"You know, it wouldn't be that hard for me to change my computing algorithms to model money instead of particles," whispered Massimo.

"Awesome," was all Sven could reply.

"No wonder you popped up on the radar of WVC, then, if you have a program that can do that sort of thing," added Lars with a grin.

"But I only just thought of it," he said in a small voice. "What could they possibly know about me?" He kept his arms tightly clasped about his chest as he spoke.

"Oh, those guys are prescient. To stay on top of the VC game you have to anticipate every trend, every technology and those guys lead the pack on Sand Hill Road, believe me." This time it was Lars who was on a roll: "If you so much as send a ripple across the space-time continuum, they're going to feel it in the strands of their all-pervasive web," he said with pride in his choice of a metaphor from Massimo's world of physics.

Massimo felt an arm encircle his waist and looked down to welcome Laura with his eyes.

"Has class finished yet, *Professore*? You guys solved all of the world's problems yet?" she smiled.

"You know, I think we may have just created a few new problems for the world," they nodded at her, in obvious cahoots with one another.

"I should have known there would be no good come out of it when I saw Massimo lecturing you both," she said.

"Hardly a lecture. These two are both geniuses."

"Well you are talking to the star of the Stanford Graduate School of Business and the star of the School of Computer Science. My friends, I might add." Laura leaned back and folded her arms, as if to say, "I told you so."

"And there I was thinking I was chatting up the barmen just to get myself a free beer," giving them a friendly nudge with his elbow. "So what happened to your guardian angel?"

"Actually, one story I'm sure you'll appreciate is that she told me how she once played for the great Itzhak Perlman when she was living on a kibbutz in Israel."

"Sounds like she's a real prima donna. I'll bet the other members of the quartet tonight weren't too happy with her attitude."

"Funny you should mention that. The first violinist did finally show up and I convinced Hildr that the two of them should go and talk and resolve the obvious tension that has built up between them. So if it's okay with you, I would like you to walk me home now. She's completely drained me."

"Of course, it would be my pleasure." Turning to Lars and Sven he said, "Gentlemen, it was an honor and an education for me to converse with you this evening. I thank you for your ideas."

There was much convivial handshaking and backslapping, to which Lars added, "Just remember us when you get recruited into the VC world for your first startup. It's all about networking opportunities for us, remember – and you owe it to us, Mass, for the beer!"

"I don't know about joining the VC world, but I'll certainly email you about how my financial simulations succeed," at which point Laura finally managed to tear him away.

Once outside he took a deep breath and looked up at the moon through the trees. "It will be good to walk some of this beer off. I'm not used to drinking that stuff."

Laura clung onto his arm, struggling with her words now that the cold air had hit her. "On my side of the kitchen we were drinking lab alcohol and orangeade. I don't know which had the higher proof rating, my drink or Hildr's conversation."

"At least pure alcohol doesn't give you a hangover, but she certainly looked like she wanted to possess you."

"She's sweet. She can be very intense but she always does so much for other people that I felt tonight I just had to support her since tonight was the first time she played in public after splitting from her own quartet in Stockholm. She was quite traumatized by the split and dealing with all the personal relationships in the musical world at such a young age, you know."

"Is she Swedish or Israeli? You said something earlier about her living on a kibbutz. Although with those looks she's got to be Scandinavian."

"Don't get your hopes up there. I'd say she swings the other way." She gave him a playful shove so that he nearly stumbled on the grass verge. "Actually, I'd say unconventional was a better way to describe her," she continued when he'd regained his balance. "Such a complicated life. And tragic, too. She lost her diplomat parents in that Swedish embassy bombing in Israel and was left to fend for herself in her teenage years living in an urban kibbutz."

He gave a little grunt to indicate that he was still listening.

"And that's when she met and played for Itzhak Perlman when he was teaching a class in Be'er Sheba in Israel. That turned everything around for her because after that a rich patron rescued her and set her on a musical career path."

"Wow, Itzhak Perlman, that's some fiddle player to have on your side."

Laura's eyes followed Massimo's gaze up towards the moon. She gave his arm a little squeeze. "You looked like you were having a good time."

"Yes, they were a most interesting pair. And smart, too. I learnt a lot from them about venture capital finance and the world of those French guys I told you about."

"Why on earth do you want to get involved with that?" she yawned. "I'm so tired. I told you my friends were all nice, if only you made the effort to meet them."

By the time they got back to the apartment it was all Laura could do to meekly brush her teeth and stagger into bed. Massimo was feeling quite amorous after the moonlit walk and snuggled in close beside her.

"Oh Massi, don't make me move, my head is spinning. Wake me up in the morning early," and she nestled her back against him. "Wake me with your tongue. I always like that," she giggled. "It must be all the languages that you speak. Such a clever linguist."

"Cunning," he corrected her, but she did not hear his feeble attempt at humor for only the soft breathing of her sleep ensued.

The bright morning sun glared unforgivingly through the shutters. His eyelids were stuck together, but he could still feel the sun trying to force its entry. A pitiful sour taste of stale beer filled his mouth to remind him of the excesses of the previous night. The pounding from the back of his head wanted to drive home the point that he should only drink wine in future. He flung his arm across the bed but found only cold empty sheets. Prying his eyes open he leaned over and saw a note propped up on the bedside table. "Good morning, sleepy head. Couldn't wake you. Gone to the library." He flopped his head back down on the pillow in disappointment and landed with his face in the crumpled nightshirt Laura had discarded there. Her lingering smell drew a frustrated groan from Massimo and he spent the next good minute feeling morosely sorry for himself over all the women in his life that he didn't seem to be able to hang on to.

# Chapter 6 – Back at Work

The subdued office lighting and dim computer screens suited Massimo's somber mood. Mulling over the events of the night before, he had to admit that the recital and party afterwards had been enjoyable. If only it had concluded more favorably. He felt that Laura was coming around again to his way of thinking, and that she loved and cared for him, but it still rarely seemed to culminate in their actually making love, and so fell a little short of the consummate relationship he was longing for. He knew it was self-indulgent of him, but he caught himself that morning ogling the short skirt of the coffee shop cashier. Hoping to settle his stomach, he had returned to his old coffee haunt to pick up a large latte and toasted bagel. A petite espresso and delicate French pastry would not have cut it after last night. The cashier seemed to have a new piercing every time he saw her, and she teased him this morning about his obvious hung-over state. Body piercings were usually quite off-putting for Massimo, but then it was not her nose piercing that he stared at either when she reached over the counter behind her to retrieve his bagel; much better to concentrate on work, he thought, than indulge in these immature fantasies. The toast and large cup of warm liquid gradually restored his equilibrium and he turned his thoughts once again to the computer simulation he had discussed with his new friends the night before. Chewing contemplatively on the remainder of his bagel he penned his new variables on the board. The felt tip board markers squeaked annoyingly as he wrote, unlike the soothing tapping of chalk on his old blackboard. The IT department insisted that the traditional blackboard had to go because of all the chalk dust extracted from his computer fans. The blackboard had often been the source of gentle ribbing from his department colleagues who would tease him that only old ideas would ever surface on his old board. They even surreptitiously mounted an ancient abacus to the top of his board with an accompanying sign expressing their sentiments.

In truth, the chalk board had been a comforting reminder of his early days at CERN when his old mentor, Hugh, had patiently stood beside him at the board. The senior Oxford Don would use the right hand half of the board to correct, in pink colored chalk, the ideas that Massimo would eagerly scrawl in white chalk on the left half. Since then, the pedagogical atmosphere that the chalkboard evoked in his office caused him to be more thorough and accurate in his derivations. Sadly, he could no longer conjure up an image of his esteemed mentor standing next to him at his new white board and delivering imagined comments and corrections as he worked.

These reminiscences made Massimo wonder if he might get an opportunity any time soon to visit his old mentor. Hugh had long since retired from CERN and returned to Oxford. For a few years thereafter he had continued to run into Hugh on the lecture circuit of international conferences. Now the only communication was an annual Christmas card reporting contentment with his gardening endeavors at his English cottage.

Massimo smirked inwardly at what Hugh might have thought of applying the math they had worked out together to this new problem of financial analysis. He gave the equations transcribed on his board one last review, and, satisfied that they would meet Hugh's stringent demands for mathematical rigor, turned to his keyboard to start programming them into his computer.

It was evening by the time the task was complete. He relaxed for a moment by switching on the small music player in his office. No one would be disturbed by it at this late hour, and he unconsciously selected a chamber recital similar to last night's Haydn quartet. He would have liked to have called Laura and told her of his accomplishments, but he still felt irked that she had deserted him in bed that morning. Not that it was her fault he had been so hung over, so there was a good measure of guilt mixed in with his thoughts as well. He should be calling her to ask how *her* work was going and how *she* was feeling. The embarrassing realization that he did not know exactly what she was working on just then inhibited him further.

The refrain emanating from the music player called to mind the Nordic violinist from the previous night. Her superlative playing and stunning appearance coupled with her strange obsession with Laura, swirled through his thoughts in time with the musical strains. Tapping his fingers lightly on the desk to the music, he contemplated the music's points and counterpoints, all mingled delightfully together. Life, he knew, was not a simple linear flow from A to B, but was fed by a myriad of tributaries, all producing their share of cross-currents and eddies, not unlike the sounds of the string quartet he was listening to. This classical music composition had condensed life's quintessential struggle into four formal movements, each of a few minutes duration. The themes were introduced, the notes danced around each other, came together and moved apart and everything was neatly resolved to everyone's satisfaction at the end. Our western artistic heritage loved this tidy summation. If only life were that simple, mused Massimo. He could go home that night and announce to Laura that their second movement was beginning and they were to play a duet. But, life was far more complex and denied him any such feeble attempts to play the role of conductor. A closer analogy, he thought, was that life was an unending series of Indian musical ragas, and he had walked into the performance midway.

The music finished and he turned his thoughts back to the work at hand. All that was missing was some real data to feed into his simulation. His program would do the financial equivalent of producing giant weather maps of the world, which showed winds and pressure systems, temperatures and flows. To do this he needed an initial set of data to start it off, a snapshot of the financial market at some point in the past to launch his program. The program would plot the data and start making predictions. If he fed it daily data it would continuously update and make new predictions based on actual trends.

Without giving it further thought, Massimo typed an e-mail to Lars and Sven briefly stating he had succeeded in creating the program and that he was now looking for ideas or suggestions on where to find test data. He had barely sent the message off and was in the process of tidying his desk when the computer chimed with a reply:

"We're on it."

Got to hand it to those guys, thought Massimo, they are keen. The instantaneous response indicated they were never away from their smartphones either. The pleasant sensation of camaraderie he felt toward Lars and Sven clouded over when he remembered that he had still not called Laura. Even though he was aware of his inhibitions, he did not seem capable of overcoming them. He had not called Laura first before calling his friends, and had to admit once more that he was negligent when it came to enquiring about her work and well-being.

With some trepidation he dialed her number and wondered what excuses he might make. All his concerns vanished the instant she picked up and he heard the warm, soft tones of her voice.

"My poor Massi. I felt so sorry for you this morning. You looked so awful and I couldn't wake you. I even tried my special resuscitation trick," she giggled. "But you were dead to the world."

Massimo's heart dropped like a lead brick.

"I feel so bad," she continued, "that I let my friends ply you with alcohol. You were right, too, that the lab alcohol I drank didn't give me a hangover. I went for a run this morning, had a good breakfast afterwards and felt fine."

Massimo groaned. "I could come over now, and you could tell me how everything's going with your work, with you…" he trailed off.

"If only you had called a couple of hours ago," she responded. "I do really need help with my statistics class, but in the meantime I ran into Hildr and she's taken me under her wing, so to speak, and said she feels duty bound to see to it that I get the correct mathematical instruction for this class."

He could hear Hildr's voice in the background calling Laura's attention back to her books.

"And there's no getting out from under her wing now," she whispered into the phone.

All attempts at getting Laura to reconsider these arrangements were futile. When Massimo tried to push the point Laura said with finality she would probably stay the night at Hildr's house since Hildr was being so helpful and set such high value on Laura staying over.

Massimo struggled to end their conversation on an upbeat note and stammered a few compliments and good wishes before sighing a last "Buonanotte, mio dolce."

The email on his computer was chiming once more as he put the phone down. Lars was asking if a year's worth of daily NASDAQ data would be suitable for the computations. Sven had sent a follow up message stating he could compile all the NASDAQ data into a single convenient computer file if Massimo could describe the data structure he needed.

Massimo drank the cold, bitter drops of the remaining coffee and put any lingering thoughts of Laura behind him. He opened the link Lars had provided in his e-mail and saw indexes to reams of market data organized according to company stock symbols. He had to follow and open many network links, but the data for a whole year of stock trading seemed to be there.

Before packing it in for the night, he sent off a grateful e-mail to Lars and Sven thanking them for their speedy response. It would take quite a bit of work to mine the data from all the indexed links they had sent him, he informed them, but he would get to work on it soon. By way of example, he sent Sven a few excerpts from his program that illustrated how he normally read in large quantities of data from file records. That done, he turned off the office lights and headed home. A brief stop at the late night market to pick up some bread and milk was the only human contact he had for the rest of the evening.

By early next morning there were already several e-mails waiting for him. Lars and Sven had evidently worked well into the night and the result was astounding. Not only had Sven created an input file to Massimo's exact requirements, but had also written a utility program that would take any set of financial index network links, on the fly, and turn them into a data stream for Massimo's program.

Massimo dashed out of the house, grabbing a half-eaten sandwich and the remains of his coffee. He could not wait to test the program with real data. The anticipation of seeing new patterns revealed, even if it was old test data, sent Massimo's physics endorphins in a rush. His colleagues recognized something must be afoot when he charged down the corridor and slammed himself into his computer chair. Some of them exchanged knowing glances and followed him into his office to see what might ensue.

In his rush, it took three attempts before Massimo entered his password correctly. Two of his colleagues leaned against the door jamb bemusedly listening to Massimo begin to curse under his breath.

"Cazzo!"

Massimo settled down once the system accepted his password and looked around abashedly to confirm that his audience was unlikely to have understood his politically-incorrect expletives in the Roman dialect.

A few minutes of furious typing were all it took to load up Sven's programming efforts from the night before. The excitement was contagious and his two colleagues leaned over the screen to see what was supposed to happen next. This was annoying. Massimo carefully reread the instructions in Sven's e-mail again to make sure he had not omitted any steps, then leaned back in his chair and with great ceremony extended his forefinger and pressed the enter key.

Something happened.

The system crashed.

"404 Error - file not found."

"E cche ccazzo!" cried Massimo loudly.

61

"I hate when that happens," nodded his colleague in sympathy.

A rich outburst of Roman dialect followed and the two colleagues backed off towards the door, agreeing that the show was probably over.

One of them briefly leaned back in the door and said, "You know, I've seen that error before. Your additional program was written on a computer with the new operating system and you just tried to run it here on our old operating system."

"Me cojoni?" exclaimed Massimo.

The door was pulled quickly shut and he thought he could hear laughter on the other side. Massimo cracked a smile that he had been able to provide some early morning entertainment for his colleagues.

It took the rest of the morning and several e-mails to the system support group to sort out the issue of incompatible versions of operating systems. In the midst of it Massimo received a phone call:

"Am I speaking with Massimo? This is Cindy, I'm Mike's P.A. I was hoping this number would connect me with your assistant so I could set up a meeting between you and Mike for next Thursday."

Massimo remained silent, trying to think who on earth Cindy was and what meeting had he forgotten.

The voice continued, "After your meeting last Saturday, Mike would like to invite you to meet the rest of the WVC team."

"Of course!" he finally replied.

"Mike thought an informal meeting at one of our after-work mixers at the Rosewood would be the best way to acquaint you with our team."

"That would be nice," he nodded into the phone, thinking that it was high time he actually paid a visit to the Rosewood Hotel, considering how close it was to SLAC.

"Shall I send a limousine for you at 5:45 p.m. on Thursday, then?"

"It's next door, on Sand Hill Road!"

"Exactly. Most people don't like to have to drive their cars for that short distance, so we find it easier just to use the limousine service."

"I'm happy to just walk," answered Massimo.

Cindy was obviously a little flustered by the response and requested he please tell the valet when he arrived that he was joining the WVC reception. She also gave him her personal cell phone number with strict instructions that he was to call her if he had any problems whatsoever meeting with them on Thursday.

Massimo wondered how much of the progress he was making in his financial analysis programming he should reveal to the WVC crowd. It was, after all, the chance meeting and conversation with Mike and Georges that had pushed him to applying his chaos theorems towards financial market behavior. Fortunately, Lars and Sven had set him straight on the futility of ever trying to predict the behavior of a large, free-trade market like the Wall Street stock exchange. The epiphany that had clinched it was that maybe small, private marketplaces like the venture capital market could be analyzed and forecast. In the parlance of math and physics, the VC market could be treated as a closed system, free of short-term external forces and should therefore behave in a predictable fashion.

The world to which WVC belonged was so different to his world of mathematical hypothesis and contemplative research. His world was all about delving into understanding the nature of how things worked. The delight came in finding neat examples of mathematical models in nature that gave insight into how our world functioned. A good scientific model, he had been taught, was one that could make predictions. The test of this new scientific theory was how well it would make financial predictions.

The neat example he had come up with of applying chaos theorems was in the turbulent flow of money. Why should the VC world be interested in the rarified atmosphere of research in Massimo's lab?

Simply stated, the consequences of making any kind of predictions in a financial market were enormous, thought Massimo.

It was late in the evening before Massimo had his program working smoothly with Lars and Sven's data. The output from the program was, to say the least, overwhelming, with thousands upon thousands of transactions for thousands of companies, each with a vector showing actual and predicted values. Massimo could extract some broad parameters for the flow, and some parameters that indicated where the flow was either deep and smooth or rough and fast. What was lacking was an overall pictorial map that would convey the global behavior of the transactions without being distracted by the minutia of the individual transactions.

His mentor, Hugh, had taken pains to explain to him that discoveries often lay in wait for those who could display data in new and concise ways, revealing the underlying phenomena. He often pointed to a copy of Minard's famous chart on his wall that showed an historic map of Napoleon's mighty army crossing Europe to Russia[14]. The width of the line marking the route denoted the size of the army, and the behemoth that departed France was graphically depicted as reducing to a dribble of wounded soldiers by the time they returned from the debacle in Russia. Napoleonic history condensed into one succinct graphical representation.

The volume of data in this case might be better served by an animated depiction, rather than a Napoleonic chart, thought Massimo. He did have access to technology that went far beyond the constraints of the colored pens and transparencies that Hugh had favored. Before finishing up for the night he checked if the media room with the wall-sized display monitors was available for the next day. It was.

The media room was part of the astrophysics institute next door. Unlike the rest of SLAC, the cosmology and astrophysics faculty had secured a large part of their funding from private patrons and benefactors. In a brilliant move they had created a dedicated room with full-sized wall monitors for displaying Computer Data. It was like an *Imax* theater for scientists. The astronomers loved it for they could display their synoptic sky survey charts on a single giant screen rather than peering at them on a small desktop monitor and having to scroll back and forth across the image. More importantly, when VIPs were taken around they could be shown in a dramatic way where their money was going. The public face of science was vital if it was to continue receiving public funding.

He used the giant screens from time to time to display his computer simulations of the workings of the particle accelerator. If you are going to show how the beam behaves as it is fired down the length of a 3 km linear accelerator, he would argue, then you also need screens a bit bigger than your usual desktop monitor. The director liked it, too, because whenever visitors were brought by while he was at work, there would be lots of "oohs" and "ahs" as his colorful graphics flashed across the screens.

Massimo was now working nearly around the clock, fed by his own adrenaline rush at seeing something no one had seen before. The display he created from his financial simulation looked indeed like a giant weather map with vast sums of money moving around like winds and currents on the globe. He could see pressure building up around certain market sectors, sending the money swirling and causing little 'financial storms' in previously barren areas. The money did circulate in eddies, just as he had predicted. When the money flow became constricted to just a few companies, it sped up and the flow broke up into smaller eddies. The established, larger companies seemed to sit in channels of regular, smooth flow of money, by comparison.

Hoping to see if it were possible to track where $1.00 would go if launched like a paper boat in the middle of the stream, he began assigning colors to all the 'flavors' of money that he could think of. The display monitor lit up to resemble something more like the neon advertising signs of Times Square.

At that moment there was a knock at the door, and in walked the director with five 'senior suits,' as he liked to call them.

"Hope we're not disturbing. Some members of the Board of Trustees are here for an informal meeting and asked for a quick tour of anything interesting that might be going on, and I saw you had the room booked. I know you always can give an impromptu demonstration," the director nodded encouragingly before turning back to his visitors.

"This is one of our principal researchers in accelerator physics. Massimo likes to use the advanced facilities of our media laboratory to display his computer simulations."

Massimo took the cue to launch into his standard five minute lecture on beam simulations, which he hastily prefaced with a short disclaimer that the results on the monitor just now were part of a 'generalized study' and not specific to the accelerator.

The trustees didn't actually have any say in the day to day running of the laboratories, but their goodwill meant a lot in terms of allocation of endowments, so it was appropriate to treat them like royalty. Someone always felt obliged on such occasions to ask an intelligent question, even though the board was rarely comprised of any scientific members, but Massimo happily answered as best he could.

One member went so far as to ask how much electricity it took to run the large screen displays. Clearly an accountant in a former life, thought Massimo as he tried to answer politely.

After two minutes the director began to gesticulate for Massimo to wrap it up, so he clicked on the screen to set the animation in motion, using one of the newly composed color schemes. The patterns of a year's worth of financial transactions swept before their eyes in glorious abstract color. Complimentary murmurs of approval sounded all around as the director gratefully herded them on to the next stop of their tour. Only a small statured, white haired gentleman hung back and motioned toward Massimo.

"You know, we had a lecture once from James Gleick[15] after he wrote his wonderful book on Chaos. I didn't understand all of it, but I did learn enough to recognize that the point you have labeled WVC on your chart is a *strange attractor[16]*!"

"That's remarkable," exclaimed Massimo. "You're very observant. I hadn't noticed that myself yet," and he leaned towards where he had pointed on the screen, wondering if the cover had been blown on his little side project, but the gentleman had already been led from the room by an eager director.

The next few days saw Massimo taking every spare opportunity to explore new ways of visualizing the data from his simulation, especially now since his distinguished visitor had pointed out a feature he should have recognized himself. Some of the market sectors and business centers had regular, periodic transactions associated with them, but the motion around just a few of them was very irregular and produced strange shapes in his displays. If you were to draw a regular trajectory, like that of a planetary orbit in the solar system, it would be a smooth elliptical curve. What he saw here was a collection of orbits that stayed in the general vicinity of some '*attractor*', but never remained on one clearly defined path. In the early days of computer-aided weather forecasting in the 1970's a researcher named Ed Lorenz had discovered just these strange shapes in his simulations[17]. They were eerily beautiful, and appealed to mathematicians of all ages, but were foreboding in that they signaled that nature could behave in such strange ways. Massimo's plots bore an uncanny resemblance to Lorenz's *strange attractor*.

When Thursday came around Massimo was caught unawares by an email from Cindy reminding him of that evening's Rosewood get together. Such significance being attached to a mere after work drink, he thought. He also now realized it had been several days since he had spoken with Laura. Not since the night of their last arguments over whether he or Hildr should be tutoring her in statistics, in fact. She had chosen Hildr for this role, and he wondered if his jealousy had subconsciously pushed these thoughts to the back of his mind.

His cell phone started ringing and he guessed instinctively it would be Laura. She had an uncanny knack for calling him whenever his mind was wracked with uncertainties over her. He looked at the incoming number, and for the first time ever since knowing her, he let it go to voice mail.

Of course, the moment the phone chimed with a notification of a new voicemail, he picked it up and listened, brokenheartedly, to her sweet voice apologizing for calling when he was probably in a meeting. She had a favor to ask of him, and that was whether he could possibly come over for dinner that night.

How could she possibly construe that as a favor, he asked himself, since he was the one who was always looking for any excuse to visit?

She continued that she was cooking dinner for Hildr that evening to thank her for all the tutoring help, and she really wanted him there for support.

"Actually, you would be doing Hildr a big favor because she has so few people she can talk to about her mathematics thesis. In fact, you're the only person I know who would even remotely understand what she might be talking about. She's also always interrogating me about you, so I'm sure you two would get on just fine. Besides," she added in a low voice, "if you're here she won't insist on staying the night. Call me back when you can. Just think, you'll be able to admire her wondrous beauty all through dinner," she laughed in conclusion, but Massimo could tell it was a little forced and not the usual, self-confident Laura.

Massimo felt very conflicted. He didn't quite know what to do, and so put off calling her back immediately. It was late in the afternoon when he finally did, and this time her phone went to voice mail. Even at the best of times he felt awkward talking to voicemail, but now he stumbled completely, trying to explain that he had a prior engagement at the Rosewood with the venture capitalists he had met at the café. He threw into his explanation bits about working with Lars and Sven on a new computer study, adding that he didn't want to let them down after all the work they had done; and then there was the very forceful reminder from Cindy who was Mike's P.A. It all came out very jumbled. By the time he had finished leaving the message, he wished he could just erase it and say that he would love to come to dinner. He looked at his watch and saw that it was already time to leave if he was to adhere to Cindy's instructions.

# Chapter 7 – Rosewood

The late afternoon sun had not yet dipped behind the hills as he headed out the main gate. The guard wished him a pleasant evening, and Massimo checked his pockets to see that he was carrying his pass to get back in later. With the cool breeze that was now blowing down from the hills, he was grateful he had donned a sports coat. It was only a five minute walk up the hill, but the fresh air cleared his mind and he began to compose some explanations of his recent work for the benefit of the WVC crowd. There was no footpath to speak of on his side of the road, so he found himself walking in the bicycle lane at the road's edge. Approaching the crest, he had to jump out of the way as a peloton of cyclists came hurtling over the hill on their evening ride.

"That's something I should be doing," he thought to himself. The Campagnolo was getting way too little use, but joining one of the Stanford cycling teams had about as much likelihood of happening as ever completing the dream of touring the Alps by bike.

"Maybe if I got Laura a nice road bike we could do some weekend tours together," but he reminded himself that this was probably also just wishful thinking, given the way things were going between them just then.

Crossing into the Rosewood parking lot he was met by an eager parking valet wearing a red cap and jacket.

"Fetch your car for you sir?"

Massimo had to explain that he had just arrived.

"I'm sorry sir, I didn't see you pull up. Did you leave the keys in the ignition?"

This time a more detailed explanation ensued with Massimo becoming less patient and the valet more puzzled. Massimo stalked off to the lobby entrance, and the valet to the office, to consult with security. Inside the lobby a large crowd was spilling out of the bar area and Massimo headed in that general direction.

In spite of its being next door to SLAC, he did not recognize a single face. At the other end of Sand Hill Road, closer to the student campus, were a couple of burger and beer bars where he could be sure of recognizing a collegial face. Here, the faces were not only unfamiliar, but the dress code followed the dictates of a culture almost forgotten to Massimo.

A fashion runway presented itself to Massimo. Elegantly dressed women paraded themselves amongst an appreciative audience dressed in business attire. The richer wives and mistresses promenaded with a self-assured hauteur, intent on displaying the relative wealth and cost of their apparel. The junior, prospective trophy girl friends were relegated to groups of smaller tables at the periphery of the lounge area. Their outfits were on the skimpier side, designed to show their youthful assets to full advantage. The established trophy wives relied on soft silks and carefully applied texture and color to achieve an alluring effect, while the downtown secretaries achieved the same end effect by leaving a blouse carelessly unbuttoned or allowing an already short skirt to ride just a little higher. They would casually look about hoping to catch the eye of a young, upcoming executive and then whisper excitedly to their companions if it looked as if they might have succeeded. The trophy wives watched carefully, knowing full well that a few years earlier they had played the game and poached a husband in a similar way.

All this Massimo took in while moving around the bar looking for a gap where he might reach the barman to order a drink. Several waitresses scurried past with trays of drinks, but none seemed to pay much heed to his attempts to order a glass of wine. Venturing through the double glass doors at the end of the lounge took him to an outdoor setting. The brocade settees of the interior lounge were replaced by fine cedar patio chairs and tables, clustered around scattered open hearths and heat lamps. Massimo had no more success obtaining a drink from the small bar at the end of the patio than he had from inside. To his amusement though, the fashion runway show was still in full swing in this new setting. It may have even been sponsored by *Ralph Lauren* or *Hermès* out here on the patio. The emphasis was now on equestrian-inspired fashion. Slit skirts had been replaced by tight fitting riding pants, and stiletto heels by riding boots.

The younger girls confined to the periphery benches were suitably attired in forest greens and beiges, somehow aware that this might appeal to the outdoor type of executive who preferred his drink on the patio deck. Their greens and browns provided the perfect foliage to the stark black and white outfits reserved exclusively for the high ranking company wives who alone were allowed to parade the central patio.

The black riding pants were not worn to facilitate the mounting and dismounting of horses, but rather to promote the sculpted thighs and buttocks, achieved at great cost and hardship with their personal trainers. The accompanying white, Italian silk blouses may not have had the same decorous necklines as the outfits inside the hotel lounge, but they left no doubt in the onlooker's mind that they contained the finest augmented breasts that money could buy. The only splash of color allowed in the strict dress code among the senior women was in their choice of Chanel scarf, knotted at their neck. Most continued the equestrian theme in the pattern of their scarves, though some blues and grays were also allowed. Even the jewelry seemed equine, with horse head brooches and tiny stirrup earrings. He wondered what message the woman who had a small mouth bit and halter secured around her neck was sending.

Of one thing he could be sure, and that was that none of these outfits had ever been soiled by the actual presence of a horse. These ladies had undoubtedly arrived in the Woodside *Range Rovers* that he had seen earlier in the parking lot. In spite of bumper stickers proclaiming 'my other car is a horse' he was fairly certain that none of the trailer hitches had ever towed a horse float.

The most striking specimen stood majestically like a proud mare at the other end of the patio. She appeared to rear up in front of an audience of admiring young colts. Outfitted in a pair of startling black, knee-length riding boots, she broke the wives club rules of color coordination, wearing a pair of light gray riding pants stretched tightly over a magnificent rump. Specimen was not a word Massimo usually ascribed to women, but this female was at the pinnacle of her species. A white blond mane had been tightly pinned back to emphasize her high cheek bones. Only minimalistic jewelry was worn to emphasize, and not detract from, a long slender neck. With her hair pulled back in that way, she called to mind the blond, vulnerable heroines of Alfred Hitchcock movies. The obligatory Chanel scarf lay untied around her shoulders, for she had no plastic surgery scars to conceal. The radiant, wrinkle-free faces of the senior wives club were a tribute to the skills of the Palo Alto surgeons.

Massimo watched in fascination for some minutes and saw how she could ripple and quiver each muscle of her body with her practiced gestures, combining them with little shrugs of laughter, so as to put all the colts into a suitable frenzy. She owned this stable.

Across the courtyard behind her was another small patio, also with glass doors behind which a private function appeared in progress. The scene appeared less hectic than in the main bar, and a sumptuous buffet table could be made out around which the guests were casually helping themselves to plates of appetizers. Someone appeared to be waving from behind the glass, and Massimo wondered what it could mean when his cell phone rang and an annoyed Cindy reminded him that he was supposed to have informed the valet that he was joining the WVC reception. He put his cell phone away and a uniformed waiter appeared behind him asking if he would please follow him. A security guard wearing an earpiece eyed him suspiciously as they walked past a sign stating Sequoia Room – Private Function. As they entered, Mike strode across the room to meet him, arm extended, and said he was glad Massimo could make it.

"Sorry if I'm late. I thought we were just meeting at the bar for a drink."

"You remember Georges?" and without waiting for a reply continued, "Did you at least manage to get a drink?"

Massimo extended his hand to Georges and smiled, "I spied a Scarbolo Pinot Grigio from my favorite Friuli region, on the menu, but so far haven't succeeded in actually securing one."

A few exchanges of light banter followed about the venue and the crowd outside before Massimo noticed a waiter standing beside him with a tray bearing a glass of the Pinot Grigio. Mike nodded to the waiter, dismissing him before asking politely how Massimo's work was going. Massimo blurted out that it was quite spectacular and that he was amazed how the financial market behavior fitted so well with his mathematical analysis technique.

At the coffee shop he had only discussed generalities with Mike on the topic of mathematically modeling dynamical systems. It was only during his discussion with Lars and Sven, after the concert, that he had actually thought of simulating money flow based on his knowledge of chaotic systems. So, he had promised himself that this evening he was going to be a little more reserved in revealing the extent of his progress, but he now found it hard to contain himself when someone seemed genuinely interested in his work. The excitement of being in this new venue added to his willingness to answer whatever was asked of him.

By the time his second glass of Pinot Grigio arrived, Mike suggested they move over to the buffet table and meet some of the others who were congregating around it. The food at the buffet had been laid out in an appetizing manner with Asian inspired spring rolls, satays and sushi at one end, transitioning to Mediterranean-style dishes at the other end.

"I can recommend the fresh artichoke hearts in aioli, they're local ones from the coast. And you might as well eat some of the foie gras while it's still legal," he added.

Massimo heaped up his plate, as was the habit of physicists at the conferences he sometimes attended, where the food would be gone within half an hour. He was struggling with the overloaded plate when he nearly spilled his wine on a woman selecting just one piece of sushi for her plate. She gave him a suffering look and explained she had to watch what she ate. Massimo sheepishly fumbled with his plate, fork and wine glass. She did indeed have a trim figure, dressed in a smart business jacket and skirt. What struck Massimo, though, as he looked up to meet her gaze, were the pair of bright green eyes and the halo of red hair surrounding her lightly freckled face.

"This is Kate from our Analysis Department," came Mike's voice from behind him.

They moved to the side of the room where a few bar tables afforded Massimo some space to put his plate and glass down, thereby allowing him to regain a little dignity.

"Kate is our Celtic tigress," praised Mike. "One of the movers and shakers of the economic boom in Ireland at the start of the new millennium."

She modestly maintained an air of professionalism and dignity as they ate. Only the mass of red hair refused to obey her completely.

"Do you suppose the eventual bursting of the bubble in the Irish economy was in any way predictable, or was the market too random to make any calls?" he asked, awkwardly making conversation and trying to remember what he knew of the boom and bust decade in Ireland at the turn of the millennium.

"It was as predictable as any incompetent move by a government ever bloody well is," she retorted in a thick Irish brogue. "We were ahead of the U.S. in IT exports, but the bastards just couldn't stand the sight of us getting rich."

"Their loss was our gain," cut in Mike in a soothing, complementary tone. "Kate had an amazing talent for getting a disparate band of industrialists, unions and government officials to work together and launch an IT revolution."

"I was only asking because I've been studying under what circumstances the dynamics of a small capital market become predictable," said Massimo.

"That's what my department is all about. We analyze financial data and try and guess what's going to happen next," she replied in a slightly less aggressive tone. "Have you invented a new kind of crystal ball?"

He launched into his lecturing mode, fully expecting to be done with his standard spiel in five minutes or so. This time it was very different. Kate called him on nearly every generality he made and always asked for a specific example and further clarification. Not that Massimo minded, he was in his element and was gesturing animatedly with his hands how money flows could be described in his model. He was just thinking that maybe he could explain it better with a little diagram and began to pat down his jacket pockets in search of a pen when Cindy appeared magically out of nowhere with a large writing pad and clutching a handful of pens. She gave him a little nod of approval that he was complying with the plans she had laid out for him this evening.

"I told you the Navier-Stokes equation analysis was worth pursuing," said Georges petulantly as Massimo jotted down a few basics.

Mike seemed to dismiss his comment with a little wave and poured a glass of wine for Massimo. A bottle of rather good Pinot had arrived at the table and there was a brief pause in the conversation as everyone raised their glasses to appreciate it.

"One of the advantages of investing in winery startups," smiled Kate. "Although they always seem to give our accountancy department the worst hangovers," which was intended as some kind of inside joke judging by the guffaws that followed.

"It's an Anderson Valley Pinot. Worth the effort I think. It certainly has much greater growth potential than the established Napa Valley cabernet makers. Just ask the folks at Roederer," said Mike with satisfaction.

"Looks like I went into the wrong profession," joked Massimo.

"Never too late to make a change," said Mike quietly.

Massimo's messy plate had been discreetly cleared away and the table was now laid with an elegant platter of small, crispy tempura. He found he could munch on these without making a mess all over the writing pad. It was as if Cindy was artfully orchestrating his presentation and dining habits from the wings.

He now reached the part in his exposition where he told them that he had, in fact, put these theories to the test with a simulation involving actual historical data from NASDAQ. He certainly had not intended to reveal this level of detail at this early stage, but the good food and wine coupled with Kate and Mike's encouraging questions made him much more relaxed about the whole business. Only Georges, who seemed to be drinking more than his fair share, got more truculent as the details of Massimo's discoveries were revealed.

No one seemed to care much as to how Massimo had gained access to all the historical data from NASDAQ, although he was careful to give credit to all the help he was getting from the student body down on campus. Nor were they particularly interested in the fact that he was running these tests at a lab setup for accelerator beam research.

"The thing is," said Massimo conspiratorially leaning over the table so that they all put their heads together, "would the VC market here on Sand Hill Road qualify, in a mathematical sense, as a closed system where predictions could be made, of the type I've been describing?"

He leaned back slightly drunkenly and with both hands flat on the table in front of him said rather directly, "Could you, or rather, do you have access to the financial transaction data in the private sector of the VC market here on Sand Hill Road?"

Mike and Kate exchanged a knowing glance. Not because they were agreeing with something Massimo had said, but because they had achieved one of their own objectives for the evening.

"You're asking a lot," said Mike quietly, and pushed the wine bottle to the other side of the table where it was no longer in such easy reach. "The whole VC industry is based on advance knowledge of technologies and growth. You don't just hand around this kind of information for free."

"But we would be doing this in the greater interests of science," responded Massimo pompously. "This would be a remarkable proof of a whole new field of mathematical analysis and economics."

"What you're asking us to do is go into a partnership with you and fund your ideas both monetarily and with patent information so that you can capitalize on this venture."

"I am?" Massimo answered with a slightly bewildered look.

"Yes. This isn't some science experiment based on a gentleman's agreement. Any venture would involve putting the appropriate instrument in place that would assign rights and ownership to the partners and protect our data, and so on."

Kate picked up her cue. "We would also have to go through the due diligence process and thoroughly vet your proposal." Mike stood up and quietly drifted to the other side of the room while Kate railed Massimo on the necessity to check out and substantiate his claims about having actually simulated so much of the problem already.

"Good heavens. Alfred Hitchcock!" exclaimed Massimo suddenly.

"Excuse me?" said Kate, both surprised and annoyed that perhaps Massimo was not taking her pitch seriously enough.

"I'm sorry. I didn't mean to say that out aloud. The woman walking towards us reminded me earlier of Kim Novak, or was it Tippi Hedren, in *The Birds*."

Before he could explain further, Mike stepped up and announced, "Please allow me to introduce my wife, Bianca."

"It's a pleasure to meet you, Massimo," she said, extending an elegant hand. "I'll take it as a compliment that you were comparing me to Hollywood actresses, even if they were vintage ones!"

"I'm sorry, I didn't mean to be so crass," he said, stumbling to his feet.

"I do believe you were staring at me for quite some time earlier this evening," she continued.

"I have to confess," said Massimo now regaining some of his former prowess, "I could not help but admire the beautiful, hand-crafted Italian leather boots you are wearing. If you were to wear these in a hotel in Rome, signora, men would throw themselves at your feet in the hope you would walk over them in such magnificent boots."

"You know, Michel, I think I'm going to like your new friend, even if he is a little strange."

The party broke up shortly after that. It appeared that Mike and Kate had achieved everything they had wanted from the meeting, and Georges seemed completely out of it by that point. Bianca was dictating to Mike their plans for the rest of the evening, and Cindy was busy with the hotel staff sorting out the formalities.

Kate took him aside and explained that the next step in the process would be that she and her team would visit SLAC and acquaint themselves with the computer simulations that Massimo had done so far to verify that this was the real deal, so to speak.

Massimo tried to think at what point he had become part of this 'process' that Kate was going to conclude with him. He was not thinking clearly enough to contradict the smooth sequence of events that Kate had apparently mapped out for him, so he just nodded in assent. Farewells were said and Massimo felt himself being propelled to the exit and questioned over the details of where he needed to be taken. Cindy would not accept his ruse of trying to walk home, and he found himself placed in a limousine. The parking valet gave him a self-satisfied look that this time the guest was being taken care of in an appropriate way.

As soon as Massimo had exited the private reception area his phone began to buzz with incoming voice mail messages. When he mentioned this to Cindy as they made their way through the hotel lobby, she explained that the banquet room was intentionally blacked out in accordance with Mike's wishes, so that no one would be distracted by outside calls. Massimo's protestations that this was a little unusual were dismissed with a wave of her hand indicating that this was simply how Mike liked to do things.

Finding himself in the back of an oversized limousine, Massimo resigned himself to the ride back to SLAC and listened to the voicemails in which Laura was a asking him with increasing anxiousness why he was not picking up his phone, and what was behind his reluctance to accept her dinner invitation that night. Each voicemail made him feel worse as he heard Laura's voice asking with mounting despair what was wrong with him and why he placed greater priority on a meeting with some inconsequential group of businessmen.

The limousine arrived at the SLAC gate and caused quite a stir when Massimo lowered the window to show his badge and explain he was only being dropped off at his office.

Back in the lab he sat moodily in his chair wondering first of all what it was that had actually transpired that evening at the Rosewood, and secondly how was he to explain it to Laura. While contemplating how to best handle the situation, he idly opened his e-mail and saw a couple of eager inquiries from Lars and Sven asking how it was going with the program. Rather than try and deal with a distraught Laura at this late hour, he responded instead to his companions and told them of his success both with the graphics presentation and of the interest WVC was showing in their venture. Their answer was immediate, with Lars and Sven both responding that they needed a strategy planning session with him and would also like to see firsthand what Massimo's graphical displays looked like.

Massimo deliberated for a few moments; he neither wished to go home at this stage, nor did he want to face Laura and possibly Hildr and have to explain himself. He chose the easy way out, and sent off an e-mail to Lars and Sven saying that if they didn't have anything better to do, would they like to come by and have a hands-on demonstration of his program.

"We're on our way!" came the immediate reply.

Massimo figured that it was probably wiser to have such a meeting afterhours if they were going to be using the media room for something that was not strictly physics. He texted them back that they should show their student IDs at the gate and he would advise the guard that he was expecting after hours visitors.

Lars and Sven acted like a couple of kids in the media room, and Sven in particular wanted to start adjusting all the settings of the monitors and servers. Like the Stanford Board Member who had dropped in earlier, Lars thought it would be a great venue to watch the Saturday game, if only Massimo would allow him to set up a keg of his special brew.

They immediately became serious the moment Massimo's data began flashing up on the screen. A barrage of questions followed as Lars wanted to understand how the underlying equations had been parameterized, while Sven wanted to know how the graphics were being generated. But they picked up on it very quickly and the questions soon turned to suggestions for analyzing and displaying the data in ways Massimo had not yet considered. By some unspoken agreement Sven was now seated at the keyboard, and as Lars was suggesting some new change, Sven would be programming it in. The simple color maps that Massimo had been experimenting with were turned into sophisticated 3D renderings and the monitors came alive in a startling new way.

Lars finally turned to Massimo and asked, "Well, what did the WVC team think of this when you explained it to them?"

Massimo answered that in hindsight he thought he had been 'handled' by them, but not badly. The gist of it was that they now wanted to 'process' him as part of their due diligence. The upshot of this would be the setting up of a venture enterprise tasked with the job of analyzing the VC market here on Sand Hill Road.

"And making some kind of forecasts about the VC startups in the area," Massimo quietly concluded.

"Seriously?" yelled Lars and Sven together.

"I knew they had the hots for you," said Sven excitedly.

"And that must be a record time for going from the pitch to the due diligence phase," added Lars.

"Wait a minute," interrupted Massimo. "What do you mean when you said you knew they had the hots for me?"

"It's like I said the other night at the party, that you must have done something on the Internet that popped you onto their radar. So I did a key word search on your name. All your physics publications popped up, but so did a whole lot of key expressions to do with deterministic chaos and predicting the behavior of turbulent flow. Then I ranked all the searches to see what your name is associated with the most in searches. There's a sort of echo effect that happens when someone else is searching and monitoring you, which makes your rating go up. Your name has market predictions written all over it."

"How can this be possible? Is it even legal?" said Massimo in exasperation.

"Sure. Homeland Security has been doing it for years, sifting through billions of emails looking for word patterns that involve bombs and terrorism. It would be easy for a firm with sufficient internet resources to search, or keep a lookout for anyone who made a breakthrough in some area of interest to them."

Lars then added, "I did tell you that anything a firm like WVC does doesn't happen by chance, but always with a purpose. So you've been discovered. That's what we all want in the end, isn't it? Who cares how it happened. Seize the opportunity!"

Lars and Sven then started talking excitedly about what still needed to be done with the program to make it ready for a full-blown demonstration for Kate's WVC team. They seemed unaware that Massimo was having serious second thoughts about the wisdom of this whole venture and how it was being approached.

Massimo finally chased them out in the early hours of the morning on the grounds he had to go home and sleep on all that had happened. They promised to come back the next night for more after hours work. Sven asked if he could also work on Massimo's code remotely during the day, and may he give himself all the account privileges he needed to do so.

There was also an implied understanding, now, that wherever this venture was going, Lars and Sven were part of the team. Massimo smiled to himself that he had two young collaborators, and was continuing the tradition that began with his own mentor, Hugh.

Before going home for the night, Massimo typed one more e-mail, this time humbly explaining to Laura that he also did not know what was going on with him. Would she please forgive him and trust him to sort this through and do the right thing. He would get back to her soon, he promised.

Laura was still up when he finally hit the send button. Unbeknownst to Massimo, she was also pulling an all-nighter for her thesis work. There was a time when this might have evoked a flood of tears, but now she just closed the email and returned to her writing with a sigh.

# Chapter 8 – The Soloist

Massimo's waking thoughts were dawdling over the mathematical concept of bifurcation. Bifurcation was a concept from his world of textbook mathematics, so what place did it have in dreams? It described how a process might diverge on two separate paths; the high road and the low road. In truth, Massimo was still obsessing over his inability to establish a satisfactory relationship with Laura; the road not taken. In such circumstances the mind will reach out for whatever means it can to put order into the world around it. Since Massimo's conscious mind was able to make little sense of his relationship with Laura, his subconscious mind, it seemed, was rummaging around for familiar metaphors. His subconscious found a suitable analogy in the form of his bifurcation diagrams. It may not have been the wisest of ideas to try and break down his personal emotions into a mathematical analysis. He knew better than to try and reduce his enjoyment of music, for example, into a series of mathematical formulae, although part of him was always itching to do so; particularly the Bach sonatas which were so appealing in their mathematical form. There was something sublime about music, and he had a feeling that if he applied the cold tools of analysis to his appreciation of it, then he might ruin the magic that music held for him.

His personal emotions and relationships, on the other hand, were something he really wanted to understand and be able to respond to more effectively. The idea behind the bifurcation diagrams was intrinsically appealing. They clearly showed that a pair of heavenly bodies could orbit each other in peace and perpetuity like the sun and the planets, the earth and the moon. But change one key parameter in this analysis by an infinitesimally small amount, and that closely coupled orbit would become unstable and the heavenly duo would fly apart onto two separate paths. The moon could come crashing down and the debris would end up looking like the rings of Saturn. Was the key parameter in his case the intensity of a relationship? Let it become too weak and it was in danger of drifting apart, whereas allowing it to become too strong could result in instability. This philosophical model did not tell him why some bodies simply parted ways in the celestial dance of time, but it gave him solace to think it was a universal phenomenon and not through any single fault of his own. If the beat of a butterfly's wings on one side of our planet could ultimately affect the outcome of a hurricane or storm on the other side then what power had he in this simple equation of life. Such were the idle thoughts of his half-awake mind.

The fact that the textbook example of a bifurcation diagram was based on something called the *logistic map*[18] did give him pause. It was not a good idea to be basing one's love life on a theory developed by a Belgian in the 19th century who had been trying to explain population cycles in terms of reproduction and famine. There had to be more to his love life than lust and hunger!

He examined his own mental state in this same light. It was not difficult to take these ideas one step further and apply them to the workings of the individual mind. He was aware of his own mood swings between the elation he experienced at seeing his work and projects succeed, and the despondency he felt when he was not sharing the success with Laura. Why not apply what he knew of chaos theory to the workings of the mind? Compare the slow, plodding thoughts of the unremarkable mind with the fast, agitated thoughts of the creative mind. Was the creative mind not exploiting the characteristics of turbulent flow to send a train of thoughts off into new creative directions, making connections where there were previously none? The slow mind, on the other hand, only moves along established channels and reaches predictable conclusions. Language was already full of metaphors describing the creative mind — with its swirling thoughts, or minds in a whirl. It sounded remarkably like the eddies he had described in his models of turbulent flow. Is genius a case where this thought process is taken to an extreme? The mind working so fast that new ideas and connections, new avenues of thought are explored with great rapidity. Little wonder that there is a fine line between genius and insanity. Was the insane mind an example of the thought processes becoming chaotic? Is the bipolar disorder an example of the bifurcation process we can observe in mathematical maps?

Enough! Massimo could picture himself descending into a maelstrom of over-analysis. Actions, he knew, would be the thing to rescue him from his state of paralysis. He had slept most of the day after the long night at the lab, but evidently Lars and Sven were already hard at work, judging by the stream of emails awaiting him. No emails from Laura, though.

As it happened, Laura was also just arising after her late night, and had not been at her computer that morning either. All of Massimo's fears and over-analysis of the chaotic nature of their relationship would have been assuaged if he had only sought the simpler explanation—that Laura was also preoccupied with completing her dissertation and working late hours.

Lars and Sven were providing new insights into Massimo's financial model and demonstrating how it could distinguish companies with growth potential from the established cash cows. What they had would already dazzle the team from WVC, and Massimo barely felt the need to interfere with the great progress Lars and Sven were making. His time would be better spent putting his own thoughts and priorities in order before he committed any more of his life to this financial venture.

A loud knock at his front door startled him, and he jumped up to answer it thinking it must be Laura, even though such a knock would have been uncharacteristic of her. After all, she still had a key to his apartment. He pulled the door open and stood, mouth agape recognizing the tall, striking figure of the Norse goddess on his threshold. Her blond hair was no longer tightly pulled back as it had been on the night of the concert, but billowed around her face in a mass of soft, angelic curls. There was no mistaking the icy blue eyes that fixed his gaze, though. Hildr pushed past him without waiting for an invitation and placed the violin case she was carrying on the settee.

"We need to talk," she said, as she kicked off her sandals, making herself comfortably at home. "I would like to ask you some questions about your work, and I need to talk to you about my dissertation. While we are at it, we will also discuss your relationship with Laura. I am not so sure it should continue."

Hildr left no doubt when she entered a room that she was in charge. It was more than just her commanding physical countenance; she also carried the arrogant air of a member of the aristocracy whose authority was simply never questioned. Massimo was too amazed to protest. Her brazenness in confronting him with such personal questions stunned him. Unfortunately, no former experience had ever prepared him to refuse entry to a stunning, mini-skirted blonde before. Her knitted dress was very tight around the hips leaving her long, bare legs exposed. He could not decide whether it was a very short dress or a long sweater that reached just below her posterior. Either way, it left little to the imagination. By contrast, the top was extremely loose with a sweeping cowl neck that slipped off the shoulder on one side. The plunging neckline could tease a male onlooker with tantalizing glimpses of her breasts, depending on the extent she leaned forward.

What young people could get away with when it came to fashion never ceased to amaze Massimo.

He glanced down at the violin case, and for want of something better to say, commented rather lamely,

"I hope that's not a gun you're carrying," remembering how her steely words alone had cut right through him the night of the concert party.

"I don't like to leave my violin behind, unattended. It's too valuable to me."

"It's certainly a splendid sounding instrument, in your hands." He should be demanding of her what she was doing here, but he somehow lost the initiative. "Does it have a treasured heritage that compels you to keep it by your side?"

Fine creases formed themselves at the corners of her eyes as she stared back at him. It struck him as unusual for someone so young to already carry such hardened features. Her eyes moved down from his face to his crotch and to his toes as she sized him up. "Laura tells me you have an uncommon appreciation of chamber music and that you have tried explaining to her the mathematical symmetry of form in the Bach sonatas."

He felt himself redden at the onslaught of her gaze. "They have a purity of form no other composer has captured since," he answered. He must have passed some test in her estimation for she opened the case and displayed to him the instrument nestled in the velvet interior.

"It is a gift from my patron. He resides in Europe," she said in anticipation of his next question. The violin had nothing shiny or new about it. The varnish had a warm, dark patina and in places had worn so thin that the wood texture was visible.

Massimo marveled at its age and craftsmanship. "A gift from your patron?" he probed gently, not wishing to reveal his knowledge of the stories and gossip he had heard from Lars and Sven.

As though unable to resist, she gently picked up the instrument, holding it with the soft polishing cloth.

"It is gifted to me for as long as I continue to play it. It has been in my patron's family for many generations and will return to his family when I no longer perform on it."

She handed the instrument to Massimo, cradling its neck as though it were a precious infant. He accepted it with due reverence and was delighted to hear how even the light tapping of his fingers on the body produced richly resonant tones. It must be a bright and lively instrument in the hands of a prodigy like Hildr.

"It would have been very difficult for you to give up a life of music performance," he said.

Her face darkened and she retrieved the violin.

"I came to Stanford to escape the demands my patron was placing on me that had nothing to do with music."

She retreated to the other side of the room.

"I do not like to be pursued by men. They have very different expectations than my own."

"I can imagine you sent some very mixed signals to your patron and your fellow musicians," he said, hinting at some knowledge he might have of her history.

"I just wanted perfection in music," she said as she crossed back to his side of the room, "and if I can't attain it in music then I will look for it in mathematics."

With disarming directness she looked him in the eye and asked, "Do you love mathematics with the same intensity as you do music? Laura has told me as much."

"What are you actually doing here, Hildr? What do you want from me? I doubt very much that we have anything in common besides my respect for your musical ability."

She sat erect on his settee, arched her back as though she were about to perform and considered his words carefully.

"It is true. I don't desire you physically. I know that Lars and Sven call me an ice queen behind my back. That is no doubt because I told them when we first met that I would never have sex with them. They are pleasant, intelligent boys, but they can't see beyond their sullied world of applied mathematics. I told them I can only be satisfied with the pursuit of pure mathematics."

Massimo was irritated by her self-important attitude. She was precise and formally correct, but he could tell English was not her first language and she didn't have the freedom to easily express herself as she did with her music. English wasn't his mother tongue either, but it grated on him that she preferred to take this stilted tone rather risk making the odd grammatical mistake or two when speaking with him.

"If the application of mathematics to real-world problems, be they physics or economics, is what you call applied mathematics, I can see no fault with that."

He continued with a musical analogy, on the off chance that it might appeal to her sensibilities.

"Not every composition can be a Bach sonata. The role of music takes many forms."

Although, as he spoke, he thought to himself that what is sometimes passed off as music nowadays can be pretty awful.

"From your point of view my own work in mathematics must appear sordid, as you put it, dealing as it does with predicting real outcomes in chaotic behavior."

He took a few minutes to explain to her in advanced mathematical terms what it was that he was working on. She regarded her long fingers as he spoke, waiting for him to finish.

"I know exactly what it is you are working on. After Laura had extolled your skills to me I read all your papers. You have ingeniously managed to find solutions to certain cases of the Navier-Stokes equations where previously there were none. I applaud you for that. I, on the other hand, want to dedicate my dissertation to the more general problem of proving whether solutions exist or not in *all* cases of the Navier-Stokes problem. I don't want to limit myself to specific solution examples, but rather to concentrate on the underlying form of the solutions. I want to express and to reveal the quintessential essence of the problem."

She picked up the violin bow from the case as she spoke and began pacing the room with the violin in one hand and bow in the other.

"My thesis professor does not understand. He claims that this is too ambitious a project for a mathematics PhD."

She raised the violin and tucked it under her chin as though about to play. Massimo could at once see the practicality, for a violinist, of the unusual cowl neckline, for it provided just the right amount of padding for the instrument to nestle comfortably against her collar bone.

"I like to play while I discuss mathematics. For me, the two are inextricably mixed. When I formulate a mathematical thought in my brain, then the other half of my brain seems to demand a musical response."

Stretching out her arm, she pointed at him with the bow, commanding him to sit so that she could pace the room more freely. He felt himself responding like an obedient dog, such was her overwhelming presence, and he dropped to the floor at the foot of the couch, not even moving to a nearby seat.

She raised her bow once more while her left hand did a deft pizzicato over the strings, checking their tune. As she did so he wondered how the loose, baggy sleeve of her right arm was not going to get in the way of her playing. At the Memorial Church recital she had worn a slim, black dress and her blond curls had been tightly pinned back. In one smooth, practiced motion, she withdrew her arm from the sleeve and the dress fell away leaving her right shoulder bare.

"Good god," he thought. "Is she going to play bare-chested like an Amazon?"

The dress did not fall off completely, but hung precipitously, at the shoulder and tip of her breast. Her shoulder now unencumbered, she began by playing a rapid musical scale on her violin. A fine adjustment was made to the tuning pegs and she followed this with a succession of arpeggios. The space around them resonated with a burst of sound such as he had never heard in his living room before. This was quite different from the sonorous acoustics of a concert venue like the Memorial Church. There was an immediacy and sense of urgency in her playing that he felt from her close proximity within the confines of the room.

"What my professor does not understand," she continued to explain between repetitions of the scales and arpeggios, "is that the Navier-Stokes problem has not been correctly and fully stated before."

A subtle change occurred as she repeated the scale in a new key and followed it with the arpeggios in that key.

"The greatest challenge in any mathematical endeavor is the correct formulation and exposition of the problem," she continued.

Massimo sat transfixed on the floor. This tall, dominating Nordic figure towered over him, hypnotizing him with the divine arpeggios she played with crystalline acuity; a minusculey attired Norse goddess was actually standing over him in his living room, her angelic face radiating with blond curls and heavenly tones, expounding higher mathematics to him. He was flabbergasted.

"The failure or inability to correctly formulate and state a problem can sometimes be attributed to shortcomings in the language employed to do so," she lectured.

Massimo noticed that she had finished playing all the major scales and arpeggios and now switched to the minor keys. Even though she was playing the same harmonic sequences as before, the mood took on an eerily somber tone.

"The greatest advances in mathematics," she said looking at him down the neck of the violin, "have been accompanied by the creation of new forms of notation, necessitated by the new field. Newton developed calculus just to fully describe his laws of motion for the heavens."

Massimo did not have a deep, scholarly knowledge of musical theory, but he recognized a repeated pattern in what she was playing. Each scale was a mathematical sequence of eight notes, starting each time on a different note, depending on the key. The arpeggios were the sequence of notes in a chord played in that key.

"My professor cannot comprehend that I may have my own notation for describing the Navier-Stokes problem."

She continued to play the minor scales, now adding modulations in loudness and rhythm. The effect was quite disturbing. Massimo was convinced now that her playing was not for musical entertainment, but was meant as an exercise or possibly a demonstration. It could even be construed as a lesson in the mathematics of music, for each note was played with a dispassionate, didactical precision. It was a lesson that he was struggling to keep up with.

"Our brains are trained to think along certain well-trodden paths. Our professors reinforce this by teaching us to explore all the known paths before we even consider venturing off alone into the woods."

At that moment she switched from the familiar eight-note patterns she had been playing to a rapid series of five-note, pentatonic scales that sounded vaguely oriental to him. She followed this with an almost incomprehensible progression made up of 22 notes, had he counted them.

"Our westernized brains can barely cope with musical scales from other cultures. The pentatonic scale sounds, at best, exotic to our ears, but the 22 note scale of the Indian raga can only be perceived as an intellectual oddity to someone brought up on western tastes."

Convinced now that she was trying to communicate something to him with her playing, he summoned a little courage to interject a question.

"Have you played music since you were a child?"

Hildr did not like to be interrupted. "I cannot remember a time when I did not play music," and she returned to playing more difficult chord progressions with increased vigor.

"Is the violin the only instrument you play?" he asked, wondering at what age a child could even hold a violin.

She paused. "I also play the piano."

Her playing now switched to a twelve-tone chromatic scale. It sounded less melodically harmonious to Massimo's untrained ear, but it was sufficiently familiar sounding that he could follow the patterns she was creating. His question seemed to pique her interest, for she continued:

"The violin better suits my present purposes. The piano is in a myriad ways the superior instrument, but it is confined to the fixed twelve-tone spacing of the keys. The well-tempered tuning of the modern piano is admirable, but not perfect. A violin allows me to choose the exact pitch of each and every note with as much precision as I choose. I am not restricted by anyone else's notion of a prescribed musical scale and I can play any sequence of pitches I choose. I also possess perfect pitch."

Then, with no warning, she reached out with one barefoot and planted it on his chest, pinning him back against the settee as if to silence any further questions. She closed her eyes for a moment and commenced to play a piece, the likes of which Massimo had never heard in his entire life. He realized that all her playing up to then had been a preparation for this performance. All the scales and arpeggios had been to rehearse him for what he was hearing at that moment. From the onset she had been coaching him how to listen to the piece she was now performing. It was at once sublime and discordant - as pure and simple as Vaughan William's *The Lark Ascending* and as frenetic as Stravinsky's *The Rite of Spring*. His brain could barely keep up with the progression as she assaulted him musically from all directions. It teased him with heartfelt melodies that were as gentle as a floating leaf, twirling at the surface of an eddy in a pond, then it would crash down on him like turbulent rapids. There were little repetitions that harkened back to their musical lessons.

Suddenly, a light went on in his brain. He realized what she was doing. If he had not still been pinned to the floor by her foot, he would have leapt up with joy to congratulate her. She had performed a musical demonstration of the mathematical form of the Navier-Stokes equation. It showed all the details of the transitions from smooth flow to turbulence and chaos. All the clumsy equations he struggled with were neatly supplanted by her composition. Bifurcation of the intervals in the musical scales showed how *period doubling* between the notes would take a simple starting melody and transform it to a complex symphony, but then transform it further into cacophony or chaos. She then reversed the process and the cacophony melted down into music and melody. This woman was either a genius or totally insane. Or both.

Her playing reached a tumultuous crescendo and he could feel his heart pounding beneath the weight of her foot on his chest. The music stopped. The silence was deafening. They were both breathing heavily. Her body glistened in a sheen of sweat. The blond hair that had loosely swung about her shoulders was now flailed in all directions, as were the strands of hair that had come loose from the violin bow. She must have looked like a dominatrix standing over him with a whip as she stood with one foot on his chest still holding the bow. All at once he realized he had been staring up at the cleft of her panties for the duration of her performance. Unlike the comfortably sporty briefs that Laura favored, he could see Hildr preferred the briefest of underwear. Straddling him as she did, he could also see that there were no tan lines to mark any boundaries on this free-spirited girl.

He was keenly aware of her smell of sweat and sexuality. If her intention had been to arouse him with her performance, she had certainly succeeded. She looked down at him with her chest still rising and falling as her heavy breathing gradually abated, the corner of her dress barely held up now only by an upturned nipple.

Her foot slid from his chest to his crotch as she asked, "Do you want to have sex with me?"

He swallowed in disbelief while staring up at her ice blue eyes. She returned the gaze quite openly. There was no maliciousness or teasing expression in her eyes, just the wide-eyed wonderment that follows having shared a significant moment with another. He held her gaze and savored the moment, still incredulous that this Nordic goddess, an angel of such disproportionate beauty should contemplate engaging a mortal such as himself. Holding her penetrating stare for a moment longer, he realized that her eyes simply did not contain the life and vitality of Laura's gentle brown eyes. When he held Laura's gaze, he could fall into her eyes and lose himself forever. It also dawned on him that Hildr's statement just then was not being proffered so much as an invitation, but as a simple question.

"Hildr," he finally responded, "just having you standing over me like this is beyond my wildest fantasies. If Michelangelo had seen you he would have smashed his statues in frustration that he had never captured your beauty. Botticelli would have slashed his depictions of angels in disgust that they could never radiate with your glow. But honestly, I must confess I would rather make love to Laura."

She smiled down at him and said quite simply, "So would I."

A loud bang at the front door caused Massimo's heart to leap. Laura had a key to his apartment and she walked directly into the living room. Massimo colored deeply, caught *in flagrante* with Hildr's foot still planted on his crotch.

"That was quite a composition you just performed, Hildr," said Laura coolly as she looked Hildr up and down. "I could hear you playing from down on the street."

Hildr refrained from delivering a decapitating blow to Massimo's head, as would have been the right of a Valkyrie in such circumstances, or at least that was how Massimo perceived the dire situation he saw himself in. Instead, she slipped her arm back into the sleeve of her dress and casually withdrew her foot from his crotch.

"It was such a raucous piece you were playing, I did not recognize the composition," Laura continued with feigned normality.

"It was a composition by Navier-Stokes," he answered quickly, and in such a confident tone that it surprised even Massimo himself.

Hildr looked up and gave him a complicitous smile, pleased that Massimo had grasped the full meaning of what she had meant to convey in her music.

Intellectually, at least, he had found an ally in Hildr. Emotionally, it was another matter.

"This is a surprise, Laura. I mean, you don't normally visit me at my house much anymore," he stammered, realizing that he was probably implicating himself more with every word he uttered.

"Hildr said I should come by when I was done this afternoon. She said you two would need a break after talking mathematics all afternoon. I can see you have been hard at it."

Feeling that he had undoubtedly been set up, Massimo quickly got to his feet, conscious all the while of what Laura must be thinking.

I know this must look pretty strange, Laura, but really, it's not what it looks like," he pleaded.

"What does it look like exactly? What has got you all worked up?" she demanded, letting her eyes pause briefly where Hildr's foot had comfortably rested a few seconds earlier.

Meanwhile, Hildr had returned the violin to its case and looked quite calm and collected after straightening her hair.

"Perhaps Hildr can explain better than me the mathematical significance of her composition and how she ended up performing it on me. No, I mean how she ended up playing it to me." He looked pleadingly from one to the other.

"I'm not sure I know what he has in mind for the three of us now," responded Hildr slyly. "Granted, you are very perceptive in both mathematics and music, Massimo, as Laura said you were, but you behave crassly like all males. As soon as the music stops the blood rushes from your brains to your penis."

"You provoked me," he protested. "First you tease me with the greatest mathematical treatise of all time, and then you taunt me with your beauty while you hypnotize me with your playing."

"I can't believe you can extoll my beauty one moment and then in the same breath tell me you want to make love to Laura. Do you want to possess two women now? Do you want to play lord and master of both Laura and myself now?" she retaliated sharply.

"What kind of creature uses her beauty and extraordinary talent to pervert a normal human response like that?" he yelled back at her.

"Stop it! Both of you," Laura shouted. "You two can argue as much as you want over mathematics and music, but don't involve me in your sexual trysts."

"Laura, darling," said Hildr, leaning closer to Laura and excluding Massimo from the discussion, "it's just as I predicted. I can only go so far in explaining my mathematics and music, but beneath it all he is just the same as Lars and Sven. You and I can be much happier without them."

"What?" Massimo exploded. "You're the one who came here uninvited, to seduce me away from Laura with your semi-naked playing. You may be an undiscovered math genius, but you are also one seriously twisted woman if you are trying to ensnare Laura."

"Enough!" cried Laura. "I'll not have you fighting in front of me. I want you to both get out. Now! How dare you treat me as some prize in your petty math competition."

Hildr picked up her violin case and walked aloofly to the door. Massimo followed, raising his arms in exasperation but unable to find any words.

By the time he reached the bottom of the stairs Hildr had already disappeared, and he was unable to tell her what he now thought of her performance. He had only gone a few steps down the street before realizing he had just been turned out of his own apartment. Indignantly, he marched back upstairs, determined to rectify this with Laura.

She was no longer in the living room, but he found her in the bedroom, lying on the bed with her back to him. Her whole body was shaking.

"Laura," he pleaded, "I never meant to hurt you. I can't stand to see you upset like this," and he placed his hand gently on her shoulder so that she would turn to face him. She rolled away from him and a muffled cry came from the pillow as her body shook.

"Laura," he said desperately, pulling her towards him. But as she turned to face him, he saw, incredulously, that they were not in fact tears of grief but convulsions of laughter that she was helplessly trying to suppress.

"Oh, Massi, you should have seen your face when I walked in on the pair of you." She began laughing all over again. "And then the look of utter bewilderment when I threw you out of your own house just now."

"Laura, you have no idea what that woman put me through this afternoon."

"Yes, I could see you were really suffering," she replied, imitating his pouting expression.

"But it wasn't what it looked like. She manipulated me!"

She gave his cheeks a gentle pinch between her thumb and fingers, and said, "Oh, you were putty in her hands, you poor thing, you."

"No, really, she had me convinced with all this doctoral thesis stuff that she was onto something. But then she just took over completely with her music, and that body of hers. You wouldn't understand how she uses it."

"Oh, yes I do," Laura smiled. "She had me nude sunbathing with her on the roof a few days ago and I think I got the same seduction routine as you."

Massimo couldn't believe what he was hearing.

"In fact, I got a rather sunburned bottom from that afternoon. Parts of me that don't normally see the sun are a little sensitive right now, so watch where you put your hands."

Before they knew it, clothes were being hastily removed and Massimo was kneeling and kissing all the places he thought had been neglected for far too long.

"Hildr tried to put some sunscreen there to protect the sensitive bits, but it all got very complicated."

"Oh, my god!" he gasped. He leapt on her with an intensity that neither of them had felt for quite some time. Their love making was intense, but also of short duration. Massimo lay back panting from the exertion.

Laura leaned over him and drew a braid of her hair across his chest so that it tickled against his nipple. "Maybe I should invite Hildr over more often if it has this effect on you," she suggested.

"I beg you, never leave me alone in the clutches of that woman again."

"Who said anything about leaving you alone with her? I'd want to be a spectator," she added, lowering her voice to a sultry whisper.

"What? What are you suggesting?" and he rolled back on top of her, his desire rising again at the thought. But she continued the roll, and he landed unceremoniously on the floor beside the bed.

"In your dreams, Massi," and she stuck her tongue out at him. "That's never going to happen."

With that, she got up and went to the bathroom. When she returned, she grabbed one of his oversized shirts from the closet, wrapped it around her and snuggled up next to him on the bed.

"You know I love it when you leave your aroma on my shirts," he murmured, "but I'd much rather see your clothes hanging in my closet again."

She sighed. "Don't let's talk about that now. One excitement for the day is enough."

"It's just that Hildr's antics have made me realize how much I miss you and need you in my life."

"Hildr's antics," she poked him in the chest, "just show you're still a sucker for a pretty face."

"I confess. Music, mathematics and hormones don't mix for me, but, honestly, Laura, she threw herself at me, and that wouldn't happen if we were living together."

"It's no use arguing, Massi. I'm going to the East Coast next month for some job interviews, now that my dissertation is nearly finished."

"How can that be possible? You've barely started writing your thesis," he protested.

"That's just it, Massi, you're so wrapped up in your mathematical world of financial forecasts, and your new lifestyle among those VC guys, that you haven't noticed what I've been doing."

His feeble objections got him nowhere.

"But, why the East Coast?" he said. "It's so far away."

"Well, Harvard is the Stanford of the East Coast, as they say, and they expressed an interest in offering me a postdoctoral position when I was finished here."

"I can't believe you're doing this to me now, after what I've just been through this afternoon."

"I told you not to bring up the subject again of living together," and she turned angrily to the other side of the bed putting an end to the conversation.

# Chapter 9 – SLAC

Cindy had already left several messages for him that morning, reminding him of the details of the WVC team visit. They were not so much requests to call her back for details, but rather a stream of orders that she just assumed Massimo would follow to the letter if he wanted a successful outcome, with WVC backing his venture.

She had a way of drawing him in, as if he was a co-conspirator in some twisted plot.

"I don't suppose you have a waiting area for the drivers, in which case you can go ahead and instruct your security people to send the limos back to WVC to wait. I don't want them parking on Sand Hill Road and drawing unnecessary attention," she said, assuming that Massimo would get right on it. He wondered how many people were coming for the tour of inspection if Cindy was discussing a fleet of limousines. The phone rang in his office, in answer to his thoughts.

"Kate will be leading the meeting, and will be arriving with her assistant," said Cindy over the phone without any word of introduction, as though continuing from an earlier conversation. "And Georges will be arriving with his assistant as well," she went on, not waiting for an acknowledgement from Massimo. "Mike will not be attending the meeting. He has left it in Kate's hands to evaluate your proposal."

Massimo broke in. "I can expect to see you all at 4 p.m., is that correct?"

There was a pause. "I hope I don't have to repeat myself all over again," Cindy said.

"No, no, I just want to make you aware that there is also a public colloquium being held at SLAC at 4 p.m. this afternoon, so there will be a number of visitors coming through the gate around that time."

Another pause ensued. "I do wish you'd tell me these things in advance, Massimo," she chided him, but then added, "Actually, I like the arrangement better because our team will be less conspicuous. A public lecture you say?"

"Yes, it's organized by the Stanford Historical Society," he happily volunteered. "It's part of our ongoing celebrations this year for the 50th anniversary of SLAC. We have a very distinguished speaker talking about all the great discoveries made here over the last 50 years."

"So long as it doesn't interfere in the business we need to conclude," she reminded him.

"It will be fine," he assured her. "I have the media room booked for 6 p.m. to follow directly on from our tour. And *my* assistants will have everything humming and ready to go."

She chose not to respond to the tone of his last remark, and rang off with a final note of warning that he was to call her immediately if any of the details were to change.

Massimo felt satisfied with the arrangements, largely because he was now enthusiastic about the idea of pursuing a startup venture.

Last night's turbulent events that had led to an altercation between him and Laura did finally come to a positive resolution. One outcome had been his new resolve to commit to the startup project. If he did commit to this project it would have to be outside of SLAC, which would mean going into the partnership that WVC was proposing.

Another outcome had been reaching a mutual understanding with Laura over their future together. He had not exactly been caught with his pants down the day before, but emotions had run high and things were said that left many a raw nerve exposed. Massimo had finally conceded to Laura's need to establish herself in her field, and listened as she recounted some of the intrigue from her burgeoning field of biotechnology. It was far removed from his endeavors in mathematical physics, but her enthusiasm was infectious and he found himself getting wrapped up in the latest developments. The projects she spoke of were all grounded in noble intentions of finding either a cure for cancer or some other global malady, but as a researcher she also found herself becoming more and more involved with issues of financial backing and expected returns on investment.

For her part, Laura now began to realize that Massimo's pursuit of financial models in the business world was not much different. No matter what the field of endeavor, there were always questions of individual integrity and making the right ethical choices.

"I like it that you're stepping outside of your comfort zone and outside the cloistered world of physics. I'm worried, though, that you may not be prepared for the extremes some people may go to."

"You mean naïve," he grumbled. At the back of his mind he was thinking that perhaps she was just saying all this so that she could go off on her own. If that were the case, he might as well do some traveling of his own, he thought. There was an international conference on advanced mathematical physics coming up that he would not mind attending. It was the only way, really, to catch up on what everyone else was doing in the field. Reading publications could only tell you so much, so there was a definite need to venture out from time to time to meet with others and talk to them in person about the challenges they faced. The downside of participating in such a meeting was the arduous process of getting there, suffering the confines of an economy class seat for 10 hours or more. No business class travel for SLAC physicists; that was a strict rule for government funded researchers. The venue for this year's meeting was London, so an added incentive would be to add Oxford to his itinerary and drop in to see his valued mentor, Hugh.

Hugh would undoubtedly give him some very candid criticisms of his work, and also would not object to slipping briefly into the role of confessor. Massimo was able to speak to Laura now, in a positive way, over his dreams and aspirations, but he still felt the need to tell a neutral, third party of his plans to move beyond the normal realms of physics.

At the outset Laura had made clear that her main objection was the unsavory type of people she suspected Massimo was now dealing with in the financial world.

"I know it's just my personal prejudice, but whenever there is so much wealth and power at stake," she had warned him, "people are going to act ruthlessly. Not only blatant exploitation, but also having little regard for human life and well-being," she had added ominously.

"What, you think someone would try to kill me for my ideas?" he had asked incredulously, trying to brush the matter aside.

Laura had countered that he was blindsided by his desire to see his mathematical analysis proven in some real world application. She had come around, though, when he argued everyone needed to face the consequences of his inventions and innovations, and he should be no exception to that responsibility.

The outcome of the protracted and long overdue conversation had been amiable, and good will prevailed. They both ended up speaking of the others' accomplishments in admiring tones. The sex had been pretty good, too, he smiled to himself. Whatever twisted intentions Hildr had visited them with, she had also triggered some deep erotic fantasies in both their subconscious minds, and Massimo was not complaining.

Over the course of the morning Lars and Sven had also been sending him lots of messages. They had a particular boyish enthusiasm that Massimo appreciated, and he felt indebted to them that they had kept the momentum going on his project even when he had faced a lot of personal doubts during the previous few days. The latest thing Sven had done was to install video conferencing on all their personal computing devices, so at the touch of a button they could all be looking at the same screen and at each other.

Massimo decided to indulge their wishes for using the latest gadget and set up a conference call to check in on the latest arrangements for the day. He was pleased to see that Lars answered the call while jogging the Stanford Dish. Good that he had the sense to balance campus life with a bit of strenuous physical exercise. Running *The Dish* was a favored pastime amongst the jogging crowd. A winding path led up the summit of the foothills where an antiquated radio telescope dish antenna still pointed its ancient eye skyward. It had become a landmark in the Stanford hinterland, and all attempts to dismantle the relic had met with fierce opposition from the locals.

Sven had also picked up, but left his video feed blacked out for reasons of "personal privacy," which raised some good natured ribbing from the other two.

The business side of their call was soon settled and they agreed that the finishing touches for this evening's meeting could all be done remotely. Lars and Sven would be at SLAC before 6 p.m. to participate in the onscreen demonstration.

By the time 4 p.m. rolled around and it was time to meet his visitors, Massimo was feeling quite upbeat. He had taken pains to dress a little more smartly and reached for the jacket hanging over the back of his chair.

"Trying to mislead the Historical Society into thinking we're a respectable bunch?" remarked his colleague.

"Never hurts to give a good impression. I'm also putting on a small demonstration in the media room for visitors afterwards," he added, in case he ran into any of his colleagues there who might wonder what the hell he was doing.

They walked across the quadrangle together towards the visitor center where some of the early arrivals were now milling around.

"I hope I don't get asked again if our experiments run the risk of creating black holes and destroying our planet," his colleague complained. They laughed and recollected how an earlier communications director for the lab had initiated a public outreach program called "Ask a Physicist." Whenever there was a public lecture like the one today, they had been asked to wear a badge proclaiming, "Ask me! I'm a physicist!" The program and the badges hadn't lasted long, but Massimo could still remember being stumped by many of the questions. School groups were the most fun because they seemed less inhibited about asking outlandish questions. Taking them down the long accelerator buildings with their rows and rows of equipment, some of it dating back to the 1960s, seemed to inspire in them questions about early episodes of *Star Trek* and *Star Wars*. They would ask all about parallel universes and whether travel at greater than the speed of light was possible. Massimo would do his best to entertain them in the hope of inspiring a future Nobel Prize winner.

Today's Historical Society members promised to be a more reserved crowd, interested primarily in getting all the names straight of the illustrious physicists who had made their mark on the scientific landscape while at SLAC. Massimo spotted his visitors and parted company with his colleague. They were not hard to spot amongst all the retirees of the Historical Society. Kate was very smartly attired in a business skirt and jacket. Her bright red hair still insisted on having a mind of its own in the light afternoon breeze, giving her a slightly tempestuous look amid her more dour looking colleagues. Massimo noticed her high heels as he approached, and began to rethink his plans for taking them clambering along catwalks through the long equipment tunnels.

"Welcome to SLAC," he smiled broadly, putting on his best tour guide demeanor.

"This is quite a crowd you've assembled today," Kate smiled, "Not just for our benefit I hope."

Massimo hastened to correct her, pointing out that there was a public science lecture as part of their gala year celebrations.

"Yes, we did our homework," she smiled again, "and know all about your five decades of Nobel Prize winning discoveries."

"The talk this evening is a perspective on that very topic, and is being given by one of our revered Nobel Laureates himself," added Massimo.

"And a good lesson for us all," she said looking her colleagues in the eye. "Not many corporations in the Valley can boast a history of staying at the forefront of their technology for anything approaching 50 years."

Massimo warmed up to her praise and added, "Much of what we do here actually fuels Silicon Valley. There are the obvious examples of companies now building klystrons and medical accelerators, but also the more subtle symbiosis with microelectronics and the whole computer IT industry."

"Though I am sure that any IT company worth its salt nowadays would have computing facilities dwarfing anything you may have here," snorted Georges, speaking up for the first time since they arrived.

Georges had not bothered to shake Massimo's hand, even when formal introductions were made for the two assistants.

"We only claim to invent new technologies, not become market leaders," responded Massimo politely as he led them in the general direction of the visitors' center.

He reasoned that since he could not take them on a whirlwind tour of the SLAC site he might at least show them some of the equipment on display in the center.

"In here we have some of the historic devices that go into making up our accelerator and the experiments that use the beam."

Georges looked underwhelmed. Admittedly the visitor center was rather small and not a great deal of money had gone into creating the displays. The lab had always directed all of its available funds into the current science programs, rather than spending it on any superfluous niceties, as one former director had put it. Try and get a window shade fixed in your office and it might take years, but come up with a new technique for hunting down a boson and the lab would find a way to fund it, no matter what.

The two assistants had been trained to ask polite questions in all circumstances and were soon pointing at bits and pieces.

"That shiny 10 foot long piece of copper in the display case is what we call a disk loaded wave guide, and it forms the heart of our accelerator."

The two assistants nodded encouragingly.

"There are roughly 1000 of those sections placed end to end to form the 2 mile long accelerator. Sort of like a giant gun barrel for electrons."

Massimo went on to explain how all of this was buried in a tunnel deep beneath their feet, and fed by high power microwaves from klystrons in the service building, but he could see Kate gazing distractedly out the window toward the hubbub of the society participants getting ready for their seminar.

"We are here for a very specific purpose," she turned to remind him. "Interesting as this all is, we came to assess your financial modeling work and computer simulations, so we shouldn't spend too much time on the general tour."

Massimo apologized for his long windedness and fumbled with his phone to text a brief message to Lars and Sven to move the demonstration forward and to come meet them in the foyer as soon as they were ready.

"Perhaps we could move to the foyer of the auditorium, and my partners will meet us there as soon as they have readied the media room for our demonstration."

It was the first time he had referred to Lars and Sven as his partners, but it felt right to do so, and he smiled inwardly at the thought.

"There are some refreshments laid out for the lecture, which we can help ourselves to while we are waiting."

The foyer also served as an overflow seating area for the lecture which had commenced and was now being shown on overhead monitors. The advantage of watching a lecture from the foyer was that one could quietly chat at the same time without the fear of disturbing the proceedings. The director was standing by one of the monitors with a small group of senior university officials and gave him a brief nod as he entered with his visitors. A long table was laid out with cakes and cookies for the attendees at the conclusion of the lecture. The graduate students always knew about the public lectures and would come and stuff themselves a few minutes after the lecture started. This time they were trying not to look too obvious in front of the director.

"Wow, this certainly takes me back to my university days," laughed Kate as she helped herself to some tea from the urn. "We were always trying to make off with an extra bun from the high table."

"Where did you study?" enquired Massimo.

"I did my MBA at the School of Business at Trinity College," she smiled, and added, "That's in Dublin, Ireland."

"That much I knew," he rejoined. "They have starving students there as well, I imagine."

"Oh, yes, a universal phenomenon. But that all seems a lifetime ago," she sighed, and busied herself with selecting a cake to go with her tea.

"Massimo," murmured the director, who now drifted by, also looking for a suitable morsel from the table, "you remember some of our Board of Regents. You were kind enough to show them some of your computer simulations during their last visit."

"Of course. A pleasure to see you again," Massimo responded graciously. "It sounds like our lecturer is in fine form this evening. I hope you enjoy the talk."

Massimo did not actually remember any of the faces except that of the sprightly, white-haired gentleman who had asked a question at Massimo's little demonstration.

The gentleman chose to speak up again and said, "I remember our speaker tonight from when he was still a young fella, begging for money for his new fangled idea for a circular accelerator." His eyes twinkled as he spoke. "We gave him a hard time back then, but I knew he was onto something great.

And look at him today - a grand old man of science. All because of that little accelerator he scrounged together out there on the parking lot." He busied himself with a plate of cookies and then looked up at the director. "We need another repeat of that success. One of those table top accelerators you've been promising. High time, I'd say!"

"Quite," muttered the director and moved a step or two away.

"Director, if I may introduce my visitors," Massimo interjected, thinking that the distraction might be welcomed.

"Of course. I'm delighted to welcome you to SLAC." Introductions were made and the director continued, "I hope after the lecture there is an opportunity for Massimo to show you around and, if you are lucky, see one of the video demonstrations of his computer analyses."

"Yes, strange attractors," chimed in the small, white haired figure once again. He was not letting the director so easily off the hook. "You should follow more closely what this chap does. Marvelous stuff. Might point to the next big discovery," he winked at Massimo.

"In fact, that's the very reason for the visit. We're hoping to get an idea of how good these simulations can be at predicting the behavior of chaotic systems," Kate replied.

"Chaotic systems?" piped up the senior regent again. "Sounds like my personal financial portfolio. The last few years that's been in total chaos. Make some decent financial predictions there and I'll let you off the hook for delivering the next table top accelerator," he chuckled merrily before walking back to join his fellow board members.

A cold finger had placed itself on Massimo's heart as the old gentleman spoke, and he wondered if everyone already knew about his little side project. Surely not, it must be just coincidence.

"Our visitors are also our neighbors from across the street," Massimo said to the director, testing the water for any recognition of his new links to the financial world. "They are with one of the venture capital firms on Sand Hill Road."

"Really?" said the director. "We don't get the opportunity very often to mix with our neighbors. We tend to concentrate rather exclusively on our world of high-energy physics."

"And it's been a banner year for you," said Kate, much to Massimo's relief. "Having the monumental discovery of the Higgs boson occurring in your 50th anniversary year is perfect timing."

The director smiled in appreciation. "Yes, it's a fitting discovery that vindicates the Standard Model for all of the particle physics that SLAC has been working on for so many years."

The director launched into a well-practiced summary of the great discoveries in particle physics.

"The Higgs discovery stands as a monument to mankind's tenacity in unraveling the complex knot that ties all matter and energy together in our universe. It started with the discovery at SLAC some 40 years ago of the basic quark building blocks. That was followed by the revolutionary discovery by this evening's esteemed speaker of the *J-Ψ* particle that gave the first clue that the building blocks came in three families. Arranging those building blocks into a sort of *Periodic Table* is what we now call the *Standard Model*[19]. The force carriers, or bosons, complete the picture[20]. The boson that generates mass for all the other particles, and is now named after Peter Higgs, who postulated its existence, is the final piece to complete this cosmic puzzle. *One Ring to bring them all and in the darkness bind them,*" quoted the Director from Tolkien, in conclusion to his mini lecture.

Lars and Sven had come in during the director's speech and now stood quietly to the side. Massimo was about to introduce them when the director made his excuses to leave and return to the waiting board members, wishing them all well one final time.

"I did a brief course in History and Philosophy of Science during my years at Trinity," Kate added when the director had left. "So I can understand your director's excitement at being around when a great theory gets proven experimentally. It's a little like Galileo finally putting to rest the idea that the sun was the center of our solar system and not the earth."

"I wonder, though, if Galileo had to justify whether there were any practical applications for his discovery," chimed in Lars from the sidelines.

Kate turned to Georges instead. "What do you think, Georges? Is the Higgs discovery worth all the fuss?"

Georges had been standing there silent for the duration, an attitude made more annoying to Massimo by the fellow's constant sniffing. It seemed to have gotten worse since the last time they had met.

"All the significant work was done 48 years ago when the mathematics for the Higgs field was laid out. It is of little consequence that physicists have only now been able to find physical evidence for a phenomenon that is so patently obvious in the mathematics," he snorted condescendingly.

"Well, be that as it may," Kate responded coolly, "it is somehow fitting that our own financial industry is now looking more closely at the tools that high energy physics has developed over the years."

Massimo took advantage of the moment to formally introduce Lars and Sven.

"My partners Lars and Sven are not actually from the world of physics but from the Business and Computing faculties on campus. We came together in our venture quite by chance."

Lars and Sven beamed in acknowledgement that Massimo was referring to them as partners.

Neither Kate nor Georges ventured any further comment and the party stood there rather awkwardly for a moment.

"I think Lars and Sven have everything prepared for our demonstration over in the media room, so why don't we head over there now, if you would like to follow me," nodded Massimo.

They made their way across the quadrangle, and as they entered the media room Massimo noticed that the monitors were already on and a bright silver logo he had not seen before was spinning across the screens. The logo had his name on one side and *Financial Analysis* on the other. Nice touch, thought Massimo, and flashed a brief smile at Lars and Sven in appreciation. Mind you, it would have been embarrassing if one of his colleagues had wandered in before they arrived and seen this blatant advertising.

Lars and Sven took up their positions by the computer controls at the back of the room while Massimo stood before the large screen at the front to give an introduction. He began by explaining again the goals of the simulation and how the data was being displayed. It followed fairly closely what he had already explained to them previously at the Rosewood, but this time he was completely sober. Consequently, his explanations were a little more rational and less sprinkled with emotional outbursts about the wonders of mathematics and chaos theory. He had also had more time to think about metaphors and analogies from the everyday world to describe what he was doing.

As Massimo spoke, Sven launched the program and initiated the loading of the data. The screen behind him gradually filled with little dots as he continued to speak. At first the dots were scattered randomly across the large screens, but as more data was loaded and the screen gradually began to fill in, patterns began to appear and the clusters took on shapes.

"Each dot represents a market transaction. The bigger the dot, the larger the transaction."

The two assistants took notes as Massimo explained.

"The position on the screen doesn't correspond to any geographic location, rather the algorithm chooses to put companies closest together that do the most business with each other."

"So, certain industries would tend to get clustered together?" one of the assistants ventured to ask.

"Yes, there is a natural scale that we can see as we zoom in and out," Massimo demonstrated. "As we zoom in, individual businesses can be identified. Zooming out shows clusters of businesses that form market sectors, then whole industries and finally, entire economies."

Sven manipulated the graphics controls in time to Massimo's explanation, and the whole screen pulsed in response, causing the audience to jerk their heads back. The black and white screen with its pattern of myriads of dots was not unlike the old op art posters of the sixties that he had uncovered once amid the junk in his parents' attic. Sven resisted the urge to play more with the graphics' capabilities and waited patiently for Massimo to continue.

"But what of the distinction between various national entities?" pondered one of the assistants, as she tapped the end of her pencil thoughtfully against her teeth.

"You're right," answered Massimo. "This representation puts businesses that trade together close to one another on the display. It effectively ignores national borders and shows the money trail instead."

Lars was smiling at the back of the room as Massimo continued. "Lars addressed this issue very effectively by assigning different colors to each country."

On cue, Sven brought up the color intensity control and the screens sparkled with all the colors of a box of M&Ms.

"Some industries have the full mix of colors, but others show up in just one or two colors, indicating the dominance of some countries in certain industries," he continued.

The selector tool ran over one sector of the screen, and at once the highlighted companies flashed their names and a few basic statistics.

"The automobile industry," he explained with this example, "is dominated by Japan and Germany, with a smaller contribution from the U.S."

"Hah, but look which country is also growing up in that sector," said Georges smugly in a comment directed at Kate, as if to settle some private argument they had been having earlier.

She chose to ignore him and asked instead, "What if I want to search out a small, specialized industry? It would be hard to find it in that mess."

Sven slid the computer controls over to Lars who typed "champagne" in the search box and manipulated a few more color mapping controls.

"Lars picked an interesting example," Massimo responded, "because we know that champagne can only originate in France."

The screen reverted to black and white again, but after a few moments various trades were being highlighted exclusively in France's color.

"Alternatively, we can add color to identify the buyer countries," added Lars gleefully, and typed furiously at the console to reconfigure the screen.

The single color of France gradually gave way to the myriad of colors of the countries around the world that bought France's famous export.

"Merde!" snorted Georges. "The Chinese really are consuming most of our champagne."

"The assignment of colors is a powerful tool that can be customized to many different analyses," continued Massimo. "Lars has been experimenting the most with that feature, so why don't I let him explain further."

"I like to think in terms of 'flavors' of money rather than individual commodities," contributed Lars. "The cost of labor can be distinguished from the purchase of goods; banking and interest charges have their own colors; service industries are contrasted with primary production and so on. There are so many flavors that I prefer to automate the color matching with an algorithm that selects from an infinite range of color combinations. The user can be given control over tint and hue, but the rest is optimized by the computer."

As he spoke, Sven masterfully added different color spectra to each flavor Lars mentioned. The two assistants clapped their hands in glee as the display began to look more like a work of art than a mathematical representation of market transactions.

Georges was less effusive, but the three of them noticed that he was surreptitiously trying to take photos of the screen with his cell phone. They exchanged private glances, puzzled at Georges' behavior since they would have gladly given him high resolution hard copies if he had bothered to ask.

Kate appeared to be the ultimate poker player: Not a single feature on her face belied her impression of the demonstration so far. She spoke in a flat, even voice. "This is a great educational tool, and I can see its role in university economics departments, but I haven't seen any evidence of its ability to predict any kind of trends, let alone the success or failure of individual companies, as you suggested earlier."

The two WVC assistants looked disappointed and a little embarrassed that they had been over enthusiastic.

Massimo noticed from where he stood that Kate had kicked off her high heels and sat with bare feet under the table. He was sure that would have some significance if he ever had a chance to look it up in the pop psychology literature, but he couldn't think what it might mean at the moment.

"What we have been looking at is a snapshot of the markets on a single day, about a year ago," Massimo responded. "You are entirely correct that no inference could be drawn from this data as to what might happen the next day, or any time in the future. However, while we have been talking, one year's worth of data is being loaded into the program."

A small progress bar at the bottom of the screen showed the data was almost fully transferred.

"Once the loading is complete, the second part of the demonstration will be to set the display in motion and watch it evolve day by day over the course of a year."

All eyes were fixed on the loading bar and Massimo walked to the back of the room to join Lars and Sven, in the firm belief that once the animated sequence began it would speak for itself. The room was hushed as the screen went dark and then moments later snapped to life. The first few frames were a little jerky as the computers assimilated the large volume of data, but then it transformed into a smooth flow. And it was, literally, a flow. All the dots that had represented individual transactions appeared to move as the money changed hands from one company to another. Some of the flows joined together, like tributaries joining a great river, others moved fast and spiraled off from the mainstream.

This time not even Kate could maintain a poker face, and a satisfied smile crossed her lips.

"Very impressive," she conceded to Massimo.

"But now I feel overwhelmed by the amount of information you're sending us, so walk me through a couple of examples of how I'm going to use all this."

Much to Massimo's amusement, he could see Kate's feet hunting beneath the table for her shoes, which had somehow slipped behind her chair. Her demeanor above the table gave nothing away of the frantic search taking place below, supposedly out of sight of the others.

"Well, my best analogy is still the weather map idea," he answered, pleased with the general response in the room. "Once you see the flow in motion you immediately get an intuitive feel as to what's coming your way and when it's likely to get here."

The two assistants madly scribbled notes as he spoke. Georges' face, on the other hand, was a mess of emotions that Massimo could not even begin to fathom. "Chaos," was Massimo's only reasonable conclusion of Georges' present state.

"Some market areas, like the automobile industry we were looking at earlier, are very smooth and predictable, so the flow confines itself to deep channels on our chart. You can predict fairly accurately how many cars will be sold each month based on some general economic thermometers. But what is more interesting is the turbulent behavior of new companies and spinoffs that break away from the main flow."

Sven obliged by zooming in on a specific market sector.

"Over here we can see that some of the money flow is being diverted into a spin off, or start up. If it is fed from several surrounding sources, it will likely grow, but this other example," said Massimo pointing at another rotating cluster of dots, "appears to be rotating too fast and will likely dissipate itself."

Georges was becoming more agitated in his seat, and finally broke in. "There is nothing new here. We have worked with several companies that promised to predict the growth potential. At most they have managed to apply some common sense rules to predicting growth."

Little flakes of spittle were collecting at the corners of Georges' mouth as he spoke.

"You have added some high-tech graphics to the analyses, but no new insight. You may have impressed Mike with your hints at finding solutions to the Navier-Stokes equations, but I see no evidence of it here. No evidence!"

Kate rose from her chair, placing a hand on Georges' shoulder to calm his outburst. She had found her shoes, Massimo noted.

"It's true," she said, "although I may not have put it in such damning terms as my colleague here, but the business of predicting the success of startups is old hat." She paused. "My own department focuses on financial analysis to make predictions based on mundane things like supply and demand, or business competency. Less than 10% of startups ever show a return on the initial investment. We want to tap into the other 90% of the funds that are circulating out there. We brought in Georges to help with the modeling and analysis because of his advanced mathematical background."

Georges sat hunched over the table like a much maligned child whose mother had to defend his mistreatment at the hands of his playmates.

"In fact," Kate continued, "it got to the point where we had to tell these small startups that they should use their professed powers to predict their own success – or demise!"

Lars and Sven looked expectantly at Massimo, waiting for him to defend their work.

"It's true," sighed Massimo, "the visual maps serve only to draw our attention to which areas of the market are interesting at the moment. We can zoom all the way from a global overview right down to the microscopic trades of a single venture. As we do so certain patterns become apparent, and the ones that interest all of us are those where the flow is turbulent," at which point he flashed his laser pointer across the screen and directed it at a small, dark eddy rotating slowly amid the flow. With a flourish, Sven zoomed the display onto the feature where Massimo was pointing. Simultaneously, Lars entered a few keyboard commands so that a new window popped up alongside the focus area in which several conventional graphs of statistical parameters appeared.

"Here is where the real analysis starts," smiled Massimo confidently. "The parameters plotted here are exponents from the Navier-Stokes solutions. They are all within the bounds that predict the eddy will steadily grow."

He swung the laser pointer to an area further away. "On the other hand, if we analyze this eddy, we can see that it is moving fairly fast, which might lead you to think it will grow faster, but the exponents that we extract here suggest it will break up and dissipate."

There were some incoherent mutters emanating from Georges, from which Lars and Sven could only discern a few broken phrases. "I'd thought of that – there are two exponents, eh! – I could've done that."

Massimo continued unperturbed. "We can now fast forward the data and see how the two companies evolve over the course of the next year."

Lars obliged by speeding up the animation and Sven added in a few new color schemes and 3D effects for good measure. It produced the requisite "ooh!" from the two assistants.

As the data played before their eyes and Massimo's "weather forecast" for the two companies proved itself correct, Kate offered her congratulations.

"I think Mike's 'prediction' of your abilities has also proved itself to be true. I must admit I was skeptical at first, having had to deal with a few young upstarts in my time who also claimed magical abilities to predict market behavior."

Lars couldn't contain himself and added, "I suppose upstarts are the downside of startups," which produced a squeal of laughter from one of the assistants, but was quickly suppressed as she slapped a hand over her mouth.

Kate shot her a dark look, but turned amicably to Massimo. "Let's get down to the business side of things. WVC would like to become an angel investor by funding a small partnership with you."

Lars and Sven did a high five at the rear of the room, but Massimo smiled calmly. "Let's discuss some of the details, and hear exactly what WVC has in mind, shall we?"

The plan they outlined was that WVC would provide the computing, and, perhaps more importantly, access to proprietary data on the venture capital market. Massimo would be required to install and sign over rights to his program and would be expected to expand the analysis and forecasting capabilities.

"You would be a joint owner of the company, and therefore hold equity and stock options, but the company would not pay you a salary," explained Kate. "That would help avoid creating any conflict of interest for you in the event you decide to continue on at SLAC while we get started in our venture. But of course, as an equity holder, you stand to benefit the most from the future success of the company."

"Who would be responsible for the running of the company?" asked Lars. He spoke with the authority of someone who already had gained experience with startups through his campus funded ventures.

"The financial responsibility is to be assigned to a CEO, appointed by WVC in a salaried position, and that will be Georges."

Georges had assumed a very superior expression, and did not even bother to turn to face the new partners at the announcement. He therefore missed the flash of distaste that crossed each of their faces at the news.

"And what of Lars and Sven?" asked Massimo. "They are essential for any further development of the program."

Kate shrugged her shoulders to indicate this did not concern her very much. "I am sure Georges will be able to find a means of funding some intern positions for a limited time."

"Perhaps I didn't make myself clear," answered Massimo firmly. "Lars and Sven will require equity stakeholder status in this venture, or there is no deal."

"If you prefer that they are not paid any compensation for helping you," Kate replied in an annoyed tone, "then I will work on a stock option scheme for them instead."

Lars and Sven flashed a thumbs-up sign at Massimo.

"Could you also look into adding in some benefits packages for Massimo?" added Lars in an equally curt tone. "He is the founder and intellectual architect of this enterprise, so I am sure some of the benefits packages made available to WVC executives can be extended to him."

Kate bristled. "I'll see what I can do. Mike might agree to include our standard company travel and transportation package. It would still satisfy the zero-salary conditions we talked about earlier."

She started gathering her things and gave a nod to her assistant, to indicate that negotiations were at a close.

"Does that mean Massimo gets a company car?" blurted out Sven defiantly.

"Yes," she replied icily. "If this gets approved, then he would have access to one of our fleet of leased cars." She busied herself with her bag and added, "Look, there's no point in going through the minutia of the partnership terms now. You will be receiving a package from our legal team shortly and it will list the terms in excruciating detail."

Massimo endeavored to close the proceedings on a positive note. He made a few praiseworthy comments in summary and something to the effect of embarking on a whole new venture together, and then made a point of shaking hands with everyone, including Georges. They shouldn't get off on the wrong foot if they were going to be working together.

Once the WVC team had departed there were whoops and hollers from Lars and Sven.

"Let's go and celebrate with a brew at the *Goose*," they shouted. "You know they have our *Whisky Hill* on tap there now."

"The Goose does very fine burgers, but I would like to treat my new partners to the best steak in Palo Alto, and a bottle of the finest *Brunello*!" exclaimed Massimo.

They made their way out to the parking lot, laughing as they went, especially about Georges' reactions during the presentation.

Kate was also on her way to celebrate. On leaving, she had sent a short text message to Mike. "Played hard to get. They went for it."

# Chapter 10 – Steak Holders

Massimo's decree that they should eat the finest steak in Palo Alto took them to the Sundance, opposite the campus on El Camino. As they walked in the door he immediately regretted his choice. Lars and Sven would have appreciated the hip atmosphere of the Rosewood scene, he thought, compared to the staid atmosphere of Sundance.

"It can't be all that bad," countered Lars. "They're showing the Giants game on the TV screens."

A young hostess at the door smiled in response to their exuberant mood and asked if they had reservations. They didn't, and were offered a table in the bar area. The table was directly under an old, wooden Stanford rowing skiff suspended from the ceiling. The glint of the mellow light reflecting off the hull matched the subdued gleam from the surrounding wooden paneling, so that Massimo did not even notice it at first.

"I can't imagine how you keep your balance in such a slender hull," commented Lars, looking up and admiring the sleek lines.

"Especially after we've each had one of the house sundowner martinis," answered Sven, surprising Massimo that he was familiar with the drinks menu and had obviously been at the Sundance before.

"Well, of course," responded Sven in answer to Massimo's next question, "they have *Stella Artois* on tap here, so I have been trying to convince them that an upscale sports bar like this needs our *Whisky Hill Brew* on tap to maintain its reputation."

"Quite a contrast to Rosewood," pondered Massimo out loud. "I would have thought the entrepreneurial style at Rosewood more your scene."

"This is definitely old money," answered Lars, looking around at the more senior crowd of retired engineers from Silicon Valley.

"But we shouldn't be guilty of age discrimination against money," interjected Sven with a grin. "After all, the money from their retirement savings accounts fills a huge part of the venture capital bank account."

Massimo surveyed the walls covered in baseball memorabilia. Glass cases with framed photographs of players were mounted next to signed baseballs, and above were slender cases with baseball bats bearing the names of icons to the game. He half recognized the names as belonging to the heroes of this great national sport. Just as the ancient Romans had adorned their walls with icons of their many gods, so, too, did these Americans worship their multitudinous gods of sport. The aging platinum blonde who sat at the bar with her trim mustached husband, and who clapped each time the Giants home team scored, may have professed her faith at the church each Sunday, but her deep loyalty lay with the heroes whose images lined the pantheon around her.

Goaded by Sven, they ordered the dirty martinis, the house specialty, and, with a little encouragement from the waitress, a dozen oysters as an appetizer so that they might peruse the menu at leisure. While Lars and Sven were exclaiming over all the different cuts of beef, Massimo turned his attention to the wine list in search of a *Brunello*. To his delight, there were four of them listed in the Italian section, but the three-figure price tag caused him to draw a sharp breath.

Lars put his menu down, his mind made up, and turned expectantly to Massimo. "See something you fancy?"

"Well, yes, my favorite *Brunellos* are here," he answered hesitantly. "And we are here to celebrate, so I am determined to treat you."

"Sounds great," answered Sven. "And we should stay clear of those Australian wines," he laughed.

"Ha! Still burning from that one?" gibed Lars.

"Why? What have you got against Australian wines? The new world is making some very reasonable wines," added Massimo, feeling that there must be a story behind it.

"I was trying to impress this Australian girl who was visiting for a semester, so I brought her here thinking that a steak and an Aussie red would make her feel right at home," he began. "Boy, she could eat like a horse. Anyway, I foolishly promised that I was going to order her the best Aussie beverage on the menu."

Lars was laughing and pointing to the menu he held open at the page of Australian Reds.

"Apparently they bottle gold down there because there's something called *Grange* which goes for the best part of a thousand bucks a bottle."

"No! What did you do?" asked Massimo incredulously.

"Easy. I told her nothing beats a glass of foaming, amber liquid with a steak, and ordered her a *Fosters*."

They all laughed.

"Tasted pretty good, too," he winked. "Maybe not as good as our *Whisky Hill Brew*, but she appreciated the gesture."

Another round of martinis had appeared at their table, along with a plate of crispy, fish things, thanks to Lars's nods and whispers to the waitress. They were not as good as the iced plate of oysters, but they did the job of sopping up some of the alcohol that was flowing.

"Well, here's to our new joint venture," said Massimo raising his glass. "I'm sure you two are going to be instrumental in us finding our true path in pursuing this venture, and discovering the road ahead," he rambled on.

Lars and Sven exchanged a puzzled glance.

"Hey, Mass, here's to our venture, no matter which path we end up on."

"Well, of course," answered Massimo, leaning forward into his martini glass. "What I meant was we have our work cut out for us figuring out where to take this venture."

The waitress had returned to take their dinner order, and some animated discussion ensued over the exact difference between rare and medium rare.

"Would you like the *Brunello* decanted now, so it can breathe a little before dinner?" she tactfully enquired. Massimo's pickiness over the cooking time for the steak gave way to an adoration of the wine and the virtues of decanting.

She was a little older than the other waitresses, Massimo noticed, and hadn't done much with her lank blonde hair. The other girls in the main dining area all wore little black evening dresses with heels. Their waitress, on the other hand, wore knee-length boots together with a short black skirt. As she walked away, he noticed that she wore long socks whose tops stuck comically out from the boots. Definitely dressed more for comfort than looks, he smiled to himself.

"This venture is taking us along a path of its own choosing, not ours," said Lars returning to the previous discussion. "Where it will take us is anybody's guess, but we are going to make the best of it no matter where we end up."

"Of course we will make the best of it," said Massimo feeling he needed to further clarify his point. "What I meant is that there is a right way to do this, and we have to find it."

"Hey, it's not a science experiment," joked Sven. "It's a business venture with many factors outside our control, so there are a great many possible outcomes, and we have to make the best of whatever comes our way."

The waitress returned with bread plates and cleared away the appetizer plate. Massimo observed that she seemed to know most of the customers in the bar area. The bartender, too, had come out from behind the bar a few times to shake hands with patrons when they arrived. He was beginning to change his mind about his initial staid impression of this place. It had a welcoming, homey feel to it.

"Have you noticed," he said, turning to Lars and Sven, "that the waitresses over in the restaurant section in their little black dresses and heels really have to work the floor."

The two of them smiled appreciatively.

"They know their tip depends on how enamored their customer is with them. But our waitress just deals with the regulars, and her tips are going to be the same no matter how she dresses, or what she says."

"Each waitress making the best of a given situation," winked Lars at Sven.

Massimo gesticulated with his hands in the air, twisting his wrists first one way then the other while he tried to think of the English words to express his thoughts.

"Now, Lars, Sven, come on," he intoned. "Our work is all about the science of prediction. We want to arrive at the truth. There can only ever be one version of the truth."

The waitress returned with three tall, crystal wine classes that she placed in the center of the table to await the *Brunello*.

"I'm sorry if I gave you a hard time earlier about the degree of rareness of my steak."

"Oh, that's okay," she smiled back down at him. "The chef is always gratified when people know exactly what they want," she added diplomatically.

"Our friend is just a control freak who suffers under the delusion that he can determine the outcome of the world around him," laughed Sven.

"He's not as bad as the ones at the next table," she indicated with a glance to one side. "They all wanted the end slice from the prime rib roast, and I had to explain that there are only so many end slices to be had."

Lars and Sven were laughing good naturedly at Massimo who was silently articulating his wrists again in search of a reply to Sven's raillery.

"But they are all going to enjoy their dinner," she continued, unperturbed. "The prime rib is delicious, and the rosemary potatoes with the jus from the roast are wonderful. And maybe they will end up sharing the end slice."

"There you go, Mass, that's true meat and potatoes philosophy for you," chuckled Lars. "Are you a liberal-arts major?" He further asked of the waitress, but she had turned her attention to the next table where they were asking for more bread.

Before Massimo could come up with a suitably witty response, his phone rang. "Ciao, Laura. – yes, it went very well today – we are here celebrating together – it's just a few blocks from your place, you could come and join us."

He filled her in on a few more of the details of the events of the day. Lars and Sven were loudly sending their greetings to Laura across the table, and adding a few ribald comments about Massimo and the waitresses, so that he had to put a finger in his ear to block them out.

"I need you to help me explain to these two rogues how the pursuit of science takes us on one path in the quest for truth."

"I don't think I could catch up with the amount you lot have been drinking," she laughed. "Besides, I'm working on my presentations for my upcoming East Coast job interviews."

That was not particularly what Massimo wanted to hear, but their food was arriving and he promised to call back later.

For Massimo, the most striking thing about the meal was the size of the portions, but Lars and Sven attacked theirs with gusto. It did complement the wine very well, though, and by the second glass he waxed poetically about the qualities of the wine, and which Popes had given their blessings to the city of Montalcino so that the future of *Brunello* would be secured.

In spite of the alcohol induced haze, a certain self-realization crept over him, namely that both Laura and these two fellows were more capable than he was of embarking on a new journey. Massimo had spent his life in search of explanations, and less so in search of choices. The young, it seemed, were in search of possibilities. He tried to explain it to them over the last few drops of wine in his glass.

"I always thought that there could only be one destination when embarking on a journey, but you guys, I see, are willing to take on any of a multitude of possible outcomes." He stopped only because his tongue was beginning to feel awkwardly thick in his mouth. "It's the journey, isn't it, not the destination," he concluded with a final gulp from his wine glass.

Lars indulged him, and said with a smile, "You can't assume that your single choice of destination was the correct one until you've actually been there to prove it."

"Opportunities are going to present themselves on any of the paths we take, so why agonize over the choice of every single turn along the way," added Sven.

Massimo couldn't remember whether they actually took him up on his offer to try the Italian *grappas* on the list of after dinner drinks. Maybe the Roman gods of baseball lining the walls around him had conspired to make the room spin so discommodiously. Even though the detailed memory of how the night finished up was a little blurred, he remembered it as a very pleasant evening.

•

The next few days were taken up with preparations for setting up their computing operations at the new site made available by WVC.

He tried to explain the setup of the new office to Laura. They managed to spend several evenings together, and, while Massimo explained all that was going on with the startup, he was equally careful to pay attention to Laura's own developments. Reviewing her presentation together turned out to be a great suggestion on his part. He learned a thing or two about her work, which he hadn't actually known, and it was good to get a complete overview for once, rather than the glimpses he had gleaned from their past conversations. For his part, Massimo was able to provide useful feedback on what a potential employer would be looking for in such a presentation. The end result was a very confident Laura, who not only knew her stuff, but was relaxed and organized in her presentation.

They sat around sharing a glass of wine after going through one of the presentations, for she had two on separate topics. One topic per evening was quite enough, and after they had been through it in great detail it was Laura who ventured to ask again about the startup. Massimo had to answer to an inverted face framed by thighs because Laura was doing yoga poses to stretch and try and ease some of the built-up tension.

"We have a media room, just like the one at SLAC, but for our exclusive use," he said, turning his head at an angle to try and match her present position. "It's driven by some very state of the art graphics processors, so Sven is in seventh heaven playing with it all. Then there is an additional set of servers just for the calculations my program does," he added.

Laura was answering in a mantra involving dogs and warriors, which he didn't quite follow, but understood it had something to do with the various positions she was twisting herself into. He found himself getting down on all fours so that he could speak to her face rather than the odd contortion of limbs.

"The most amazing part of the setup is the network connectivity. It's like we're right at the center of the Internet, and everything comes through our node in the blink of an eye. Lars only has to think about accessing some exotic data and it downloads immediately," he said, with a face turning red from his sudden inversion.

"What are the chances," he said, now panting from the exertion of holding a lunge position as he mimicked Laura's stance, "of walking into a setup as perfect as this for the studies I want to do?"

Laura's slow, even breath, in contrast to his rasping, made her words come out with deliberation and poise. "I think you have to seriously consider that they were expecting you."

"Don't be silly," he said collapsing onto the floor, unable to keep the same balance as she had. "How could they possibly know beforehand that we were going to pass all their assessments of our abilities?"

He was hoping she might repeat the doggie stretches, or whatever she called them, where she wiggled her buttocks provocatively in the air, but she chose instead a meditative pose in the Lotus position. She bade him do the same and hushed him from speaking further.

"Let your body relax and allow your mind to travel to great heights," she whispered.

"That's what I want to talk to you about," he said too loudly. "All of me is going to travel to great heights. I've decided to fly to London to attend the conference while our new office is setup."

A sigh of resignation issued from Laura's lips as she realized that even a brief minute of mutual meditation was unlikely with Massimo. But a warm tone of encouragement followed and she asked, "That's nice. Will you take some extra time to visit your old friend?"

"Yes, I'd like to. Since the conference is in London this year, that was one of the factors that finally made me want to go."

"And what were the other factors that made you choose to go?" she inquired, raising an eyebrow and trying to draw a little more out of him.

"Well, it's the primary conference in my field at the moment, but I guess the main reason is that you will be traveling to the East Coast and I didn't want to be left here feeling sorry for myself."

"Are you feeling bitter about that?" she probed a little further.

"I confess I was at first, but I've gotten past that. I think the change of scene will do me good. I've also decided to take heed of Lars and Sven's wise counsel, and open myself up for new opportunities."

Laura rolled onto her back and endeavored to stretch her thigh by raising one leg while trying to grasp the ankle with an outstretched arm, but she failed in a most comical manner, much to Massimo's amusement.

"Don't just laugh at me. You can assist me with this stretch by helping to keep my leg straight and leaning with your torso against my thigh."

He complied as best he could, but started laughing at the sublime expression of release that crossed her face as he leaned forward. He lost his balance and toppled on top of her, producing a loud 'oof' as he landed. Instead of pushing him off, he felt both of her legs slip down and around him, pulling him closer.

"There's definitely something to be said about opening yourself to new opportunities," she murmured, snuggling her mouth down into his neck.

# Chapter 11 – London

The line was long at San Francisco International Airport as Massimo waited to check in to his flight for London, Heathrow. A soaring edifice of beams ranged high overhead like the wings of a great bird poised for flight. A bird whose legs were securely shackled to the ground, thought Massimo, recollecting articles he had read on the seismic construction of the new international terminal. Like most San Franciscans, he lived in denial that the geological gash beneath their feet would one day rend the land asunder.

Only at idle times as these, trapped in some public space, would such morbid thoughts cross his mind. Would he dive under the narrow airline counter if at this instant the ground were to heave and roll? His eyes wandered down the line of already bleary travelers and stopped at the family with two toddlers. Absurd thoughts once more took hold: there would not be room under the narrow airline counter for the stroller if the quake struck now. As if in answer, the rambunctious two-year-old, who evidently considered himself too old to be confined to a stroller, began to holler at his exasperated parents. Massimo cringed and looked once more at his ticket and seat assignment in the rear most economy cabin on the plane. A passing spirit would have heard a chorus of prayers rise into the air above the terminal pleading not to be seated too close to the little darling.

The line shuffled forward and he was finally directed to a counter where the surly attendant wordlessly took his documents. The attendant examined the passport and computer screen for the longest time, tugging in frustration at his ill-fitting waistcoat livery, before finally giving up and calling a senior assistant. She took a further minute to type in codes and confirmations before looking up and apologetically smiling at him.

"I'm terribly sorry for the inconvenience, sir, but please step this way."

"What now?" he grumbled to himself as he followed her along the counter and found himself standing now at an almost identical counter as before, with the exception of the square of red carpet beneath his feet.

"I do apologize once again, sir, but the system was slow to recognize your million mile flyer status," she smiled meekly at him. "But I've taken care of that now and your business class upgrade is confirmed."

"What!" he blurted. "Business class upgrade for a million mile status, I don't understand," but cut himself off abruptly with the realization that he was vehemently protesting a dream upgrade.

"I know, sir, I do apologize," she said crestfallen. "First class is completely full, but I have given you the nicest business seat in the upstairs, forward section."

She slid his passport and boarding pass across the counter and left her fingers resting on his as she continued,

"I could personally escort you to the First Class lounge, but we will commence boarding in just a few minutes, so you might be more comfortable going directly to the gate."

"Well, that will have to do," he said, a little more gruffly than he intended and pocketed his passport.

"Please take the first entrance at the end of the counter to passport control," she said coyly, "and have a wonderful flight, sir."

Not believing his luck, he sailed through passport control and security, bypassing all the economy class lines. He was greeted by name as he boarded, and the flight attendant stowed his jacket and bag before showing him his seat and explaining all the recliner functions. He stretched back luxuriantly, unable to even touch the bulkhead in front with his toes. There were stacks of gadgets and magazines that preoccupied his attention for the next several minutes.

"Here's a glass of the champagne we're serving in First Class, sir. Please accept our apologies again for the mishandling of your check-in." She bent rather stiffly to place the champagne in front of him, and did not make eye contact.

He sensed from her attitude that all was not well, and took pains to explain he really was happy with his seat in Business Class.

"It's just that my girlfriend, Monique, at the check-in counter said you must've been pretty ticked off with the way your ticket had been handled. So I just assumed you would be coming on board with an attitude and probably give me hell for the entire flight."

The champagne was remarkably good by the usual airline standards, and he found himself quite enamored with this young woman now that she was turning on the charm.

"Once we're airborne I'll come back with a proper drink and some hors d'oeuvres from First Class for you, Massimo," she said, pointedly dropping the "sir" in favor of his first name now.

True to her word, she plied him with cocktails and fine wines from the First Class cabin throughout the flight. The food was brought out nicely arranged on a tray with real glassware and plates. About half way through the flight he felt decidedly woozy from the over indulgence and passed out blissfully in his seat.

A sickening plunge woke him from his slumber and the captain announced they were over the Irish Sea and would be experiencing a little inclement weather on their final approach to Heathrow. The tray and little liqueur bottles had been cleared away, removing all evidence of his excess, but his stomach knew the truth of it, and as the horizon disappeared into the clouds and the plane gave one final lurch he lost it, reaching just in time for the convenient paper bag in his seat pocket.

As he disembarked at Heathrow there was no sign of the tall, attractive flight attendant. It was probably just as well because he was still feeling green about the gills and would have reacted rather sheepishly had he met her again. Perhaps she had extracted her revenge on him after all by plying him with alcohol during the flight, or in reality was he just a novice business class flyer reacting greedily to all the free liquor?

A hotel shuttle bore him to the center of London, and he excused himself immediately upon checking in to collapse on the hotel bed. An antiquated, but thankfully warm shower partially restored his humanity after which he spent the next two hours lying indisposed upon the bed trying to recollect the purpose of his mission.

A welcoming supper and reception was being offered downstairs for the arriving conference delegates. He was beginning to feel well enough that he entertained the idea of going down and mixing with a few colleagues; that, plus the pangs of hunger that were beginning to awaken in his stomach, having lost most of his previous meal on the plane.

In spite of still feeling a little rough around the edges, he made it down to the reception room and went through the registration procedure to obtain his badge and complimentary shoulder bag before being permitted to the inner room with the tables of refreshments. As he entered he saw that the food was all laid out at the far side, and he would be forced to navigate the throng of attendees.

There is a certain dance that one must perform at the opening of every international conference: Known as the dance of the badges, it is as significant as any mating ritual you may see on a wildlife documentary. It begins for each participant as he enters the room, and it serves to establish his ranking in the hierarchy of the conference. Each delegate will pirouette around the room hoping to greet and engage in conversation the most eminent people first, and not be distracted by underlings who might lower their ranking. The problem is that many of the shortsighted mathematicians and scientists may not recognize the changed features of their colleagues that might have occurred over the intervening years since they last met. Confirmation is therefore sought by bending at the waist to read each name badge before looking into the eyes of the wearer. A comical dance ensues in which the ducking action is executed with subtlety, so that if one recognizes the name one can feign surprise,

"Heinrich, so good to see you again. I have some questions about your last paper...."

Or, if the name is not recognized, one should feint and transform the duck into a checking of shoelaces, or the dismissal of some imaginary dust fleck. This works smoothly most of the time, but can occasionally cause embarrassment when an Asian delegate misinterprets the duck as a bow of respect and a flurry of returned bows between complete strangers ensues.

Massimo did make it across the floor to the food table without too many embarrassments, and only had to skirt the Italian delegation, whom he knew would detain him at length, trying to discover the latest gossip in their community. He piled up a plate with what was on offer, which turned out to be mainly meaty things with lots of pastry. The morsel he was biting into he remembered from previous visits as a sausage roll, although it bore no resemblance to either a roll or a sausage as he knew them in Italy. He was looking for a place to dispose of the remainder of them from his plate when an American voice from behind said,

"God, they're awful aren't they. Try some of the Chicken Tikka over there; at least it has a kick to it."

He turned to face a dazzlingly well-dressed woman in her mid-thirties who looked decidedly out of place amongst the rest of the conference delegates.

"Thank you," he said as he peered at her name badge. "I don't think I've had the pleasure of meeting you in person Dr., um, er Jones," he smiled weakly. "I think I might stick to some salad if I can find some that's not drowned in this mayonnaise dressing."

"Good luck with that. The bowl of cherry tomatoes is about all that's been spared the mayonnaise dressing. No, you wouldn't have come across my name before. This is my first time at this conference, and it's Jenna. Ms., not Dr., I'm a headhunter, not a mathematician."

"Well, I'm a delighted to meet you, Jenna. I don't think I've ever met a headhunter before. No bone in the nose either," he chuckled.

"Gosh, I haven't heard that one before. I must remember it," she said unblinkingly.

"Sorry. So, where are you from? Um, your company name isn't listed on your badge."

"Hmm, I'm guessing you just flew in from California this afternoon," she said, forking some chicken into her mouth, and ignoring his question. "You have that pasty, jetlagged look that blanks even a West Coast tan." And then she added, "No, I'm from a private company on Wall Street."

"Well, you look chirpier than even the locals, so I gather you've been here a few days already."

"No, I just got in this afternoon. But I just pop an *Ambien* when I board in JFK, and then I wake up fresh as a daisy in Heathrow."

"Remarkable," he replied. "I think I should be more careful about my hydration when flying."

"That usually means not drinking all the free booze," she laughed.

"But you haven't told me what you are doing here, at this conference, I mean. – Sergio, ciao, good to see you. I'll catch up with you a little later," he nodded at the group congregating nearby.

"Oh, this is where we do all our recruiting for the fodder for financial analysts positions. Mathematical physics is not dissimilar to what we need on Wall Street, but I don't need to tell you that."

That icy feeling of uneasiness came over him again, but he tried to dismiss it as another symptom of his jet lag.

"How do you mean?" his voice unconsciously rising in pitch.

"Oh, you know, we regularly recruit from the graduating Stanford classes. It's not hard to lure them away with the promise of bright lights and the Big Apple."

"Ah, I see," he sighed, visibly relieved.

"And, of course, you are already spoken for, seduced into the arms of WVC."

Massimo's jaw dropped.

"Don't worry. Your secret is safe with me. You were on my recruiting list until I got wind of your new joint venture with WVC," she winked.

Massimo couldn't think of a rejoinder.

"How do you put up with living on the West Coast?" she said condescendingly.

"It's not Milan or Rome, but I've grown accustomed to the Californian lifestyle."

"I can't imagine a life without the Metropolitan Opera."

"Well, I had hoped to catch a performance at the London Opera while I was here, but there seems little chance of snagging a ticket this week."

"I have tickets," she said with a little smile.

"I envy you then. There was an article in the in-flight magazine on Covent Garden that got me quite enamored with the idea of attending."

"Actually, I was proposing we go together. I'd much rather share my seats with an opera buff than some bored new recruit who only wants to talk statistics."

"I don't know what to say. Of course I would leap at your offer, but surely you have a more deserving friend."

"No, I'd be flattered to be in the company of a dashing Italian gentleman. The only catch is that the performance is next week, after the conference."

"That's not a problem," he replied, getting excited now at the prospect. "I'm going to Oxford for a few days after the conference to visit an old friend, and will return to London next week."

"That settles it then. I'll e-mail you the details of the performance and where I'll be staying."

With that she gave a little wave and excused herself to go mingle and recruit a few new souls for her collection.

The moment she left, the Italian contingent pounced on Massimo to interrogate him on his charming new companion and pump him for gossip on the goings on in America.

"What, you don't want to hear first about our latest results from SLAC?" he teased them.

"No, we will ask the deeply probing science questions tomorrow when you give your talk," they chorused. "Tell us first some juicy stories about what keeps you from returning to Italia."

Massimo happily complied. It was good to relax and speak in his native tongue for a while.

Massimo's new acquaintance was notably absent the next day during the technical sessions, and he found himself craning his neck from time to time in a vain search for her. Perhaps her promise of a night at the opera had not been meant seriously. As he wandered around the poster sessions he began mentally chastising himself for habitually chasing after young, attractive women.

The poster sessions he was walking through were there to allow participants to present their work in summary form even if the program committee had not recognized it as important enough for an oral presentation in the main auditorium. They were usually manned by eager young students who were keen to break into the field and launch their research careers. Occasionally there would also be an oddball character who had failed to launch into the mainstream, but would make perennial appearances in the poster sessions of any conference he could get into.

Massimo admitted to himself that if it had been a frumpy dowager making the offer of free opera tickets, he wouldn't have been nearly as keen.

"But a mature, attractive lady who knows what she's about," he almost muttered out aloud. Plus the enticing aspect that she was from his new world of financial trading. "Who could resist?" he actually blurted out aloud this time.

"That's my point exactly!" came a nasal voice directly in front of him.

Massimo blinked to find himself staring at a shoddily presented poster lacquered with acronyms and indecipherable charts. The voice belonged to a small, greasy man whose unkempt features matched the careless layout of his poster.

"It's just a matter of time before all of Wall Street will be clamoring for this kind of analysis," the nasal voice continued.

"I'm not sure I follow, exactly," Massimo replied, and looking down now recognized the face as belonging to someone he studiously strived to avoid at all meetings such as these. The owner of the face was notorious on the conference circuit for his half-baked ideas and for trying to sell the ideas of others as his own. He rarely lasted at an institution for more than a year or so, and whenever Massimo saw his name listed at a conference it would be affiliated with a new organization. Lately, the names had become more outlandish and he suspected they were largely made up. Today the fellow wore a badge bearing the name Trans Global Institute for Quantum Analysis.

"No, it's just like you said," he simpered. "Who could resist a cloud-based app that lets someone carry around the power of quantum computing in his pocket, giving him the latest stock market forecasts?"

"Who, indeed?" Massimo almost sneered, disgusted at this fellow's audacity to string a few acronyms and buzz words together and promote it as science.

"But this time I'm letting my friends in on the ground floor," he sniveled. "It's all going to be open-source, so my close friends like you can contribute."

"Contribute?" answered Massimo in horror.

"I'm generously allowing my friends this time to contribute one of their analytical tools which I would incorporate into my app."

"So your 'friends' would be doing all this work for nothing," he trailed off, his eye now catching the dribble of food stains covering the awkwardly knotted tie hanging around the fellow's neck. He wished he hadn't looked so closely, for now his eye became fixated on the protruding Adam's apple that bobbed up and down as it continued to spew out more of the rubbish.

"You're lucky that I have grasped the role of OSS in the scientific-financial marketplace today," he babbled on. "Once your name becomes associated with my new FasDAQ and MyDOW apps then you are going to be in demand, my man, with developers everywhere. In fact," he continued, solicitously tapping a bony finger to an elongated nose, "there is a recruiter here who is highly placed among the top financial firms on Wall Street. Play your cards right and I will introduce you to her. I have important contacts you know!"

Massimo couldn't stand it any longer. "Look, I'm just here to catch up on developments in high energy physics. I'm sure I have no place in your lofty financial circles," and with that he turned and walked away.

"Well, I'll catch up with you later," he shouted after him, but Massimo had managed to engage himself into the group of Italians and secured his escape. A few appropriate rude comments in Italian were voiced over the despicable fellow and Massimo felt purged of the encounter.

Not surprisingly, the conversation amongst the Italians soon turned to dinner plans for the evening and Massimo was swept up in a group outing to a nearby Italian restaurant. It would not have been his first choice for an evening in London. Something more traditional, even an English pub would have been preferable, but it was a small price to pay in exchange for the warm camaraderie with which they welcomed him into the group. The restaurant fitted the stereotype image of an Italian trattoria, with red and white checkered tablecloths and straw covered Chianti bottles, but, regrettably, over-cooked pasta. He cringed when his boisterous companions teased a Pakistani waiter over his lack of knowledge of Italian cuisine.

Some of the Italians also knew Donatella from his days at CERN when they were still a couple, and he had to skillfully deflect questions over their separation, for he didn't want word to get back to Italy regarding his new relationship with Laura.

Being slightly on the defensive all evening took it out of him, and he was definitely feeling bleary by the time he returned to the hotel. He was standing in the dimly lit foyer waiting for the elevator when his phone chimed with an incoming message.

"Join me in the piano bar for a nightcap –J.J."

His heart skipped a beat when he realized JJ could only be Ms. Jenna Jones, and he peered towards the even dimmer end of the foyer where a petition of potted plants and the tinkling of piano music suggested there was indeed a hotel bar. Drawn by the music, or some other fatal attraction, he ventured down toward the bar. He hadn't noticed the bar area during the day, but now the cozy glow of flickering table candles drew him closer. Plush seats were scattered around the lounge in little islands to allow for discrete after-hours conversations. The barman stood behind his counter polishing glasses and looking bored, for there were only a few couples still lounging around at this late hour. Massimo was about to turn and go when he spied a pair of long, stockinged legs protruding from behind a potted palm at the far corner of the lounge. One stiletto shoe dangled provocatively from an extended foot, somehow beckoning him to come over.

"I'd almost given up on you when I spied you returning from your evening outing," came a dusky voice, still concealed by palm fronds, as he approached. The voice sounded much smokier than he remembered from the previous day's encounter.

"Ms. Jones? What a surprise. I looked all over for you this afternoon at the conference. That isn't to say I was searching for you. I meant that I was keeping an eye out for you in case there was an opportunity to talk, about work of course, I wasn't trying to stalk you or anything, but I was surprised you were not at the conference sessions today." Massimo was embarrassed to notice that his voice had gone up in pitch, whereas hers maintained a mellow, relaxed tone.

"Now, why don't you sit and keep me company for a while."

He relaxed the grip on his jacket that he was clutching to his chest, and awkwardly sank into the seat she indicated beside her.

"It's Jenna, remember. Ms. Jones is just for business formalities," she smiled, with the slightest flutter of her eyelids. "I kept out of sight at the conference, but I was keeping tabs on who was chatting with whom."

"Ah, yes, it can be quite exhausting all that mingling and chatting: especially if you are used to a quiet academic life." He thought again of the distasteful encounter with the opportunist at the poster session whose name he could not even remember now.

"I thought there might be a palm court orchestra when I heard the music," he said changing the subject to something lighter. "But now I notice it is just a player piano. We don't even merit a real performer."

"Yes, and if it plays *The Girl from Ipanema* one more time I shall slam its lid," she laughed. "But the redeeming feature of this bar is their excellent selection of Single Malts," she said, raising a nearly empty glass to her lips.

"I'm not familiar with them," he apologized with a shake of his head.

"You can't visit this little island nation without trying its single greatest product." She raised her glass a little higher this time: a heavy, cut crystal tumbler that caught both the gleam from the bar light and the barman's attention.

"I could tell you about Grappa," he shrugged, watching the refractions of light from the crystal tumbler cut across her face, "but I wouldn't know a Single Malt from a glass of Scotch."

"Then you are in for a treat, laddie," she exclaimed in a fake Scottish accent.

Sounds of laughter and loud voices that he instantly recognized came from the other end of the lobby. The rest of the Italian group were returning from the restaurant and noisily bidding each other *buona notte*. He had excused himself from the restaurant earlier on the grounds that he was tired. It would be embarrassing if they now discovered that his tiredness had magically disappeared in the company of an elegant American woman at the bar.

The doors of the elevator slid shut and the noise subsided. They had not discovered the bar, and his reputation was safe for the time being.

Ms. Jones, however, was staring icily over his shoulder.

"Ehh," came a rheumy, nasal voice from behind, causing him to jerk around in surprise.

"Ms. Jones, I apologize that I haven't had a chance to discuss my work with you earlier." It was the malodorous fellow from the poster session earlier in the afternoon. "But I know you will be very excited to hear about my new FasDAQ and MyDOW apps we are developing."

She continued staring at him icily and didn't say a word in reply.

He glanced at Massimo looking for support, and even though he found none he continued awkwardly,

"But I'm glad in the meantime you have met my colleague here, and one of my top programmers, I might add. He can give you details of some of the analytical tools he will be adding to the FasDAQ and MyDOW application suite."

Massimo was able to add only a gaping look to her icy stare.

"But I'm unable to stay and talk now," a note of desperation rapidly becoming more apparent in the interloper's voice. "I have important conference calls to make with New York, the time difference you know. Massimo can fill me in on any details or questions you may have in the morning."

With one more phlegmy sniff, he turned and left.

"Thank god, he's left," muttered Massimo.

"You don't know that weasel do you?" she laughed contemptuously.

"God, no. The nerve of that fellow. I just happened to stop in front of his poster this afternoon," but he was cut off by the arrival of the barman, who, with a white gloved hand, discreetly removed the empty whisky glass. From his silver tray he then placed two ornate tumblers on the table, together with a small water jug. He replaced the candle on the table before withdrawing, and its glow now illuminated two generous pours of amber liquid in the glasses.

"What have we here?" Massimo exclaimed, a little over eagerly.

"I want you to try my favorite of all of the Scottish whiskies," an impish glint now returned to her eyes. But Massimo had also witnessed the icy coldness that had been there when the interloper had stood before them.

"I thought New Yorkers always had their scotch on the rocks."

"First of all, this is not scotch, and secondly I would never put ice into a ten year old Single Malt whisky," she smiled tolerantly. "The correct way to do it, *laddie*, is to take it with just a splash of water," and she put her hand on his wrist to stop him taking a gulp before she could pour a little water from the jug into his glass. "The water will cut the alcohol so that instead of burning your throat you will actually taste this, the most female of all whiskies."

"Female?" he said with surprise.

"Well, taste it first, before I tell you more," she commanded.

She was right, cutting it with water meant that it didn't burn his throat, but he took a correspondingly larger gulp than he might have, and a warm glow rose pleasantly from the pit of his stomach to envelop him.

"Whoa," he said appreciatively.

"You're drinking a Single Malt crafted by the great and famous Bessie, the only whisky in all of Scotland to be made by a woman."

146

"Well, hats off to Bessie," he said with a giggle, and noticed that their knees were touching as they leaned over the table to clink glasses.

The second taste filled his mouth with smoky flavors of vanilla and oak. The smokiness, she explained, came from the peat fires used during the whisky making process. There were other flavors, too, that he didn't recognize from his repertoire of wine drinking experiences.

"This time, before you swallow," she said with a wicked look of pleasure in her eyes, "keep it in your mouth, breathe out through your nose, and tell me what you experience."

He closed his eyes and did as she directed, but then almost choked as he finished the swallow.

"Wow, that's incredible," he said when he recovered.

"What did you taste?" She smiled.

"No, it wasn't so much the taste, as the amazing recollection from my childhood it triggered, quite out of the blue."

She leaned forward and rested her chin on her hand to hear what he had to say.

"I suddenly had a flashback to an instance when I was very small and on a beach holiday with my parents. My mother was so young then," he said dreamily. "Anyway, I was running ahead of my parents towards the tide pools and my mother was yelling to be careful. Of course, I slipped on this green slimy stuff and fell headfirst into a pool. The salty, green water all went up my nose, and then I felt a hand pull me out of the water and into the arms of my laughing father. But my mother held me and told me it was okay to cry because it would clear away all the water from my nose. And she wiped away all this green stuff as it poured out of my nose, and she cried, too."

"All that," he added, "flashed back in an instant, just then when the smell came up the back of my nose."

She had an indulgent smile on her face as he pleaded his case, and waited a moment before speaking to make sure he had finished with his story.

"Whisky aficionados will try and tell you that *Laphroaig* whisky picks up the taste of the sea because it is aged in barrels right by The Bay and the wind carries the salt and smell of seaweed directly into the aging stores."

"That's amazing," he replied.

"But I also have a strong personal recollection that hit me the first time I tasted a *Laphroaig*. For me it tastes like a woman."

"Do tell," he said, drawing closer and trying his best to imitate the smoky, mellow tones of her voice. He raised his glass to his lips and looked expectantly at her over the rim.

By way of reply she took two fingers and dipped them into her glass, lazily stirred them and then salaciously rubbed them over her upper lip before sucking off the remaining drops of amber liquid.

Massimo's glass hovered at his lips, his eyes transfixed.

"The taste of *Laphroaig*," she whispered, "reminds me of the first time I tasted the sex of another woman."

Massimo choked for a second time on his whisky, but she continued, unfazed by his obvious amazement at her forthrightness.

"It has that same smoky, salty, seaweed nuance, coupled with a sweet vanilla flavor and a slightly bitter aftertaste," she finished with a smile, delighting in the shocked reaction she had caused.

She drained the rest of her glass and then moved to gather up her things.

"I suppose I should be getting back to my hotel," and she gave a little, polite yawn.

"Oh, you are not staying in this hotel?" he said disappointedly, and then wondered why he had blurted that out.

148

"I won't see you tomorrow, but I will e-mail you the details of the opera performance and the hotel I'm staying at. When you come back from Oxford, book a room at my hotel. It's much more conveniently located for the opera and then we can also have dinner together."

"Yes, of course. I am looking forward to it. And dinner would be excellent."

"You should also check out the Italian suit store adjacent to the lobby of my hotel. They have *Armanis* and all kinds of suits I'm sure you'll just love."

"Um, okay," he said, a little taken aback.

She stood to go, but placed her hand on his shoulder so that he would not stand and follow her.

"I hope you enjoyed the *Laphroaig*," and as she walked around the back of his chair to depart, he felt her fingers brush lightly against the back of his neck, sending goose bumps down his arm.

"Whisky will never taste quite the same again," he assured her.

She smiled and departed without another word, leaving him staring at two empty glasses, wondering what the hell was going on.

Glancing around, he saw that he was the last patron in the bar, so he gathered himself together and shuffled toward the barman and the waiting elevators beyond.

"Good night, sir. The drinks bill has already been taken care of."

Massimo nodded and heard the lights click off behind him.

That night he dreamt of his mother for the first time in many years. She held him to her breast as he cried his salty tears, and he could smell both her and the sea. Then, as dreams sometimes do, when he had dried his tears it was Donatella's face he looked up at, and she scornfully reproached him for crying. When he finally emerged from the dream he thought it was Laura's voice shouting that she did not like whisky. The pillow was quite damp from his nocturnal harassments.

# Chapter 12 – Oxford

The remaining conference day passed uneventfully. He avoided any further corrosive encounters with the weasel, as he now thought of him following Jenna's comment, and departed the conference with a perfunctory farewell to his Italian colleagues.

Massimo dug out Hugh's last e-mail with details of how to find his cottage in the Oxfordshire countryside. The journey began with boarding the Oxford bound train at Paddington Station. Thereafter followed a barrage of directions for making bus connections to the little village of Horspath where a room was booked at the King's Head pub. The fact that Hugh had not even considered Massimo might prefer to rent a car for the journey made him smile.

"Why take a car when there's a perfectly good train and bus connection?" he could hear Hugh reprimanding him for even entertaining the thought.

The train was late departing, but he secured a compartment in first class and settled back in the seat with a clutch of new math papers from the conference, admitting to himself that this probably was better than driving. A few of the papers dealt with financial models, and he eagerly read ahead to see if anyone else was doing anything remotely like his work. Most of it was old, well-established formulae for pricing derivatives. Nothing new there. A rogue paper, evidently from someone in the banking industry described the algorithm for bundling loans together and then selling the package at a price higher than the sum of its parts. A companion paper then described that far greater profits could be made in the short term by subsequently betting against the bank and buying credit default swaps from an insurance company. There was no limit apparently as to how many such insurance policies you could buy, so that when those packaged loan bundles you were selling all tanked, you could rake in quite a profit from the insurance. Not unlike insuring members of your family many times over, and then encouraging them to go and behave recklessly. If the algorithm was applied on a large enough scale, the insurance companies would eventually be driven into the ground, the paper concluded, but in all likelihood the governments would be forced to bail them out, and the profit taking would have succeeded in its goals.

He could appreciate that someone with a mathematical mind had made the effort to clinically layout the calculated scheming of the profit takers that had brought the world's banking system to its knees. It was still highly distasteful, though; much as if a respected medical psychology journal were to publish an article on enhanced interrogation techniques at Guantanamo, and how they could get you any confession you wanted.

The indignant thoughts of reprimand beat inside his head in time to the clacking of the rails. He could hear Hildr's violin pick up the beat and create her strange musical patterns that typified a mathematical flow that grew faster and larger until it exploded into chaos and collapsed to almost nothing. Why was Hildr here in the carriage with him? She had said nothing about attending this conference. How could her wild theory of musical chaos be performed at a conference like this? Laura was shaking him and yelling something about needing a ticket for Hildr's performance, at which point he flung his arm out and managed to strew the papers he was reading all over the compartment.

"Sorry to startle you sir," said the conductor, "but I need to see your ticket."

151

Massimo retrieved it from his breast pocket and a relieved conductor left him to sheepishly gather the strewn papers.

Arriving in Oxford, Massimo was hard pressed to find the correct bus stop for his connection to Horspath. He did spy an off-license liquor store on the opposite side of the road named *Ye Olde Malt Shoppe*, a name blatantly chosen to appeal to North American tastes. It occurred to him that he had no gift for Hugh, and that his new found knowledge of whisky could be put to use. As luck would have it, he spied a bottle of *Laphroaig* upon entering and pointed it out to the sales assistant.

"La-froyg," repeated the assistant, trying to be helpful with the pronunciation. Feeling quite pleased with himself over the purchase, he decided to splurge and take a taxi the remaining way to Horspath. Hugh need never know that he hadn't caught the bus.

The taxi deposited him in the graveled forecourt of the King's Head hotel. The black enameled sign swinging noisily in the breeze above the inn's door proudly proclaimed the age of the establishment. Massimo finally felt he was getting his money's worth in terms of an authentic English cultural experience. The pub was just how the tour books described a typical English hotel, with its austere stone walls and small casement windows. A knowledgeable guide would immediately have recognized the hodgepodge of additions that had been layered on the original coach house over the centuries. But to Massimo its disposition was just 'English' and he rejoiced in the simple differences that set it apart from an Italian castello. He felt reassured that even the dour smoke that clung to the drapes in the lobby must have come from fires of ancient logs of magnificent English oak and yew. The proprietress, sensing how enamored Massimo was, turned on her charm, repeatedly referring to him as 'love' or 'pet' as she explained the vagaries of the heating and plumbing in his room.

"The professor, he's such a dear, told us you've come all the way from California, and that you'd be expecting a room with a private bath," she said as she sashayed up the steps in front of him.

The small room was at the front of the inn and there was barely enough space for them both to walk around the bed to the window. No doubt it was because the charming lady insisted on thrusting her ample bosom forward whenever she turned to speak, but Massimo was much too enthralled with the leadlight window overlooking the courtyard to notice the disproportionate dimensions of either her bust or the room.

"Do come down when you're ready and avail yourself of some refreshment in our parlor lounge," her voice echoed on departure with a sweetness as artificial as the honey blond hair on her head.

"All part of the atmosphere of staying in a pub," thought Massimo, as he transferred a few belongings into the creaky wardrobe.

The rain had started coming down and the vista from the leadlight window turned a uniform gray, dispelling any ideas of going out for a saunter around the village before dinner.

Perhaps he should go downstairs and 'avail himself of some refreshments', as the landlady had suggested. He could picture a cozy fire downstairs with a comfortable armchair where he might while away an hour gazing out of a window at the rain sweeping across the courtyard.

The cozy log fire turned out to be a hissing gas radiator around which two lone patrons huddled in the parlor. The comfortable chair was in fact a hard bench by a drafty window, so he chose a padded stool by the bar. The two gentlemen nodded and said something he couldn't comprehend so he just nodded and smiled in reply, hoping that would suffice.

"You know, I've always wanted to try a Ploughman's," he said when the barman finally took his order.

"I'm sorry, sir, we stopped serving lunch two hours ago, but I could fix you a nice cheese sandwich if you're hungry."

"Cheese. That sounds wonderful," he replied, thinking it might be a fine country cheddar, or possibly some stilton. "And what would you recommend I drink with that?" he continued with an air of expectancy that he might be in for a local village specialty.

"I'd recommend a pint of bitter, sir," sighed the barmen, reaching for a glass and placing it under the spigot. The beer did not spurt forth, foaming into the glass like the ale Lars and Sven had served him back in California. Rather, it had to be coaxed from the tap by the barmen pumping on the handle. Nor did it taste anything like Lars and Sven's beer. It was surprisingly flat and not at all cold. Massimo thought he should reserve judgment until the bread and cheese came along.

Alas, the hearty slab of cheddar and chunk of crusty farm house bread turned out to be a single serving of processed cheese between two slices of limp white bread, garnished with a single pickled onion. He took a bite just to see if it would change the taste of the ale. It didn't.

Meanwhile the two gentlemen were once more smiling in his general direction and muttering something about the weather outside.

"Perhaps you can give me some advice," struck up Massimo in a friendly tone. "If the weather is a little more cooperative tomorrow I'd like to walk to my friend's house," he said, showing them a piece of paper with Hugh's address on it.

"Oh, that's very kind of you, sir," said the older of the two gentlemen, holding up an empty pint glass.

"Please, allow me to buy you both drinks," he said after the briefest of pauses, once he realized what they were hinting at. "Then we could look at this little map I've got and see if it's any good for finding the way," he said, unfolding another of Hughes notes from his pocket.

"I'll have 'arf," chimed the other companion.

"Ar, he'll be wanting to walk to Monks Wood from here then," said the pint drinker, peering at the map he was holding at arm's length and pointing with his other hand.

"Aye, but if he goes that way he'll end up in Brasenose Woods and have to double back around over here," argued the half-pint drinker, snatching the map away from his friend.

"Do I understand you want to visit the professor's house tomorrow?" came a more refined English voice from the gentleman who had recently entered the bar. He was the epitome of a well-dressed country squire in his tweed jacket and he sported the most English of mustaches that Massimo had ever seen.

"Yes, I was hoping to enjoy a little of the English countryside and take a stroll to my friend's house if it's not raining tomorrow."

"Oh, the weather will be Piccadilly fine in the morning, you'll see," he replied in his perfect Oxford English. Understandable that he should speak so, considering they were in the heart of Oxfordshire, but Massimo was still having a hard time understanding what the two beer drinkers were saying, especially now that the landlady had joined in.

"Now, don't you go sending 'im all the way over to Magdalen Wood," she pleaded. "No good will come of it, I warn you. Not after that unpleasantness."

Massimo looked alarmed.

"There's nought 'arm never come to nobody in them thar woods," countered the pint drinker.

"Aye, not in the daytime, maybe," muttered the second into his half-pint glass.

"Well, 'e's not goin' out in night time, is 'e!" said the first in exasperation.

"Oh, do please ignore them," insisted the country squire. "I'm sure they put it on just for the tourists."

He ordered another large gin from the barman, and offered Massimo one as well, which he politely declined.

"Now, if it's a country jaunt that you want, you'll have a jolly nice time of it if you head off down this lane here," he indicated on the map with a little mark, then added as an afterthought, "and pack a knapsack with an apple and some chocolate, along with your 'tosh."

"And if you keep to the right of the stone wall here, you will be crossing a stile here and here," making little annotations as he continued, "Until you finally make it to the professor's cottage in about forty minutes, at a brisk pace.

The other two just muttered.

"And our landlady will be happy because you only cut across the corner of Monks Wood here, and won't be anywhere remotely close to Magdalen Wood."

"What happened in Magdalen Wood?" Massimo asked, wide eyed.

"Oh, a couple of priests were murdered there, we believe."

"Murdered! Hugh never mentioned that in his emails, ever."

"Well, I should think not," said the squire stroking one finger across his mustache. "It all happened centuries ago, but you'd think it happened just last week if you listen to our thirsty friends over there," he winked conspiratorially.

"Now we'll not have any more talk about the unpleasantness," came the landlady again as she bustled back into the room. "Cook's prepared a lovely Cottage Pie if Mr. Massimo cares to stay in for dinner. And we'll be serving a very nice house claret with it in the dining room this evening."

Massimo smiled in acquiescence, but had given up on any hope of grand country gastronomy after the experience with the cheese sandwich and warm beer.

The map was put away and everyone returned to their drinking. Not much for it, thought Massimo. He wouldn't be going out in this weather, so the dining room would be his fate this evening.

Contrary to what its name suggested, he saw absolutely no resemblance to a pie in the mush he was served, and could only speculate that the filling might have been once used as mortar in the construction of cottages. Pushing the unfinished plate aside, he thought he might rejoin the others in the parlor for a nightcap rather than sit alone in the dining room. The squire's face had reddened considerably in the meantime from several more gins and he made no reply to Massimo's greeting, but gripped the bar rail

156

tightly lest he should topple from the bar stool. The beer drinkers had also departed, so Massimo mounted the stairs to retire quietly to his room.

The sporadic wireless internet connection in his room was just strong enough that he could download and read his emails. He felt more comfortable once he was under the large bed quilt, for the leadlight window was not very effective at blocking out the weather. He had exchanged very few emails with Laura in the course of the trip since she was also travelling, and their times were out of synchronization. Each waited twenty four hours, it seemed, before responding to the last email. He read eagerly of the successful presentations she had made, and felt a pang of guilt when she added that she hoped he would find time to attend his beloved opera in London. Sending an email reply proved even more difficult with the weak internet connection in his room, but he didn't feel like venturing out from underneath his warm quilt to the lobby downstairs, so his reply to Laura was quite terse, informing her only of his visit to Hugh the following day.

Lars and Sven's emails were bright and frequent in comparison. The first few enthusiastically reported good progress with their market analyses and asked if he would be returning soon, or was he too busy enjoying the pub life in Merry Olde England. A message from Sven raved about the computing resources they now had at their disposal and how he had never had access to so much data, and with such speed as well. It ended cryptically, though, with a reference to whether Massimo ever missed his old fashioned messaging on his phone. It aroused his curiosity sufficiently that he powered up his cell phone for the first time since arriving in England. When it finally connected to its roaming network, a stream of messages were downloaded, much to Massimo's initial dismay at the thought of the data roaming charges he would now have to pay. They were all from Lars and Sven, with the exception of one from Laura wishing him happy landings when he arrived in England. Lars and Sven's emails were all from a masked internet server, but the subject matter left little doubt whom they were from.

Sven wrote that he didn't want to alarm Massimo that he had been snooping around on their new employer's network, but he had been deploying some of his private network diagnostic tools just to ensure peak performance of their own software. In doing so he found that WVC's network penetration was much greater than you would think was permissible. "They monitor networks without necessarily asking permission of network hosts or service providers," Sven explained. "They have more fingers in other people's networks than you would believe, and it's amazing that they can get authentication. Their tools are straightforward enough, but they can achieve this degree of penetration by scaling their network connections to a very large size and becoming a super hub. It is hard to imagine that someone has installed that much network capability."

Massimo thought back to the ridiculous amounts of optical fiber he had seen being installed beneath Sand Hill Road, plus the satellite dishes at WVC, and it began to make chilling sense.

A second email from Lars was even more foreboding. It alluded indirectly to an earlier conversation he remembered with Lars as to why a certain someone would ever take notice of the likes of Massimo. He knew Lars was referring to the conversation as to why Massimo had shown up on WVC's radar, even though his email now was written as though he was talking about some adolescent girl-boy relationship thing. "*She's* got copies of emails and drafts of things you've written which I am sure you would never have left lying around," Lars had hinted.

A third email from 'anonymous' warned Massimo not to reply to any of these messages, for although they could send him anonymous messages it was likely that all his replies would be monitored.

He sank down beneath the quilt and shuddered at the thought of what might be going on. Lars and Sven might be blowing this out of proportion. This was big business after all, and people were expected to play hardball, but it was unsettling to think that big brother might be monitoring their every move. There wasn't anything he could do about it now. He couldn't email anyone and discuss his fears.

He sent one short email to them both and feigned a cheery tone, telling them of his unexpected flight upgrade and how WVC must have "great connections" to get his frequent flyer status raised to such an astronomical level with the airline. It would serve to let them know he had read their hidden emails.

He tried to focus his thoughts instead on what he might tell Hugh in the morning. "If I ever find the place," he mumbled to himself, doubting whether the inebriated instructions from the pickled squire were worth anything at all. He had his phone out, so it occurred to him that he might as well try programming its GPS with a Google map. Sure enough, it came up with a very direct route that looked a lot simpler to follow than the annotations of the squire. "Lars and Sven would be proud of my resourcefulness," he thought as he settled himself back against the pillows and stared at the play of light coming from his leadlight window and dancing across the curtain.

He awoke next morning to a blue sky studded with fast moving clouds. Any kind of weather might be possible with that outlook, and indeed, a little bit of everything was in the forecast. No wonder the English always talked about the weather. He risked a quick shower with the fickle hotel plumbing, but was in luck and emerged feeling refreshed and ready for anything.

The English breakfast awaiting him downstairs might have been the best meal so far. Hot tea, toast, eggs and bacon with grilled tomatoes all tasted particularly good, but he passed on the baked beans and black pudding. He was hungry after only picking at last night's dinner. The proprietress very kindly packed him a satchel with a leftover bacon and egg sandwich and an apple. He was tempted to ask if she could include some chocolate, as the squire had suggested.

Out in the courtyard he compared his cell phone GPS with the annotated map from the squire. The squire's map indicated he should turn left coming out of the pub, but the GPS indicated a right. Massimo marched confidently down the narrow lane to the right. The path took a slight turn as it went up the hill and walls gradually rose on either side of him, so that he could no longer admire the countryside. After about half a mile a stout gate barred his way and a large sign declared "No Trespassing." Evidently Google maps knew nothing of private property laws in England. On the way down the hill he nodded a curt good morning to the people he had passed on his way up, and stomped back towards the pub's entrance where he fished out the hand drawn map again and this time headed off on the inebriate squire's trail.

Although he was still not totally convinced that he was heading in the right direction, this trail was decidedly more countrified and he took delight in speculating over the history of the bramble covered walls that jutted off at odd angles to the path. What a contrast to California, his adopted home. Here it was all about how many shades of green could coexist in one visage of the landscape. In California the rolling hills were golden browns and only flecked with grey olive greens of scrub oaks. But here the dark green shadows of the mighty oaks contrasted with the brightest emerald greens the eye could perceive. Only the dull grey stone of the rambling walls provided any relief to the eye from the avalanche of color, but even there, if the eye dwelt too long, a myriad of moss greens could be discovered in the crannied stone. Even his homeland hills of Rome and Tuscany offered a more subtle palate of olive greens and taupes amidst the vines and cypresses. The decadent joy in the brightness of it all was at once doused by a sudden morning shower. The sun could still be seen on the far hill, so he didn't feel oppressed by the thought that the glory of the day was over. He stood under one of the sheltering oaks and munched on an apple while it passed.

> *Time, never wand'ring from his annual round,*
> *Bids Zephyr breathe the Spring, and thaw the ground;*
> *Bleak Winter flies, new verdure clothes the plain,*
> *And earth assumes her transient youth again*

In his schoolboy days he'd thought Milton was an Italian poet when he had to translate from Latin the lines of this *elegia*[21]. Later he read that Milton had met his first wife right here in Oxfordshire. He might have first seen her running across this very field in the dappled sunlight, he mused. She was only sixteen when they first met, less than half Milton's age. But who was he to criticize, when he thought of his own age difference with Laura? Donatella had been such a stickler for the proper age difference between spouses, claiming that the man should ideally be two years older, but that hadn't worked out particularly well for them, had it?

The clouds moved on and so did Massimo's thoughts as he resumed the path that would hopefully take him to Hugh's cottage. The map indicated a stile was to be crossed, and when he found it and negotiated its awkward steps, he felt a slight elation that perhaps he was on the right track after all. The path struck out across a featureless field and he wondered if he might lose the way again, but a well-trodden track led him along his way. There might be a lesson to be learned here: people's motives and actions have been the same for centuries, even if the setting changes from priests and monarchs in Oxfordshire to financiers and CEOs on Sand Hill Road. All he had to do was follow the well-trodden path towards wealth and power, and he might better understand the events unfolding around him. He would run that thought by Hugh, who would surely expound on such a theme. And maybe the high tech tools like Google maps were not always the best way to go. One could go much further with simple rational thinking and a little local, insider knowledge. He was even beginning to think like Hugh now. It must be because the cottage was in close proximity, and he quickened his step.

The path turned down towards a copse of trees and the warbling of birds in the meadow gave way to a damp silence of dripping leaves as he entered beneath the boughs. It hadn't looked like much from a distance, but the trees now closed around him shutting out the sunlight. Monks Wood, no doubt. He shivered and pulled the anorak from his pack. As he pulled it over his head, he caught himself peering into the dark spaces between the trees for any sign of murderers who might still be lurking there. The bacon and egg sandwich in his pack had smelt good, but he wasn't about to stop for a picnic anywhere around here.

As he emerged from the wood the path wound up a small hill and he could see a group of cottages at the top, marking his final destination. It had been a good forty minutes since crossing the stile after the rain shower, so his pace could not have been very brisk by the squire's measure. The only question now was which was Hugh's house out of the half dozen dwellings spread out around the little crossroad where he now stood. A creaking of ancient bicycle pedals and the swish of a stiff corduroy skirt came up behind him.

"Good morning!" came a very forthright voice, warning him not to get in the way of the bicycle's path.

"Good morning. Would you be able to tell me if the Professor's house is anywhere near here?"

"Well it's right here, dear. Oow, if you were any closer you would burn yourself. That one on the corner." And with a tinkle of her bell and a further swish of corduroy she pedaled off. "Enjoy your gardening!"

Disregarding her last remark as that of an eccentric old lady, he pushed open the little wooden gate and then had to lift it to close it again behind him. The house was charming but didn't have the thatch roof that Massimo had imagined. Climbing roses sprawled across the front door and found a home under the eaves. His eyes roved around the collection of plants and the profusion of flowers pushing up around the flagstones. A scraping noise coming from the side of the house caught his attention, so rather than knock on the front door he made his way around through the garden. There stood Hugh with his back to him. A baggy pair of work pants was cinched at his waist with an old leather belt. He looked a little frailer than when Massimo had last seen him, but he still had a full head of white hair that curled up at the collar of a thick Shetland sweater.

"My boy, my boy," he said as he turned around. "How good of you to come all this way just to see an old man," and he thrust a bony, tanned hand into Massimo's.

"Good to see you looking so well, and you know me, I always have questions when I come to see you." Massimo was grinning, happy to see his old mentor, and amazed to see him in this totally new setting.

"I thought you would have been here an hour ago. I've already had my morning cuppa' and so I've started work in the garden."

"Well, it's quite a walk, it took me over an hour." But not wanting to sound like he was complaining, he added, "It's a very beautiful walk and I really got a feel for the English countryside."

"You must have come by a very scenic route because it takes me only twenty minutes to walk into the village."

"No, no," said Massimo impatiently and tugged the map out again from his pocket. "How could that be? The gentleman in the pub showed me very clearly on the map here which way to go, and I'm sure I followed his directions exactly."

Hugh peered for a moment over the map before chuckling and folding the paper to hand it back. "He sent you on a wild goose chase, though admittedly a very pretty and leisurely stroll for a tourist to take. I thought you would have just looked up the address on a Google map and followed your GPS, otherwise I would have sent you a map myself."

"Argh!" Massimo felt totally like a student again, and that he'd been caught making a stupid mistake on the board. "I did follow my GPS but the path ended at a gate with a 'No Trespassing' sign, so I walked all the way back and followed the map in the opposite direction."

"Oh, *that* sign. Nobody takes heed of that. Some chap from London thinks he can stick up a sign in the middle of a public right-of-way just because he bought the property around it."

Massimo felt appeased by the soft look of forgiveness in Hugh's grey eyes.

"But now that you are finally here, I wonder if you wouldn't mind giving me a hand in the garden with a couple of heavy things that I couldn't manage on my own."

He followed him round to the rear of the garden where a row of large sacks leaned up against the shed.

"I need you to put those sacks into the wheelbarrow and we're going to spread manure on the vegetable garden."

The wet manure was certainly heavy, but Massimo happily complied, albeit rewarded for his effort by getting it all over his shoes and slacks.

"Whew! There it's done," he said wiping his brow, for the sun was at its zenith now and the work was making him quite hot.

"We're not done yet. There's a branch I need you to lop off and I don't trust myself on a ladder anymore when I'm on my own."

Massimo found himself ten feet up a ladder with a rope and a small hand saw facing a large limb that was brushing the eves of the house.

"We have to plan the cuts so that the branch falls away from the house and doesn't take you with it," Hugh was shouting from below.

Massimo swung a leg over the branch and sat there laughing. "Your neighbor on the bicycle was right when she said I should enjoy the gardening." He gave the trunk a little slap. "I have to be honest with you, Hugh, I haven't eaten since breakfast and if you want me to continue, I need to eat something first."

"Well stop all that malarkey and come down and I'll make you a sandwich, then."

Hugh brought out a tray to a table on the little patio at the rear of the house. Massimo visibly relaxed at the sight of the food, and stretched out on the chair that he'd placed in the dappled sunlight under a fruit tree.

"I can see why you like it here, but don't you miss the intellectual stimulus of work, and your colleagues?"

Hugh sawed off the crust of the loaf he was holding, using a large serrated knife. "I can always read, and I keep in touch with emails and the internet." He flipped a thick slice of crusty white bread onto Massimo's plate. "And the people important to me come and visit me here."

He lifted a tea towel from a platter that held remains of a large leg of ham. The serrated knife was less efficient at thinly slicing the ham, so the result was a generous chunk of the meat that he slid onto Massimo's plate.

"Try it with some mustard," Hugh instructed. "It's hotter than the mustard we used to get in Geneva, so be careful."

"Mmm. Much better than the egg sandwich they packed for me at the hotel. Why can't they serve decent bread like this at the pub?" he added, getting crumbs all down his shirt as he bit off a chunk now slathered with ham and mustard.

"It's just from the local baker and the ham is from our neighborhood butcher, but the pub now belongs to a large global chain and it gets all its food prepackaged and delivered from a central warehouse somewhere."

"The cost of globalization, I suppose," and he thought of the venture capital companies and banks he was now involved with. This is really what he wanted to talk to Hugh about, but he wondered how to broach the subject.

Hugh did it for him. They talked at first about a few generalities of Massimo's work at the lab and whether he had made any headway on his new interest in the application of chaos theory.

"But why do I get the impression you are not wholly engaged in the high-energy accelerator aspect of it anymore? I get the feeling your intellect has been aroused by some new application, am I right?" Hugh probed.

"I think you might be surprised where this has taken me," Massimo began. "I've made some new friends on the Stanford campus and they've introduced me to the world of investing and economics. Then, quite coincidentally, I met up with some of our neighbors on Sand Hill Road, and somehow I now find myself in the midst of a burgeoning enterprise to do with economic forecasting."

Hugh wiped the mustard from his fingers with a well-worn cloth napkin that he folded and then put aside to refocus his attention on Massimo's revelations.

"I haven't seen the connection yet to nonlinear dynamics and your interest in chaos theory," Hugh observed, raising one bushy, white eyebrow.

Massimo took Hugh through the details of how he had discovered that his mathematical modeling tools could be applied to monetary flows. He took pride in explaining that Hugh's lessons in the correct graphical representation of data had paid off and that he was able to observe many new features in the money flow and investment cycles when he displayed it on the computer.

"These students, Lars and Sven, sound exceptionally gifted chaps," Hugh commented. "It's a pity they weren't lured into physics at an early age, or we might now be discussing the chaotic flow of dark energy, or some such, instead of venture capital," he chortled.

Massimo explained a little more of the circumstances of meeting Lars and Sven through Laura, and how the Stanford campus was something of a melting pot for many different disciplines. It wasn't just science and math that Stanford was famous for, there was the business school of course, but also the arts and music, all of which provided a wonderful opportunity for cross fertilization of ideas. He thought of Hildr and her wild ideas of music and mathematics. He still couldn't decide whether it was a genius or madness, but acknowledged to himself that it was a brilliant example of cross disciplinary science.

"And I take it that Laura is significantly more than just a friend right now," Hugh interrupted.

Massimo conceded that Laura was, indeed, an important factor in his life right now, but it wasn't that easy for him dealing with a modern young woman who held very strong ideas about who she wanted to be and where she was going.

"Quite the opposite of Donatella," he sighed.

"Donatella was always very gracious to me when she invited me to your home in Geneva," Hugh said. "But I saw then that her conservative social and religious ideas might cause problems for you both in the future."

Hugh refolded his napkin and moved the plates on the table to some new alignment. "I'm no expert in matters of the heart, but I'm delighted, my boy, that you've taken me into your confidence explaining the twists and turns your life and your work are taking." Little creases had formed around Hugh's eyes. "For a brief moment I thought you may have launched yourself into the mathematics of musical theory. I recall that was always a favorite after-dinner topic of yours. The idea of exploring economics comes as a bit of a surprise, but an intriguing one!"

"It's funny you should mention that," Massimo mused. "I've had the strangest interaction with a friend of Laura's who wants to use music to explain mathematics, rather than using mathematics to explain music."

He went on to tell of Hildr's obsession with trying to demonstrate the famous *existence theorem* for solutions to the Navier-Stokes equations. It sounded very farfetched now that he was recounting it in his own words.

"But her musical demonstration with a performance of a Navier-Stokes composition and decomposition was very convincing," he said shyly. His subsequent description of the performance carefully omitted mention of the more 'physical' aspects of his last encounter with Hildr.

"You certainly seem to deal with as much chaos in your personal life as you do in your professional studies," said Hugh, clearly seeing through Massimo's attempt to obscure the full truth.

He began to clear away the lunch dishes. Massimo followed him into the house, looking to restore his friend's faith in him.

"I really wanted to discuss my concerns about working outside of the physics community and getting involved in the business world where huge fortunes are at stake."

Hugh stood with his back to him at the sink. "I suppose there's a whole new set of ethical concerns for you to get into trouble with."

"Not really," said Massimo valiantly. "Scientists have always faced the ethical dilemma whether their discoveries will be used for good or bad. Isn't it the same situation if a new financial tool is developed?"

Hugh remained silent.

"My concern right now," Massimo continued, "is how to deal with my suspicions that not everything is completely above board with the new people I am involved with."

Hugh's shoulders unhunched as he turned and dried his hands on a tea towel. "Look, I'm not much good at giving advice about the business world, or questions of ethics for that matter, but let's get back to the garden and if it helps for you to have someone to listen to your concerns I'll gladly do so as we work." He rested one hand on Massimo's shoulder and gently guided him back to the ladder leaning against the tree.

As Massimo climbed the ladder and straddled the tree limb once more, Hugh called out from below, "You know, if you are going to go out on a limb with this venture capital thing, make sure you're sitting on the right side before you start cutting."

Massimo chuckled to himself. Just like Hugh to be witty with his advice.

"On my way over here," he called back, "I was thinking something similar. The motives for wealth and power haven't changed much over the centuries. If I just follow those well-worn tracks of greed and ambition, they'll point the way fairly clearly to who is manipulating things for their own ends."

As he spoke, Massimo looped the rope over the far end of the branch and fed the remaining length down to Hugh.

"Give a man enough rope ...., is that what you are trying to say?" said Hugh, pulling the rope taut.

"You 'taut' me well," replied Massimo, trying to keep up with Hugh's dry repartee.

He began the arduous task of sawing through the limb with the handsaw which was in his opinion far too small for the job. "The idea," he said breathlessly between cuts, "is that you keep the rope taut so that when the branch starts to give you can pull it away from the house."

"Steady, even cuts there, my boy," Hugh called up.

"You concentrate on training your rope and I'll deal with sawing," muttered Massimo.

"What was that?" said Hugh, feigning a little deafness.

"Oh, never mind," replied an annoyed Massimo, but then suddenly there was a loud crack as the tree limb broke.

Such was the suddenness of the limb parting from the tree that Hugh was sent stumbling backward across the yard, ending up on his backside in a pile of leaves.

The tree trunk shook with such violence from the recoil that Massimo dropped the handsaw and clung to the tree for dear life. The ladder, however, was flung away from the tree trunk and Massimo was left suspended some height above the ground.

"My boy, my boy!" cried Hugh, scrambling to his feet. "Are you alright?"

"It wouldn't be the first time," said Massimo dryly, "that you've left me dangling after giving me one of your hard problems. But in this case, would you mind putting the ladder back up?"

"Of course, of course," said Hugh with relief that his young protégé was both unharmed and still had his wits about him. "I could never bear to see you dangling out on a limb by yourself for very long," he said as he guided Massimo's feet towards the rungs of the ladder.

"Well, I'm relieved that you're alright," said Hugh brushing away some twigs and slivers of bark from Massimo's shoulders.

"We made a good job of it, though," said Massimo admiring the enormous limb now lying at their feet.

"I'm afraid we're not done," said Hugh, resuming a more matter of fact tone. "We can't leave it here blocking the path. It will have to be cut up into pieces that I can stack on my wood pile."

"What, with this?" asked Massimo, holding up the little handsaw he had just been struggling with.

"You know what they say," said Hugh ducking briefly into the garden shed. "If you fall off your horse, you should get right back on it. But, in your case it's a saw horse." He came out of the shed holding an enormous bowsaw above his head. It had ferocious sharp teeth that seemed to leer at Massimo standing there with the little saw in his hand.

"Why didn't you give me that one to begin with" he exclaimed, "instead of this piddling little thing?"

"You would have cut your leg off! Besides, it takes two hands to operate this thing, so you wouldn't have been able to hold onto the tree trunk, and then where would you be now, hmm?"

The bowsaw was indeed a formidable tool and made short shrift of the cuts once Massimo got the hang of it. He was actually enjoying the work, watching the sawdust pile up beneath the log and inhaling the resinous sap with each cut. But he wasn't about to admit as much to Hugh, who was busy lecturing him about the time it would take for the stacked logs to season so they could be split and used in the fireplace.

"I suppose you want me to come back next year and do the splitting for you, eh?"

"That wouldn't be so bad, would it?" said Hugh in almost a whisper.

Massimo smiled at the old man, and they continued their work in silence for a few minutes.

"You know," said Hugh breaking the silence, "there's an old adage that if you want to find where the power really lies, then you should follow the money trail. Well, it strikes me that you have the ideal tool with your program to map the money trail. Your graphics sound like they could reveal and track the money flow like no one has been able to before."

The afternoon sun was dipping low and a damp chill had returned to the air. Massimo gave a little shiver. "You know, I hadn't thought of it that way, but if we get this program into the public domain it could add a whole new level of transparency to the banking industry."

"You might run into some opposition there," said Hugh. "The last thing the banking industry would want is transparency."

"Therein lies the problem," said Massimo, carrying the last log over to the wood pile.

"I think we're just about done here," said Hugh eyeing the path around them. "There are only these twigs and leaves remaining, and I can sweep them up tomorrow. Why don't we go in and have tea by the fire. We can toast some muffins over the fire; I think you'd enjoy that."

Hugh oiled the bowsaw blade before hanging it up again in the shed. Massimo observed the neatly arranged gardening tools hanging on the shed walls, and then followed his master into the house.

The fire crackled back to life as Hugh stoked the embers and added fresh logs. "I always find a mixture of pine and oak works best for a good fire."

The wisps of cyprus smoke reaching Massimo's nostrils brought pangs of nostalgia for his childhood visits to aunts and uncles in Tuscan farmhouses.

"Make yourself comfortable, lad, while I fetch the tea things."

Massimo settled in an old wingback chair whose crinkled leather stroked him like an old friend. He gazed up at the bookshelves and saw that Hugh's old reference books for physics and math were relegated to a high shelf where they were hardly touched. The lower shelves were cluttered with books on gardening and local history and all manner of rural topics. Hugh had moved on, Massimo thought.

It wasn't that he'd given up on physics, but more that he'd opened new chapters in his life. I'm about to do the same, he thought, giving a little nod.

"This is a muffin toasting fork," said Hugh bustling back into the room. "And these are pots of homemade jam and clotted cream. A combination I've always had a weakness for, I'm afraid, ever since my parents took me on holidays to Devon as a child."

Massimo had never imagined Hugh with parents, or as a child. He had always been the white-haired mentor to Massimo.

"The homemade jam comes from my neighbor. I believe you ran into her this morning, outside on her bicycle. She spends quite a bit of time here," he said with a twinkle, "but I think your visit scared her off today."

Now there was something else Massimo had never imagined: Hugh with a romantic life!

"I almost forgot," said Massimo reaching for his satchel. "I brought you a present."

He proudly placed the box with the bottle of Laphroaig on the table before Hugh.

A look of gloomy disappointment crossed Hugh's face. "I'm sorry, Massimo, but I can't accept that," he said and slid it back toward him.

"Why, what's wrong with it?" said Massimo pushing his hair back dejectedly.

"My constitution doesn't tolerate strong alcohol anymore. It's best if you take it back so I'm not tempted," he said, giving it another little shove in Massimo's direction.

Massimo felt awful at his own lack of sensitivity and for not carefully considering whether Hugh would appreciate something like a bottle of whisky.

"Now don't be like that," Hugh chided. "I don't need a gift from you. Your coming here to visit was a treat in itself, and you did all that work in the garden for me."

"I suppose I just got carried away after I was introduced to this malt whisky the night before last by the headhunter lady who's taking me to the opera tomorrow night."

"Now hold on there, young fella. Is this yet another floozy you're consorting with now?"

"No. It's not like that at all. She is just someone I met at the conference, who is a recruiter for Wall Street firms, and we happened to get talking about opera and she happened to have a spare ticket." Massimo sounded less convinced himself now as he said this.

"What? And you believe these are just coincidences in this new hardball world of big business you move in now? Must you always unbutton your trousers and look for trouble? God knows you have enough trouble hanging onto relationships without going out of your way looking for complications."

Massimo was completely taken aback by Hugh's directness. He had never spoken to him like this before, but he had to admit that Hugh had a point, and he stared despondently into the grate.

"Don't pout. Now eat your muffin before you burn it to a crisp."

The homemade jam and clotted cream revived his mood.

"Look, it was the temptation of going to the London Opera that lured me into this. I've always wanted to see it. I'll be careful. Even if she is some kind of industrial spy, I'm not going to tell her anything about my new work."

"Ah, yes, the opera," Hugh reminisced. "I was quite the concertgoer in my day, you know." He rose from his chair and slipped out of the room.

"Here, I want you to have this," he said as he returned to the room. "It's my old evening scarf that I used to wear with my black tie to all the concerts in Oxford. I don't venture out anymore and it would please me greatly if a little part of me was to accompany you on your excursion to the opera."

Massimo admired the creamy white silk of the scarf, draping it around his shoulders and feeling the coolness of the silk on his neck. "Thank you. I'm touched. It's a beautiful gift that I shall wear with pride to the opera."

They sat back down to finish the muffins. Massimo took care to fold up the scarf and put it in his jacket pocket so he wouldn't get jam on it.

Finally, he said, "I suppose I should be heading back to the hotel now, before it gets too dark. I have an early train to catch tomorrow."

They went out into the hallway for Massimo to gather his things.

"Here, I'll give you a torch in case you lose your way again," he said rummaging in the hall closet.

Massimo imagined a burning paraffin torch that was meant to light one's way in the wilds, but Hugh pulled out an old, cylindrical metal flashlight instead.

"Oh," said Massimo when Hugh switched it on and a dim yellow beam sputtered on the floor.

"Not to worry. I have some new batteries for it somewhere," and he fumbled for them in the hallway table drawer.

The flashlight made a loud screeching noise of metal on metal as he unscrewed it and the two halves separated.

"There. Good as new," he said as he flicked it on and an only slightly brighter beam emerged. "Just leave it with the proprietress at the pub and I'll pick it up next time I go by."

Massimo stuck out his hand to bid his professor, mentor, friend goodbye.

"I thought Italian men always embraced each other," said Hugh clasping Massimo's shoulders firmly.

That was something Hugh had never done before either.

The direct route back to the pub with his GPS was indeed much shorter, and it took Massimo only fifteen minutes at an accelerated pace before he tromped in through the hotel front door and up the steps to his room.

"It's Shepherd's Pie tonight, dear," the proprietress called after him. "If you're interested. And we'll be serving a nice Chilean hearty burgundy with it."

Massimo decided he could quite comfortably last until morning on his supper of muffins with jam, and forgo the mystery of which parts of a shepherd were used in the making of another non-pie.

# Chapter 13 – The Opera

Thoughts of Hugh preoccupied his mind on the journey back to London. It was all sage advice that Hugh had given. Not that they weren't things he hadn't considered himself, but Hugh had a way of bringing things out and forcing Massimo to consider them rationally. At the blackboard, he remembered, Hugh had an uncanny knack for making him discover the solution to mathematical problems for himself. When they were making new and original contributions to their field, Massimo was sure that Hugh would plant the germ of an idea, so that when he worked out the details he would feel he had discovered it himself.

Was he doing the same now in regard to Massimo's relationship problems? What was that all about? Really! Hugh had never spoken up like that before, he thought indignantly. Massimo felt that he was only going to the opera with this woman, after all, so why all the fuss? Although, somewhere at the back of his mind was a little voice asking why had he omitted to tell Laura of the invitation. Wouldn't she be pleased to hear that he had the opportunity of going?

That morning over breakfast, however, when he was checking his e-mail, it wasn't Laura's missives that drew his attention. Rather it was one from Ms. Jenna Jones that garnered his attention. She wanted to inform him that she had reserved a room for him at her hotel. The performance at Covent Garden started at 7:30 p.m. she instructed, so they would be going to the Champagne Bar before the performance and taking supper together after the show.

When he went online to complete the hotel reservation, it came as a shock to discover that the room was more than twice as expensive as the one he stayed at for the conference. She obviously had a more generous expense account than he had, for his meager physicist's travel budget would never cover that. He couldn't complain though because he was getting a free ticket for the opera and the value of that was at least equal to the difference in room rates.

And so his thoughts went round and round on the return train journey to London. They weren't thoughts about computer modeling or anything work related, it was Hughes stern warning to keep his personal affairs in order, and not let chaos rule that irked him. What had Hugh said? "Keep your trousers buttoned."

He bit pensively on a fingernail, staring out at the gray landscape as they approached the Greater London Area. Actually, he also bit on a sticky bun, courtesy of British Rail, since he had declined the offer from the pub to pack him another egg sandwich. They were very friendly at the pub, he thought, wishing him a safe journey and hoping he would return again soon. They even gave him a souvenir mug bearing a likeness of the Monarch with an inscription *Golden Jubilee 2002*.

This time at Paddington Station he didn't even consider a bus connection, but went straight to the taxi cab rank.

The hotel was quite a bit plusher than the last one, and he was delighted to see American-style plumbing in the bathroom; no doubt a significant factor in Ms. Jones's choice of this hotel. The bags were taken up to his room by the hotel porter without his being asked, and he was a little embarrassed to see his shabby valise assigned to the pedigree *Samsonite* and *Inox* luggage kennel as it went up the elevator.

A monitor screen in his room somehow knew to start playing a welcome message when he first entered. He fumbled in his pocket for a tip, but could only find a 1 pound coin, which he thought was a bit much for one bag, but the bellhop evidently thought the opposite.

The screen continued to play its welcoming address as Massimo unpacked, and it made sure he was aware of the selection of shops conveniently located at the lobby level. He looked up as the acclaimed Italian men's suit shop was mentioned, and recalled Ms. Jones's advice that he should check it out. It wouldn't hurt to look. The last time he had shopped for an Italian suit was with Donatella in Milan. He hung up his jacket in the wardrobe, unable to ignore the college-issue faux leather elbow patches. He really did need something smarter for a night at the opera.

A saunter down to the street and shops might be in order, he thought, after he finished unpacking and exploring the amenities of his fancy room. Downstairs, an arcade branched off perpendicular to the main hotel lobby. The hotel reception provided him with a map and shopping guide for the area, and handed him a message from Ms. Jones instructing him of their rendezvous time in the lobby that evening.

The hotel arcade housed an assortment of shops. A coffee shop was done up in dark wood tones and the smell of fresh beans wafted out of the door as he passed. Two elderly female patrons with hats that could only have been styled in tribute to some royal personage, given the prim ornateness of feathers and fabric, sat alone in the window forking at pieces of cream bedecked sponge cake. Alongside, a jewelry store with polished brass window frames displayed the usual assortment of rings and brooches under the rhinestone glare of tiny lamps. To reassure the shopper that this display of costume jewelry was truly an authentic offering of Covent Garden, the eye was drawn to a centerpiece display of tiny crystal ballerinas mounted on a raised platform that twinkled and turned under the lights. He couldn't see anything that might remotely appeal to Laura, and stepped back a little to observe what else might be on offer in this sheltered shopping niche.

Three mannequins leered at him from the opposite window. Their slim suited forms beckoned and sneered like young Davids, ready to grope any female passerby. He had found the Italian suit store. Inside, rows of suits hung from racks like unfinished men. Muted glows reflected from the wool and silk fabrics. Somewhere, deep inside, a dormant fashion gene that could be traced back through Massimo's family roots, was stirred back to life. Nobody rushed to serve him, so he could finger a lapel here and let a silk necktie slip through his fingertips there, quite undisturbed, except perhaps for the uncanny feeling of the eyes of the mannequins upon him, following him along the row.

"Signor, we can help you," came a voice from a dark corner. "I see that you have been living in the States for some years, but perhaps your discerning taste is now calling out for something more fitting."

Massimo stepped back slightly and sought support by placing his hand on the firmly padded shoulder of the jacketed bust at his side.

"The sack-cut jacket favored by college professors and Midwest business men gave you away. And those shoes, if you will forgive me, signor, could only have come from the West Coast of America."

Massimo looked down at the nubuck suede of his sturdy walking shoes. They were the most comfortable shoes he had ever owned, but they did look a little out of place amongst the finely pleated trouser cuffs cascading from the hangers.

"I was thinking of a new suit for a special occasion, but I'm not sure," he half answered.

"We hope to be of help in advising you, signor, but please understand that only our main store on Saville Row can serve you with a bespoke suit, whereas our little branch store is more for emergency services only."

"Emergencies?" said Massimo, not understanding.

"Our location here in the Covent Garden means that quite a few of our visitors come in because they've realized their street clothes aren't going to hold up against their partners' outfits for a gala night at the opera."

"That seems to be my situation," said Massimo scratching a finger to his forehead.

"And when is our performance at the opera to be, signor?"

"This evening," answered Massimo.

"That gives us just a couple of hours, then, to find something suitable," he said, producing a measuring tape and reaching it around Massimo's waist. He called out the readings to an unseen assistant in the shadows as he walked around holding up the tape to shoulders, arms and all manner of places that would guarantee a snug fit.

"Signor has not completely lost his youthful figure, so I am confident we can find something suitable on the racks."

Massimo felt a pointer stick firmly placed up his crotch as his inner leg dimensions were read.

"It would be best if signor were to disrobe entirely, down to the underwear, so that we can start building up the ensemble."

Massimo's jacket was slipped from his shoulders as he was led into a changing cabin.

"I am sure your American jacket with the sack cut and unpadded shoulders is quite comfortable, but it does nothing to create style or contour," said the salesman, holding Massimo's jacket out at arm's length. "And those pocket flaps..." He shuddered.

"What about an English suit?" Massimo countered, thinking that the choices shouldn't all be left to the salesman. But his comments were dismissed as he was handed a shirt to put on.

"We'll begin with a plain white shirt, signor, for the purposes of trying the suit and matching the collar style, and then we can return to the color when we come to selecting the tie."

The fine cotton fabric slid smoothly over his shoulders and buttoned snugly at the neck. He was also handed a pair of black socks to replace his thick woolen walking socks.

"The English suit, signor," the salesman condescended to reply, "is only for military types or circus performers. The shoulders are padded too wide and the waist pulled in too narrow, so that it is either made to look overbearing, or becomes entirely too whimsical, depending on the cloth. We will try and show you that an Italian suit has a contoured fit to accentuate the natural lines of the body and has just enough padding and taper to create a style."

With that he handed him a pair of dark trousers that Massimo found were exceedingly light and comfortable about the hips. The curtain was pulled back and Massimo was shown a pair of pointed black leather shoes he should slip on before coming out of the fitting area.

"We will concentrate on either a dark blue or black for this evening," said the salesman with a smile, pleased at his progress in transforming Massimo.

"It's all about the vee," he continued, as he adjusted the lapel on the first jacket Massimo tried.

For Massimo's benefit, he indicated towards one of the suited mannequins, "The first vee is formed where the lapels come together when the jacket is buttoned. The second is an inverted vee formed by the shirt collar. Together they direct the eye first to the face and then to the hips."

The idea of geometric symmetry appealed to Massimo and he allowed himself to be swept up in the salesman's elaborate explanation.

As several jackets were slipped on and off his shoulders in quick succession, he was reminded of a time in Milan where it had been Donatella commanding which was the right combination he should choose.

A midnight blue was settled upon and the assistant was sent scurrying in search of the matching pair of trousers.

"I think we will stick with a white shirt collar, but the shirt front can have a light pink stripe like this one," said the salesman, now completely in charge of the choices.

When Massimo returned wearing the new shirt and trousers, the salesman held forth a tie for him to put on.

"A gray silk tie with some pink thread running through it should do nicely."

Massimo complied, and the salesman then redid the knot, with a little lesson in achieving the right amount of dimple beneath the Windsor knot.

As the coat jacket was once more slipped over his shoulders, the salesman again elaborated on the layering of vees formed by the jacket lapels, shirt collar and now the tie.

Massimo beheld himself in the full length mirror with approval, though hardly recognizing what he saw. The salesman was busy adjusting the trouser cuffs and explaining that it should just touch the midpoint of the shoe.

"If signor cares to go next door for a quick haircut and shave, we can complete the final adjustments," said the salesman stepping back and nodding at his handiwork.

Massimo ran his fingers up the back of his neck and shrugged in acquiescence. He had gone this far, why not finish the job.

As he left the store he passed the coffee shop, and whom did he spy but the weasel sitting there. Facing him, with her back to the window was a woman who, as he strode quickly by, looked a lot like Ms. Jones. Odd, he thought. He couldn't imagine Ms. Jones wanting to have a meeting with the weasel. Whoever she was, she appeared to be handing over an envelope. He thought no more about it and hurried on towards the barber's.

The gentleman's barber, situated just off the hotel lobby, managed to turn a quick trim into a full styled cut that was much shorter and more angular then the floppy tresses he was used to brushing out of his eyes. He winced at the bill that they cheerily told him he could sign to his hotel room.

This was nothing to the shock that awaited him at the suit store where his suit, shirt, socks, tie and shoes were all neatly packaged in a black and gold carry bag. When Massimo was handed back his credit card, he saw that the bill for this extravagance amounted to four figures. Just the cost of the shoes alone was more than he anticipated paying for a suit. But it was a fait accompli: he could not possibly go back to wearing his old jacket now with its elbow patches, nor was there time to run down to a department store and grab some mass produced article for $300. He hadn't protested once while the salesman had customized the fitting for Massimo, so now he was stuck with the extravaganza and he must sign for it bravely.

The salesman wished him a pleasant evening at the opera and, as he swung the suit bag over his shoulder, Massimo took the philosophical approach of not thinking any more about what he had just done.

There was barely enough time to go and get ready for the evening's engagement. A thought raced through his mind whether he should buy some kind of gift for Ms. Jones to show his appreciation for the invitation. He could not think of anything appropriate other than offering to pay for dinner after the evening's performance.

Just before leaving his hotel room he reached into the wardrobe for Hugh's scarf. The aged, creamy white silk added a touch of seasoned elegance to his otherwise brand new outfit. The idea of a gift for Hugh had not worked out, so it was probably best to avoid any misinterpretation that Ms. Jones might construe from receiving one.

Ms. Jones was already waiting for him in the foyer lounge as he came down the elevator.

"Well, you do clean up nicely," she said stepping in closely and running an approving finger down his cheek to rest for a moment on his chin.

She was dressed in an elegantly simple, long black gown that was slit and cut away to be revealing in all the right places.

"It's only a short distance to the opera house, but we will take a cab that can drop us at the entrance," she said, taking his arm and leading him through the foyer.

He would have liked a walk, but one look at Ms. Jones stiletto shoes told him they would not get very far on the London pavements. The London taxis were still a fun novelty, and he did not mind clambering into the back of one for the short ride.

"Damn sight easier to get in and out of than a New York cab when you're dressed like this," she said appreciatively, stretching out a leg and revealing a long length of thigh.

Massimo attempted to make some small talk about the anticipation of the coming show. It seemed appropriate to talk about which opera they were about to see, but Ms. Jones didn't seem to attach much importance to it. He had seen performances in some of the big opera houses in Italy and tried to explain the attraction of attending something in an English setting, but he was cut off by their arrival at the steps.

The Champagne Bar was located in a tall, elegantly marbled atrium adjacent to the main hall.

"It reminds me of New York's Grand Central Station," she said as they made their way through the crowd towards the bar. "If you get close enough to catch the barman's eye, order us a couple of glasses of the *Ruinart*, or better yet, a bottle, so we don't have to go back twice," she shouted above the mounting noise.

But as they worked their way towards the front of the throng it was Ms. Jones, of course, who was able to catch the roving eye of the barman.

"I also ordered us a plate of hors d'oeuvres," she said hauling off the bottle and two glasses towards a vacant table. "Could you pick them up from the end of the bar?"

As they stood at their little bar table Massimo caught sight of his reflection in the long window opposite. He saw a suave fellow chatting up a femme fatale, clinking glasses and checking out who was looking at them. Surely this could not be him. He tried to steer the conversation back to the thematic matter of the opera, but Ms. Jones kept directing him to comparisons between here and the Met. The bottle of *Ruinart* Champagne melted his intellectual ambitions and he fell in with her, making asinine observations on the degree of fashion extravagance here, versus Milan and New York.

When the bell rang to indicate they should start making their way towards their seats, she took his arm and said quite openly,

"I suppose I should be pumping you for information on your new venture with WVC, but you know what, screw them, I'm just going to enjoy the evening."

"Phew, that's a relief," he joked. "I thought I was going to have to give you one of our marketing pitches tonight."

They wound their way up the steps and corridors to find their box. An usher opened the door and stood aside as they entered the narrow box.

"That's quite something," said Massimo, impressed with the vista of the horseshoe shaped hall beneath them. A large domed ceiling arced overhead and three tiers of galleries were spread before him.

"This box is perfectly located. We have a commanding view of the stage," he said.

"And a commanding view of all the other audience members," she added. "This is the kind of seat you only get if you know someone with connections!"

"I should have brought opera glasses," he said, gazing down at all the patrons who appeared to be peering up at him through their opera glasses.

"Sometimes there's more intrigue in the audience than on stage," she smirked.

"The problem is this new suit is rather form fitting, and doesn't have any decent sized pockets for useful things like opera glasses."

"I was going to compliment you on your suit," she said, giving him a little nudge as they slid down into their seats.

"*Cosi fan Tutte*[22], sort of an ironic title in this day and age," he said, steering the conversation to the subject of the opera. "Women, they're all like that!"

"Hmm?" she replied, only half listening while she made one final check of her messages before silencing the phone in her purse.

"The title, it roughly translates to *They're all the Same*," he said. "Mozart was implying that women are always fickle when it comes to choosing partners."

"Just the women are fickle, you think?" she answered. The house lights dimmed and the noise around them subsided. "We'll see about that."

Massimo settled back in his seat and let the overture wash over him.

At one level it was a trite, old-fashioned story with characters easily duped by droll disguises. The cynical old Don Alfonso was making a bet with the two gentlemen that their fiancées could be seduced if they were to go away and return in disguise as new suitors. A silly story, but Mozart's music took it to a whole different level. The best thing would be to ignore the farcical plot and sit back and enjoy the music, but the constant references to infidelity and capriciousness of feelings made him fidget in his seat. He rubbed the silk of Hugh's scarf between his fingertips, and the tassels, like rosary beads, evoked Hugh's litany.

How could the conniving Don Alfonso sing such a transcendent trio together with the two beautiful sisters? They sang so sweetly wishing their departing fiancés a gentle voyage. It was incongruous that Mozart should write the most sublime piece of music in the opera and then sarcastically put old Don Alfonso in the middle of it all.

"Sunday, Bloody Sunday," whispered Ms. Jones.

"What?" he whispered back.

She leaned closer to his ear. "*Sunday, Bloody Sunday*, this is where they got the music from."

He shrugged, having no idea what she was whispering about.

The seats in the box were angled such that Massimo sat to her left and slightly behind her. It meant he had to gaze past her slender neck and the curve of her shoulder to see the stage. The dress she wore beguiled him. The simple black pleats of the silken cloth were very proper at first glance, but when she moved in certain ways they split open in a most alarming manner.

Despina, the maid of the two forsaken sisters came out onto the stage. She was the most grounded of the characters in the story and provided a little comic relief. She wasn't flighty like the two sisters, nor bitter like the old Alfonso, and certainly not a naive romantic like the two fiancés. She set about convincing the two lovelorn sisters they should not worry, but then lamented it was men who were always unfaithful. They go to other countries and have affairs, she wailed. Why did he have to choose an opera based on infidelity and men choosing to have affairs when they travelled overseas? Massimo was so restless in his seat that Ms. Jones shot him a sideways glance to shush him.

The lights came up at intermission and she said, "I think we should go downstairs for some more champagne so you can move around a bit, or you'll never sit still through the second act."

"Sorry," he replied. "The music is out of this world, but the silliness of the story has gotten me annoyed."

They fought their way through the crowd to the bar and Ms. Jones managed once again to get served instantly.

"Was it the betrayal of romantic young love that irritated you, or just the cynicism of old Alfonso?" she asked after they had procured their drinks.

Massimo swallowed his champagne in one gulp. "It's the banality of the story," he shrugged. "I mean, really, fancy not knowing whom you are in love with."

The shortness of the intermission precluded much further conversation and they rejoined the surging crowd once more up the stairs to find their seats.

He was pleased to be sitting comfortably back in their box. Glancing over the program at the names of the performers, his gaze eventually rose back to the stage, where it had to first pass over the curves of Ms. Jones' shoulder, teasing him beneath the wispy folds of black silk.

The storyline of the second act was even more annoying than the first. The two soldiers returned in mustached disguises and agreed each would try and seduce the other's finance. To their surprise they both succeeded and much confusion between the characters ensued. Massimo no longer cared; he was so elevated by the music that he even wished happiness on the old Alfonso.

This time as he wriggled further down into his seat Ms. Jones shot him an approving smile.

On stage the story resolved itself. The players revealed who they really were to their lovers and eventually all was forgiven. It was a little puzzling, though. If he was not mistaken there had been a little wife swapping going on, and it wasn't completely clear who was going to marry whom in the end.

What is it in human nature that makes us crave the beauty of music? The search for beauty is as instinctive as the urge to live and reproduce. The beauty of music can reach across time, and it allows us to forgive the tritest of storylines and lyrics.

"People no doubt thought it a little risqué in its time," was Ms. Jones's comment after the clapping and cheering had finally subsided.

"Do you have a preference where we should go for supper?" Massimo politely asked, harking back to his desire to thank her for inviting him to the opera.

She took his arm as they descended the staircase.

"I have made a table reservation at the hotel restaurant," she said. "I didn't want to go traipsing over town for supper after the opera. And it's easy for me to put it straight onto my expense account there."

"I would have liked to have invited you some place special to thank you for taking me to the opera," he said.

"That's not at all necessary. Besides, I think you will find the hotel restaurant quite cozy. The food is on the conservative side, but well prepared. And the wine list is excellent."

"Still, I am in your debt for a really wonderful evening."

"I'm sure I'll think of a way for you to repay me one day," she said, giving his arm a little squeeze.

In the taxi on the way back to the hotel, she powered on the phone in her purse and started to scroll through the messages that had arrived in the meantime. Massimo stared out the window and casually remarked," Funny thing, I thought I spied the weasel at our hotel this afternoon."

"Mm?" she replied, still distracted by her cell phone.

"That despicable fellow from the conference. I wonder what he was doing hanging around here?" he asked.

"Oh, he was probably looking for me. Wanting to get his payoff," she answered, still intent on reading a message on her phone.

"His payoff?"

"Yes, sordid isn't it. That weasel is only good for gossip and snooping. His ideas are crap, but I subsidize his conference attendance in exchange for his collection of rumors and hearsay."

"Doesn't sound a very reliable way of collecting information about people," he muttered.

"Look, I'm not a scientist, but if I hear the same rumor from two or three independent sources, then something's behind it. How do you think I found out about you and WVC?"

Massimo twisted in his seat and looked out the window again.

"Relax. I'm only exploiting you because you look good in a suit at the opera. – Hey, I'm teasing," and she took his arm and held on to it for the remainder of the taxi ride.

As they exited the taxi and made their way across the hotel foyer to the restaurant she said,

"They're all the same."

And since Massimo only looked at her with raised eyebrows, she added, "*Cosi fan tutte* – they're all the same."

"Women are?" he asked.

"No, I think Mozart was being more universal and meant all people are fickle, not just the women."

They entered the restaurant of the hotel. It was an elaborate Victorian dining room with polished wood tables bedecked with ornate tableware. The maître d' rushed towards them as they stepped through the door.

"Ms. Jones, I trust you had an enjoyable evening at the opera. Your table is right this way," and he led them across the room to a comfortable corner table elaborately laid out with crystal and silverware for two. As the chairs were slid under them, and the maître d' departed, she leaned forward and said,

"I'm always tempted to call him Jeeves. Don't you just love the potted palms? It's so English."

"What do you mean, all people are fickle?" he said, not wanting to let her previous pronouncement go so easily.

"That was the point of the opera, wasn't it? Our choices of partners are often capricious, dictated either by social expectations, or worse, by naive romantic notions," she answered.

The headwaiter arrived and discreetly placed a card in front of them with the evening menu.

"Ahem," he quietly announced, waiting to see if their conversation had finished. "The soup this evening is mulligatawny; our fish is a poached smoked Scottish haddock; and of course we have our usual traditional offerings of beef."

"I think we should move straight to the main course, don't you Massimo, considering we already indulged on all those hors d'oeuvres and champagne." Without waiting for a reply she said to the waiter, "I really want my companion to sample your wonderful beef. What do you recommend this evening?"

"If I may suggest the Fillet Mignon for madam, and perhaps the Beef Wellington for the gentleman."

"Sounds perfect," she said, handing the menu back to the waiter, giving Massimo only the slightest glance to indicate he should approve of her choice.

Massimo gave a little shrug. He could remember a time in Italy when it was not uncommon for a man to do all the ordering. Laura had disavowed him of that habit in California, reminding him that she did actually have her own set of tastes and preferences. Now the tables seemed to have been turned and this New Yorker was making all the decisions for him. He didn't protest, though. He couldn't; the choices were exactly what he would have selected.

"I will send the sommelier over to you, madam," said the waiter as he departed.

"So if our choice of partners is largely capricious," she said, picking up the thread of the conversation again, unfazed by the waiter's interruption, "then we can hardly be affronted when later there is a change of mind, can we?"

"And this was reflected in the music, you think?" he said, for this was all, he decided, he cared about now.

The sommelier arrived and addressed Ms. Jones directly. "Will you be continuing your campaign with the French Burgundies this evening, Ms. Jones?"

"Indeed, I will be. Thank you, Henry," she said as he handed her the wine list opened at her page of choice, and then withdrew.

"What was that all about?" laughed Massimo.

"I'm working my way through their collection of Burgundies. Each time I dine here I try a different one. It's a real blast," she said.

He thought she might be dismissing his conversation again, for she turned her attention to her cell phone for a moment.

"Ah, yes, here we are," she said after a minute. "They have a *Vosne Romanée* and I was just checking it against Robert Parker's rating. We should try and go for the 2005 and not the '06 listed on the menu."

The sommelier returned when she closed the menu and placed it beside her, indicating that she had made up her mind.

"Henry, I've decided on the *Vosne Romanée, Champs Perdrix, Domaine Bruno Clair*," she said to him, "But do you have any of the 2005 left? I really want the '05 and not the '06."

"I think we may have set aside a few remaining bottles of the '05, Ms. Jones. Allow me to check for you."

"Ah, the music kicks the legs out from under you, doesn't it?" she said, immediately returning to their conversation about the opera when the sommelier left. She expounded a few of her favorite arias and Massimo became hopelessly ensnared in the web of conversation she threw around him.

The sommelier returned once more and stood to one side of his small trolley, laid out with tools for slitting the foil capsule, extracting the cork and pouring the wine into a crystal decanter. Massimo watched as the red liquid was poured through a small silver funnel into the neck of the decanter.

He brought the decanter over to the table and placed a small silver dish with the cork next to Ms. Jones before announcing,

"The '05 *Vosne Romanée, Champs Perdrix, Domaine Bruno Clair*," and then poured a splash into her glass.

She twirled it around and sniffed it before taking it into her mouth.

"Thank you, Henry. Leave the decanter there. I think it will open up nicely by the time our meal arrives," she said.

The sommelier left and she picked up the conversation again on the music, but Massimo jealously stared at the decanter, disconsolate that he had not been able to taste the wine and would apparently have to wait until dinner before he could.

"What was it you were saying to me in the first act?" he said, looking up suddenly. "Something about Sundays?"

"Ah, yes, the music from the beautiful trio. It was used as the theme music in the movie *Sunday, Bloody Sunday*," she said.

"I don't know that one. Sounds like an odd choice of music for a gangster movie, though," he said.

"Just because I am from New York doesn't mean it has to be a gangster movie," she laughed. "Quite the opposite, it's about relationships between three people, and the music fits it perfectly."

The wine in the decanter was still eyeing Massimo with its rich, red glint, but he managed to stay focused on her movie retelling.

"The film starred Glenda Jackson; she was my idol when I was a teenager growing up in the Bronx. It was made in the early seventies, but you should look for it. It's a real classic."

"I will," he said. "It sounds interesting, especially now, in light of the music."

"The Glenda Jackson character has a lover, but she doesn't have exclusive claim on him, for he openly has a second lover and splits his time between the two of them. That's where the issue of Sundays comes in," she explained.

"A consenting love triangle," commented Massimo. "And this was made in the seventies, you say?"

"The twist to the story is that the second lover is not another woman, but a man. It was the first mainstream movie to depict a bisexual relationship and show men embracing and kissing on the screen."

192

"I bet that caused quite a stir at the time," he said. "How did the story end?"

"The bisexual character dumps them both and heads off for New York," she laughed.

Their laughter was interrupted by the squeaking wheel of the serving trolley being rolled toward them by the waiter, with the maître d' following close behind.

"Your fillet mignon, served very rare, madam," said the maître d', lifting the silver covers from the chafing dishes. "Would madam care to choose a side vegetable from the trolley? The roasted potatoes, perhaps?"

After Ms. Jones had made her selection, he carved a slice of the Beef Wellington with great aplomb. "And which vegetable would the gentleman prefer?" he asked.

Massimo indicated that he would also like the roast potato, but the maître d' gave a brief waggle of his fingers and pointed discreetly at the glazed carrots with his serving fork.

"The roasted carrots, then," Massimo replied.

"Excellent choice, sir, and perhaps a few green beans as well," said the maître d'.

Last of all, the wine from the decanter was poured, much to Massimo's relief, and 'Jeeves' withdrew.

"Wouldn't you love to have him as a butler?" she said, as they clinked glasses.

"I'm not sure he would have me," he answered, tucking into the superbly pink piece of beef adorning his plate. He hadn't realized how hungry he was at this late hour, having only picked at the small offerings with the champagne earlier. His beef was crusted in a golden brioche pastry, beneath which was a steaming layer of duxelles mushrooms and a coating of foie gras. What a heavenly aroma.

They both attacked their food with gusto. Ms. Jones's fillet was seared with a peppercorn crust, but the inside was not pink, but blood red.

"Oh, this beef is so juicy," she said in a swoon, but she said it with her mouth full, and a trickle of the blood red juice escaped the corner of her mouth and dribbled to her chin. In the brief instant before she wiped it away, an image of red lips, white teeth and the trickle of blood registered itself on Massimo's brain, but it was too fleeting for him to grasp on to, and it vanished as he shook his head in disbelief.

"What are your thoughts on this wine, then?" she asked, unaware of what had just flashed before Massimo's eyes.

He regained his composure and cleared his throat as if to launch into one of his discourses on wine.

"The English language has the usual words to describe the tastes of berries and fruits in a wine, but it sadly lacks expressions like we have in Italian, and the French also have, for describing the character, the personality of a wine as magnificent as this…"

But she cut him off, raising her glass to eye level, and gazed through the viscous red swirls clinging to the sides of the glass.

"This wine is red lingerie beneath a black velvet dress," she said duskily.

Mouth agape, he quietly put his glass down, and then, pressing his fingers together, said, "I guess that proves me wrong about the language aspect. What I was going to say doesn't really amount to much now."

Massimo was unable to make much conversation after that. The remainder of the meal was still very agreeable: the wine was superb, but her description of the wine haunted his every sip.

"I think the movie fell short of the mark in one aspect, though," she said returning to the conversation about *Sunday, Bloody Sunday*[23].

"What was that?" he answered, wondering whether he was being asked as a movie critic or a social critic.

"It was the male character in the movie who was allowed to break out of the accepted social norms and explore his bisexuality," she said. "Imagine how the story would have unfolded if it had been the Glenda Jackson character who was bisexual and divided her time between a male and a female lover."

"Would it have been that different?" he pondered.

"Absolutely! The whole social tone of the movie would have been completely different if it had been a woman who was empowered and the male was subjugated to her whims," she said forcefully. "But a movie like that would never have made it into the mainstream media."

"Why not?" he asked. "It sounds like a good story."

"If it really was the woman who was willful, and it wasn't portrayed as some sexual ménage à trois for the titillation of the male audience, then it would have been far too threatening for the male world," she said, waving a fork around. "The male dominated film distribution industry would never have allowed such a radical film to be released, especially in the seventies."

The subject obviously meant more to her than she wanted to reveal, so she calmed down by asking him a few polite questions about his trip to Oxford.

The waiter came in and cleared the plates away at the end of their meal, leaving them with just the two wine glasses and what was left in the decanter. He stared at the last remaining sip in his glass, not wanting to finish it, for then it would all be gone.

"When I was in Oxford," he finally spoke up, "I wanted to get my old friend a gift, and I happened to come across a liquor store that sold single malts, so I bought him a bottle of Laphroaig."

"You remembered our little lesson on whisky, how sweet," she remarked. "What do you think, are you interested in dessert after all that?"

"I'm not sure," he answered. "How about you?"

"They're serving trifle tonight. It's made with cake soaked in Sherry. Not really my thing. Now, if it had been soaked in whisky, laddie, that would be different! That's the one shortcoming of this place, they don't have a decent single malt to speak of. 'Jeeves' will tell you all about the Sherries and Ports in their cellar, but no whiskies," she lamented?

"The sad thing was that when I gave the present to my friend, he handed it right back to me," he said.

"Why'd he do that?" She asked.

"Said his constitution couldn't handle strong alcohol anymore. It made me feel really bad about not being more considerate in selecting a gift," he said.

"What did you do with the bottle of Laphroaig?" she asked.

"I brought it back to London with me," he said.

"So, all this time you've been teasing me not telling me you've got a bottle of Laphroaig in your room. Come on then, laddie, let's go. We'll skip these trifles and get ourselves a proper drink," she said, gathering her things and standing to go.

Massimo didn't know what to make of the situation. He had not intended to invite her back to his room, but she was now insisting, and he felt in her debt after the night at the opera, and for the dinner and the wine as well.

"What a perfect evening this is turning out to be," she said as they rode up in the elevator to his room.

When they entered his room he handed her the box with the bottle of Laphroaig and she said, "Why don't you hang up your coat and tie, make yourself comfortable, and I'll pour us a couple of drinks."

He did as she suggested, and when he turned back toward her she had kicked off her heels and stood with toes curling in the carpet. In each hand was a tumbler of whisky.

"You're much shorter without your heels, more like my height," for he could now look directly at eye level into her face. "But tell me, what are you really doing here? I'm very flattered by your attention, and all that, but someone as attractive as you could get whatever you want in life, I am sure."

"I have a confession to make," she said, looking away from his gaze for a moment. "The bottom has pretty much fallen out of the recruiting market for me, ever since the stock market crash of '08."

She took a swig from her glass before continuing. "Wall Street lost faith in the math and physics geniuses who developed all those financial models that failed so miserably to predict the crash, so that now they don't want to hire them anymore."

Massimo sat down on the edge of the bed to listen to what she had to say.

"That means there's no market for all the quants I used to recruit from all the university math and physics departments, and bang go all my commissions."

"Times are tough, I understand completely," he said. "You would like me to pay for my opera ticket."

"No, no," she laughed. "That's not it at all. The tickets and dinner were all paid for. No, it's just that I didn't want you to think too badly of me afterwards, that's all."

"I don't think badly of you at all," he protested.

"Then why aren't you drinking with me?" she said, holding her half empty glass out toward him.

"I was waiting for you to add a splash of water, as you so carefully instructed me last time," he answered with a little smile.

"There are times," she said with a wicked gleam in her eye, "when you want to drink it neat, and enjoy the full force of the alcohol." She clinked his glass and bade him drink. "If we had been in New York I would have taken you to the Met. You would have enjoyed that, too, but we would have probably eaten a hotdog from a street vendor afterwards. I'm a different person in New York."

"I'm sure I would enjoy it," he said, clinking her glass this time.

"But a girl's got to live," she said with a sigh, "and I've found new and creative ways to earn my commissions."

"The whisky tastes different doesn't it, when you drink it straight, a little more bitter," he said slightly drunkenly. Her last remark didn't even seem to enter his consciousness.

"Here, let me show you something," she whispered, leaning in very close to him. She took her two fingers and swirled them around in his drink, and then swung one leg over him so that she now sat straddling him on the edge of the bed. This time she rubbed her two fingers over his upper lip and slid them into his mouth so that he should suck off the remaining drops of whisky.

"Now drink down your glass in one gulp," she whispered.

He did not protest, and stared back up into her eyes when he had drained the glass. "That's a good boy," she murmured, and pushed him gently back down onto the bed. The empty glass fell from his hand to the carpeted floor. He felt her body cover him. His face now buried in the folds of that dress that had intrigued him all evening. All those pleats and folds that now split open before his eyes and spilled warm, fragrant flesh across his cheeks. Red lingerie beneath black velvet, the beautiful music of Mozart's trio filling his years with promises of love, the laughter of old Alfonso singing 'they're all like that' - cosi fan tutte. The lights of the room began to spin through the veil of black silk of Ms. Jones's dress covering his eyes, until all went dark.

He awoke to the jarring ring of the bedside phone, the glaring light from a half open curtain falling across his face.

"Good morning, sir," came the voice from the hotel reception. "We are just confirming if you are still checking out this morning."

"What time is it?" croaked Massimo.

"It's 11:00 a.m., sir. We can extend your checkout time until noon, but after that we need to make special arrangements."

"No, noon is fine, I'll be down shortly," and hung up.

He must have drunk too much the previous night. All that whisky, he wasn't used to it. His first thought was to call Ms. Jones immediately and apologize, for he must have passed out in her arms. How embarrassing. He reached over for the phone and dialed reception.

"Could you put me through to Ms. Jones's room please, she is also staying here."

There was a brief pause. "Ms. Jones checked out late last night, sir."

He put the phone down. With his other hand he reached down. His trousers were still buttoned.

He groaned at the lingering pain at the back of his head. There was nothing he could do now to make amends, and he had a plane to catch in a few hours. He struggled to his feet to make his way over to his computer to confirm his flight and check his e-mail. Apparently he couldn't even remember where he had left his laptop the night before, because it wasn't on the table. He stumbled over towards his briefcase, but it wasn't in there either.

"Christ, why did I pack it away in my valise already," he muttered, banging the wardrobe open and pulling out the bag. But there was no sign of his computer.

He searched around the room in exasperation and then noticed that the charger for his laptop lay unplugged on the table. Two empty glasses and an empty whisky bottle stood where his laptop had been.

Someone must have taken it, but who? Laptops weren't that valuable nowadays. Had Ms. Jones left his room unlocked when she walked out in disgust, and had someone come in during the night?

He had no time to dwell on it now, and quickly showered to change into his travel clothes before a hurried departure for the airport.

At least he had his wallet and passport, which he now clutched as he waited at the check-in counter. There had been no time for breakfast or a coffee. Just a mad rush to catch the hotel shuttle to the airport, and his head hurt all the way.

"I'm not going to drink all that free booze this time," he thought to himself. "Just some coffee and a little something to eat and I'll probably stretch out and sleep most of the way back."

When the agent handed him his boarding pass Massimo looked at it and exclaimed, "But this is a seat in the economy section!"

"Yes, sir, you have an economy ticket," the agent replied.

"But what about my frequent flyer status?" Massimo almost howled.

The agent took back the boarding pass and pointed to the bottom line printed on it. "You have our bronze frequent flyer status, but with just three more transatlantic trips you will qualify for our silver, economy executive status," he smiled, handing back the boarding pass and nodding to the next customer in line.

Massimo thought of sardines in a tin can as he sat bolt upright, squished in the center of the row at the back of the plane. At least they got to lie flat in their can.

## Chapter 14 – Double Take

The exit doors spat Massimo out into the arrivals hall at San Francisco International terminal, as though they were just as glad to be rid of him as he was of them. Expectant eyes gazed upon him to see if he was a long-awaited passenger for whom they were holding up name placards. Families were being reunited in front of him. He skirted past and wondered what it might be like if, one day, a little girl were waiting for him, clutching balloons saying "Welcome Home Daddy."

"Hey, Mass, over here!" came a shout.

"Lars, Sven, what are you guys doing here?"

"Nobody had heard from you in a while, so we were worried if you were okay," they answered.

"Sorry about that, but I was unable to send e-mail in the last day or two," he said sheepishly. "How did you know I'd be on this flight, then?"

"Laura sent us the details," yelled Lars, for he had taken Massimo's wheeled bag from him and was already striding ahead. Sven had grabbed the suit bag and was twirling it over his shoulder, leaving Massimo with just his empty laptop bag to carry.

"We also wanted to talk to you privately, away from snooping ears and watchful eyes, before you came into the office," Lars said.

"We're a little paranoid at the moment after all the things we've been uncovering on the company network," Sven added.

"Yes, your messages were very disconcerting, but I'm still in two minds as to whether this is just the hard reality of working in a competitive business environment," he said.

Lars and Sven looked at each other. "You need to see it firsthand," they said. "But we need to agree beforehand what we talk about in the office, and how we dig into these things without looking like we're snooping."

The fluorescent light overhead was buzzing loudly, flickering on and off as they walked through the parking garage in search of Lars's car. It was unnerving to watch his friends advance through the stroboscopic flashes of light and see them appear to move jerkily forward. His eyes and brain registered their presence during the brief flashes of light, but all their motion as they maneuvered between the cars occurred during the intervals of darkness when he saw nothing.

"And Georges is always hanging around, prying into what we're doing. You can't leave anything lying around and not expect him to start reading it," they complained.

"Well, he is our boss," said Massimo, not really wanting to excuse Georges' behavior. "But we can always swamp him with useless information and then he won't have time to figure out what we really do."

"Yeah, just be careful what you say in front of him," said Lars, opening the rear hatch of a faded red Subaru. He shoved aside some sports gear to make room for Massimo's bag. "We did some shopping for you," he said, pointing at a supermarket bag stuffed in behind the sports gear.

"Hey, I really appreciate you guys picking me up like this. It's no fun having to take the shuttle home after a long flight. And very thoughtful of you to do some grocery shopping for me so I don't have to go out again," he said.

"We thought you'd be expecting limousine service after enjoying First Class on the flight," joked Sven, as he clambered into the back seat, allowing Massimo to sit up front.

"I'm afraid that didn't work out for my return flight and I was back in cattle class again," he said. "Do you suppose someone in the company was really able to reach into the airlines computer system and tweak my frequent flyer status, and then, apparently tweak it back again?"

"That's nothing compared to some of the stuff we've seen," said Lars, swinging the Subaru out of the parking garage.

"It's just hard for me to imagine that it's possible, but you guys are the experts," shouted Massimo above the noise of a leaky exhaust silencer, as Lars accelerated up the freeway on-ramp.

"101 South, San Jose" the sign stated, which, to Massimo's relief, meant they were heading directly to his home, and not going via the office, which would have required cutting across to the 280 Freeway.

Sven had his long legs sprawled diagonally across the small back seat. "It's not like I was intentionally prying," he shouted back, "but I just ran my usual suite of diagnostic programs on their system, and they came back with such fantastic numbers for speed and bandwidth that I began to poke around a bit more."

Lars's moved into the carpool lane so that they could zip by all the single-occupancy cars choking up the slower lanes in the late afternoon rush hour. "By the way, I'm supposed to say 'hi' from Laura. She said to call her once you're back on California time. She's staying a few days longer on the East Coast. I think they must be going to hire her, by the sounds of it."

Massimo just nodded silently.

"Dude, you need to fix that muffler," said Sven after a few minutes. "The smell of exhaust back here is even worse than your sweaty sports socks."

Neither Lars nor Massimo responded, so he cracked the rear window open, but was immediately yelled at for making the noise worse.

"I don't think the company people realize that we are equipped to probe their network capability to such an extent," shouted Sven, ignoring Lars's verbal abuse. "Once I began to see what I could do, I throttled back on my probing, so it wouldn't draw their attention."

"We need a fast and powerful network to efficiently run our programs, though," countered Massimo.

"Yes, but wait until you see what their search features are capable of turning up. You could embarrass your grandmother by what they can dig up on her," chipped in Lars.

The car pulled up in front of Massimo's apartment and they helped him up the steps with his bags and the shopping.

"Get a good night's rest and we'll see you at the office tomorrow," they bid him.

He opened windows and blinds and carefully hung up the suit bag in his closet. He still didn't like to think too much about how much he had spent, but he was also quite proud of his purchase, and he straightened the pants on the hanger before zipping up the black and gold bag again.

In the kitchen he saw that Lars and Sven's idea of food supplies was a couple of frozen pizzas, a six pack of 'Whisky Hill' beer and a packet of chips. The beer tasted pretty good, though, as he dropped his remaining clothes into a laundry hamper and headed for the bathroom for a long, hot shower.

He spent a restless night tossing and turning in bed, churning over thoughts of what a chump he had been and whether this fitted in with the unexpected goings on at his new company office. By 4:00 a.m. he was fully awake, so he powered up his old desktop computer to check his e-mail. Back in familiar surroundings, his thoughts turned to Laura, and how nice it would have been if she had been waiting at home for him. Would he have behaved in the same way in London if he knew she was waiting at home?

He sent off a long e-mail to her explaining that he had lost his laptop, but apart from that he'd had a wonderful time seeing Hugh in Oxford, and even got a chance to catch an opera performance in London.

Laura's reply came back very quickly, for her day was just getting started on the East Coast. She was glad that he was back safe and sound, and that Lars and Sven had picked him up. There were further hints that she was accepting one of the job offers since she mentioned driving around and being shown potential places to live. They had been wining and dining her, for she also commented how he would like the restaurants and food there. She closed saying how she looked forward to seeing him in a few days' time.

The rest of his emails from SLAC, with various meeting announcements, could be dismissed since he was now taking an official leave of absence from the lab to concentrate on the new venture.

Surprisingly, there wasn't anything in his new company mailbox. He thought they would be all over him with directives about what was expected of him, but for now they seemed to be letting him just get on with it.

Pangs of hunger were beginning to awaken in him. It was early, but his stomach was still on London time. A slice of cold pizza from last night did little to help, and he opted for a more satisfying breakfast at the coffee shop. There was even time to bicycle there, and then on to the office. It might be good to bring a little exercise into his new daily regimen.

There wasn't any laptop to carry now, so he could fit a change of clothes in his backpack. He cycled through the early morning traffic and came to the French café, or at least to where it had formerly been, for it had now closed. Damn, he was looking forward to their croissants. Mike and Georges had apparently been true to their word and withdrawn their financial backing. He wondered what had happened to the two brothers who had found a winning combination in pastry baking and the art of brewing great coffee. Maybe they would find some benevolent investors to back them and allow them another chance.

He cycled back toward his regular coffee shop and stood with the throng of early morning commuters getting their morning fix.

"Hi Ma-th-imo" the cashier cheerily greeted him.

He thought she'd come up with a new way of making fun of him, but then he noticed she had developed a strong lisp.

"Would you like your usual cappu-th-ino?" she asked.

"Yes, and a breakfast bagel please," he replied.

We haven't seen you in a while. I thought you might have de-th-erted us," she said.

I've been traveling," he said. "How about you? You seem a little … different?"

She opened her mouth wide, to reveal a large silver stud in the middle of her tongue.

"I'll bet that must've hurt," winced Massimo, as he moved over to Carlos's counter to await his order.

"Hey, Massimo," said an overwhelmed Carlos, "you want to come and work here for a few hours each morning to help us out?"

"I don't know about that," he grinned.

"I teach you how to make a latte-for-the-ladies, Carlos-style," he said, wiggling his hips. "You earn really good tips, and I get propositioned all the time, man," he winked.

"If my new business venture doesn't work out, I might take you up on that," said Massimo with a little wave, as he took his cappuccino over to a small corner table. He thumbed through a copy of the Palo Alto weekly lying on the table. A headline called out at him: "Another Doomed Coffee Shop Closure." It described how the French café had only been open a short time, but had become wildly popular with locals. The writer bemoaned the modern tendency to condemn any venture as financially unsound if the patrons actually sat around and took their time to enjoy the fare on offer.

The cashier brought him his breakfast bagel. "My boyfriend really likes it," she said, taking a little extra time to arrange the knife, fork and napkin in front of him.

"Don't get tongue tied with his piercings," he laughed.

She gave him a little nudge before leaving him in peace to eat his breakfast.

The bicycle ride up Sand Hill Road got his heart rate up and he felt good entering the new office. He was the first to arrive so he took his time looking around at the office layout Lars and Sven had created in his absence. The main area was equipped with terminals and networking gear, forming a pit with a conference table at its center, now strewn with coffee cups and empty food cartons. Large screen displays were hung around the walls so they could monitor their programs. The screens were dim now, but the winking lights on the servers and network switches told him there was a lot of number crunching going on in the background. A private office had been kept aside for Massimo, as a place he could retreat to if he ever wanted to do some thinking on his own. He entered and dropped his backpack on the couch. In the middle of the room was a writing board on moveable wheels. Not a white board, but a glass board that you could see through. That will take some getting used to, he thought, picking up the tray with assorted crayon markers. Someone had written $\$=mc^2$ in the top corner as a joke.

He changed his shirt then settled down behind his new desk to try out this amazing new computer system that Lars and Sven had been raving about.

A loud gurgling noise from the other room startled him and he jumped up to see what was going on. A coffee machine had switched on in the kitchenette and was burbling forth brown liquid into a pot. Moments later, Lars and Sven burst through the door.

"Hey, Mass, good to see you up so early," they said, noisily bashing into chairs and the table as they crashed into the room like a couple of kids. Lars brushed off all the trash from the table into a bin with one sweep of his arm. Sven headed straight over to the coffee maker.

"How do you like our machine? It has the fastest network connection in the world for a coffee maker. I wrote a phone app so I can switch it on remotely when I'm on my way to work," he said, waving his phone in the air so that Massimo could see the coffee cup icon on its screen.

"I suppose you wrote it in Java," he said.

They soon had all the monitors powered up so that they could observe the progress of the previous night's downloads and analyses. Massimo was visibly impressed by the speed with which the system flashed the data upon the screen. They had been at it for about an hour when Georges strolled into the office. He didn't say much and just helped himself to coffee and sat down to busy himself with his laptop, sniffing annoyingly as he clicked through web pages. Lars and Sven just shrugged in Massimo's direction and ignored him, continuing with their demonstration of what could be done on the new system.

Massimo was more surprised when Mike and Kate walked in. They all got to their feet, still feeling indebted to the pair for giving them this opportunity.

"Don't want to disturb you," said Mike pleasantly. "Just came by to make sure you had all the facilities you need to get started."

"Well, as you can see we have the system up and running and we're right now seeing what we can learn from the real-time data that's streaming in," said Massimo, proudly pointing to Lars and Sven's handiwork.

Georges, who had been trying to ingratiate himself as soon as Mike and Kate had entered, attempted to cut in.

"Yes, I told them to stop all the theoretical simulations and get on with analyzing some real data!"

Apart from a filthy look from Lars, no one paid him heed.

Mike, on the other hand, looked impressed with the progress and ventured to put his hand out to click on a few of the displays, zooming in on some of the details. "Kate told me how impressed she was with your demonstration at SLAC. I can see she was right to recommend that we support this venture."

When the hubbub of congratulations died down, Kate spoke a little more seriously, "We're not here to play video games, though," she said, raising an eyebrow at Mike, who was now getting more adventurous at the controls, scanning the timelines back and forth.

"We have a business plan to execute," she said, plopping down some folders on the desk with a thud to indicate she meant business. "Our commitment, you may recall, is to come up with a robust pricing model for our future IPOs."

"Yes, all these fancy graphics are meaningless if we don't produce hard numbers," said the toady Georges, interjecting once more.

Massimo sat back down at the table and eased open one of the folders, but couldn't make much sense of the corporate gibberish written there.

"Setting the Initial Public Offering price just right is very important in determining our profit margins," she continued. "Set it too low and it may take off in subsequent public trading. All the profit goes to the speculators," she glared. "Set it too high and it may plummet in public trading, and our initial investors get burnt and everyone with stock options hates us. People lose confidence and the price falls even lower than the fair price. I don't have to remind you of the recent fiasco with the IPO of a certain prominent social networking company," she said, jabbing the table with her finger.

Georges was looking pained.

"It's critical that we restore public confidence in our next few IPOs," she said, belaboring the point. "So come up with a pricing model and you will have earned your keep," she smiled. "Then we can get on with some of the more fanciful propositions in your analysis."

There were general murmurs of agreement, and Georges felt it was once more necessary to make some fawning remarks how he would see to it that 'his team' kept on course with the corporate mission.

"I also have some incorporation documents here," she said, placing another folder on the table. "These specify the subsidiary functions and terms of incorporation with the parent company, limitation of liability and so on."

Massimo flipped open the folder and found the language of the documents even more incomprehensible than the first set of folders.

"And before you ask," she said looking at Lars, "you will find therein details of a corporate vehicle use plan for Massimo, together with a stock option package for the office assistants, in the event that this little startup ever goes public."

She flipped the binder shut so that she could get Massimo's full attention again. "Remember, we haven't just hired a bunch of quants to crank the handle on some tired old formulae for pricing options. We bought an innovative analytical system, and we expect results."

Mike, who had let his attention drift back to the console screens, now stood and readied himself to go. Reaching out a hand to Massimo, he said, "I have a good feeling about this. Great things are going to happen." He gave a brief nod to Lars and Sven and headed for the door with Kate. Georges followed, bowing and chanting words in obeisance.

"What a sycophant," muttered Sven as he turned his attention back to the program screens.

Georges didn't even bother coming back in, but stayed outside to smoke.

"Time enough to read all about our stock options later, if they ever do take us public," said Lars, idly flipping through a few of the documents left behind by Kate. "Not much use to us before then, are they. There is a piece of paper here for you, though, Mass. It says, if you hand this in at reception down in the foyer, they will give you the keys to one of the fleet cars in the parking garage."

"Wow, I can hardly wait," said Massimo sarcastically. "Do you think I'll get a Buick or a Hyundai?" Although at the back of his mind he wondered why he didn't give as much due diligence to such things as work contracts as he did to mathematical rigor in his analyses.

Sven rolled his chair toward them and said, "Hey, while Georges is out of the room we should show Massimo some of the 'extended' search features of the system here."

He spun back around to the keyboard and began typing:

```
grep -l -r "massimo|chaos|modeling" *
```

After the briefest of pauses the monitor spilled forth a long list of emails, files and documents.

"Hey! How did you get into my emails without entering a password?" protested Massimo.

"Our point exactly," said Sven. "And it's not just limited to Stanford accounts, either."

Sven hit the erase key in response to the sound of the door opening and Georges returning.

"I'm going back to my other office," said Georges in his superior tone, "where I can get some more serious work done. I need to write a mission statement." He looked very red-eyed and Massimo wondered if he suffered some kind of allergy.

"Do you think they're ever going to show us around the rest of the WVC corporate headquarters?" asked Lars after Georges had left. "I notice that people need pass keys to get in all the corridors beyond the reception desk."

"We have a pass key to get in here," said Massimo holding up his new ID badge.

"Yeah, but they only open this door, and no other entryway," said Sven. "I already tried."

"Well, there's a lot to think about," said Massimo. "I'm going to take this business plan document of Kate's into my office and see if I can make any sense out of it."

In reality, the first thing he did when he shut his door was repeat the search function Sven had just performed. It came up blank this time, so it seemed to be a capability of the superfast network node in the other room.

He turned his attention back to the business plan documentation Kate had left, and began scratching out a few of the IPO pricing algorithms on a pad next to him. After a couple of hours of this he stuck his head back into the pit room, for he thought he could hear new voices.

The mass of blond hair, even though tightly entwined in two Wagnerian braids, was unmistakable.

"Hildr! What are you doing here?" he exclaimed.

She looked decidedly more conservative compared to the last time he had seen her in that mini-skirted sweater outfit. She was attired in simple jeans and a gray sweatshirt with a large maroon colored Stanford "S."

"We made a bet with her," said Lars, "that we could present mathematical elegance in this 'applied math' example that even she could appreciate. It's been an ongoing debate in our statistics class as to what constitutes pure mathematical form."

"So here I am," said Hildr, "with an open mind, to see what you guys have been working on."

"No musical instrument today, I see," said Massimo, the memory of his last encounter still stinging.

She didn't take his bait. "I'm not just looking for pretty graphical displays, but for elegance in the application of mathematical solutions."

Lars and Sven seemed to be diving into the programming code with her, so he left them to it and retreated to his office. A short time later there was a tap at the door and Hildr stuck her head around.

"I have a favor to ask regarding my dissertation," she said plainly. "I know I can't expect much after the way I behaved last time, but I'm hoping your interest in the subject matter will allow you to overlook my indiscretion." He nodded that she should come in and make her case.

212

"This is a copy of my dissertation proposal. It outlines how I would approach the age-old problem of general solutions to the Navier-Stokes equation. I try and show why existing mathematical notation is inadequate and where I think I can make a new and original contribution." She lay a folder down on the table in front of him. Massimo eyed it, but made no attempt to reach out for it:

"I can make no promises, but I will try and look at it when I have time."

"That's all I ask," she said, standing to leave, not wishing to disturb him anymore.

He stared at the folder for a good five minutes after she left before yielding to his curiosity. What he saw when he finally did open it were pages of tiny, neat handwriting. He could make out recognizable features and equations on the first page, but subsequent pages diverged into what looked like group theory and then evolved into something more like the gauge theories his experimentalist colleagues at SLAC dabbled in. This was going to take more than just a casual reading to make any sense of. There were also small, cryptic notes scribbled in the margins that, for the life of him, looked like it had to be musical notation.

He wasn't able to face the complexity of it this evening, so he pushed it to one side and reached instead for Kate's business plan to take home and read. It was already twilight and he didn't have lights on his bicycle so he hurried out the door, yelling a quick good night to Lars and Sven.

A true racing bike isn't allowed to have lights or other superfluous accessories attached to it, but he was willing to concede that these new helmet mounted lights might be a good idea. He sped down the hill and nearly rear-ended a car that cut in front of him to make a right hand turn at the bottom of Sand Hill Road. Most definitely, he should get one of those bright LED cycle lamps, he thought.

The bicycle ride home ended in a tree-lined street, where he found himself cycling in and out of the darkening shadows into orange pools made by the street lights. A childish impulse steered him into a neatly raked pile of leaves that scattered in his wake. His first bicycle as a child had been equipped with a dynamo, driven by the front tire, whining and growing brighter whenever he sped up. The memory of cycling in the lanes behind his house in the evenings came back to him. As a 12 year old he would cockily ride hands-free and puff on a cigarette stolen from his uncle, his mother calling out to come in and eat dinner.

Tonight it would just be a simple pasta on his own, and he tried not to spill tomato sauce on Kate's documents opened up next to him at the table. Jet lag overtook him at an early hour, and he found himself dozing off on the couch with Kate's folder, still unread, lying open on his chest.

Waking up early wasn't a bad thing, though, and he enjoyed getting into the office again before the others. Coffee in hand, he resolutely opened Kate's folder again, determined to make sense of it. He persevered for about 10 minutes before he reached for Hildr's notes instead, so that he could deal with its far more interesting mathematical challenge.

He could hear Lars and Sven banging around outside complaining about something. He preferred to let them deal with it on their own and he kept reading. There was a knock at his door, but it was Mike who entered.

"Glad I caught you before Georges came in. I need you to help me with a presentation we are giving tomorrow for some potential investors. They need a technical introduction to the work you are doing, and you will clearly come across as more of an expert than Georges ever could." Mike drifted over to the window and gazed out at the young Redwood trees planted there.

"Yes, I suppose I could do that," Massimo answered. "But I would need some guidelines as to how many slides to prepare and what level of detail I should get into."

Don't worry about that," Mike said, turning back towards him. "My office is preparing all the slides with the level of detail that we want to show. These types of presentations are very carefully vetted by management. We just need to make sure the person making the presentation sounds very knowledgeable and is able to answer questions competently."

Massimo hadn't been in that situation before, but he guardedly agreed to what was being asked of him.

"Don't worry, you will get a copy of the presentation slides this afternoon to review in plenty of time. Also, you need to wear a suit. The investors are coming from a consortium of banks in France, Germany and Switzerland, so we need to follow their dress code. No sloppy college clothes."

As he returned from seeing Mike out the door, Lars and Sven seemed to be squabbling about something.

"Your physicist computer programming skills leave much to be desired," grumbled Sven.

"It seems parts of your program are hogging all the computer resources and slowing everything way down," said Lars.

"I tried debugging some of your programming code, but I can tell you never had any formal training as a software engineer. Have you never heard of writing comments in your code?" he said, pushing aside some of the accumulated trash of wrappers and coffee cups, as though that would magically fix things.

They argued back and forth for a while, Massimo maintaining that his programs had worked fine up until then, so why would they suddenly go haywire. Sven ran all his system diagnostic tools again to prove to Massimo that there was a problem.

"I can't believe it!" He suddenly shouted. "There's a second version of the program running, and it evidently has a higher priority in the system than ours."

They all peered intently at the monitor screens while Sven listed all the processes that were running, There was clearly a phantom program that they had not launched themselves.

"I may not be able to stop this program, or change its priority in the system," said Sven, "but I can get it to display its output here on our screens for us to see."

They stared back in amazement, for what they saw was an exact duplicate of the original program, busy analyzing reams of company data. But there was a twist: whereas all the company information was the same, the financial transaction data was totally different.

Everyone agreed quickly enough that none of them had copied and launched a second version of the program, so that left the vexing question of who was doing it and why.

"What puzzles me," said Massimo, "is how someone managed to make an unlocked copy of the program. I'm in the habit of keeping track of all the versions of my program by using an encryption key. That way I don't accidentally run old versions of my programs with new data, which is important in the research world."

Lars and Sven just nodded, for they knew exactly what he was talking about.

"The point is," he continued, "that without my encryption key you can't duplicate the program or modify an old copy."

"So, where do you keep the encryption key?" Sven asked.

"It's on my laptop, burned into the flash memory, so it's even off the network," he said, mashing his knuckles against his lower teeth, a habit he had picked up to stop biting his nails.

"And where is your laptop?" asked Lars pointedly.

"God damn it!" yelled Massimo, first kicking the table leg, and then walking to the other side of the room to hide his embarrassment.

Lars and Sven said nothing.

"Okay, it was stolen! Alright?" he said uncomfortably. "This happened just a couple of days ago in London."

They didn't say a word, figuring that this was somehow a touchy subject for Massimo.

"Ms. Jones knew exactly what she wanted to get from me." As an afterthought he added, "and apparently she figured out exactly how she could lure me into letting her into my room late at night."

Lars and Sven were failing to suppress their laughter now.

Massimo felt compelled to relate a little of how he had met Ms. Jones and her posing as a recruiter.

"Well, it's obvious, she's a squid," Lars rejoindered. Sven nodded in agreement with this assessment.

This wasn't helping Massimo's mood. "What's a squid?"

"She's bound to be working for the vampire squid crowd. They'll do anyone's dirty work, jamming their blood funnel into anything that smells like money." It was evident that Massimo had no clue what they were talking about, so Lars added, "It's how we refer to the Silverman Sax investment bankers on Wall Street. Their actions are always suspect."[24]

"Oh, very poetic." Massimo's mood was even darker now. "The point is, why would WVC go to all this trouble? They own us, after all, so why be subversive about copying the program? I mean, it has to be WVC, doesn't it, because the phantom copy is running here on their system?" He paced up and down, not expecting any answer to his question.

A loud bang at the front door startled them and Sven immediately blanked the monitor screens to hide the evidence of what they had just uncovered.

"Oh, it's you Hildr," said Sven, restoring the displays to the monitor screens again. "Come to admire the mathematical elegance of our work again?"

"Sorry, I didn't mean to disturb you guys," she said. "I just wanted to ask Massimo if he'd had a chance to look at the work I left him."

"You're not disturbing," Massimo answered, pushing around some papers on the table to settle himself. "We've just uncovered a bit of intrigue here, and were trying to figure out what's going on."

They reviewed the situation, explaining it to Hildr as much for their own benefit as hers. There is something about confronting a new and startling situation that makes you want to share it with whoever is around. She got swept up in their concern and listened attentively. Massimo decided he could handle her presence far more easily when she was dressed just in her student sweats.

"So there you have it," summarized Lars. "Here is all this company transaction data streaming past us, but it bears no resemblance to the data we've been analyzing. It's like this phantom program lives in a parallel universe."

Hildr looked studiously at the screen and helped herself to the keyboard where she began typing in some of her own programming expressions.

"Is it okay if I run some of my statistical tests on this data?" she asked, her fingers already tapping across the keys.

"Sure, go for it, we're at a loss what else to do," said Massimo.

Lars and Sven began arguing about some detail of system priorities, and why the phantom could not be overridden. Massimo just watched Hildr's look of intense concentration, and her blonde plaits bob around as she typed.

Finally, she sat back and said, "You know what I think? I believe that what we are looking at here is fake data."

"How do you mean?" They all said, crowding around her.

"If it were real data," she said, "It would exhibit a certain randomness, akin to the real world. But this data looks synthesized, or contrived. If you throw a dice you know statistically that a double six is only going to come up a certain number of times. In this data, the equivalent of a double six is coming up way too often, according to my statistical tests."

"That's great," they all chimed in, admiring her initiative in questioning the validity of the data. But Hildr began to look bored as they started arguing why WVC would want to use fake data when they had unique access to so much real data. Massimo could see that the discussion wasn't going anywhere and suggested they needed to figure out WVC's motives behind all of this first.

"Tell me this," he said to Sven, "do you think that WVC is aware that we know about the phantom version of the code?"

"No, they went to some pains to conceal it from the normal system view. That's why, at first, I was convinced that it was your programming at fault. It was only when I ran my stealth system tools that the phantom became visible," replied Sven.

"Good, then let's keep it that way," he answered. "The only advantage we have in this game they are playing is our inside knowledge of their actions. Let's watch and wait for a while."

Lars and Sven grumbled, but agreed there was not much more to be done for now, and went to get coffee. Massimo suggested to Hildr that he could show her the notes he had made on her proposal. He hadn't got very far with the notes, but he wanted to do something in appreciation for her insight into the validity of the fake data being spewed out by the phantom program.

To make up for the brevity of his notes, he began writing on his new glass board, starting with the well-known Navier-Stokes equation, and then borrowing from her group theory notation to describe the sets of solutions to the equations. He rehashed some of the standard textbook stuff on why the existence of solutions could not always be guaranteed for the Navier-Stokes equation. It served to get Hildr involved in a lively defense of her proposal and she soon took up a crayon and started writing on the other half of the board.

"That's why we need to make use of a gauge theory," she said emphatically. "It's the only way to compare, or gauge, dissimilar objects, like apples and oranges, if you will, within one equation."

Massimo wracked his brain for what he knew about gauge theories from his experimentalist colleagues. It was, after all, a fundamental key aspect of the Standard Model that predicted the now famous Higgs Boson.

"Think of it as the mathematical equivalent to a key change in music," she said, writing now in her new notation that she alluded to in her proposal.

It was at this point that Massimo suddenly realized that, although he could read everything perfectly fine that she wrote, Hildr was in fact standing on the opposite side of the transparent glass board.

He walked around to the back side of the board where she stood. From her side the writing appeared back to front.

"Hildr, you're accomplished in writing mirror script," he said in amazement.

"Oh, that's nothing special," she replied, tucking a rogue strand of blonde hair back behind her ear. "I taught myself that in school, just to annoy my teachers."

But Massimo was impressed. He recalled his own school days when he first read in textbooks of Leonardo's great inventions that he described in his journals in a mirror script to keep them secret from prying eyes.

Voices could be heard in the other room and Massimo excused himself to see what was going on, saying he would be right back.

Mike had returned to give him a copy of his presentation slides for tomorrow on a memory stick. It was a read-only version that could not be copied. Mike explained that, with confidential presentations like these, they didn't e-mail them around, for security reasons. Massimo thought that was a little ironic, considering what he knew about WVC's computer systems.

"So how are things going otherwise?" Mike casually asked when they had finished discussing the presentation.

"We're having a few little technical difficulties just at the moment," he answered, equally casually. "The guys think my programming skills leave a bit to be desired so they're rewriting part of my code so that it will run more efficiently."

Lars and Sven made a few hand signals to Mike, indicating they thought his programming left a lot to be desired.

"Don't be too hard on him; we were expecting you to have some teething problems at the beginning," laughed Mike. "By the way, how was your London trip, did you have any time for some fun stuff?"

"The trip was for the large part successful, and I did get a chance to go to the opera, which was a special treat for me," he answered, forcing himself to maintain a friendly tone.

"So you're a music lover, are you?" said Mike. "I'm a bit of a music fancier myself. Though for me it's more about collecting. Some people collect art, I collect musical memorabilia; I suppose that's what you would call it. You might like to see some of the things in my collection some time," he said, placing an arm on Massimo's shoulder, like an old friend would, as they walked toward the door.

"Yes, that would be nice," said Massimo, squirming, but trying to keep his tone light.

"Bianca was saying we should have you are over to the house sometime. I'll let you know." He gave a little tug at Massimo's jacket lapels along with one final reminder about the dress code for the next day's meeting, then turned and left.

"Damn, that means I won't be able to pick up Laura at the airport tomorrow morning," he said to no one in particular, as he reentered the room.

"Was that your boss?" said Hildr, suddenly emerging from the shadows of Massimo's office door.

"Yes, sort of. He's from the parent company that is funding our startup," he answered.

"The big shot manipulator," she said, holding onto the door frame.

He wondered if she was making some general observation about types like Mike, and why she seemed to take it so personally. "Are you okay? You look very pale."

"*I* will be picking Laura up at the airport tomorrow," was all she said. She swung her bag over her shoulder and stormed out of the office.

"Women!" was Lars's only comment when the door slammed.

Massimo distractedly cleared some discarded jotting paper from the conference desk into the trash, wondering what it was that had upset her. He wandered slowly back into his office, pondering whether it was something he had criticized in her proposal that had set her off. He saw that she had written the last part of her notation on his board neatly in red crayon and then underlined it several times with bold strokes.

$$\oint \Sigma_b^s \left( \frac{\partial J}{\partial t} + J \cdot \nabla \right) = -\nabla_b^s + \nabla \cdot T + f$$

The strange notation still wasn't completely clear to him, and he picked up the red crayon that now lay smashed on the floor. Alongside the cryptic equation she had also written:

*OEΔ !!!*

He left the writing on the board, figuring it might eventually mean something to him if he read her notes again. Glancing back to the other side of the board, where he had written his own version of the Navier-Stokes equations, he noticed that Hildr had also scrawled something diagonally across his own writing. It was not her usual neat script, and was difficult to read superimposed on top of his writing. He snapped a picture of it with his phone, thinking it was all Greek to him, but he might be able to make more sense of it later. Staring at the phone, he rotated the screen a few times and thought he could make out the following symbols:

نۊۘۢۯۣ

For now though, he would have to turn his attention to the slides for the upcoming presentation. The computer screen flashed up an angry red warning when he slipped Mike's memory stick in, advising that no attempt was to be made to copy or disseminate the contents.

It took several hours before he was confident enough with the contents of the slides to make a half decent presentation of it the following day. The slides were worse than he feared, littered with pie charts and glib, proselytizing corporate mantras. Very little of it he could actually recognize as having originated from his own program and analysis routines.

By the time he was done, Lars and Sven had already left. There wasn't much for them to get on with until they had all figured out what to do about the phantom lurking in their midst. It was late, and he didn't feel like cycling home in the dark. He wouldn't be cycling in his suit tomorrow either, so Massimo figured he might as well make use of the company car.

He dutifully handed in the piece of paper at reception and received the keys after signing more papers and having his ID badge carefully scrutinized. The elevator took him down to the underground parking, and he was left standing in front of a silent row of cars as the elevator doors thud shut with an echo behind him. He realized he had no clue which one was his, but ventured to press the button on the key. Lights flashed and a horn blipped at him from a car concealed from view behind a pillar. He walked around and stood in front of the car, pressing the button once more. The lights flashed at him.

It was a Tesla.

# Chapter 15 – Overtaken

Massimo took extra pleasure in waking up early the next morning. He had the presentation to give and would be driving into the office that morning, but be damned if he was going to go by the usual city streets. He would take a winding detour up into the hills, through the redwoods and up to Skyline before coming down onto Sand Hill Road from the west. It was time to put this Tesla through its paces.

Like a small boy rushing to play with his new toy, he did the buttons up all wrong on his shirt and had to start over again. His tie didn't receive the carefully dimpled Windsor knot that he had given it for the opera, but it would do for now. Only when he slipped the jacket on and caught sight of himself in the full length mirror did he straighten up and grin at its transformative effect.

He took the steps down to the street very casually, pulling at the shirt cuffs to adjust them beneath his jacket as he walked, so that you might have thought him a suave Italian runway model. At least that was Massimo's self image as he clicked the ignition key so that the Tesla would wink its lights at him. A midnight blue Italian suit to match the metallic dark blue of the Tesla. Perfect.

So was the drive around Portola Valley, up through the hills and back down into Woodside. He would snug down into the cockpit as he paced himself into the tree-lined turns, arms stretched out in the ten-minutes-to-two steering wheel grip, Italian racing driver style. The lack of engine roar as he accelerated out of the turns was the only thing preventing this ride from being a *Mille Miglia* experience for him.

"Whoa, look at you," chorused Lars and Sven as Mr. Italian suit walked into the office, still grinning from ear to ear.

"Laugh all you want," he replied. "You are not going to believe what my new ride turned out to be."

"Oh, he must have gotten the Toyota Camry, Special Edition," said Sven sardonically, getting up from his chair to check out Massimo's suit from another angle.

There was no way he was going to convince them about the car without taking them down to the parking garage to lay eyes on it for themselves.

"Just take a look at that," he said, proudly flashing the car lights with the remote. "And if you 'office assistants' learn to show a little respect, I might consider letting you borrow it."

Lars and Sven were all over it, popping the hood to see where an engine should have been, and poking around to find the battery compartment. Sven was already lying on the ground trying to get a glimpse of the drive train.

"It might be a good idea to plug it in," he shouted from beneath the car and then scrambled to his feet to give Massimo a congratulatory slap on the shoulder.

"Right," said Massimo, feeling rather foolish. "I hadn't even thought of that."

They all had a good laugh at the thought of Massimo being stranded at the side of the road with a flat battery on the first day he took ownership.

"It does have a range of 300 miles or something, but I suppose it makes sense to keep it fully charged," he agreed.

"You know what I think?" Sven added, leaning in towards his friends so that they could hear him above the noise of the garage exhaust fans. "This car is going to take a place in history, like the first Apple Computer did. I was just reading about the original models in my Computing History class: how expensive they were when they first came out, and the laughably small memory storage they had."

It made Massimo feel old when people talked about the first personal computers as though they were from a bygone era. He could remember experiencing firsthand the shortcomings of early personal computers. Some of his colleagues at SLAC still talked about their participation in the Home Brew Computer Club at SLAC, here in Silicon Valley, and how it was instrumental in shaping the way people thought about and interacted with the very first personal computers.

"It's true," said Lars. "People loved the Apple, and put up with its shortcomings because they saw in it the wave of the future. This Tesla has the same 'cool' factor, and in a decade from now the battery technology will have advanced so much that people will smile fondly at the memory of having to charge it every couple of hundred miles. As they go sailing past, electric car owners will be laughing at the gasoline powered cars still having to fill up every 300 miles or so."

"You may be right," said Massimo looking at his watch. "In fact, I have to go make a presentation to some venture capitalists about our work, right now. You never know, they may be the very people about to invest in the future of battery technology!"

The reality of it was that he would have to sit through some very dry and tedious meeting presentations this morning. He looked at his watch again as he hurried off to the meeting room, thinking that he would much rather be at the airport now to greet Laura, thus denying Hildr the pleasure.

Cindy was at the meeting room to greet him and acquaint him with the workings of the high-tech podium for presentations.

"Your slides are set to advance automatically after a fixed number of seconds," she advised. "That way you can't dawdle over some technical detail, and will have to stick to the topic to finish in the allocated time." She looked at him fixedly as she spoke.

The room had the smell of new, polished wood furnishings. The indirect lighting above the fined grained wall paneling suffused a rich glow to the room.

"If there are any questions from the audience," she continued, "I can pause the slide advance of your presentation. If it advances to the next slide it is because Mike does not want you to answer that question in more detail. "I will be in control," she said, leaving him in no doubt.

When the meeting started he was introduced to everyone present, but the reverse introductions were not made, leaving him in the dark as to who they were exactly. He came to realize that his presentation slides had been sanitized to be so content free that the audience was too bored to ask any questions. After his presentation commenced, Cindy began handing out a printed prospectus to the meeting attendees. Massimo was not given one, but he could see from a distance that it contained much more analytical data in the form of graphs and tables than his slides did. He had to pause his presentation while some of the attendees asked Mike whispered questions about the content of the prospectus.

At the end of his presentation he was politely thanked and then Cindy escorted him from the meeting room, indicating that his part was over for the time being.

He came back into the office slamming doors and complaining to anyone who would care to listen that it had been a complete waste of time, adding that it was humiliating to be paraded out like that if he wasn't even party to all the information being discussed at the meeting. Not wanting to further burden Lars and Sven with his frustration, he retreated to his office to vent, but he wasn't alone for long. Georges stormed in a few minutes later and made a beeline for Massimo.

"What's the meaning of giving a presentation in Mike's meeting without clearing it with me first?" he screamed.

Massimo tried to explain that he had been asked directly by Mike to give the presentation, but that he would have gladly relinquished the responsibility to Georges had he known what it would entail.

Georges, who was far from appeased, railed some more at Massimo about betrayal of trust, and not working for the common good.

"And what is more," he fumed, "I've had my own team of analysts checking on what you have been doing the last few days, and they tell me you have been hiding the important data with a secret version of the program."

Massimo was about to explain that he had no idea about the origin of the phantom version of the program, but they had managed to ascertain that the data was meaningless. Instead, he said, "How can you stand there and talk about trust if all this time you've had another team of analysts scrutinizing our data and probing our system?"

"That's beside the point." Georges was bristling. "If I didn't keep close tabs on you I would never know what you are up to. You just proved my point!"

Massimo had been in some heated conversations before with research colleagues over the validity of some theory or other, but he had never encountered someone as acrimonious as George. He crossed to the other side of the room so that the glass board was between them, signaling subconsciously perhaps that he would like to return to the classical world of mathematics and equations that Hildr had left there.

But this was a mistake, for Georges became further incensed by Massimo's retreat, and crossed the room in one stride. "How dare you take it upon yourself to formulate an approach to solving the world's most challenging mathematical problem," he hissed. "This is not your domain!"

At this point, Georges somehow realized he had overstepped the mark and faltered. "Your mission here is to set up your program on the WVC servers and use it to justify pricing schemes for IPOs. That is all!"

He was shaking and backed toward the door lest Massimo should hurl some rational, reasoned argument at him for which he had no defense.

When he finally left, Lars and Sven stuck their heads in the door. "What was all that about? We thought we might have to turn the fire sprinklers on to douse the sparks."

"I have no idea. But if this is typical of the venture capital world then I am having serious doubts about having made the right choices."

"Well, there's one piece of good news I can give you," said Sven. "The performance of our programs on the server has been restored. The phantom program has disappeared and we have top priority on the system once more."

They followed him out of the office, eager to see their programs once more running at full capacity.

"What do you suppose happened?" asked Lars.

"I don't know, I doubt we will ever find out. But if it means we can quietly get on with our work again, then I'm not going to ask any questions," said Massimo.

With that, he returned to his room and tried to resume work, hoping to put the morning's unpleasantness behind him. Laura's phone call came as a welcome distraction, and he was delighted to hear that she had arrived safely and fancied an early dinner. She was still on East Coast time and was used to eating 3 hours earlier than he was, but if that meant he could get out of the office early, then all the better.

He passed by the men's room on the way out and assessed his appearance in the mirrors above the wash basins. The fine cut Italian suit was still a novelty for him and he tugged here and there to make it sit just right. The Windsor knot would have to be redone to achieve the full effect, he thought.

As he was fiddling with his tie Mike appeared behind him. "Hey, nice suit. Great job on the presentation this morning. I think you made a good impression."

"Well, I don't know," answered Massimo. "It's not what I expected, or thought …"

"Don't think about it," interrupted Mike who was relieving himself noisily at the porcelain. "If you're not aware of all the facts, you probably shouldn't try and make any conclusions. I'm sure you science guys have a technical term for trying to predict an outcome from incomplete data."

Massimo futilely tried to respond, but was at a loss for words as Mike briskly washed his hands at the sink next to him.

"I meant it about the suit, though. Nice cut." He reached across in front of Massimo for one of the folded towels stacked in a small basket. "But you're right, you should redo the tie," he said, giving Massimo a little slap on the shoulder as he walked out.

Massimo didn't know whether to be annoyed or not at the last remark, but undid the tie and started over again, reproducing as best he could the knot that the salesman had shown him.

Parking in front of Laura's house a short time after, he walked across the grass to her front steps, slightly self-conscious about his new appearance. Smiling as she came out of the front door, she hugged him warmly before pulling away to take a second look.

"What happened to your hair?" she said, reaching up and running her fingers across his forehead at the place she was accustomed to pushing the locks away from his eyes.

"I had it trimmed in London," he said, taking her hands in his, "but it turned out to be more of a trendy hair salon than I had anticipated." He started leading her across the lawn towards the street and his parked car, but she held back for a moment and appraised the rest of him, holding him at arm's length.

"And this suit! Wow! I'm going to feel completely under-dressed sitting with you at dinner tonight." She ran her hands up and down the arms of the jacket, then the lapels and finally the tie, letting it slip slowly through her fingers.

Massimo didn't know whether to feel proud or embarrassed of his new couture. "I had a business meeting today," he said, taking a neutral stance.

"I had to wear formal business attire for my presentation to some European investment bankers." He took her by the hand and tried again to lead her toward the car.

"Investment bankers? You do move in exclusive circles, now." She let go his hand and straightened the bodice of her simple outfit, no longer looking him directly in the eye.

"Now, don't tease," he said, taking her by the elbow and propelling her forward this time. "You know I'm not one for superficial appearances." They reached the car and he opened the door with his other hand, helping her inside before she had time to speak, then running around to the other side to climb in beside her.

"What's this? An Italian sports car to go with the new lifestyle?" she said, running her hand over the smooth leather of the dashboard.

"It's not Italian, it's a Tesla electric vehicle made here in California. And I didn't buy it. It's part of the deal that goes with the new company," he continued, putting the car into drive, and pulling out from the curb a little more boldly than perhaps he should have. "And it's very environmentally friendly, being electric," he added when she didn't make any further comment.

They drove in silence to the restaurant, until she finally remarked, "It's very quiet for an Italian sports car."

Detecting what he thought was a slight smirk, he didn't correct her, suspecting she was trying to goad him on the sensitive topic of ownership of Italian sports cars. Instead, as they pulled into a parking garage off University Avenue, he said, "I suppose we can use one of these spaces at the front, reserved for electric vehicles." Normally, they had to circle around for ages looking for a parking spot, competing with all the other diners looking for a space within easy walking distance of the University Avenue restaurants.

"I suppose that's one thing in its favor," she conceded.

He hadn't gotten around to making a table reservation at any of their favorite haunts, which meant they had to settle for walk-in seating at one of the larger restaurants. As soon as they were settled in at their table and the waiters were satisfied that they'd been given their menus and requisite glasses of iced water, he asked her whether her trip had been a success. She answered him with extraneous details of the flight, and where she had stayed, but all the time tugging and twisting at a long strand of loose hair that curled down beside her cheek. He sensed that she was having difficulty telling him the most important part, so he lay his hand on hers and quietly let her take her time.

"Oh, Massi, you would have loved it there. All the wining and dining, and meeting new people eager to talk to you about your work and your ideas."

The enthusiasm expressed in the words she spoke did not match her countenance which looked pained as she spoke of the people she had met and the wonderful time they had given her.

"You must still remember the excitement you felt when you were first offered your job at CERN," she continued.

"I do," he smiled, trying to sound supportive, yet still perplexed at what she was obviously holding back.

"But you had someone at that time to share the excitement with. Someone to discuss all the plans and possibilities with. Someone who was going to be accompanying you to your new job, and sharing in all the new adventures to come," she said with finality, sitting back in her chair and withdrawing her hand from his.

"Ah, so that's it," he replied. He sat there with his lips pinched together in a pained expression. It was difficult to know how to respond. He could tell her to stay with him and look for a less exciting job, but she certainly wouldn't want to hear that. Nor could he tell her that he would drop everything he was doing and follow her to the East Coast. Not with all his commitments.

"It's not an easy situation," was the best he could answer. "We could try and visit each other as often as possible and earn ourselves a whole lot of frequent flyer miles."

She was slightly mollified by his answer and sat forward in her chair, placing her hands back on the table, but stopping short of picking up his hands once more.

"Let's order," she said. "I'm starved. Remember I'm still 3 hours ahead of you."

"We should get a bottle of Champagne to celebrate your success," he offered.

"That's a nice thought, but honestly," she said, "I'd rather have a trusty Californian red. Too many people have been toasting me with Champagne these last few days."

Massimo felt a pang of jealousy, topped with an equal measure of guilt at the recollection of his own indulgences at the opera.

With the food and wine ordering out of the way, they could return to the discussion of her job offer and what exactly she would be doing. A basket of bread and some dipping oil had been placed between them. Laura had at least stopped tugging at the rampant strand of hair, but was now breaking the bread into smaller and smaller pieces and stirring it in the oil, hardly bothering to eat it, in spite of her earlier proclamations of hunger.

"We could make promises to visit each other at every opportunity," she murmured. "But how long would that last? Realistically? You've said it yourself that you're no good without a woman's company. So how long would it be before the next pretty face catches your eye? I'm only in the picture now because you split up with Donatella. You're not the type to stay on your own for very long. I'll bet you were even flirting around in London."

Massimo felt his ears become very hot, just as she raised her face and looked him in the eye.

"You did, didn't you? I can see it in your face," she said, squeezing the last piece of bread into an inedible, doughy ball.

"It wasn't like that at all," he stammered. "I had some dealings with people, but nothing like you are suggesting. In fact, to use Hugh's expression, I can categorically state that I kept my trousers buttoned."

"You sound about as convincing as Bill Clinton," she said with a shake of her head. "But it says something, doesn't it, that even your old mentor has to advise you to keep your trousers buttoned."

Massimo was saved further embarrassment by the arrival of the food.

"So what did you get up to in London?" she asked, her mood slightly improving after a few mouthfuls of steaming pasta. "You said you visited Hugh, and that there was also an opportunity to visit the opera."

He actually got her laughing as he recounted his gardening episode with Hugh, and the mess-up in walking directions.

"I hope to meet Hugh one day, he sounds nice, and he's always been there for you," she said.

"I'm sure he would also like another visit, one day," he replied. "And you're right, he had sage advice about this new financial venture and dealing with people like the recruiter I met."

"And who would this recruiter be?" she asked, twirling the fork in her pasta, but not raising it from her plate.

"Ah, yes, well, I ran into her at the conference, where she acted very charmingly, even offering me a companion ticket to the opera, which turns out, by the way, to be impossible to get otherwise."

She stopped twirling her fork. "Go on."

"Well, the tickets were for a performance on an evening after I got back from visiting Hugh in Oxford, so she suggested I stay at her hotel."

"Massimo! You stayed at her hotel?" she said with raised eyebrows.

"In separate rooms, of course," he hastened to add. "She said it would be more convenient for the opera and dinner afterwards."

"You had a late night dinner with this woman in her hotel? Was she attractive?"

"Um, she wasn't exactly frumpy, if that's what you mean. And she somehow also convinced me to visit a Saville Row tailor shop and buy this suit," he said with a pleading shrug of the shoulders.

"Wow. She certainly sounds like she had you wrapped around her finger. I don't think I could have ever convinced you to buy a pink tie," she added sarcastically.

"I know, I know, and I spent much more than I meant to. But she made me feel guilty about accompanying her to the opera wearing my old jacket. It does turn out, though, that I'm expected to wear a suit like this from time to time for business meetings," he added defensively, even though he hoped he would never have to attend another one like that morning's.

"I hope the opera was worth the cost of a new suit," she said.

He started to tell her about the performance and the fabulous box seats beneath the dome of the grand theatre, but he could tell she wasn't really interested in the details.

"It would have been great if the evening had ended after the opera," he said finally.

"Why, was the dinner so unbearable?" she said, pushing the remnants of her food to the side of her plate.

"No, it was sumptuous - both the food and the wine. And all paid for on a company expense account," he said. "She worked for a big Wall Street recruiting company that hires mathematicians and statisticians they find at conferences like these. Or so she said, because the whole thing was really a ploy for her to get into my room."

"Oh, come on, Massimo! You seriously expect me to believe that?" she said, clutching at a napkin and balling it up as though she were about to throw it at him.

"Look, this is deeply embarrassing for me, but I want you to understand, stupid as I was, that I was completely manipulated."

Laura stared at some imaginary spot on the floor to the side of the table. "So what happened?" she asked solemnly.

"She insisted on coming to my room for a nightcap after paying for dinner, and the opera tickets, of course. She must have slipped something into my drink, like a date-rape drug, because I passed out almost immediately. When I woke up next morning my laptop had been stolen." He tried to catch her eye so that he might gauge if she believed him or not, but she kept her gaze fixed on the floor.

"I'll save you the embarrassment of asking what 'almost immediately' entails, but honestly, why would she go to so much trouble just for your laptop?" she said when she finally looked at him.

"I assure you, when I awoke the next morning, with a splitting headache I may add, I was still fully dressed." He then proceeded to tell her about what they had since discovered at the office with the phantom program, and how the copy could have only been made by someone with access to the encryption key that was hard coded into his laptop.

"Well, that's alarming," she said, almost forgiving him. "Why are you still hanging around with these people if they are so ruthless? We talked about the potential dangers of this job."

"They don't know we discovered their phantom program, so we're keeping quiet, waiting and watching to see what they're up to."

"That sounds even more infantile and stupid than being seduced by some woman in a London hotel," she said, giving him the most cutting of looks. "I suppose there is some modicum of truth to your story, though. Hildr told me on the way back from the airport that she'd helped you uncover the fake data from the phantom program."

"O, yes. Hildr came by to look at Lars and Sven's work, and then I offered to read her dissertation proposal. I wanted to thank her for her help in looking over our data and identifying it as fake."

"So what the hell did you do to her to make her so upset? She was so distraught in the car on the way back from the airport that I could hardly make any sense of what she was saying. Did you try and seduce her again, or make some indecent proposal?"

"No, I've never tried to seduce Hildr. And Lars and Sven were in the office the whole time I was discussing her mathematics dissertation with her," he added indignantly.

"Well, it had something to do with the music thing that's going on between you two," she retaliated. "Her whole musical past seems to have opened up like an old wound, and she was raving on about integrity and fate."

"I'm as baffled as you are. She didn't have her violin with her, so she didn't play anything like she did on the previous occasion. We were just discussing her dissertation at the board in my office. I stepped out for a minute or two to discuss my presentation with Mike, and after he left, she stormed out of the office without any word of explanation, save for a few cryptic lines of math on my board."

The waitress had come and discreetly left the check on the table, not wanting to encroach on their heated discussion.

"It must be just the mad delusional mind of a genius," he added as an afterthought. "Sad, really, because she can truly see things that other people can't. But, wow, it must get all twisted up inside that head of hers."

They made their way out of the restaurant, and Laura walked with arms tightly folded across her chest, keeping some distance away from him.

The drive home was in silence, made even more palpable by the quiet cabin of the Tesla. Massimo fiddled with the radio to put on some mellow jazz, hoping it would soothe her. "I don't suppose you'd like to come back to my place for a nightcap?" he suggested, after one or two tracks had played.

"You're pathetic," was the only answer he got.

In retrospect, it probably wasn't the most appropriate suggestion he could have made, given the Ms. Jones story. Pulling up outside Laura's apartment, he jumped out to open the door and walk her to her apartment, but she reached out, planting a hand on his chest, and said, "It's not a good idea for you to come in tonight. With all these revelations, I need time to think. Perhaps, with me going away, it's time to rethink our relationship altogether. Maybe it's run its course and it's time to go our separate ways."

Massimo stepped back, walking in a small circle, raising his arms and letting them fall helplessly to his sides. He knew better than to argue with her.

"Just call me when you can," he said to her retreating figure.

The next morning Massimo was not the first person into the office. He dawdled going in, having lost some of his enthusiasm as a result of the previous night. Even Georges was in before him, and there seemed to be a buzz of excitement around the place.

Georges was pacing up and down, gesturing with a coffee mug in one hand that Lars and Sven should bring up various displays on the computer for him to examine. Massimo retreated quietly into the kitchen for some coffee, but Georges was right behind. His mood was unnaturally exuberant, especially considering the vile altercation he had engaged in the day before.

"Let me tell you this," Georges said, speaking very fast. "A lot of changes are going to be taking place. All for the better, I might add." He took the coffee pot from Massimo's hand, apparently unaware that he already had a cup on the counter, and poured himself another one. "You show me the appropriate loyalty and we can advance together. But if you don't, then there's not going to be room for you, if you catch my drift." The rapid outpouring of words didn't leave any room for a reply from Massimo, but apparently none was required or even desired by Georges. "And you should leave the advanced mathematical thinking to me. You should concentrate on deriving something more practical like IPO pricing formulae."

Georges' euphoria suddenly transferred itself to Lars and Sven and he dashed back into the computer room to tell them to try something completely different from what they were just doing. He gulped down one of the cups of coffee he was holding, and Massimo cringed at the thought of how hot it was.

"I have to go out and think," he said excitedly, and raced from the room.

"What's going on?" said Massimo.

"We have no idea," answered Sven. "He's been like this since he arrived an hour ago."

"We were hoping you would turn up and rescue us," added Lars. "Maybe he is wildly looking for the missing data stream from the phantom program"

"And that hasn't resurfaced since it disappeared yesterday, I presume?" Massimo inquired.

They were able to calmly discuss the last twenty-four hours of data analysis for a few minutes without any frantic commands or interruptions from Georges.

"The only conclusion I can come to about the phantom program," Massimo said finally, "is that it was intentionally run in reverse to create fake market data, possibly to convince someone to believe that this particular venture capital market sector is behaving very differently to the way it really is."

"If something fraudulent is going on," he continued, "then I want to take steps to prove that we haven't been involved."

Lars and Sven made the point that it was going to be difficult since the program had now vanished and they hadn't been able to make any permanent record of its actions. Furthermore, they pointed out, Massimo hadn't actually examined the prospectus that Mike had handed out in the meeting, so they couldn't go around making accusations all of a sudden.

"Maybe they were just doing it for educational purposes," suggested Sven.

"With a stolen program," Massimo muttered angrily.

Georges burst back in through the door. His eyes were bloodshot again, so much so that Massimo wondered why he insisted on going outside if he suffered such allergies.

"I find I must go back to my office to get some work done, so I'm afraid you'll have to carry on without me for a while." He began shuffling through some random papers on the desk, as though he was deciding which of them commanded his immediate attention. In the end he took nothing and abruptly left.

"The guy's snorting coke, like nobody's business," said Sven contemptuously.

"He is?" said Massimo, wide eyed.

"Isn't it bloody obvious," said Lars. "At least we won't have to put up with him for the rest of the day now."

"Well, let's try and focus on our own goals, here," said Massimo, scratching his head for a bit, and deciding to not even drink coffee from the same coffee pot as Georges had been drinking from.

They agreed there wasn't much to be done about the phantom program now that it was gone, nor should they spend time worrying over Georges, so it was back to their original business plan. Massimo retreated into his office and gazed out at the stand of young redwoods outside his window. Even though they couldn't be more than 10 years old they were already well over thirty feet tall. Things can grow fast in the Valley once they take root.

His reverie was short lived because a text came through from Laura asking if he could come around and see her as soon as he had time. After last night's unhappy ending, he immediately hoped she'd had a change of heart.

"Anything you guys need me for here? Otherwise I'm going to go and help Laura with something."

"Nah, we've got it covered," said Lars.

"Yeah, go improve your golf swing, or something," grinned Sven.

"Right-oh. Probably see you tomorrow, then," said Massimo and marched out the door with a little swing in his step.

Laura didn't look at all happy, though, when he arrived at her apartment.

"I've had some startling news about Hildr," she announced immediately. "Are you sure there isn't something you're not telling me about the two of you?" Laura sat opposite him on a chair with her arms folded and legs crossed under her, waiting for him to reply.

"Why, has something happened to her?" he ventured to ask. "I told you she came to our office a couple of times, ostensibly to see Lars and Sven, but I suspect she mainly wanted my advice on her dissertation. Is she okay? She seemed fairly contrite when I spoke to her."

Massimo was puzzled why Laura would interrogate him like this again, and looked around to see if she was at least going to offer him a drink.

"Hildr has quit Stanford," she said blankly. "Why would anyone quit Stanford? I was hoping you would have some insight. Nobody quits Stanford."

Massimo mashed his knuckle into his lower lip, as was becoming his habit lately.

"Well, what did she say when she quit? She must have given a reason to you, and what did she say that makes you think it involves me?"

"She didn't say anything, that's the point, she just upped and left." Laura now stood and paced about the room, pausing only at the table to pick up a large envelope. "Student services called to say she had left this envelope for me, and that's how I found out she had quit."

She pulled a folder out of the envelope, being careful not to allow the remaining contents to fall out, and thrust the folder at him. The cover of the folder was scrawled with the words 'For Massimo' and the interior was filled with her neat but dense mathematical notation. He couldn't tell much from his precursory glance, but it was clearly related to her dissertation topic.

"Was there a note or something?" he asked.

"No, just some photographs of me that she took when we were sunbathing on the roof."

When Massimo tried to take a closer look, she clutched the envelope to her chest keeping them well out of his reach.

"Why can't I see them?" he said, almost laughing. "I get a benign folder of mathematics and you get some interesting photographs. How come I'm in the hot seat?"

Laura walked out of the room, and he could hear her open and slam shut a draw. "Argh ..." came a frustrated groan. He sat there in silence and waited.

"Would you like a cup of tea?" she finally asked.

"Certainly, if it will calm you down and if we can talk some more," he proffered.

"Don't think for a moment that I've forgiven you," she said, but then quietly added, "I'm going to miss you, though, when I leave. And this business with Hildr suddenly disappearing is disconcerting."

She busied herself with tea bags and mugs. "I'm just blaming you for everything at the moment. I never expected you to follow me to the East Coast, but that doesn't mean I'm happy with the way things are turning out."

She banged a mug down in front of him, startling him. He sensed, though, that now she was more annoyed at herself than at him.

"Can we try talking this through, at least? If we list everything we know about the situation, we might figure out what's going on," he suggested.

"No! I don't have time right now," she said, jumping up again. "I have publications I need to submit before I leave, I have my thesis defense to prepare. I don't *care* that Hildr quit. Why did she have to do it *now?*"

He walked around the room following her as she paced about, trying to put his arm around her, hoping that a little show of affection might calm her, but she wasn't having any of it.

"Are you *sure* you didn't engage in one of her little musical performances again?" she said, turning abruptly to face him. He didn't answer, and she continued. "Already on the way back from the airport I could tell she was upset. She was complaining about something to do with musical performances, but I was too tired to understand or bother asking questions."

When he didn't reply she picked up the folder again and handed it to him. "Take this and leave me to get on with my work before I blow a fuse."

She gave him a brief hug and brushed her cheek against his; leaving him to think that perhaps their relationship was not totally beyond redemption.

He couldn't decide whether to return to work or go home and possibly look over Hildr's thesis notes. He chose the latter, thinking that a bottle of wine, even if he was on his own, wouldn't be a bad way to unwind. Settling down on the couch, he soon found that the notes were just as incomprehensible as before. Perhaps he should take a cue from Hildr and listen to some music while he worked through the pages. He selected some Bach, the Goldberg Variations, but although it was a very interesting evening with the wine and the music, he couldn't honestly say he made any headway deciphering the work. However, he did come across one interesting note scrawled in the margin towards the end of the document:

"This will prove that solutions must always exist for N-S, up to dimension 3, but not beyond."

It was written next to the same mathematical-musical notation she had left on the board in his office:

$$\oint \Sigma_\flat^\sharp \left( \frac{\partial \natural}{\partial t} + \flat \cdot \nabla \right) = -\nabla_\flat^\sharp + \nabla \cdot T + f$$

How intriguing was that? These notes might one day become as famous as Fermat's manuscript[25]. If only he could understand it now, he thought to himself as he drifted off. Centuries ago, Fermat had scrawled a margin note claiming that he had discovered a marvelous mathematical proof, and it wasn't until the end of the 20th century that his claim could be finally vindicated, albeit with the aid of powerful computers. Was Hildr also way ahead of her time? Massimo could only speculate.

A phone call the next morning jarred him awake. Lars and Sven were telling him he should come in at once because they couldn't get into the office. Their explanation didn't make a whole lot of sense, and having consumed a whole bottle of wine on his own the previous night probably wasn't helping either.

He high-tailed it into work, figuring he could go out again afterwards for some coffee. When he pulled up at the office park, however, there was a security guard to greet him. It was a new security firm and the guard examined his ID closely and only then allowed him to proceed and park. At the entrance to the building he found Lars and Sven who exclaimed that they had been locked out of the building. Another security guard at the door explained that everything would be fine if they would kindly go down to the foyer office where a transition team would explain what was required of them.

The transition team was also from an outside HR firm that was usually called in to make layoffs when a corporation shut its doors for good. In this case, they explained, WVC had been bought out by the much larger investment banking firm, the Megateck Corporation. The three of them were handed a stack of documents to read and sign once they had sat through a formal presentation. The presentation was prerecorded so there was no opportunity to protest or ask questions.

At least they could make comments to one another as they sat alone in a room watching the astonishing news of the takeover unfold before them. After the usual platitudes about new strength and efficiency came the more brutal news about the inevitable redundancy layoffs that would occur. The three of them sat on the edge of their seats to see whether their startup would become one of the shortest lived in venture capital history.

WVC had an ornately complex corporate structure. Their startup was a separate entity, but it had been swept up in the overall buyout. Then came the shocking news that Mike and Kate's team were out. As of today they were excluded from the new corporate entity. They had been summarily fired by the new owners. Massimo looked at Lars and Sven, waiting for the certain news that their little startup would not survive.

But it was not to be. There it was, on the new corporate org chart, and it had even been given a new name, QDOT. That sounded like a name Georges would have come up with. And it would have been just like Georges not to consult with them on a name for their new company.

Their relief and elation was short lived because the next slide in the presentation revealed that Georges had received a huge promotion in the reorganization, and while he was still their boss, he was going to be several levels higher than they were in the management structure.

"How could they promote such an incompetent idiot?" asked Sven in amazement.

"Everyone rises to their level of incompetence – the Peter Principle[26]," offered Lars.

"At least he won't be getting under our feet anymore as he'll get a lofty new office," said Massimo.

The presentation ended, stating that by signing the documents in front of them, they were acknowledging the new organizational structure and accepting Megateck as their new owners. Following that, they could resume occupancy and go back to work.

The three of them walked together across the office park towards their building. They passed a group of business-suited executives huddled in conversation a small distance away. One of them turned and looked across his shoulder at them, head thrown back, staring down his nose with hauteur. It was Georges, dressed in a brand new, stylish suit of dark blue, remarkably like the Italian cut of Massimo's suit. He even copied the pink tie.

"The guy can't do anything original," muttered Massimo, and he wondered how Mike must be reacting to the news right now.

# Chapter 16 – On the Outside

The company logo for the Megateck Corporation looked like a herd of stampeding steers, and it was now emblazoned above the main entrance of the company offices. It was presumably intended to convey the same sentiment as the iconic charging bull of Wall Street. But since it was a Texas based investment banking firm it was probably also supposed to communicate that with more bulls, Texas business was bigger and better than Wall Street.

On the day the buyout was announced, Texas Governor Rick Perry released a statement praising the move, saying it was a sign of the times that Texas was luring big business away from California.

Someone had submitted a posting to the company online bulletin board showing the response from California Governor Jerry Brown, calling the Texas takeover 'barely a fart', but the posting was very quickly taken down.

Massimo thought the logo reflected the cowboy attitude of the new investment bankers, since they were literally stampeding off in some random direction. The very next day the company had announced that it was going ahead with an IPO of the WVC Group of companies, an IPO that included Massimo's little startup. The company memo had called it a bold and forthright move, indicative of the strength and dynamism brought by Megateck. Gone were the days of conservatism and holding back on new ventures as had been favored by WVC in the past. The new company had immediately recognized a profit potential when it saw one, was seizing the bull by the horns, and was not going to stand about and wait for competitors to catch up.

Massimo was certain some of the words in the company memo had been lifted directly from Georges' mission statement. That didn't appease him one bit.

What took Massimo completely by surprise was the price at which the initial public offering was to be made. He had, after all, been working on the pricing formula for this himself, analyzing what he believed to be the real market data for the companies in question. The price that Megateck was describing in this confidential, internal memo was three to four times higher than what the stock was worth, by any stretch of the imagination. If the IPO went ahead at this price it would be an unmitigated disaster.

He took his concerns to Lars and Sven, but they could offer little more than to say it all looked like a setup.

"If it is a setup," said Massimo, "then I want to know who's behind it. Who's got the power here?" He reiterated Hugh's advice to follow the money trail, adding that they had the perfect tools on hand to do it. Lars and Sven began flipping up displays of the data in question.

"Can you create that display again with the highlighting, where we tag $1.00 and track its motion across the board?" Massimo asked them.

Once they brought it up it revealed a swirl of activity around the companies, but oddly enough, no real economic growth. Lars's keen eye discovered that a single commodity was simply being passed back and forth between a small group of companies. Nobody was actually doing anything with it, just selling it back and forth between themselves at inflated prices, giving the illusion of a large revenue stream for the group of companies involved.

"But over here," said Lars pointing at one area of the screen, "we do have an injection of about $100 million in funds, fairly recently, too.

"That could well be Georges' personal investment," Massimo pointed out, peering closely at the numbers on the screen. He related to them what he knew of the story of Georges' grandfather giving each of the grandchildren $100 million to invest on his behalf. Whoever succeeded in achieving the greatest return on his investment would head his new venture capital firm in the Valley.

"Georges must be very confident to put all his eggs in one basket like this," said Sven. He didn't hold Georges in very high regard, and the looks he was exchanging with Lars made it pretty clear that neither would shed a tear if Georges lost it all.

"Let's bring up the 'weather map' display again," suggested Massimo. He liked to call it that because the colorful computer animation showed the money flow swirling around in the little whirlwinds and gusts of a busy economy. During times of lively economic growth, powerful jet streams would sweep across the display, snaking back and forth like a giant fire hose providing wealth and prosperity.

Not so today, though. The money was going in circles, gyrating around the WVC Group of companies, building up in intensity and speed, creating a bubble that had to burst somewhere.

"WVC is still a strange attractor," commented Massimo, harking back to his earliest observations when they first began describing the money flow in the terminology of chaos theory. "And what's more, the orbital motion of funds around this select group of companies has *period three*!" he said jabbing the screen with his fingers to emphasize the point.

The whites of Lars's eyes glowed in the light from the monitor screen. "And what's the significance of that?"

Sven was frowning. He didn't like Massimo putting his fingers on the monitor screens and leaving messy prints everywhere, but he held his tongue.

"*Period Three Means Chaos*," answered Massimo. "That's the title of a seminal paper written by the 'Father Christmas' of chaos theory, Jim Yorke, and his student Tien-Yien Li[27].

Lars stared at the monitor with the masses of dots rolling around the screen, like dark clouds, boiling and heaving. "A perfect storm," he said, also remembering the words he had used when Massimo and he had first talked about it at the party.

"You guys are making me nervous," said Sven, wiping away Massimo's fingerprints with a box of wipes he kept on the desk for that purpose. "What are we supposed to do about this?" He rubbed a little harder at the screen than was necessary. "I didn't count on any of this when I bought into this deal."

"I'm not sure there's anything we can do," said Massimo opening his laptop, subconsciously looking for some distraction to the rising tension in the room. "Our job has been to monitor things and make predictions," he continued. "But clearly Georges doesn't want to heed our IPO forecasts, and prefers to go with his own predictions."

"Dude, will you stop polishing that screen!" Lars yelled at Sven. "We may not be able to do anything about this, but don't forget when this bubble bursts our little startup is right here at the epicenter.

"Hey, I don't believe it!" Massimo interrupted. His head was in his emails, and he was not paying Lars and Sven much attention. "I just got a party invitation."

"Well, bully for you," said Sven with a sniff, and rolling his chair away from Lars.

"No, it's from Mike," he said. "It just arrived on my SLAC e-mail account. There's to be some kind of thank you party for the time he spent at WVC, and apparently also to celebrate some other events. It's going to be some fancy affair, though, up at his estate in Woodside."

"You should go," said Lars, sitting up and taking an interest. "He might be more willing to talk about what's really going on in WVC now that he is out of it. You might learn something valuable that could help us cover our asses."

Sven responded with just a "Hmph" from the back of the room, but he seemed to be in agreement with Lars that Massimo needed to do this.

"But I hate the idea of going to a formal garden," groaned Massimo at the thought of having to stand around and make small talk with people he hardly knew.

"Nah, just put on your fancy suit and drive up there in your Tesla and you'll fit right in," snickered Sven.

Massimo shot him a sidelong glance, but decided not to berate him for the implication that he was now somehow part of the elite class.

"I'll see if Laura wants to join me," he grumbled. "I notice you guys were not invited," he added, trying to get the last word in, but the two of them were just giggling like a couple of kids.

Unfortunately, Laura declined his invitation when he called her that evening, citing, as usual, that she had too much work to finish before her departure. However, she was willing to talk about it with him and offer her opinion as to whether he should attend. Although she didn't hold the venture capital crowd in very high esteem, she did agree with Lars's view that he should try and get some insight from Mike into what might be going on.

"It's not going to be just a backyard barbecue," he told her. "Probably more of a formal affair, judging by the invitation."

"You'll have a good excuse to wear your fancy-schmancy suit, then." This last remark set him wondering if Lars and Sven had called ahead and set him up.

On the evening of the party Massimo's assumptions were proved correct. Valet parking was provided as he discovered when he drove up in his Tesla. He had no idea where they were taking the cars to because Mike's estate was at the end of a narrow country lane, devoid of any large empty lots to park cars. It was hard to imagine that any of the neighbors would volunteer their driveways, not when property prices were in the one hundred million range. The Woodside estates were home to vineyards and horse stables, hidden behind tall Cyprus hedges. The footpaths along the roadside were made into horse trails so that the privileged residents would feel they were at home in the country.

The gravel crunched beneath his black Oxfords as he made his way up to the house. He didn't feel at all underdressed as he caught sight of the splendid raiments of his fellow guests. An attendant in waiter's garb directed him to the pool and garden area, where banquet tables had been laid out. Judging by the bulges beneath the waiter's too small jacket, he also served some security function, keeping people out of the private areas of the house.

The serving tables were laid out as culinary islands, each one focusing on a particular cuisine, so that guests could pick and choose. A French contingent was clustered around a colorful assortment of crudités. Behind them was a tasting bar for wines of the region. Massimo headed there first. Woodside had its own little appellation, and a local winemaker was proudly pouring his selection. The tasting bar was a good place to station himself, for here he could watch the comings and goings of the guests and listen in on some of the conversations. English seemed to be a minority language, so it was not always easy to follow the eavesdropped conversations.

Massimo didn't even try to comprehend what the party of Russians might be talking about. The boisterous laughing and the pained expressions on the faces of some of their women companions led him to guess that their comments were more than a little ribald. They were helping themselves to the contents of a dish set in a block of ice. Small mother of pearl spoons were provided to ladle out the translucent gray contents of the dish onto little squares of bread. As he moved closer to investigate, he also spied an ice bucket with the chilled vodka bottles and a neat stack of shot glasses.

"Michailovich, come and drink a toast with us."

Massimo turned to see whom they were addressing.

"I see you found the caviar." It was Mike who had walked up behind him, laying a friendly hand on his shoulder.

A frosted glass of vodka was thrust into both his and Mike's hand. The toast and resounding cheers were made in Russian, at the conclusion of which everyone tipped back his glass in one gulp.

"Quite a party! Though I hadn't realized it was going to be such a formal affair." Massimo was commenting on Mike's suave, white dinner jacket. What, with the boisterous Russians, and Mike dressed like that, Massimo felt he might have walked into a scene from James Bond.

"Oh, that's just to appease Bianca. She likes to make an occasion of it, especially if she's showing off one of her musical discoveries.

Massimo took a generous bite of the caviar he had heaped onto a wedge of bread. "Mm, this is good." He clicked spoons with one of the Russian women when they both simultaneously reached for the caviar dish. She looked up and smiled at him. It was the first time he'd seen the surly expression lift from her eyes. "I suppose you're used to eating such a fine delicacy." He was only trying to make polite conversation, and perhaps offer a little camaraderie to compensate for the macho leanings of the Russian males. She blushed, looked down and stepped away without answering. Perhaps she doesn't speak English, he thought.

"Be careful, Sergei is the jealous type," Mike whispered discreetly in his ear.

This time it was Massimo's turn to be embarrassed. He quickly sought to change the subject. "I see we're in for a musical treat." Massimo pointed to a group of musicians setting up on the other side of the terrace near the pool.

"That's right, you're a music aficionado. I remember I wanted to show you my music collection inside."

Mike led him across the garden through the French doors into a stylishly furnished parlor. A grand piano, with its lid closed, stood in silent repose at one end, and around the walls were paintings of mighty steeds. Massimo drew in his breath as he passed by portraits of quivering flanks and flaring nostrils. He could almost smell their equine breath on him as he passed.

"This is Bianca's garden parlor. My study is at the rear of the house."

They passed down a stately corridor to the east wing of the house. It opened into a large wood-paneled room. Unlike Bianca's sunny garden study with its bright French windows, the only light here suffused its way down from skylights. The walls were completely lined in glass enclosed bookcases.

"On this side I have some original manuscripts, scores and librettos," Mike waved dismissively at the glass cases. Massimo peered through the glass doors at some of the items on display. Before he could comment on the names of the venerable composers, Mike led him over to the other side, where several antique instruments lay ensconced in their glass cases. The most prominent instrument stood in the center of the room in its own glass cube; a magnificent cello lit by a single spotlight, glowing in rich, warm wooden tones.

Mike casually laid one arm on the glass case. "It's a Stradivarius, you know. Most people think of violins when they hear the great Stradivarius' name, but he also made some of the greatest cellos of all time."

Massimo crouched down in front of the case. He felt he was in a museum, not someone's private library. "Is it still played? I mean is it taken out from time to time, or is it just for show?"

The question may have come across as impolite, for Mike did not answer at once. He walked over to the other smaller glass cases. Some were notably empty. "The cello is my particular favorite. It was last played by Mstislav Rostropovich, and its tonality is probably the closest of all instruments to the human voice. Yo Yo Ma already has the exquisite Stradivarius Davidoff cello, so for now this instrument remains here. Each instrument must find its rightful player."

The realization that he was standing amongst some of the world's finest instruments was overwhelming for Massimo. "How did you come by such a collection? This was not acquired overnight?"

Again, Massimo's question may have been a little too direct, but Mike tolerated it. "Some of them have been in my family for generations, others I have acquired over the years. Some people invest in art; I choose musical 'memorabilia'. The cello alone would probably pay for this place, not that I would ever part with it."

It was hard to discern whether the answer came from someone who valued the musical history of the instrument, or simply its monetary worth. Either way, he held Mike in a new regard.

Massimo was about to get all sentimental and tell Mike how sorry he was about the sudden takeover by Megateck, and how shortsighted they must obviously be to have cast Mike loose like that, but he was cut short.

"I must get back to our other guests, I'm afraid. I'd leave you alone here to peruse the collection longer, but the alarm system isn't set up for unaccompanied visitors"

They walked back along the long corridor towards the terrace. Doors clicked shut with a metallic finality behind him, leaving him in no doubt that his passage down the corridor was one way.

Out on the terrace the string orchestra was playing innocuous melodies that drifted across the pool.

"Enjoy the food and wine. I must go and entertain some of Bianca's guests. But make sure you stick around for the little performance she has arranged for later. I think you'll appreciate it."

The opportunity to thank him for his efforts was lost once again as Mike was swallowed up in the throng. The numbers had swelled at the party, and each of the culinary islands was in full swing, serving all manner of sizzling and steaming dishes.

The pool had become the centerpiece of the terrace now that the sky was fully dark, and the water was illuminated in azure blues. Ornate mosaics lined the bottom of the pool, their lines drawing the eye to the far end where their pattern rose out of the water and continued into a shell like structure arching over a small stage. The decorations did not include any leaping dolphins, but were limited to subtle geometric motifs in a classical style.

What a shame the string orchestra did not make use of the shell structure and the stage at the end of the pool, for it would make a perfect acoustic reflector for their performance, much like a miniature version of the Hollywood Bowl.

His question was answered just a few minutes later when Bianca finally made her grand entrance. She walked around the pool towards the small platform beneath the shell dome. The orchestra stopped playing and someone dimmed all the garden lights, save for one spotlight focused on the stage. Bianca took her time crossing to the stage; nodding graciously to the guests she passed. Her stark black and white outfit perfectly matched the backdrop of the evening sky. The stars in the cloudless firmament lending just the right amount of formality to the artfully staged tableau. Her white silk blouse and its daring décolletage shimmered under the spotlight. He could remember how she had looked at the Rosewood with those tensed muscles beneath stretched riding pants, waiting to pounce on the young colts. The boots and stretched pants were now supplanted by more demure black culottes.

A hush spread gradually across the garden. Bianca was in no hurry. The chefs stepped back from their grills, the bartenders stopped pouring. Finally someone tapped a crystal wine glass and all eyes turned expectantly to Bianca.

She thanked everybody for coming and hoped they were enjoying the food and wine.

"I especially want to thank you all for the continuing support you have shown my husband, Michel. Your loyalty means a great deal to us." She turned to face the spot where Mike stood in the crowd, putting her hands together so that everyone would give him a little round of applause.

Then, to Massimo's surprise, she continued, "Michel's foundation, with your generous support, continues to take thousands of homeless children off the streets each year. Its goal is to put a musical instrument into the hands of every institutionalized child. Michel has pioneered venture philanthropy in California and we hope you will further embrace our latest dream that a hand holding a musical instrument will never hold a gun nor deal a single drug."

This time the applause was much louder and Massimo was heartened to see a look of genuine pride flash across Mike's face.

Massimo placed his hands together, but did not clap. He stood there pondering this new revelation. A small statured woman standing nearby looked up admonishingly and said, "And at that time shall Michael stand up, the great prince which standeth for the children of thy people."

He blinked and looked down at her with a wrinkled brow. "Excuse me?"

"It's from the Hebrew Bible[28]. We should all praise that Michael is doing God's work here amongst us."

"Oh," was all that Massimo could reply before being hushed so that Bianca could continue.

"We also have a very special musical treat for you this evening. This is someone you're going to be seeing and hearing a lot of on the New York concert stage in the coming weeks. She is someone very close to my heart, and I am delighted to say that after an extended absence she has chosen to return to our fold. Ladies and gentlemen, I will let the music speak for itself."

She stepped to one side, and out of the dark shadows stepped a youthful figure dressed identically to Bianca. The same white silk blouse open all the way to her navel, and the same elegantly cut black culottes fell to the tops of finely strapped black stiletto heels. Bianca had filled her outfit with a toned and sculpted body, but the guest endowed hers with a vitality and advantage that only youth can possess.

Massimo snaked his way through the enraptured crowd towards the front. There was no mistaking the tightly bundled blond hair and the tall, arched body of the Nordic goddess. Hildr had returned.

She stood before them all on the raised platform, violin in her left hand, bow in her outstretched right hand, poised to play. The eyes of every male in the audience were upon her and the minimal thin white silk of her blouse. Massimo noticed just a single difference in their outfits in the form of a braid of finely spun gold rope around Hildr's neck, tied in a small knot at her throat, with the long end of the cord left dangling tantalizingly between her breasts and reaching all the way down to her navel.

She raised her bow and the unmistakable opening notes of Paganini's Caprice number 24 spilled out across the garden. A hushed gasp arose from the audience as she executed the scales and arpeggios composed of $1/16^{th}$ and $1/32^{nd}$ notes with breathless speed and precision.

Executed was an apt expression, for Massimo always found the piece to be completely devoid of any polychromatic complexity or emotion. It had been written by Paganini two centuries earlier as a vehicle to show off his own unparalleled virtuoso skills. The composition had since become a benchmark performance piece for a violinist to capture the world stage. Nevertheless, Massimo's heart clenched within his chest to hear such a beautiful instrument played with such perspicacity. The pizzicato passage machine-gunned over the audience. It finished with an incredible flourish and the crowd went wild.

"Bravo, bravo!" cried the vodka and caviar Russians from earlier, pushing Massimo aside and almost toppling him into the pool. No one looked more proud than Bianca, now beaming quietly at Hildr's side.

She raised her hand as the applause quelled. "Thank you, thank you. This is just a taste of things to come. If you want to hear more I hope you will follow us to New York for Hildr's concert tour, where I just know Hildr is going to take the world by storm." More applause followed, to which Hildr gave only the tiniest bow of acknowledgement.

"I also want to acknowledge the efforts of my dear friend Jenna from New York who is putting together this whirlwind musical tour in New York at such short notice."

A woman in an elegant black dress and neatly coiffed hair, standing in a nearby group, returned a reticent wave.

It was dark, but Massimo was struck by how much the woman looked like the Ms. Jenna Jones he knew from London. She had disappeared back into the shadows, clearly not wishing to be seen. Apparently Ms. Jones had multiple creative ways of supplementing her income with Mike and Bianca.

The applause died down and Bianca a made a final vote of thanks to everyone for coming. In the brief instant before she turned to step off the stage, she reached towards Hildr's bare midriff and gave an almost imperceptible tug to the gold rope fastened around Hildr's neck. If Massimo eyes had not still been transfixed on Hildr, he would have missed the subtle play altogether. Hildr silently and obediently followed Bianca off the stage into the darkness. Not once had she made eye contact with anyone in the audience.

The Russians were clearly enthralled with the performance, and as soon as the garden lights came back on, they were raising their glasses and making toasts to Nicolò Paganini, the violin, and beautiful women in general.

The Frenchman to Massimo's left was less enamored, and turned to his companions, saying, "It is reminiscent of a poodle dancing on its hind legs. One applauds not because it is done well, but because it is done at all."[29]

Mike was just freeing himself from a group of guests, so Massimo once more seized the opportunity to try and thank his host.

"I take it that was a violin from your collection we heard in that extraordinary performance just now?"

Mike came over with a look of satisfaction on his face.

"Indeed, the violin is one from my family collection, but the beautiful violinist belongs to Bianca."

The garden lights glimmered in the blacks of Mike's eyes, yielding no clue as to the depth of intrigue that lay behind them.

Massimo wasn't sure if it was appropriate to reveal he knew Hildr. "She is certainly a gifted performer. How did you discover her?"

Mike did not answer at once, but looked Massimo critically in the eye. It wasn't clear if he didn't want to answer Massimo's question, or whether he already knew of their connection. "She is entirely my wife's project. We discovered her in Be'er Sheba, Israel of all places. Unusual I would say, considering Hildr is Swedish. Itzhak Perlman had recognized her talent during a class he was teaching at the community center there and enthusiastically commended her ability. If Itzhak says someone has talent, my wife pays attention. I was only there to discuss the succession of the *Soil Stradivarius*, which you may or may not know was passed on from Yehudi Menuhin to Itzhak. It is the most beautiful red violin."

Massimo nodded appreciatively, but then added, "A Swedish violin prodigy surfacing in Israel, and there to be discovered by Itzhak Perlman, is certainly an amazing story."

"Bianca discovered her when Hildr was just a child prodigy. She groomed her, trained her, hired private tutors for her. She even kick started her musical career in Europe. There was a very strong bond between the two of them for many years."

More bondage than a bond, thought Massimo when he considered the gold noose about Hildr's neck.

"So it is very gratifying now for Bianca to have Hildr return to the fold after her unfortunate breakdown and disappearance."

"I didn't mean to pry."

"No, no, that's perfectly fine. Bianca is delighted to tell everyone that Hildr is making her North American debut." Mike's eyebrows gave a little upward twitch. "On the other hand, I wouldn't ever want to be the one standing between Bianca and her Hildr."

Massimo felt a cold constriction around his own throat, as if he were wearing one of Bianca's nooses. It would be wise to change the topic. "It's most gracious of you to throw a party like this in light of what has happened at WVC. And I want to congratulate you, if that's the right sentiment, on your philanthropic efforts with your foundation. It sounds like a very noble cause. Especially that you are still pursuing this after the, er, WVC affair."

Mike considered this for a moment, his crafted, genial smile never leaving his face. "We have much to celebrate. There is Bianca's musical debut. We had a banner year at WVC, and selling out to Megateck may or may not be a bad thing in the long run. And setting up your little endeavor is something to be proud of, isn't it?"

"But the takeover seemed so sudden and cutthroat," Massimo countered. "I'm concerned that Georges' actions may not be completely above board." He stopped short of revealing that they had uncovered the phantom program, but hinted at the idea that Georges might be using contrived data to support his actions.

"How is old Georges doing?" laughed Mike. The blacks of his eyes flashed, but it was impossible to tell if it was anger or mirth that lay behind them.

"Georges seems to have done remarkably well in the takeover. He is now quite highly placed in the new management organization." Massimo was trying to get some kind of indication from Mike whether he also suspected something was amiss.

All he got was a derisory laugh. Mike pulled him closer by the lapels so that he could say in a low voice, "Do you want to know how to make a small fortune on Sand Hill Road? You start by giving a large fortune to Georges!"

Massimo was clearly less amused than Mike by the sarcasm, and asked him now, point blank, what he would do in Massimo's position.

"Ride it out," was Mike's advice. "Even if the Megateck IPO is wildly overpriced, it's not going to harm you personally." He laid a hand on Massimo's shoulder and propelled him back towards the food and drink, indicating that the discussion was over. It was time for Massimo to thank his host one last time and take his leave.

As he walked across the garden back towards the driveway to where he supposed his car would be, a figure stepped out of the shadows to make sure he knew which way to go. It was another of the bulging security types, dressed for this evening in waiter's attire, but making sure no-one stepped out of the permitted areas. His car pulled into the driveway at the same time he did. Clearly, the movements of the guests were closely monitored for them to know in advance which car to bring to the driveway.

The drive home gave him time to mull over what he had learned that evening, but was he any the wiser as to what was going on? On the other hand, he'd had a pretty good education in how the privileged and wealthy class lived.

Next morning he didn't feel particularly compelled to go to the office early. When he did finally arrive, he was surprised to find Laura chatting with Lars and Sven.

"I thought I should come by at least once before I leave to see where you guys hang out nowadays, and what you do." Her voice was a little more nasal than usual, and Massimo noticed she had a number of tissues wadded into her sleeve at the wrist.

Massimo stood behind her and gave her a friendly squeeze at the waist. "I'll make you some tea with lemon. You should drink plenty of fluids to help fight off your cold." He moved around them and into the kitchen to search for a clean mug and some tea bags. Half a lemon lay forlornly in the refrigerator, wrinkled with age, but it would do fine in a mug of tea. He could hear them chatting in the other room as he boiled the water for tea.

"I hear that Hildr also came to visit you guys a couple of times to see what you do here." Laura was obviously not going to let go of the topic of Hildr's sudden departure.

"Yeah, she thought it was pretty cool," Sven cut in brightly, "but we all know that it was just an excuse for her to see Massimo."

Laura looked daggers at them both. Lars was quick to realize her misinterpretation and added, "What he means is that all Hildr was thinking about was her crazy dissertation topic, and she thought our *Professore* here could save her."

Massimo returned to the room bearing two steaming mugs of tea. "I think I now know why Hildr quit Stanford," he said, placing one mug down in front of Laura. "Here, I squeezed some lemon into your tea and I even found some honey, so I think it will be quite soothing for your cold."

Laura ignored the tea. "Why? Have you heard from her? What happened?"

Massimo slid the tea a little more across the table toward Laura, indicating she should drink it. "It's a long story, but it all makes sense now, so drink your tea and I'll try and explain."

Lars and Sven also stopped what they were doing and sat down on either side of Laura to listen.

"I saw Hildr last night at the party," he began.

"What? Why on earth would Hildr attend a party for investment bankers, of all people?" Laura immediately interrupted.

"Well, if you let me finish, I'll explain. Now drink your tea." He laid his hands flat on the table, enjoying the theatricality of the moment, their eyes all fixed on him in suspense.

"Quite simply put, Hildr is returning to the concert stage to take up her musical career again. At the party last night she gave a short recital as a sort of preview to her upcoming New York concert tour."

Sven let out a short whistle. "No kidding!"

Laura took a gulp of tea in astonishment, and realized too late how hot it was.

Massimo continued. "The intriguing part is that we all knew about the story of her early musical career in Europe, and that it came to a stormy end."

"Yes, she left to get away from her patron. He was probably a dirty old man trying to take advantage of her." Laura blew in annoyance across the too hot tea, spilling some on the table which she then wiped with her clutch of tissues.

"Not so fast. It's more complicated than that." Massimo waited a couple of seconds in silence, admonishing her to not interrupt his storytelling. "What we didn't realize was that her patron followed her here to America, or possibly just came here to the same place by coincidence, and now Hildr is reunited with her patron."

"So who is this patron? Get to the point will you. You're so annoying when you drag out a story like this." She looked to one side to cover her embarrassment that the cold was making her more short tempered than usual.

"It turns out that Mike's family had been her patron, and that's why she was giving her American debut recital at his party last night."

Lars lifted his head in a moment of realization. "That's why she stormed out of the office last time she was here. Not because of Mass and his mathematics, but because she was in the office when Mike came by and she saw and overheard them talking together; she must have realized her past had caught up with her."

Sven also ventured forth with an opinion. "If she was really paranoid, our Ice Queen would have thought that Mass was in some kind of conspiracy to hunt her down and hand her over to her patron. Her past would have looked inescapable to her."

Laura looked skeptical. "You want me to believe that your Mike followed her all the way to America and set this all up just to get her back?"

"No, I don't think it was quite like that." Massimo pondered the question. "Mike is a wealthy man, and if he had ambitions to invest in America, it's quite natural that he would come to Sand Hill Road where all the venture capital companies preside. He may not have known that Hildr was next door at Stanford enrolling in a math program."

Laura grimaced. "Ugh, I never held these capitalist financiers in high regard, and now I hear that he's the one who tried to take advantage of poor Hildr."

"Hold on a moment. There is another twist to the story. It is not Mike so much as his wife Bianca who was actually Hildr's patron. You've never met Bianca to appreciate what a character she is. Hildr had been under Bianca's wing since her adolescence, at least according to Mike. Her violin comes from Mike's private collection, but the musical training and tutelage was all taken care of by Bianca. There is quite a strong 'bind' between the two of them, I believe."

Laura looked perplexed. "If Bianca was the patron, then why all the drama of the stormy separation when Mike was not the one exploiting her?"

"Ah! Hildr may have gotten herself tied up in something that led to a rather intimate power struggle between herself and Bianca." Massimo told them first how Bianca and Hildr were dressed almost identically, like twins, and then how Hildr wore a gold braided rope around her neck which Bianca had tugged at like a leash.

Lars and Sven were in stitches. This was too much for their juvenile little minds. "Our Ice Queen was really a Bondage Queen?" They roared with laughter. "It sounds like something from *The Story of O*."

"Do you think she had a bondage studio right here on the Stanford campus?" laughed Sven.

Laura's face went bright red.

Lars and Sven didn't notice, for Sven was jabbing Lars on the arm. "Did she have you in knots, buddy?"

Massimo noticed. He sat across from Laura looking directly into her face and tried to suppress a little smile.

Laura leaned her head over the table so that her brown curls fell forward and covered her face. "This head cold is getting me all flushed," she said, excusing herself to go to the bathroom.

Lars and Sven went back to their work, their conversation punctuated with occasional bursts of laughter as they thought of new circumstances in which Hildr may have practiced her craft. Massimo took the tea mugs back to the kitchen and was washing them when Laura returned.

"The photographs?" were the only two words he uttered.

"Never you mind." She leaned back on the kitchen counter. Her jeans looked tighter than normal, and she had on a turtle neck sweater that flattered her soft brown curls. Maybe, in spite of her reddened, stuffy nose she looked more becoming to Massimo because he was so tickled pink by her reaction to the exposé of Hildr's secret life.

"It's not what you think," she finally began when Massimo had managed to refrain from saying anything for a whole minute. Laura was about to continue when they were interrupted by a cry from the other room,

"Oh no, not again!"

Massimo stepped back into the other room, and was met by groans from both Lars and Sven. Laura followed, pleased that she didn't have to answer any more questions for the time being.

Lars sat there glumly. "All our programs are running at an excruciatingly slow pace again."

Sven had pulled out his box of screen wipes again, as if that was going to magically help. "At least we know what to look for this time." The commands he began typing in rapid fire contained a lot of back-slash characters, and that key had developed a loud click on his keyboard in the last few days. Everyone in the room became mesmerized by his syncopated typing.

Lars started jabbing at the monitor screen. "There! There, it's back again, see."

Sven was on to him at once. "Would you stop poking at the screen with your fingers. I hate it when you do that." He had his screen wipes at the ready.

Laura was standing behind the three of them, arms folded, amazed that the mood in the room could change so quickly. "Would someone please mind telling me what's going on?"

"It's the phantom," Massimo replied. "The phantom copy of our program has returned and is once again hogging all of the computer system so that our version of the program can't run anymore."

Lars was now keeping his hands in his pockets to avoid Sven wrapping his knuckles for touching his precious screens again. "We may as well take a look at whatever fake data it's analyzing. We can't get to our own data while this is running."

For Laura's benefit, Massimo then added, "Last time this happened we discovered somebody was running a stolen copy of our program, but running it backward so that it generated fake data rather than analyze the real world data. Hildr helped us figure out that the data was completely synthesized."

Massimo cracked a little smile. "She really tied it up for us."

Lars's came back with an immediate rejoinder. "She was bound to get it right."

Sven couldn't resist either. "We were shackled by that problem."

"Oh, for heaven's sake, give it a rest." Laura pushed back the curls from her head, but she knew there was not going to be any mercy from this lot.

The monitor screens filled with data as Sven completed his typing. "There. That's what the phantom is doing right now, in real time."

"It doesn't much resemble the data we were looking at last time," said Lars, peering closely at the screen, but still keeping his hands in his pockets so Sven wouldn't get upset with him.

"Let's run Hildr's test. That'll show us quickly enough whether someone is up to the same tricks again." Massimo sat down in front of them and started methodically typing.

"I got it," said Sven, charging in ahead of Massimo. "I saw how she did it last time."

Massimo wondered why he bothered sometimes, with these two lightning kids around.

"I can tell you now," said Lars stepping back from the screen, "this is a completely different kind of data set than last time." He plunked himself down in a swivel chair in front of Massimo to make his point. The chair pivot sank all the way to the bottom of its travel under the sudden weight. "The fake data last time was all about transactions outside of WVC. They were trying to make the WVC group of startups appear to be more valuable in the marketplace. This time it is all internal data from Megateck that we are seeing."

Massimo held his chin between thumb and forefinger, scratching the stubble he found there. He hadn't bothered to shave that morning. "What do you think, Sven, is it real data? What does the Hildr test tell us?"

Sven's fingers were still dancing over the keyboard. "Hang on, I'm almost there. Gi'me just one sec."

"Do you think it's the same people?" asked Massimo, thinking aloud.

"No doubt about it," answered Sven, still busy with the last bit of data. "It's the same piece of code, with the same authentication key."

"But why would someone first want to generate fake market data for a group of companies, and then start running the program on internal data for the Megateck corporation?" said Massimo, still trying to make sense of it all.

"Bingo," said Sven, leaning back at last from the keyboard. "Hildr's little test tells us that this is not fake data like last time, but real world data for the Megateck Corp.."

"But that would be highly confidential corporate data, not available for public viewing," protested Massimo.

"Yes, but we are inside the Megateck firewall now. They took us over, remember?" said Lars.

"Atchoo!" came a loud sneeze from Laura. "I'm sorry," she said with her nose in a bunch of tissues. "I bet I picked up this cold virus on the East Coast, and it lay dormant until I got back to San Francisco before attacking me."

Massimo felt sorry for the sore nose she was carefully dabbing with tissues. "Can I get you another hot tea with lemon? Do you want to put your feet up?"

"Some organisms have evolved ingenious methods for depositing their genetic material inside a host. I hate the fact that this cold virus has got the better of me, but as a biologist I have to admire its skilled strategy," she said with a pitiable sniff. "That's what you guys are. Just carriers of a disease."

"What…?" said Massimo, bewildered. "We made you sick?" He looked at Lars and Sven to see if they knew what she was suddenly talking about.

"You guys and your little startup are just a Trojan horse," she answered, looking up and slowly opening her eyes in a way that suggested the stuffiness was also giving her a pounding headache.

"The ancient Greeks were never able to broach the mighty city walls of Troy so they left an irresistible gift outside its gates before they departed. The Trojans claimed this beautiful carved, wooden horse with its belly full of soldiers as the spoils of victory and took it inside their city."

They all looked at her in amazement.

"The Trojans were history after that," she concluded with a little smile.

"Do you realize," said Lars, "that twice now, it has taken a woman to come in here and figure out what the hell is going on."

"I'll tell you what," Sven answered to Lars. "I can tell you which part of the horse you are!"

"This is too much," said an exasperated Massimo. "Are you telling me that this whole venture has been a ruse to get access to Megateck's confidential internal financial data?"

There was a gloomy murmur of agreement and nodding of heads as the truth sank in.

Massimo lost interest in fingering the stubble on his chin and slammed his fist on the table. "Why?" Laura gave a little jump at his sudden outburst, realizing how much this must be hurting his pride.

"What do they possibly hope to gain by this elaborate deception?" he ranted.

"We have front row seats to watch what unfolds and find out," said Sven, pointing at the screens. "We can see all the company dealings from here, in real time."

"Do you think they know that we are watching?" asked Lars.

"They might, but I don't think they even care," was Massimo's reply.

# Chapter 17 – The Players

The narrow leather saddle of a Campagnolo bicycle is supposed, with time, to conform itself exactly to the contours of its owner's body. The true, hardcore cyclist will always claim the narrow leather saddle is superior to the squishy gels of a modern commuter bicycle. The worn and sculpted leather will recognize its owner and allow the bike and rider to meld as one. This bicycle seat knew Massimo. It knew exactly where all the pressure points in his backside were and it was now mercilessly probing them one by one as he cycled over the rolling hills just above the Stanford campus

This was just the warm-up phase, he reminded himself, for he was setting out to do the major loop up to Skyline and along the ridge of the Santa Cruz Mountains. The pain would subside. The leather of the seat would become more supple as it warmed up, and so would his backside, he hoped. There was a sense of determination in his hope, and a certain perverse pleasure in the pain he was feeling. With each downward push of the pedals, he stretched out the knots in his calves and felt himself doing penance for all the turmoil of the last few days.

It had been a tumultuous 48 hours since he had to come to the realization in his Sand Hill Road office that his startup company and his brilliant program had been a façade, a Trojan horse to get inside the Megateck Corporation.

A strenuous bicycle ride into the hills was just the thing to purge his mind and soul and put events into perspective.

A single coil of hard spring steel beneath the leather saddle was the only cushioning between him and the pavement. Every undulation, every bump in the tarmac was going to transmit itself to his frame and shake out any feelings of self-pity he may have accumulated in the last 48 hours.

The route he had chosen was a good one, he thought. He'd set out along Sand Hill Road to the west, over the freeway, but instead of heading straight up into the hills he'd turned right onto Whiskey Hill Rd, toward the town of Woodside. This would give his untrained body more of a chance to warm up on the gentle hills before tackling the steep grades.

Whiskey Hill Rd had inspired the name of Lars and Sven's beer. They had remained with him in the office for the previous 48 hours, watching events unfold.

As he cycled along the shoulder, only the dust from the horse farm rose in his peripheral vision; a midweek morning in the Stanford Hills and not a car in sight.

The markets had been quiet as well when they had opened on that Monday morning. The quiet before the storm.

Lars had called him early Monday morning before Massimo had even come into the office. Obviously, Lars had his antennae out listening to every news feed that was even remotely connected with activities at WVC.

"Tune your TV to the cable news Business Network," he had advised. "There is a show being broadcast right now, featuring an interview with Kate, talking about the Megateck IPO."

Kate's bright red hair was unmistakable on the TV screen when he found the right channel.

"I think the WVC Group of companies was on a sound footing," she was saying. "But in answer to your question, an IPO may still be considered by some to be premature at this stage."

The camera had switched to footage of exuberant Megateck executives at the time the IPO had first been announced. If Massimo was not mistaken, that was Georges in the background sporting a wide brimmed Texan hat.

The presenter was trying to goad Kate into revealing more.

"I think Megateck is a lucrative investment bank with a lot of strength from their vast holdings, but their fast-track tactics here are questionable, to say the least."

"If you wouldn't mind, Kate, walk us through what happens in a typical IPO, and just how this one is different."

"Certainly, Larry. There's a lot at stake here and I want to congratulate your show on doing the best job at keeping the investing public informed." A loud crash occurred somewhere off screen and a startled look crossed the presenter's face, but Kate was unfazed. "The job of the venture capitalists is doing all the due diligence necessary to bring a company to the public. Venture capital firms not only find the new and exciting nascent technologies, but we nurture them with seed money and put them on a sound business footing."

"But it doesn't stop there, does it Kate?" fawned Larry, flashing his whiter-than-white teeth at the camera.

"Indeed, Larry, there are several stages of funding we go through to really prove that the company has a sound business model before we even approach the Securities and Exchange Commission with an application to list a new company on the exchange. And even then, the application process with the SEC can take upwards of a year."

"But that is not what's happening here, is it Kate? We'll be right back with more of our in-depth coverage of today's top story."

Massimo had called Lars back during the commercial break. "She's very cool and collected considering she just got ousted in the takeover." He could hear Sven shout in the background that the show was back on already.

The presenter had theatrically removed his jacket to convey that he was really getting down to business; he had an annoying way of barking his commentary at the camera to hype up the news story, but Kate didn't bat an eyelid. "The investment bankers at Megateck are bypassing our rigorous protocol and are doing a backdoor IPO, Larry. It really is audacious of them."

"Tell us what a backdoor IPO is, Kate. You're doing such a great job at explaining these technicalities to us 'Street people. I'll have to watch out, I hear you might be looking for a new job yourself."

Kate's eyes flinched ever so slightly at the last remark. "A backdoor IPO, Larry, if you're not up on your 'Street jargon, is when a shell company is used to list the new venture on the stock market. A reverse takeover of the shell company by the startup gets them a place on the trading floor."

"Is that something typical, Kate, which you West Coast people do nowadays with your IPOs?"

"No, Larry, it's not." She paused to let the severity of the situation sink in. "Backdoor IPOs are something we've only seen with some questionable Chinese startups trying to get listed on the American exchanges. Backdoor IPOs are part of an ongoing SEC investigation right now over the legality and ethicality of such tactics. You won't find that anywhere on Sand Hill Road, but if you are looking for something closer to home, check with your squids, Larry, right here on Wall Street."

"Whoa! Remember folks, you heard it right here on the morning show on the business network. We'll be right back with the fire-breathing Kate to see if she'll give us a 'Street definition of a squid."

In retrospect, Massimo decided as he leaned forward in the saddle, Kate had filled in many of the gaps in his knowledge of financial practices with that interview.

Whiskey Hill Rd led Massimo past the old Pioneer Saloon into the center of the town of Woodside and its single stop sign. The general store at the crossroads had made way for a gourmet grocery store, more in keeping with the needs of the current residents. Only the Pioneer Saloon served as a reminder to the bygone era when the town was named for its whisky still. Ironically, Whiskey Hill owed its nefarious reputation in part to Stanford's no-alcohol policy within one mile of the campus perimeter. The consequence of which had been a burgeoning of bars and liquor stores in locales at the one mile marker point. Whiskey Hill was at the western boundary, and Whiskey Gulch, another den of iniquity, had stood at the eastern portal, down by the Bayshore.

Hard to believe that all now, as Massimo cycled along Woodside Rd, past the present day exclusive residences. The road, as it exited the town was still flat and uneventful, just as the financial markets had been that opening morning. After watching Kate take her stance in the interview, he had driven in to join Lars and Sven at the office to watch the further unfurling of events. The road ahead was about to get steep, but Massimo was warmed up now, and his legs beat a steady rhythm.

Rather than take the main road to the summit, his route was going to loop back towards Sand Hill Road by turning left onto Portola Rd. His goal was to take the Old La Honda Rd to the Skyline ridge, a road less traveled and far more circuitous than the highway. A fitting tribute to events of the last few days, with its hair raising 180° hairpin bends to be negotiated en route to the summit.

Portola Rd was lined with giant eucalyptus trees, another legacy from Leland Stanford's railroad baron years. Introduced from their native Australia, they had proven to be a terrible construction timber in the railroad industry, but their prolific growth in the California soils provided Stanford with a ready source of firewood. Apparently, they were free of pests here, and grew unchecked to great heights so that they now towered over his head. Perhaps herds of ferocious koala bears should be introduced into California to cull these boisterous gum trees!

Mike shared quite a bit in common with Leland Stanford. They were both entrepreneurs who played by their own 'unconventional' rules in developing whole new industries and markets.

Stanford had gone on to become California's first republican governor, and may even have had aspirations to the Presidency of the United States, but spent his fortune instead on the founding of a university. It was debatable what cost more, running for president or founding a university. And which resulted in greater power and left a more significant mark on the land? At least the country would be spared a bid by Mike for the Presidency, given that he hadn't been born in the United States; just like the country had been spared the last Republican Californian Governor's aspirations for presidency because of his Austrian heritage.

There had been no sign of Mike during the TV interviews, but it was clear that Kate was doing his bidding. When the IPO hit the trading floor nothing had happened, but it was ominous. The price held steady, but the volume wasn't there; nobody was buying.

Portola Rd, along which he was now cycling, lies in a slight depression which is actually part of the fault zone of the San Andreas. To his left lay the Stanford campus and Sand Hill Road, smugly attached to the American Continental plate, but the hills rising steeply to his right were part of the Pacific plate, pushing and grinding its way along the fault line. This foreign, geological intruder wanted to shake Stanford and Sand Hill Road to its core, and it did so with regularity every 100 years or so. Eventually, this piece of the Pacific plate would tear itself loose from California and make its way north. The way Massimo was feeling now he would have preferred to go with it, leaving Sand Hill Road far behind.

Massimo had been able to watch the opening day of market antics from an insider's perspective with unprecedented clarity, courtesy of the phantom program, still spewing out its data on the screens in their office. An offshore hedge fund consortium, it appeared, was buying the majority of the IPO shares, but only at a trickle, just enough to make the share prices rise modestly. At any moment now the fray was supposed to step in and the price would take off in a buying frenzy; a magnitude 7, or greater, on the Richter scale of market movements.

At the end of Portola Rd, his cycle route briefly rejoined the stately Sand Hill Road, but not for long, for then he veered off onto the narrow, winding route of Old La Honda Rd. The leisurely part of the ride was over and a grueling assent lay ahead of him. There were 1500 vertical feet between Stanford and the summit of Skyline. He took a deep swig from his water bottle, knowing that he would soon be breathing hard and it would be more difficult to gulp down water. No doubt some of the Stanford athletes regarded this route as an easy lunchtime hill climb. But, just as with his foray into the financial markets, he felt a little trepidatious about tackling this hill for the first time. It was daunting to think that these hills had been formed by mighty seismic forces beneath his feet, acting out of sight of the surface inhabitants, but ready to tear the land apart.

On their computer screens, what Massimo, along with Lars and Sven had seen, but the rest of the world had not, was that Megateck was moving to take a long position on the IPO stock. In other words, they were betting the house that the new stock offer would continue to rise sharply in price.

Sven began to get very excited as he crunched some of the numbers. "If Georges' model is correct, then Megateck stands to make a record profit at this rate. No wonder they were so keen to act on this quickly."

Lars was less enamored. "*IF* Georges' model is correct. Georges' numbers are garbage."

"But evidently the rest of the market doesn't know that," Sven had muttered.

"What's more," Massimo had added, "by the time the market does find out, Megateck will have already made a killing. By taking a long position, they're double dipping, and are going to be feeding like pigs in a trough."

Lars was still not convinced. "They stand to make a record profit, but they are also leaving themselves very exposed. Even if it's for a very short time, and nobody catches on to what they are up to, it's a tremendous risk to take, not to mention that it's totally illegal."

Massimo encountered the first hairpin bend as he made his way up the narrow reaches of the road. Fortunately, very few cars used this road. It was strictly for residents' cars only. At the apex of the turn the pavement was very steep, and Massimo had to rise from his saddle and stand on the pedals to get around the bend. Confusingly, he was now heading in the opposite direction than before, and the sun in his eyes was making it difficult to see the road ahead. The steep grade would turn him around several times on this route, so that he would lose track completely of where he was heading. Of course, on a narrow, windy track there is only one way to go, namely up, but it is disconcerting to discover you can be so mistaken as to which direction you are actually heading.

Massimo, Lars and Sven had no option but to watch the Megateck market strategy play itself out, even though they were also without a clue which direction they were actually heading.

A new play abruptly started on the sidelines, away from the main action, and initially unobserved by Megateck. The hedge fund that had been buying up the IPO stocks suddenly changed its strategy. It was now taking a short position on Megateck shares. In other words, it was betting that the value of Megateck shares would drop at some time in the near future. By taking a short position the offshore hedge fund had the option of buying up Megateck shares if the price ever dropped and then immediately selling them back again and getting the present high price. This was a very unusual strategy to take for someone buying the shares from the IPO that Megateck was brokering.

Megateck didn't seem to notice this change in strategy. Their eye was on the ball in play, namely the IPO itself, and not someone tossing a ball around on the sidelines.

The second hairpin was coming up. Massimo was breathing heavily, but enjoying the endorphin rush from the exertion. This time he executed the steep turn adroitly, not missing a single beat as he rose out of the saddle. He thought he was now heading south, but couldn't really tell with the stand of trees rising up around him to swallow the sky.

If the offshore hedge fund's strategy for shorting the Megateck stock had seemed a little odd, its next step was truly bizarre. It suddenly did an about face and began to take a very large position in shorting the same IPO stock it had just been buying. It appeared as if the hedge fund was shooting itself in the foot. Normally, when an IPO is made, people who believe in the stock will vie for the shares and push the price up. The nonbelievers don't buy and don't exert pressure on the price, but it was counterintuitive for someone to actually bet on a negative outcome. The offshore hedge fund was doing more than this. They were dumping a huge amount of money into this short position. It could have a destabilizing effect and all the money it had invested in its earlier buying of the IPO shares could be lost.

Such an action is hard to keep secret for long, especially if someone is taking such a large position. The market can get easily spooked by such rumors and everyone starts running away from the stock.

Not quite the stampede that Megateck would have envisioned for themselves.

Massimo figured he was about half way up the climb. The endorphin rush had worn off, and now it was just a slow, steady slog.

Sven had looked worried as their monitors had revealed the apparent about turn in events. "If the IPO does well, our stock options are worth more, right?" It was a rhetorical question, for what he was really saying was that if the IPO tanked, then there would go their chances of cashing in.

"I hate being beholden to Georges' planning," was Lars's only comment.

Massimo was beginning to catch on to what was really going on. "This offshore hedge fund is intent on manipulating things to its own end. This is not an IPO anymore, but a play for power."

Indeed, the hedge fund suddenly stopped buying. Minutes ticked by and nobody else appeared to be buying either. The last transaction price hovered unchanged on the screen for several minutes. Then it dipped, first a little, and then a precipitous plunge.

"Whoa! What's going on?" came Sven's hoarse voice.

Lars had also caught on to what was really going on. "The hedge fund is dumping all the IPO stock it just bought this morning."

Sven was unprepared for this. "What a waste. It'll lose millions."

As the price approached the marker point that Massimo had originally set for the stock offering, the plunge appeared to level out. The offshore hedge fund didn't appear to care that it had lost money on its initial stock purchase; it had a more ambitious plan in mind.

All this replayed itself through Massimo's mind as he cycled up the last stretch of the Old La Honda grade. His lungs were rasping now, his calves burning and his body was soaked in sweat, but he was determined to get to the top, to push through to the end.

Sven had not done well that morning. Although none of them had actually lost money, it was still painful to have a large sum dangled in front of their noses and then see it turn to smoke.

"Is that it, are we safe now? Are we going to at least be hundred-thousand-aires if we can't be millionaires?"

Lars was more wrapped up in the financial mechanics of what was going on, and paying less attention to the tally of how much was going to end up in their pockets.

"It's not over yet," he had said. "The price has only stabilized because Megateck is buying the stock themselves in an attempt to stop the free fall. But they are doing it at a tremendous loss because of the long position they took at the beginning of the day when they bet the store on the price only going up."

Massimo had walked up behind the two of them and placed a hand on each of their shoulders.

"Gentleman, I believe we have just witnessed our Trojan horse opening the city gates of Troy from within, to allow the invading army to enter."

Lars and Sven turned at the same time to look up at him.

"The offshore hedge fund that has been doing all the buying and selling is clearly using our program here to monitor every move by Megateck from within. It lured them into taking a vulnerable position, and now that they have over extended themselves I think we are going to be privy to a financial *coup d'état*."

The grueling bicycle ride finally reached the summit. The narrow, one lane road broke out from under the canopy of trees and into the sunshine of Skyline Boulevard. Massimo leaned back on the bicycle saddle, briefly letting go of the handlebars while he coasted along the flat. He was able to take a few tentative sips from his water bottle as his breathing gradually subsided. He would have dearly loved to have thrown himself onto the grassy roadside verge, but he knew he would never be able to remount his bicycle if he did. His muscles would stiffen in the cool breeze blowing across the ridge line and he would barely be able to stand, let alone cycle back down the hill. Instead, he cycled graciously along the ridge, maintaining just enough pace to keep his muscles warm, and allowing his shirt to dry in the breezy sunshine. He fumbled in his pocket for a Cliff Bar, the one piece of sustenance he had brought with him. He hoped it would quell the internal shaking of his over exerted body.

The ridge line road offered spectacular views over the Bay. It presented him with a new perspective as he slowly made out familiar landmarks in the hazy distance. The Hoover Tower marked the Stanford campus, and the familiar two-mile long east-west line of the SLAC linear accelerator could be seen ducking under the 280 freeway. Beyond, he could make out the Dumbarton Bridge, and further to the north, the San Mateo Bridge crossing the Bay.

It was uplifting to take in the big picture after having been so intently focused just a few feet ahead on a narrow, steep trail.

When he had finally seen the big picture on the trading floor it had also come as a relief. Not because the damage that had been done was any less, but because he could finally see what all the players were doing. The IPO and the sale of the startup companies had never been the issue. The prize all along was the fat, asset laden hulk of the Megateck Corporation.

Shortly after Massimo had elucidated his theory to Lars and Sven that the hedge fund must be using the phantom program to penetrate Megateck, the carnage had begun. The hedge fund dumped all its remaining IPO stock, and in the panic that ensued, every single financial institution that held the IPO shares dumped theirs as well. There was no way that Megateck could buy back all these shares, and the price plummeted to below $1 per share. Trading ceased. It was all over.

"Bloody hell," was all that Lars had managed to say when the IPO name disappeared from the listing of publicly traded companies on the exchange.

Massimo looked at them sympathetically. "I'm afraid it's still not over."

Sven just grunted. "What else is left?"

"Think about what this will mean for Megateck stock price. Who's going to want Megateck shares after word of this fiasco gets around."

The hedge fund was obviously waiting for this to happen. It had invested on a short position for Megateck, betting heavily on Megateck stock going down. It left nothing to chance and gave the herd a nudge by selling off a reserve of Megateck shares it had cunningly acquired for this purpose. The price fell just a little, but that's all it took to spook other investors to follow suit.

By the end of the day Megateck shares had closed at about 50% of their starting value.

Massimo's muscles had warmed down nicely as he cruised northwards along Skyline Boulevard. The Cliff Bar had hit the spot, and he'd nearly emptied his water bottle. He had now reached the Kings Mountain Rd turnoff, where his route would take him back down the mountain. He allowed himself a brief stop, not dismounting, but just resting back on his saddle to gaze out through the trees at Silicon Valley spread out below: the source of unimaginable wealth and enterprise. He imagined he could see the dust rising in the distance from the Megateck bulls stampeding in retreat.

At the close of that fateful day of trading, Massimo had believed that it was now all over, but it was Lars who announced what would happen next.

"It doesn't end here for Megateck. There will be afterhours trading by all the financial institutions involved. We may not get to see the final bloodletting, but there is sure to be a *margin call* after this trading disaster."

Massimo had asked what exactly a margin call was. Lars was in his element.

"Megateck placed a bet, but worse than that, they made it with borrowed funds. It's like going to the track with $10 and being so certain your horse is going to win, you borrow $100 to place the bet so that you can win so much more. The bookie agrees because you're a reliable customer with a good bank account. Unfortunately for Megateck, the offshore hedge fund made the opposite bet that Megateck shares would go down in value. They can buy up any Megateck shares at the low, closing price, then take them to the broker and get paid the original high price for them.

The broker, in order to cover his losses, will go to Megateck and demand immediate repayment of their debt.

That's the margin call.

In order to raise funds to pay the broker, Megateck will be forced to sell off even more of its stock at the unfavorable price. It will be a vicious spiral for them because the hedge fund will snap up all the shares they can buy and be paid full price for them.

A lot of wealth is going to change hands very quickly."

Lars had enjoyed the fact that he could explain in simple terms something of great enormity, but the impact it was going to have on their own little enterprise made him turn white as a sheet.

Sven, in turn, panicked.

"Lars, what does it mean for us? Lars! Lars, what's going to happen?"

In silence, Lars had reached forward, flipped off the switch to the monitor screen, and walked out of the room.

At the top of Kings Mountain Rd Massimo gave a little squeeze to the brake levers. It was a long and steep descent. The ride down would be exhilarating and raise his adrenaline level. Not so for Megateck. Their decent was equally fast, and without the benefit of any brake levers.

Already on the first sharp turn Massimo narrowly avoided a patch of loose gravel and dangerously crossed the centerline as he pelted down the hill. A sobering experience that reminded him to take the rest of the hill a little more cautiously.

What had Mike told him at the party when he had asked his advice concerning the takeover? – "Just ride it out." That's what he was doing now. Events had gathered such momentum that there would be no stopping until he reached the Valley floor.

The next morning after the trading day massacre, Massimo had received another early phone call from Lars and Sven.

"It's happened. We're locked out of our offices."

There was a sense of déjà vu when he drove his car up to the office entrance and the guard asked to see his identity card before allowing him to pass. It was a different security firm from the previous time, though.

Lars and Sven were waiting for him at the building entrance where another guard instructed them once more to go to the main office to receive further clearance.

To their surprise it was Cindy who greeted them, all organized and businesslike, with a stack of forms and papers, as though she had never been away from the premises during the last few weeks.

This time, instead of being invited to sit down and watch a video, she escorted them to a small meeting room to explain in person the new order of things.

"The Megateck Corporation has been taken over by a private consortium," she began. "The previous management structure of the publicly traded Megateck entity has been dissolved, and a new private consortium, headed by Mike and Kate will take over."

"The little fish turned around and ate the big fish," chuckled Sven.

"I think there may be some misunderstanding of the relative sizes of the fish involved," she said, looking back at him over the rim of her glasses.

She pushed a number of forms over the table for them to sign.

"These are for you to acknowledge the new ownership of the company, and the dissolution of the previous organization."

"Yes, we know," said Massimo scrawling his signature over the bottom of the forms. "We've been through this procedure once already."

Cindy ignored the remark and pushed the next bundle of forms toward them. "These are to reaffirm the intellectual property rights that you agreed to when you joined WVC; namely that all software programs, financial analysis tools and data are the exclusive property of the new WVC Corporation."

Lars rolled his eyes as they were instructed to initial each page and sign the last one.

"And finally, these are non-disclosure statements, stating that you will not discuss the findings of any financial analysis outside of WVC."

"Is that it?" said Massimo, bored and exasperated. "Can we get back to our office now?"

Cindy pulled all the signed papers towards her, putting them back in neat piles and binding them with clips.

"I'm afraid it's not that simple. Your QDOT Company doesn't exist anymore."

Massimo had been standing up, readying to go, but sat down again with a thud.

"What? How can that possibly be? Companies can't just suddenly disappear." He was both angry and frustrated that there was some further twist of betrayal he had not seen.

"You may recall that your company went public yesterday with an initial purchase offering. The IPO failed and the company listing was removed from the exchange. The new WVC consortium then bought up the remaining stock and has now privatized the holdings."

"So where's the problem? Isn't it back to business as usual, just like before the Megateck nightmare?" Massimo was annoyed that he was still not grasping the complete picture, and dropped any semblance of politeness towards Cindy.

She pulled back from him, the signed papers now safely tucked away. Her tone was cold and detached.

"Under the reorganization Mike and Kate decided that your company no longer fitted in with the goals and mission of the new WVC consortium."

Lars stared at her through narrow, slitted eyes. "All the programs and data will remain with WVC, though?"

"That is correct," she answered.

"And under the terms of the non-disclosure statement you made us sign, we would not be able to go to another company and work on a similar program?"

"Correct."

Sven was squirming, unable to believe that he was about to lose access to the greatest computer system he'd ever laid his hands on. The three of them looked from one to the other in silence. Massimo made one last ditch effort.

"Can't we discuss this with Mike, at least?"

But Cindy was immovable.

"Both Mike and Kate are in Switzerland, meeting with the new consortium. Their instructions were absolutely clear."

"That's it, then," said Massimo finally. "It's over."

"There will of course be a final disbursement of any remaining equity from your former company, and you will be advised of the outcome in due course."

Massimo felt nothing but contempt.

"Pah! Equity. What's that if we don't even have the rights to our computer code anymore?"

"Any personal effects on the premises will be packed and sent to the private address we have for you on file. Coffee mugs and such like. The security gentleman will escort you out."

She turned and left without so much as a farewell handshake.

Massimo had felt totally hollowed out that night. His departure from WVC and farewell to Lars and Sven was now just a blur. He could not even remember what he may have said as condolences to them. Clearly, a total reevaluation of his career was in order. Possibly his whole life, now that he was feeling sufficiently melodramatic about it all. A return to SLAC would take some time and negotiation since he had taken an extended leave.

That's when the idea of finally doing the epic bicycle tour of the mountains occurred to him. The mighty Sierras and Lake Tahoe lay in wait. He would have to get in shape, though. He could picture a slimmed-down, spandex covered version of himself whizzing over grades and mountain passes, undaunted by sun or snow.

And that is how he now found himself on his first foray into the foothills. A mere 27 mile training loop that had taken him four hours, and he was exhausted. On the other hand, it had cleared his mind, and put things in perspective. Freewheeling down the mountain, leaning into the turns, watching the redwoods flash by, he felt he could still appreciate nature. Nobody could take mathematics and physics away from him. He would just have to admit to himself that he had been gullible in his dealings with the financial giants of the venture capital world. Life would go on, and eventually he would be able to say to himself that he had learned a valuable lesson.

When the mind is at rest, the stomach soon follows. The Cliff Bar was the only thing he had eaten all morning, and a sandwich and salad at the SLAC cafeteria didn't sound like a bad idea. He could also drop by his old office and see which work colleagues might be about.

Those were his thoughts as he cycled down Sand Hill Road, approaching the SLAC main gate. The office park workers were also returning from their executive lunch meetings, always in a hurry to be ahead of the next market announcement. An armada of German engineering sped past him. A black BMW slowed down as it passed him, regarding him with the soulless eyes of its dark tinted windows. Instead of pulling away, it suddenly cut in front of him, into the bicycle lane and slammed on the brakes.

With no room to maneuver, Massimo's hands instinctively reached forward. His fingertips just reached the brake levers as, first, the high pressure bicycle tire, then the lightweight rim and high tensile spokes contacted the rear of the car and crumpled like paper. Massimo's body hurtled forward in a ballistic trajectory over the car. Even without guidance from a physics textbook, in the half second that he was airborne, his body executed a perfect parabolic arc. Somersaulting through the air, at the apogee of the arc, his eyes faced skyward for a split second glimpse of a perfect blue Stanford sky. Perfect, save for one rogue cloud scudding across it, the harbinger of chaos.

He was facing downward when his head crashed to the pavement. All light vanished, all brain activity ceased under the insult of impact. Time no longer had any meaning in the darkness and void. Blood continued to beat within the warm tissues of the brain, and it attempted a reboot according to some primordial instruction set, buried in the firmware of the cortex. A single pinprick of light came on; a one dimensional entity within the limited processing power of his awareness. As more of the brain awoke, the single point pulsed and extended into a line in a two dimensional world. The line gradually took on color, yellow against a black background. His face lay across the lane marking on Sand Hill Road, and he became aware of the taste of blood and bitumen with his tongue draped indecorously across the tarmac. Sound also returned as each of his peripheral sensory organs was reenergized in turn. Someone was shouting at him to not try and move, that paramedics were on their way.

The ability to move any muscle had not yet returned, and all he could see were pairs of ankles clad in bicycle shoes clustered in a concerned group a few feet from his head.

"Don't worry, we're holding the bastard until the police arrive. We saw it all happen from behind."

Massimo could hear incoherent screaming coming from the direction of the car.

"The solution to Navier-Stokes is mine. – No one else has any right to the Millennium Prize."

This was too much information for Massimo to process. His pain receptors were stirring into life and his body was faced with a choice of waking up to what had happened to it, or falling back into the arms of Somnus. The latter was definitely the better choice, for it allowed his brain to begin the more serious business of rechecking all the synapses and purging all the data corrupted by the impact, unhindered by the constraints of rational consciousness.

Not without strange dreams, though. He kept the nurses attending him amused with shouts that his wheels were buckled, that his frame had to be straightened. They sent him to the blissful land of poppies and warmth where he made one last feeble cry for a shiny new bell.

## Chapter 18 – The Next Chapter

When normal consciousness returned, the warmth was still there. The smell of poppies was replaced by a more familiar scent that pulled him to the surface and opened his eyes. A soft brown cascade of curls spilled across his shoulder.

"Laura?"

Sighs and murmurs of forgiveness and concern followed as Massimo gradually returned to the world of rational thought and expression.

Once he was fully awake and asking what had happened, she explained that Georges was being held in custody. He had gone quite out of his mind and somehow blamed Massimo for everything that had happened. Why he was so fixated on Massimo she did not understand.

Massimo was more interested in talking about why Laura was still in Stanford and not winging her way to the East Coast.

"I had to make sure you were okay." She brushed the matted hair away from his forehead. It was beginning to grow back but she couldn't quite run her fingers through it in the same way as she could before the London fashionistas had groomed him.

He was enjoying the fuss and attention when a commotion outside signaled the arrival of Lars and Sven. The bed bounced as they rushed into the room and leapt to his bedside.

"Mass, look at you, you're a mess."

Massimo hadn't actually looked at himself, but the bouncing of the bed made him feel for the first time that he was badly bruised and broken.

"The Stanford cycling team told us they were right behind you when it happened."

Sven was already eyeing the instruments and monitors hooked up to Massimo, but, under the glare of Laura's eyes, he put his hands in his pockets so that he wouldn't be tempted to adjust any dials.

"They said Georges was completely coked out, raving on that you were trying to steal his glory for the Millennium Prize by solving the Navier-Stokes problem."

Massimo tried to pull himself up a little in the bed so that he wouldn't feel like a complete invalid.

"It was Hildr's equations he saw on my board. Thank god he didn't take it out on her, or the world might have lost its newest violin virtuoso."

Lars propped some pillows under Massimo's head to stop him from sliding down.

"We ran the old version of your program on the SLAC computers, before they cut us off. Georges lost everything of his own investments, on top of getting kicked out of WVC."

"Georges was an asshole, but I can't help but feel sorry for the guy. He was being exploited just like the rest of us." Massimo was sweating from the effort of trying to sit up in bed. Laura held a glass with a bent straw so he could sip on some water while she dabbed at his forehead with a cloth.

"I'm really sorry about the mess I've got you guys into. It's all my fault because I let my vanity get the better of me, thinking my program was somehow going to revolutionize the financial world."

"We went into this with our eyes open," said Lars, bending forward so that his face was in Massimo's line of sight, and Massimo wouldn't have to strain to see him.

"I would have beaten the crap out of Georges if I'd been there." Sven was standing at the foot of the bed and gripping the rail so tightly that the bed shook again.

"The good news, though," said Lars, laying a hand on Sven so that the bed would stop shaking, "is that we got our severance package from WVC already. It turns out that our stock options weren't completely worthless after all. Even though they only fetched pennies on the dollar it still added up to something. We're not going to be millionaires or anything, but let's just say that Sven and I will be able to pay off all our Stanford student loans, and that's quite something."

Sven slapped his hand on the bed rail again making it shake. "Not bad for a summer internship, hey!"

This time it was Laura who unhooked Sven from the bed rail and led him to a chair beside her, lest he start using the bed as a trampoline in his exuberance. Massimo smiled weakly. At least Mike hadn't screwed his friends completely. He wouldn't put it past him, though, that money grabbing son of a bitch.

"And you didn't do so badly, either," said Lars, looking down and trying to suppress a grin.

"How so? I wasn't classified as an employee under the terms of the contract, remember?"

"Tangible assets, man," said Sven trying to leap up, but being firmly restrained by Laura.

"Turns out our startup had only one tangible asset, and you get to keep it." Lars was grinning ear to ear now. "The Tesla. It's all yours."

Massimo sat bolt upright in bed, and immediately regretted it. "Woo-hoo. Awesome," he said, half laughing and half crying. Shooting pain or not, he felt like giving them a high five.

Laura rolled her eyes at their idiotic behavior. At least she was convinced now that, in time, he was going to make a complete recovery.

A nurse came running in to see why all of Massimo's monitors were flashing red. She glared at Lars and Sven.

"I think visiting hours are over."

Massimo slid back down under the sheets as the nurse adjusted his drip and sent a cocktail of sleepy, calming painkillers coursing into his vein. Only Laura remained by his bed.

"Your being here is better than any prize Tesla," he murmured. "And you have much better battery life."

Laura came to visit him regularly over the following days, watching over his steady recovery. He did manage to tactfully ask once more about the photos from Hildr. Laura insisted that they were innocent enough; she was just putting on 'costumes' to entertain Hildr after they had been sunbathing and sharing a bottle of wine on the rooftop. She thought they might be misconstrued now, in light of Hildr's unconventional behavior.

With that question out of the way Massimo's thoughts returned to the enigma presenting itself in Hildr's thesis. The notes she had left him contained cryptic hints of something just beyond the grasp of his perception and understanding. He asked Lars and Sven to bring Hildr's dissertation notes from his apartment the next time they came to visit him in the hospital. She had expressly left the notes in his care, but how he was meant to use them was unclear. Was she presenting her completed proof, and that's why she was now moving on to other things, or was she still seeking the correct formulation, and had possibly given up in frustration?

Perhaps if he were to compare the portfolio of notes she had left him with the notation she had written on his board on that last day in his office, he might see some new connection, gain some new insight. Not that he was ever going to be able to get back into that office, and the board was surely erased and dispensed with by now. Whatever had been written there had certainly incensed Georges into mistakingly believing that Massimo was on his way to solving the famous Navier-Stokes problem. He wasn't about to ask Georges his opinion on the topic, but he could ask Lars and Sven to blow up the photos he'd taken with his phone of Hildr's handiwork on the board. Lars and Sven were more than willing to help, but in return they now badgered him during the hospital visit with questions about what Hildr's strange symbols might mean.

"Or, maybe it will give us some insight into why she gave up on her Stanford doctorate so suddenly, and why she felt the urgent need to return to her former world of music and performance," was Laura's sarcastic response to the situation, obviously still peeved that Hildr had departed without so much as a hint of explanation.

Massimo was tugging at his bandages trying to get at an itch. "Music is pivotal in Hildr's life. She may be brilliant at mathematics, but it's not what drives her at an emotional level." A look of relief came over his face as his fingers managed to reach the infuriating itch beneath the bandages.

"Mathematics is an intellectual exercise for her, but music possesses her. It takes over her soul when she plays. I've seen it in her eyes."

Laura raised an eyebrow at that last remark, but didn't respond; she merely shuffled the copies of the enlargements she was holding that Lars and Sven had made of Hildr's handwriting on the board. "All this you inferred from her dissertation notes?"

Massimo wondered if he had said something out of place, but continued. "She seems to have developed her own mathematical-musical notation. The same equation appears both in her notes and again on the board."

Sven grabbed the notes from Laura's hands so that he could look, too. "You mean here, where she underlined it to make some point?"

"Yes, it's exactly the same 'equation' that appears in her dissertation notes. It uses a combination of math symbols together with musical notation, but I'm afraid it's all Greek to me," he sighed, tugging at the annoying bandages once more.

"But what about the symbols $OE\Delta$ written at the bottom? Those are Greek letters aren't they? Do they spell something?" asked Lars, trying to take a look at the sheets that Sven kept moving just out of reach as he tried to grab them.

Massimo stopped scratching and attempted to sit up. "You're right, of course. I didn't recognize them at first, but they stand for *hoper edei deixai*, which is what the ancient Greek mathematicians like Euclid and Archimedes would write at the bottom of their mathematical proofs. It means *what was required to be proved*."

A glazed look of polite interest passed over Lars and Sven's eyes as Massimo insisted on continuing with a full discourse on the subject. "The phrase was later translated into the Latin *Quod Erat Demonstrandum*, or *QED*, which is what we were taught to conclude the proofs we wrote out in our geometry lessons at school."

Laura also stifled a yawn. "And how does this tell you anything about Hildr's state of mind?"

"Well, if you can first give me a pencil I will try and explain."

Laura rummaged in her bag, cringing at the thought that Massimo was about to start writing out one of Archimedes' proofs.

Instead, he inserted the blunt end of the pencil under his bandage, gingerly sliding it down until a look of pained pleasure crossed his face.

"Ah, that's better. Sorry. What it means is that she was convinced she had solved the Navier-Stokes problem, and if Georges had also seen the letters $OE\Delta$ on my board, he would also have interpreted this as a declaration that a proof had been found."

He retracted the pencil and held it out to Laura.

"No thanks, you can keep that one."

Massimo shrugged and continued. "I think Hildr was frustrated that her work would never be accepted or acknowledged as a proof in the traditional mathematical sense."

"So, if she was trying to explain and justify her proof to you, why would she scrawl this other stuff over the top of your writing? It looks more like graffiti," Lars observed.

Sven thrust his smart phone under their noses. "Here, I did some color filtering of the image so you can more easily distinguish her writing from yours. Is it more Greek?"

Massimo chuckled at Sven's dexterity with the technology on his smart phone which speedily helped him decode what Hildr had written on his board. "It is like deciphering a Greek Palimpsest. Did you know that SLAC once analyzed a thousand year old document using the x-rays from our synchrotron to reveal the obliterated writing in one of Archimedes' lost texts? In later centuries monks had scraped off the writing from one of Archimedes' book so that they could reuse the parchment for their own texts, but the beam from the synchrotron was able to reveal the barely visible original text with great clarity[30]. This doesn't look like Greek writing, though."

Laura reached over and took the phone away from them so she could look at the screen. After rotating it a few times she handed it back. "It looks more like Hebrew writing, but I think it is back to front because you photographed it from the wrong side of the glass board."

"I can fix that. I can just flip the image on my phone." Sven leapt up as he spoke, escaping to the other side of the room so that no one would take away his precious phone.

"There," he said holding up the screen for all to see. "This is what she actually wrote."

# מִיכָאֵל

"I wonder if Google can translate it for us?" he added, gleefully turning his back on them once more and tapping away at his phone before anyone could reach out for it.

"Yes, yes it recognizes the image as Hebrew text characters **מִיכָאֵל** ." He held up the phone briefly for them, but no one could really see anything before he was scrolling further down the screen. "And those text characters translate into '*Who is like God?*', or more literally, it says '*Who is like El?*' " Sven had a bewildered look on his face, but scrolled further down the screen to see what else he could elucidate from the search result.

"So the Hebrew text can be read as **Mîkhā'ēl**," he added, no longer bothering to even show them the screen as he read further; but then his face brightened. "Which is written in English as Michael, and apparently the Biblical origins of this name mean '*Who is like God?*' "

He moved over to the side of the bed for Massimo to see, adroitly sidestepping Lars who was also reaching out for the phone to see the search results for himself.

"Well, that's one mystery solved." Massimo was smiling as the phone was passed around so that each of them could see the Hebrew text once more and the explanation beneath of the name's origin. "And it does give some insight into Hildr's state of mind," he said, looking Laura in the eye.

"I have to grant you that," she nodded, and added, "It must have come as a complete shock to her to suddenly discover Mike in the other room. The irony in the meaning of his name didn't escape her either, so she splashed it across your board, that fate, or God, would never let her escape her bond with Mike's family."

Lars was biting a fingernail and looking skeptical. "It's still a bit of an unlikely coincidence that Hildr should happen to cross paths again with Mike, right in our office."

"It's not that unreasonable," Massimo countered. "Hildr wanted to enroll in the top mathematics program available anywhere, so she came to Stanford. Hildr met Laura, Laura knew me, and I met Mike. That's two degrees of separation. It can be mathematically proven that there are no more than six degrees of separation between any two people on the planet, so the probability of two degrees of separation shouldn't be that hard to figure out." He craned his neck looking for the pencil again, and perhaps a piece of paper.

Laura discreetly hid the pencil from view. "No more math lectures. Please. We believe you."

"Well, anyway," he replied with a little sniff, "given what we know about Mike, it's also natural that he ended up on Sand Hill Road. If you have ambitions in venture capital, this is the place to come."

The hospital visit ended on a positive note. Laura seemed convinced now that Massimo had nothing to do with Hildr's abrupt departure. She joined in the laughter when Sven insisted on answering every question with "Elementary, my dear Watson," reprising his role of sleuth detective.

After they had all left, Massimo found himself still staring at Hildr's notes. He would never know if she had found the key to solving the Navier-Stokes problem. Was it just mathematical doodling with musical symbols, or had she indeed found a new mathematical notation? The same doubts he had always harbored regarding Hildr's ability remained: maestro or madwoman, genius or insane? She did have a proclivity for being cryptic, as evidenced in the way she had portrayed Mike's name. Her notation was intentionally cabalistic, he decided, deliberately constructed to obscure its true meaning from mere mortals such as him. His first impression of her as a Norse goddess, had been right, he decided, as he put her notebook away.

Laura didn't speak of Hildr again during subsequent hospital visits. When it came time for him to begin some physiotherapy, she did finally say it was time for her to depart for the East Coast. To cover the obvious sadness they both felt, she said she wouldn't be able to bear his swearing and cursing when he had to coax his legs and body back into action in the physio sessions. There were professionals, she said, who knew how to handle the likes of him.

Lars and Sven oversaw his eventual return to his apartment and got him re-established in his normal routine. He wondered how much he would be seeing of his friends now that their paths would be diverging.

His return to SLAC was uneventful. Everyone assumed his foreshortened leave of absence was due to the bicycle accident, so he didn't have to explain what had happened to the startup.

Walking with a cane was difficult, so he chose to go to the cafeteria only after the midday crowd had dispersed. It was easier that way, carrying a tray with one hand and not bumping into everyone. It did mean that he usually sat alone to eat his lunch, but he didn't mind being alone with his thoughts.

He pushed the glass swing door awkwardly open with his shoulder, pivoting his body and the food tray around so that he could go outside and eat on the benches in the open air. The sun was hot and he headed for his usual table under the shade of an oak tree. Only when he got close did he notice a solitary figure still sitting in the deep shadows.

"Mind if I join you?" he said, sliding his tray across the table and putting the cane alongside while he swung his leg, still with some difficulty, across the bench.

"Of course, glad to see you are on the road to a full recovery."

"Mike? I never expected to see you again. What are you doing here?"

"I wanted to make sure you were doing okay; and to tell you that we never intended Georges to go so completely crazy." Mike had been eating a burger and fries from the cafeteria, and now pushed the remaining fries to one side of his plate.

"But screwing Georges over big time was part of your plan." Massimo had lost his appetite and forked aimlessly at his salad.

"Georges had it coming. And he quite happily joined the opposing team, you may remember."

Massimo didn't answer but kept his jaw clenched.

"Your interns, Lars and Sven are doing okay now? They were a bright pair. I'm sorry to lose them."

"Thank you for at least taking care of my friends so they got some remuneration for their efforts."

Another painful silence followed.

"You didn't like the Tesla we gave you?"

One part of Massimo wanted to hit Mike over the head with the cane.

"Of course. You know my tastes, like I'm sure you know most things about me. But look, either you answer some straightforward questions, or you can get the hell out of here."

Mike dipped one of the cold fries into some ketchup and bit off the end.

"Here, I brought you a present." Mike slid a hardcover book across the table. It was a copy of Alan Greenspan's memoir *The Age of Turbulence.*

"It was published on the eve of the 2008 stock market crash. I thought you would appreciate the irony of the title. Greenspan never grasped the significance of turbulence and chaos in the marketplace like you have. The 2008 crash is a testimonial to that."

Massimo flipped the book around so that Greenspan's face leered up at him from the cover.

"I take it this is not a book on the mathematical theory of chaos."

"No, but I just loved it for promoting the deregulation of banks and financial markets. It gives me a sense of hope that there is so much more money to be made."

Massimo was fed up with Mike's cynicism.

"Tell me this, if you lay so much value in the theory chaos, why did you derail our enterprise and stop us from pursuing this further?"

"Two things, really." Mike pushed his plate aside and rested his chin on his clasped hands. He looked Massimo up and down, assessing how much he wanted to reveal. "We wanted to acquire Megateck, and you were a convenient means of getting it at a bargain price." He pulled the book toward him and stood it on its end.

"Your theory of analysis is all about predicting the future behavior of markets. We, on the other hand, are about maintaining the status quo." He slapped the book down in front of Massimo again. "If there is one thing better than being able to predict the outcome of markets, it's being able to *control* the outcome."

Mike sat back to let the words sink in, then added,

"There are boom and bust cycles, and I have made my fortune by manipulating those cycles. It would ruin everything if you were to come along and start predicting them for everyone. I had to put a stop to that."

Massimo had felt like standing up and walking away in disgust. Partly, it was vanity that kept him there, the idea that he would not have looked in command, struggling to his feet and hobbling off. He had also wanted to hear, in Mike's own words, what ultimately motivated him to do what he had done.

There was also something appealing in all of this, from a physics point of view, that any act of observation, any attempt to predict the outcome of an event, would change the very outcome.

Giving up on the idea of any show of bravado, he asked, "Why Megateck? What's so special about them? There are a lot of fat companies you could have taken down."

Mike was not prone to revealing his business strategies to anyone. He operated on a strictly need-to-know basis. But there was something about Massimo's calm acceptance and intellectual grasp of the situation that lured him to reply,

"Energy."

Massimo blinked, and waited for him to continue.

"Megateck is strategically placed within the petroleum sector in Texas. Those huge price fluctuations you see at the pump aren't because either the world supply or demand for oil is dramatically changing. Prices are lowered to put someone out of business or raised to rake in the profits. That's a market WVC could thrive in."

Massimo seemed to forget for a moment that it was this very attitude that had defeated him.

"But petroleum seems such an old fashioned technology to be getting into in this day and age."

"Exactly."

Mike seemed to forget, too, that he was revealing plans to someone who might, logically, want to extract revenge for all that had happened.

"That's why we want to control the energy sector from here in Silicon Valley. We are at the cusp of a new age in energy technology: solar, biochemical, wind, to name but a few. There is going to be a lot of money flow in the venture capital energy sector, and I want to be here to control it."

Massimo contemplated Mike's words.

"Solar?"

"You bet," said Mike, rising to leave. "You should get down to the pool again. It doesn't look like you're going to be able to get back on a bicycle for a while."

"How is Bianca's musical prodigy doing? Was the New York tour a success?"

Mike turned back to him. "A stunning success. They're still in New York embarking on an even more ambitious tour."

"I know she was a Stanford scholar. Some people are quite shocked that she gave up a promising career in mathematics to return to the stage. Do you think she might return to the world of mathematics one day?" He tried to keep an even gaze that wouldn't betray whether he had known Hildr in the past.

Mike sat down again, his own expression like that of a poker player. "I can imagine Hildr might have created quite a stir in your cloistered world of math and science. But I don't think she will be returning any time soon, at least not if Bianca has her way."

"That's a pity. People say she was a brilliant student."

"Well, since you ask, I can tell you that at quite a young age Hildr was recognized as a prodigious savant. But it was always music that dominated everything she did, to the point of obsession. Her tutors also recognized she had an uncanny knack for solving mathematical puzzles. But the biggest revelation came when they recognized that she was using her innate musical ability to solve math problems."

Massimo lost any semblance of the poker face he was trying to preserve, and eagerly leaned forward to hear more.

Mike gave a little, all-knowing smile as he continued. "There is a brain condition called synesthesia where people associate colors with certain sounds, or sometimes it can be certain smells or tastes. A sort of cross-wiring of the senses. It's more common than you think because people either don't want to admit to it, or simply don't recognize it as anything out of the ordinary. Then there is an interesting variant called ideasthesia where concepts can evoke perception-like experiences."

"Yes, yes, I know." Massimo heard himself voicing some of the same frustrations that Laura must have felt when he was the one guilty of dragging out a story. "Richard Feynman was a famous example of someone who would identify numbers and mathematics with a particular color. He was one of my heroes, and it was his famous *Lectures on Physics* that convinced me to pursue physics."

Mike took his time replying, teasing Massimo a little, and constantly checking himself as to how much to reveal in conversation. "Well, Hildr's brain is even more complicated. When she 'sees' mathematics her brain 'hears' musical chords. She will process a math formula as though it was a musical score and something very different goes on than you or I could ever comprehend."

"But that's amazing. What if she were able to solve some of the greatest mathematical challenges of all time with such a talent?"

Mike shook his head slowly in response to Massimo's wild gesticulations. "Bianca maintains that it is best to keep Hildr isolated from mathematics. It overstimulates her brain and she becomes excitable and unreasonable, and worse, her musical performance ability suffers."

Massimo couldn't sit still. In spite of his stiff leg he stood up and pointed an accusing finger at Mike. "What gives you the right to deprive the world of a mathematical brain like that? History tells us we need great geniuses like her."

Mike also slowly got to his feet. "But it's not your call. The world also needs great musical performers. And I can tell you the contributions to my charitable foundations skyrocket every time she does a concert tour." He stepped in close and lowered his voice. "Go down to the pool, Massimo, get yourself healed again and return to your world of physics. Don't interfere." He took his hand from Massimo's shoulder and quietly turned and left.

Frustration welled up inside him. Mike had blatantly announced that he had designs on controlling the energy market; he had revealed that he was fully aware of Hildr's uncanny mathematical ability, and had arrogantly assumed that Massimo would subserviently keep his nose out of it all.

He threw himself back down onto the hard bench, annoyed that his leg still hurt and that he had not made all the clever rejoinders that now rushed through his head. To make matters worse, the overhead power lines seemed to be leering down at him, telling him that here was SLAC at the mercy of the National Power Grid, and there was Mike about to take control of the energy distribution in this country.

Leaning down on the bench, his head lolled back and he continued to stare at the high tension transmission lines dipping gracefully across Portola Valley, delivering 200 kilovolts to the SLAC accelerator. "Ironic, isn't it," he mused to himself; "those power lines look just like Hildr's musical staff." And that's when the penny dropped, or rather, that's when the notion slapped him in the face. He sat up abruptly. Energy flow through the grid was just like Hildr's fluid flow equations. It was all there: the humming of the wires, the music of the spheres, Navier-Stokes' ancient equations and Hildr's musical score that orchestrated every instrument, every utility on the national grid. A brief maniacal, but infectious laugh burst from his lips, had anyone been there to hear it.

Mike obviously had no idea what he had let slip through his fingers by taking Hildr out of the world of mathematics. The distribution of energy over the power grid was an incredibly complex mathematical problem that defied analysis. A power outage on one breaker at one utility could ripple across several states and wreak havoc with blackouts. A chaotic system if ever there was one, just ripe for analysis, if only someone had the right tools. Hildr's tools, and Hildr had entrusted all her notes to him!

The giant energy corporations had long been suspected of manipulating energy prices by creating energy shortages on the grid. Mike thought he was about to step up and take control of this lucrative market.

But you can't fully control what you can't understand and analyze, thought Massimo. This venture was not over yet.

Yes, he would go down to the pool and swim some laps. He did his best thinking when he was swimming.

And maybe one of Carlos's espressos afterwards to celebrate.

# About the Author

Patrick Krejcik works as a physicist at the SLAC National Accelerator Laboratory on Sand Hill Road, adjacent to the Stanford University campus. He has witnessed many growth cycles over the last 25 years, both in the high-tech enterprises surrounding the University and Silicon Valley, as well as in his own field of high-energy accelerator research. His interest in the Venture Capital world was sparked when his son became an investment analyst, and he took a closer look at the world of the financiers across the road from SLAC, admittedly, though, from the perspective of a physicist. The comfortable Californian lifestyle, with its emphasis on outdoor recreation, good food and wine, plus the ubiquitous coffee shops of the San Francisco Bay Area have always provided an entertaining source of anecdotes and inspiration for his writing.

# Acknowledgments

The author wishes to thank his friends and family who read the first drafts and added their insightful comments and criticisms. None of this would have been possible without my wife Jennifer's support and tireless editorial work. Special thanks to my sister Catharine for her contributions, to Carol for her thorough reading of the manuscript, to Jackie and Phil for their critical reading and advice. Thanks also to my son and 'financial advisor' Adam who set me straight on many aspects of IPOs and the world of venture capital.

# Bibliography and Notes

Some books that I read in the course of writing this story include the following:

1. *The Misbehavior of Markets: A Fractal View of Financial Turbulence,* by Benoit Mandelbrot and Richard L. Hudson. Publisher Basic Books, 2007. ISBN 0465004687, 9780465004683.
2. *The Fractal Geometry of Nature,* by Benoit B. Mandelbrot. Publisher Macmillan, 1983. ISBN      0716711869, 9780716711865
3. *The Black Swan: The Impact of the Highly Improbable,* by Nassim Nicholas Taleb. Publisher Random House Digital, Inc., 2007. ISBN 1588365832, 9781588365835.
4. *Chaos: Making a New Science,* by James Gleick. Publisher Open Road Media, 2011. ISBN 1453210474, 9781453210475.
5. *The Physics of Wall Street: A Brief History of Predicting the Unpredictable,* by James Owen Weatherall. Publisher   Houghton   Mifflin   Harcourt, 2013. ISBN 0547618298, 9780547618296.
6. *The Age of Turbulence: Adventures in a New World,* by Alan Greenspan. Publisher Penguin, 2008. ISBN 1440635692, 9781440635694.
7. *The Visual Display of Quantitative Information,* by Edward Rolf Tufte. Publisher Graphics press, 1984. ISBN 10: 0961392142 / 0-9613921-4-2 ISBN 13: 9780961392147.
8. *Musicophilia: Tales of Music and the Brain,* by Oliver Sacks. Publisher: Alfred A. Knopf, 2007. ISBN-10: 1400040817

Some of the graphical illustrations in the notes below were created using the *Matlab* program distributed by MathWorks, Inc.

---

[1] TEDx are the individually sponsored venues of the TED Talks (Technology, Entertainment and Design) that have become popular in recent times, and TEDx happens to rhyme with teddy in Jimmy Kennedy's 1932 lyrics to "The Teddy Bears' Picnic".

[2] A name popularized by Nassim Nicholas Taleb in the book *The Black Swan: The Impact of the Highly Improbable.*

[3] Chaos theory is a field of study in mathematics, with applications in several disciplines including physics, engineering, economics, biology, and philosophy. Chaos theory studies the behavior of dynamical systems that are highly sensitive to initial conditions, an effect which is popularly referred to as the butterfly effect (something so sensitive that the beating of the wings of a butterfly on one side of the planet may trigger a hurricane on the other side). Small differences in initial conditions (such as those due to rounding errors in numerical computation) yield widely diverging outcomes for such dynamical systems, rendering long-term prediction impossible in general. This happens even though these systems are deterministic, meaning that their future behavior is fully determined by their initial conditions, with no random elements involved. In other words, the deterministic nature of these systems does not make them predictable.

[4] A fractal is a geometric object that is similar to itself on all scales. If you zoom in on a fractal object it will look similar or exactly like the original shape. This property is called self-similarity. The length of a fractal boundary, like that of a coast line, is indefinable because it becomes longer and longer the more you zoom in and the more detail you include.

The term 'fractal' was first coined by Benoit Mandelbrot, a Polish/French/American mathematician who spent most of his career at the IBM Watson Research Center in Yorktown Heights, N.Y. He developed a 'Theory of Roughness' and published his influential book, *The Fractal Geometry of Nature*, in 1982. An image of the now famous Mandelbrot set appeared on the cover of Scientific American in 1985. This was about the time that computer graphical displays were becoming widely available. Since then, the Mandelbrot set has stimulated deep research topics in mathematics and has also been the basis for an uncountable number of graphics' projects, hardware demos, and Web pages.

The Mandelbrot set is the region in the complex plane consisting of the values $z_0$ for which the trajectories defined by

$$z_{k+1} = z_k^2 + z_0, \quad k = 0, 1, \ldots$$

remain bounded at $k \to \infty$.

The overall geometry of the Mandelbrot set is shown below. Its boundary is rich in detail, and the more you zoom in, the more filamented it becomes.

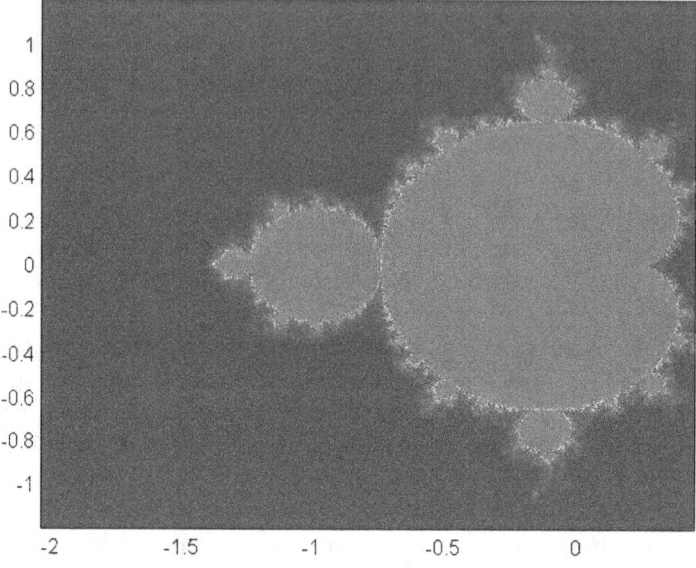

The second picture zooms in by a factor 100 on the previous picture and reveals self-similar detail as the boundary replicates itself on the microscopic scale.

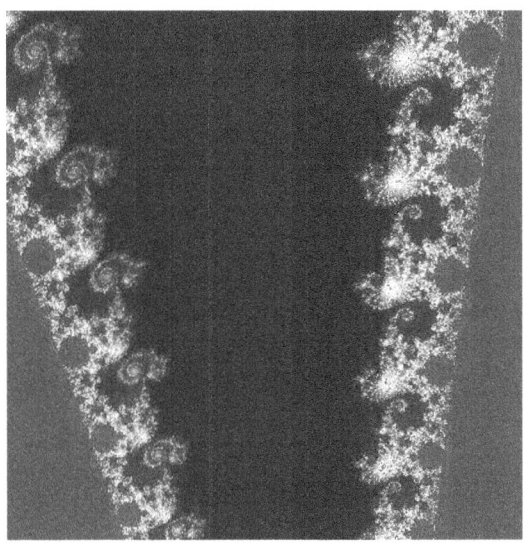

[5] Douglas R. Hofstadter, in *Metamagical Themas: Questing for the Essence of Mind and Pattern.*

[6] SLAC National Accelerator Laboratory, sometimes referred to as Stanford Linear Accelerator Center, is funded by the US Department of Energy and is operated by Stanford University. Built in the 1960s, it was conceived on the campus as Project M (M stood for Monster). The two-mile long linear accelerator is the longest in the world and is said to be visible with the unaided eye from outer space. Research at the accelerator has led to the awarding of several Nobel Prizes over the decades. SLAC has always been at the forefront of technology and innovation as well. Many now famous members of the Home Brew Computer Club met at SLAC in the early days of personal computing. SLAC also set up the first web server in America in 1991 after the World Wide Web was developed at CERN by Tim Berners-Lee.

[7] CERN is the European Organization for Nuclear Research (*Conseil Européen pour la Recherche Nucléaire*) in Switzerland. There has always been a healthy balance of collaboration and competition between SLAC and CERN.

[8] Claude-Louis Navier and George Gabriel Stokes developed the mathematics in 1822 to describe the motion of fluids, which is summarized in their famous equation

$$\frac{\partial v}{\partial t} + (v \cdot \nabla)v = -\nabla p + \upsilon \Delta v$$

It is used to model a variety of phenomena such as ocean currents, weather or the flow of air over an aircraft wing. Turbulence and chaos are important factors in characterizing any flow!

[9] Andrey Nikolaevich Kolmogorov was a Russian mathematician who introduced the concept of a universal scale in modeling turbulent flow. At the Kolmogorov scale, viscosity dominates and the turbulent kinetic energy is dissipated into heat.

[10] The Millennium Prize Problems are seven problems in mathematics that were stated by the Clay Mathematics Institute in 2000. As of March 2013, six of the problems remain unsolved. A correct solution to any of the problems results in a $1,000,000 prize (sometimes called a Millennium Prize) being awarded by the institute. The Poincaré conjecture, the only Millennium Prize Problem to be solved so far, was solved by Grigori Perelman, but he declined the award in 2010.
Mathematicians have not yet proven that in three dimensions solutions always exist for the Navier-Stokes equations, or that if they do exist, then they do not contain any singularity (smoothness). These are called the Navier–Stokes existence and smoothness problems. The Clay Mathematics Institute has called this one of the seven most important open problems in mathematics and has offered a US$1,000,000 prize for a solution or a counter-example.

[11] Georges Frederic Doriot (1899 – 1987) was one of the first American venture capitalists. An émigré from France, Doriot became director of the U.S. Army's Military Planning Division, Quartermaster General, during World War II, eventually being promoted to brigadier general. In 1946, he founded American Research and Development Corporation, the world's first publicly owned venture capital firm, earning him the sobriquet "father of venture capitalism." ARDC is credited with the first major venture capital success story when its 1957 investment of $70,000 in Digital Equipment Corporation (DEC) would be valued at over $355 million after the company's initial public offering in 1968 (representing a return of over 500 times on its investment and an annualized rate of return of 101%).

[12] Jane Lathrop Stanford played a significant role in shaping the future of Stanford University. It was under her direction that there was a strong focus on the arts, and she also insisted that the university be open to women. She fought strongly for academic freedom and laid the groundwork for open and public research, which is the hallmark of Stanford University today. Great mystery surrounds her death from strychnine poisonings and the cover-up that surrounded her death.

[13] The uncertainty principle is often confused with a somewhat similar effect in physics, called the observer effect, which notes that measurements of certain systems cannot be made without affecting the systems. Heisenberg offered such an observer effect at the quantum level as a physical "explanation" of quantum uncertainty. It has since become clear, however, that the uncertainty principle is inherent in the properties of all wave-like systems, and that it arises in quantum mechanics simply due to the matter wave nature of all quantum objects. Thus, the uncertainty principle actually states a fundamental property of quantum systems, and is not a statement about the observational success of current technology. It must be emphasized that measurement does not mean only a process in which a physicist-observer takes part, but rather any interaction between classical and quantum objects regardless of any observer.

[14] Charles Joseph Minard (1781 –1870) was a French civil engineer and pioneer of the use of graphics in engineering and statistics. He is famous for his *Carte figurative des pertes successives en hommes de l'Armée Française dans la campagne de Russie 1812-1813*, a flow map published in 1869 on the subject of Napoleon's disastrous Russian campaign of 1812.
The graph displays several variables in a single two-dimensional image:
- the size of the army - providing a strong visual representation of human suffering, e.g. the sudden decrease of the army's size at the crossing of the Berezina river on the retreat;
- the geographical co-ordinates, latitude and longitude, of the army as it moved;
- the direction that the army was traveling, both in advance and in retreat, showing where units split off and rejoined;
- the location of the army with respect to certain dates; and
- the weather temperature along the path of the retreat, in another strong visualization of events (during the retreat "one of the worst winters in recent memory set in".

Étienne-Jules Marey first called notice to this dramatic depiction of the fate of Napoleon's army in the Russian campaign, saying it "defies the pen of the historian in its brutal eloquence". Edward Tufte says it "may well be the best statistical graphic ever drawn" and uses it as a prime example in his book *The Visual Display of Quantitative Information.*

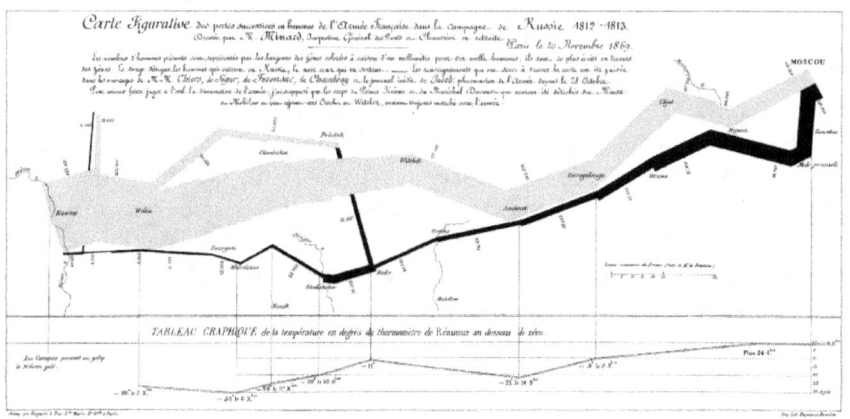

[15] *Chaos: Making A New Science* is the best-selling book by James Gleick that first introduced the principles and early development of chaos theory to the public. It was a finalist for the National Book Award and the Pulitzer Prize in 1987, and was shortlisted for the Science Book Prize in 1989.

The first popular book about chaos theory, it describes the Mandelbrot set, Julia sets, and Lorenz attractors without resorting to complex mathematics. It portrays the efforts of dozens of scientists whose separate work contributed to the developing field. It remains in print and is used as an introduction to the topic for the mathematical layman.

[16] An attractor is a set towards which a variable, moving according to the dictates of a dynamical system, evolves over time. That is, points that get close enough to the attractor remain close even if slightly disturbed. An attractor is called strange if it has non-integer dimension. This is often the case when the dynamics on it are chaotic, but there also exist strange attractors that are not chaotic. The term was coined by David Ruelle and Floris Takens to describe the attractor that resulted from a series of bifurcations of a system describing fluid flow.

[17] Edward Lorenz's first weather model exhibited chaotic behavior, but it involved a set of 12 nonlinear differential equations. Lorenz decided to look for complex behavior in an even simpler set of equations, and was led to the phenomenon of rolling fluid convection. The physical model is simple: place a gas in a solid rectangular box with a heat source on the bottom.

Lorenz simplified the Navier-Stokes equations and ended up with a set of three nonlinear equations:

$$\frac{dx}{dt} = P(y - x)$$

$$\frac{dy}{dt} = Rx - y - xz$$

$$\frac{dz}{dt} = xy - By$$

Where $P$ is the Prandtl number representing the ratio of the fluid viscosity to its thermal conductivity, $R$ represents the difference in temperature between the top and bottom of the system, and $B$ is the ratio of the width to height of the box used to hold the system. The values Lorenz used are $P = 10$, $R = 28$, $B = 8/3$.

These three equations may seem simple to solve, but they represent an extremely complicated dynamical system. If one plots the results in three dimensions the following figure, called the Lorenz attractor, is obtained.

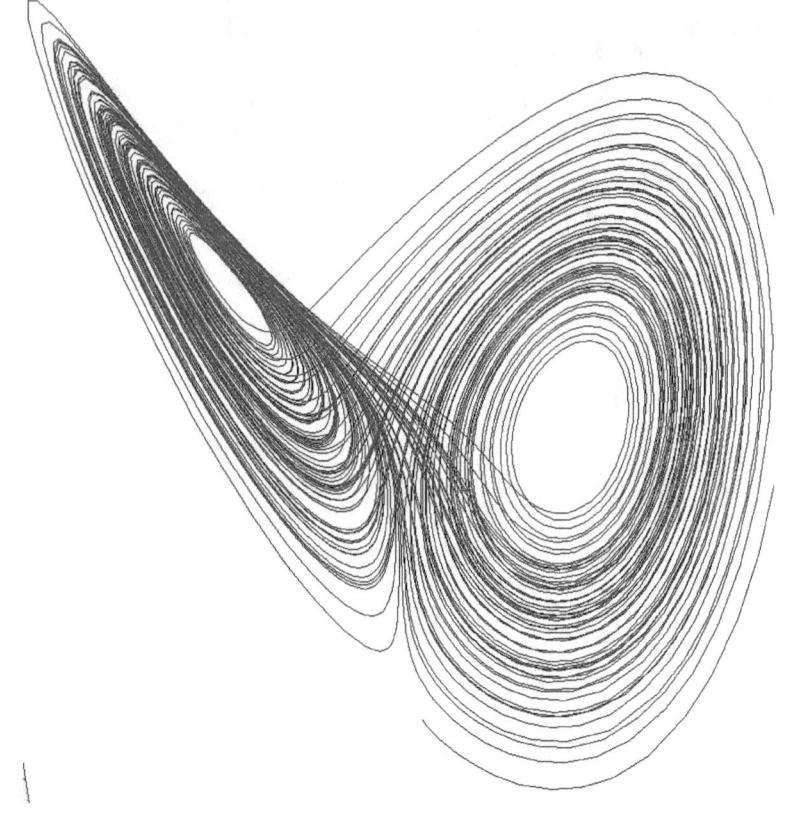

The Lorenz attractor is an example of a strange attractor. Strange attractors not only look aesthetically attractive but they are unique from other phase-space attractors in that one does not know exactly where on the attractor the system will be. Two points on the attractor that are near each other at one time will be arbitrarily far apart at later times. The only restriction is that the state of system remains on the attractor. Strange attractors are also unique in that they never close on themselves — the motion of the system never repeats (non-periodic). The motion we are describing on these strange attractors is what we mean by chaotic behavior.

[18] Pierre François Verhulst (1804 –1849) was a Belgian mathematician and a doctor in number theory from the University of Ghent. Verhulst published in 1838 the population growth equation:

$$\frac{dx}{dt} = rx\left(1 - \frac{x}{K}\right)$$

where $x(t)$ represents number of individuals at time $t$; $r$ is the intrinsic growth rate and $K$ is the carrying capacity, or the maximum number of individuals that the environment can support. In a paper published in 1845 he called the solution to this the logistic function.

We can replace this with the quadratic recurrence equation

$$x_{n+1} = rx_n(1-x_n)$$

Then, in the illustration below we show a bifurcation diagram of the logistic map obtained by plotting as a function of $r$ a series of values for $x_n$ obtained by starting with a random value of $x_0$, iterating many times, and discarding the first points corresponding to values before the iterates converge to the attractor. In other words, the set of fixed points of $x_n$ corresponding to a given value of $r$ are plotted for values of $r$ increasing to the right.

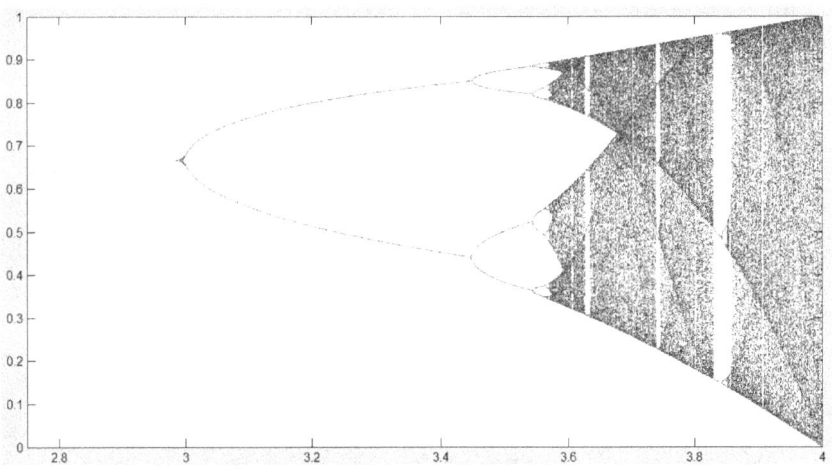

[19] The Standard Model may be summarized in a 'periodic' table that shows

the elementary particles grouped in three families, together with the forces that hold them together:

| Three Families of Matter | | I | II | III | H<br>Higgs boson | |
|---|---|---|---|---|---|---|
| **Quarks** | +2/3 | *u*<br>Up | *c*<br>Charm | *t*<br>Top | γ<br>photon | **Force Carriers** |
| | -1/3 | *d*<br>Down | *s*<br>Strange | *b*<br>Bottom | g<br>gluon | |
| **Leptons** | | *e*<br>electron | *μ*<br>muon | *τ*<br>tau | Z<br>Z boson | |
| | | $v_e$<br>electron<br>neutrino | $v_\mu$<br>muon<br>neutrino | $v_\tau$<br>tau<br>neutrino | W<br>W boson | |

[20] Bosons are particles generated by a field to carry a force from one object to another. They are named after *Satyendra Nath Bose*, who made a famous "mistake" in describing the statistics of such particles.

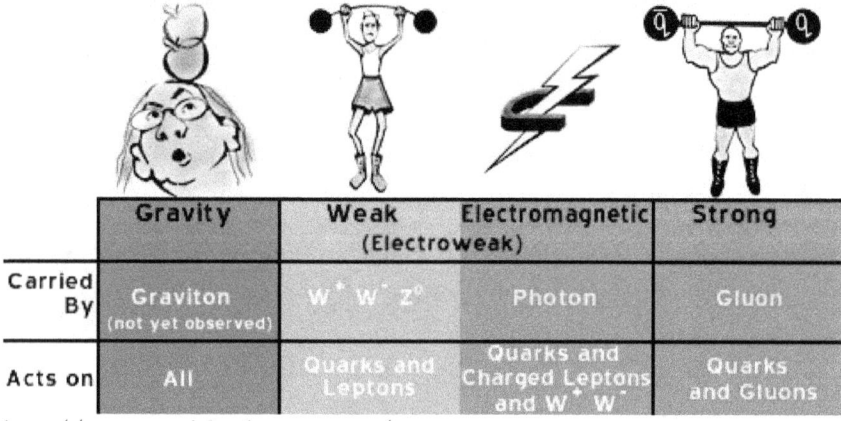

| | Gravity | Weak<br>(Electroweak) | Electromagnetic | Strong |
|---|---|---|---|---|
| **Carried By** | Graviton<br>(not yet observed) | W⁺ W⁻ Z⁰ | Photon | Gluon |
| **Acts on** | All | Quarks and Leptons | Quarks and Charged Leptons and W⁺ W⁻ | Quarks and Gluons |

http://www.particleadventure.org/

[21] John Milton (1608 –1674) was an English poet best known for his epic poem *Paradise Lost*. At the age of 20 he wrote The Fifth Elegy, *On the Approach of Spring*, quoted by Massimo in the story. Milton wrote in English,

Italian and Latin. The original Latin reads:

> *Elegia quinta, Anno ætatis 20.*
> *In adventum veris.*

> *In se perpetuo Tempus revolubile gyro*
> *Jam revocat Zephyros vere tepente novos.*
> *Induiturque brevem Tellus reparata juventam,*
> *Jamque soluta gelu dulce virescit humus.*

Milton travelled widely in Italy, and even met the famous Galileo, so it is fitting that in the story Massimo would have had an attraction for Milton, and even believed at one stage that Milton was Italian. In June of 1643, Milton at age 35 did in fact pay a visit to the manor house at Forest Hill, Oxfordshire, where he met and married the 16-year-old Mary Powell. The marriage lasted about a month!

[22] *Così fan tutte*, Köchel-Verzeichnis 588, is an Italian language opera buffa in two acts by Wolfgang Amadeus Mozart first performed in 1790. The libretto was written by Lorenzo Da Ponte. The title, *Così fan tutte*, literally means "Thus do all [women]" but it is often rendered as "Women are like that". The words are sung by the three men in act 2, scene 3, just before the finale. The subject matter of fiancée swapping did not offend Viennese sensibilities of the time, but throughout the 19th and early 20th centuries it was considered risqué.

[23] *Sunday Bloody Sunday* is a British drama film directed by John Schlesinger and starring Glenda Jackson, Peter Finch, Murray Head and Peggy Ashcroft. The film makes extensive use of the musical trio *Soave sia il vento* from Mozart's opera *Così fan tutte*. It was made in 1971, just after Schlessinger's Acadamy Award winning *Midnight Cowboy,* and was itself nominated for four Academy Awards.

[24] Matt Taibbi wrote in Rolling Stone magazine on July 9, 2009, "The world's most powerful investment bank is a great vampire squid wrapped around the face of humanity, relentlessly jamming its blood funnel into anything that smells like money. In fact, the history of the recent financial crisis, which doubles as a history of the rapid decline and fall of the

suddenly swindled dry American empire, reads like a Who's Who of Goldman Sachs graduates."

[25] In 1637 Fermat wrote his Last Theorem in the margin of his copy of *Arithmetica*, stating
"I have discovered a truly marvelous proof of this, which this margin is too narrow to contain."
referring, of course, to the famous Diophantine equation $x^n + y^n = z^n$
(You may recognize this as the Pythagorean Theorem when $n=2$). A proof was finally found and published in 1995.

[26] The 1969 book *The Peter Principle*, is a satirical treatise on the "salutary science of hierarchiology" and stated "Employees tend to rise to their level of incompetence."

[27] Tien-Yien Li and James A. Yorke, *Period Three Implies Chaos*, The American Mathematical Monthly, Vol. 82, No. 10. (Dec., 1975), pp. 985-992.

Yorke is also known for his jovial character and sometimes dresses like Santa Claus at department holiday parties.

[28] *"And at that time shall Michael stand up, the great prince which standeth for the children of thy people: and there shall be a time of trouble, such as never was since there was a nation even to that same time: and at that time thy people shall be delivered, every one that shall be found written in the book."*

Daniel 12:1, Authorized King James Version of The Bible.

[29] The original quote is from The life of Samuel Johnson by James Boswell : "Sir, a woman's preaching is like a dog walking on his hind legs. It is not done well; but you are surprised to find it done at all."

[30] In the 10th century, an anonymous scribe copied Archimedes' treatises in the original Greek onto parchment. But three centuries later, a monk "palimpsested" the parchment: he scraped away the Archimedes text, cut the pages in half, turned them sideways, and copied Greek Orthodox prayers onto the recycled pages. Adding further injury, forgers in the early 20th century painted religious imagery on several pages in an attempt to elevate the manuscript's value. The result was the near obliteration of Archimedes' work, except for the faintest traces of ink still embedded in the parchment.

In 2006 a team at SLAC used the bright x-ray beam from the SPEAR3 synchrotron to scan the pages and reveal the underlying text with a technique called x-ray fluorescence. It revealed previously unread sections of Archimedes' greatest treatise, *The Method*, including a once indecipherable page of Archimedes' *On Floating Bodies* for the first time (Eureka!). The same experiments also brought to light the identity of the priest who erased the Archimedes texts. His name was Johannes Myronas, and he finished transcribing the prayers on April 14, 1229 in Jerusalem.

Full details of the Archimedes Palimpsest Project can be found at

www.archimedespalimpsest.org.

www.ingramcontent.com/pod-product-compliance
Lightning Source LLC
Chambersburg PA
CBHW070216260626
47160CB00002B/572